STRICTLY COME DATING

KATHRYN FREEMAN

One More Chapter
a division of HarperCollins*Publishers* Ltd
1 London Bridge Street
London SE1 9GF
www.harpercollins.co.uk

This paperback edition 2020

First published in Great Britain in ebook format
by HarperCollins*Publishers* 2020

A catalogue record of this book is available from the British Library

ISBN: 978-0-00-836586-8

Printed and bound in Great Britain by
CPI Group (UK) Ltd, Croydon CR0 4YY

This one is for Strictly fans everywhere (and that includes you, Charlotte and Bethan – thank you both so much for your invaluable input).

For anyone with connections to Blackpool (hello Shelley, Kath, Karley, Kirsty and Hayley).

It's also for Mum, who spent many happy hours dancing with Dad in Blackpool Tower ballroom.

This one is for South Jim's everywhere (and that includes you, Charlie and Debbie — thank you both so much for your invaluable input).

For anyone with connections to Blackpool: Hattie Shelley, Kath, Karley, Kirsty and Hayley.

It's also for Mum, who spent many happy hours dancing with Dad in Blackpool Tower ballroom.

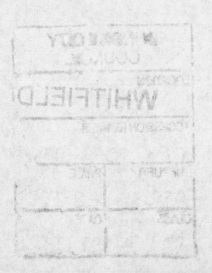

Chapter One

M aggie took a look around the room, her mouth curving in an unconscious smile. God, she was blessed. Her daughters, Penny and Tabby, sat cross-legged on the floor, their hands wrapped around slices of pizza, laughing with Hannah, the nanny who'd become a close friend. On the armchair was Alice, Maggie's closest friend, and the twin sister of Sarah, whose house they were all currently occupying, and who sat next to Maggie on the sofa. Both her friends sported vibrant sequinned tops that put Maggie's tame black effort to shame. Also with them was Alice's daughter, Rebecca, who was nine like Penny.

Everyone was waiting in front of the TV for their programme to start.

Some more patiently than others.

'I'm bored of this.' Seven-year-old Tabby turned her nose up at the show currently trying its hardest to entertain them. 'How much longer?'

'Five minutes.' Maggie gave her youngest an indulgent smile. 'Just time for you to demolish that last slice of pizza and wash your hands.'

Tabby frowned. 'Washing hands is for before you eat.'

That was Tabby. Always ready to argue any point. 'True. It's also for after you eat if your hands are covered in pizza goo. It stops the goo ending up on your clothes.'

Her daughter glanced down at the pretty rainbow tutu she was wearing, and gave her a toothy grin. 'I guess.'

A few minutes later, Penny lunged for the remote control on the coffee table and sent the volume shooting up. 'It's about to start!'

Instantly Sarah's living room was filled with the distinctive toe-tapping, body-wiggling theme tune for *Strictly Come Dancing*. Yes, tonight, was the now traditional Saturday night Strictly Fest. The only people missing from their usual gang were Jack and Edward, Alice's husband and eight-year-old son, who'd chosen to go ten-pin bowling, as they did now and again. In Edward's words, watching dancing was okay, but bowling was better.

As they settled in for an hour of the best entertainment Saturday nights could provide, eyes glued to the sixty-inch-wide screen, the front door opened, then banged closed, and a man walked into the room.

'Bloody hell, that's loud. Are you trying to give the neighbours a heart attack?'

All of them turned to look at the intruder. Tall, athletic-looking, with sharp cheekbones, tanned skin and shaggy blonde hair, he wore black tracksuit bottoms and a white T-shirt. On his left wrist were several braided leather wrist straps. Further up his arms were... muscles. Maggie couldn't help but notice them: the corded muscles of his forearms and the bulge of bicep as he strained to carry the gym bag he'd flung over his shoulder.

His eyes settled on the girls, and he winced. 'Ah, didn't see the kids. Sorry for the bad word.'

'We're trying to watch television,' Alice answered him pointedly. 'So butt out.'

The intruder tutted. 'That's not very friendly.' Then he frowned at the television. 'Strewth, is that *Strictly Come Dancing*? I can't believe it's still going. Haven't viewers had enough of watching people prance about in lycra and sequins by now?'

Tabby stood up and placed a finger on her mouth. 'Shh.'

Maggie bit into her lip to stop herself from laughing. Probably she should reprimand her daughter for being rude, and to a stranger too, but what she really wanted to do was high-five her.

Looking more amused than annoyed, the man flashed Tabby a grin. 'Hello, I'm Seb. What's your name?'

Tabby huffed, raising her eyes to the ceiling. 'I'm Tabby. But you're not allowed to talk while we're watching the dancing.'

'Oh, okay.' He nodded towards the double doors that divided the sitting room from the kitchen. 'Am I allowed to get myself a drink?'

'I suppose. If you're quiet.'

His lips twitched. 'Yes ma'am.'

Seb. Maggie ran the name around in her head, and realised who the guy was. 'Your brother's staying with you?' she whispered to Sarah.

Sarah nodded, eyes fixed on the television where Tess Daly was coming into view. 'I'll tell you later.'

A loud crash from the kitchen made them all jump.

'What the hell?' Sarah let out a strangled noise of sheer exasperation.

'Oops.' Seb's face appeared, framed by the double doors, looking anything but sorry. 'Don't worry, everyone, no need to leap up and check on me. I haven't hurt myself.'

Alice stood, grabbed the remote control and pressed pause. 'For God's sake, Seb. What have you broken?'

'Hey, relax. It was just a glass. I'll clean it up. You guys can get back to your programme.'

'Well, as you've already disturbed us, I guess I might as well make the introductions. Everyone, if you haven't guessed already, this is Seb, our annoying baby brother.' Alice swung her eyes over to Seb. 'And brother dear, the people whose evening you keep interrupting are Maggie, our friend from uni days, her children, Tabby and Penny, their nanny, Hannah. And I assume you recognise your niece.'

Seb winked at Rebecca before skimming his gaze over the rest of them. When it connected with Maggie's, she experienced an unexpected jolt. Wow, even from this distance, she could see his eyes were a vivid blue. Together with the tan, the sun-bleached hair and the laid-back appearance, it gave him a sexy surfer vibe. If he hadn't come across as such a dick, she might have been tempted to try and set him up with Hannah. The girl could do with a bit of excitement in her life.

'Ladies.' Seb bowed his head. 'And my sisters. I apologise for interrupting what is clearly an... absorbing evening of entertainment. From now on I promise to keep the noise down. I wouldn't want you to miss anything... crucial.'

Sarcastic bugger. Maggie swallowed her words. After all, he was Alice and Sarah's brother.

'Oh, bugger off.' Alice, as usual, said what others were thinking. 'Just because it isn't twenty men running around a field getting sweaty doesn't mean it isn't entertainment.'

'I think you'll find it's twenty-two men, though I suppose you could argue the goalie doesn't run, so—'

'Seb.' Alice ground out the word.

'Shut up. Got it.' He waved a hand at the television. 'Carry on. I'll be quiet as a monk in here.'

Maggie had to bite into her lip again. There was nothing about the six-foot-plus, brash male that suggested he could mimic a monk in any way.

'God, he's annoying,' Sarah muttered as he closed the doors.

'Hey, I heard that,' came a shout from the kitchen. 'You guys missed me really though. You're just too stubborn to admit it.'

Sarah rolled her eyes, but Maggie didn't miss the smiles she and Alice tried to hide. Seb might be the annoying younger brother, but he was clearly loved.

5

Holy fuck, how many pieces could a glass shatter into? Seb brushed yet another shard into the dustpan, his eyes searching the floor for stragglers. He didn't want to be responsible for any of the party in the living room getting cut feet. Especially not the cute little firecracker sat on the floor with his niece who'd told him to shush.

He'd not expected to find a house full of women when he'd come back from his workout. Not that he was against the idea – he was all for the other sex. No, it was more that, after only three days being back in his home town, crashing in Sarah's spare room, he felt the life slowly being strangled out of him. And coming home to a house of females watching dancing on the television only reinforced the direness of his situation. He ached for the sea, the surf, the *freedom* he'd left behind.

A life where he hadn't been introduced as 'our annoying baby brother'. Where nobody asked him when he was going to 'grow up, knuckle down and get a proper job'. Yep, those were the very words his father had said to him this morning. *Thanks, Pop, way to make me glad I've given up my life in sunny Oz and moved back to the dreary UK.*

It hadn't helped that his dad had looked so terribly ill. Always on the chubby side, he'd lost weight since the heart attack that had nearly killed him a week ago. Now he looked unwell, his skin a horrible grey colour. A man on borrowed time.

Seb pulled himself up short. Nope, he wasn't going to

wallow. What he needed was a distraction. He glanced towards the closed double doors, smirking at the sound of Bruno Tonioli giving his usual flamboyant feedback. Jeeze, how old was the guy now? He'd been a judge on the programme back when Seb had been forced to endure it at boarding school.

Decision made, Seb tucked the dustpan and brush back under the sink, opened the doors and squeezed himself on the sofa between Sarah and the fair-haired woman he clearly remembered Alice saying was Maggie.

'Excuse me, ladies.' He shuffled his backside further back.

Sarah narrowed her eyes. 'Really?' she hissed. 'You're going to watch this with us?'

He gave her a sunny smile. 'Well, you obviously enjoy it. Thought I'd see what all the fuss was about.' He glanced at the television. 'Where's the old guy?'

The girls on the floor turned their heads towards him, Tabby giving him that evil eye again.

'You're meant to be quiet, Uncle Seb.' His niece did at least smile when she said it.

'Sorry, Beccs.'

'Rebecca,' Alice muttered.

He smirked, knowing Alice hated it when he shortened his niece and nephew's names. 'Look, just put me out of my misery and tell me what happened to the old dude. You know who I mean. He was the funny one.'

'Bruce Forsyth passed away.' Maggie angled her head and gave him a rather cool look.

7

'And a great loss he was, too.' *See*, he wanted to add, *I knew that*. 'I always had a soft spot for him. But I was talking about the other dude, the one who used to say seeevvvvveeeeerrrrn!'

'Len Goodman left in 2016.' This time Maggie didn't bother to look at him, and maybe he *was* still the immature kid his family had him down as, because her polite formality made him want to wind her up. Ruffle her feathers a bit.

'That's a real shame,' he replied, ignoring the deep sigh from Sarah on his other side. 'I seem to remember he was quite a character.'

'You used to watch it then?' He had Maggie's attention again, and had to admit the way she arched her brow, the wintry grey of her eyes, the subtle beauty of her face... she was quite intimidating.

'I had no choice. At boarding school, it was watch that, or watch nothing.' Immediately he regretted the words. It wasn't bad enough his sisters calling him baby brother, now he was making *himself* sound like a schoolboy still. 'Of course, that was a long time ago,' he added, which, yes, on reflection, just made the whole kid vibe Alice had started even more obvious.

'I suppose it depends how you define *long*.' Maggie gave him a small smile before turning her attention back to the TV screen.

It left Seb to sigh inwardly and decide to keep his mouth closed for a bit.

'She looks like a fairy princess,' Tabby piped up five

minutes later.

Seb wondered what her dad was like, because she certainly didn't get her chatty genes from her mum. They shared hair colour, and the same eye shape, only Tabby's were a pretty hazel, not a wintry grey. 'I thought we weren't allowed to talk?' he couldn't resist saying.

She rolled her eyes in that way kids have of making adults feel two feet small. 'You can if it's about *Strictly*.'

'Right. So I can say she might look like a princess, but he looks like a…' Dick, prat – he wasn't sure what was appropriate for a kid of Tabby's age. 'He looks like a turkey wrapped in tin foil.'

Tabby, bless her, started to giggle, and Seb felt a rush of warmth, and of gratitude towards her. One bright spot in an otherwise pretty shitty day. Her eyes sought out her mother's. 'Can he say that?'

Maggie smiled at her daughter – not the watered-down version she'd given him, but a really lovely smile. 'He can say it.' When she turned to him, the smile dimmed though the grey of her eyes was less frosty. 'But we don't have to agree with him.'

Alice, lounging on what Seb liked to think of as his armchair, even though he'd only lived at Sarah's for three days, snorted. 'People rarely agree with Seb. Usually because he enjoys being deliberately provocative.'

'Hey, it's not my fault you're so easy to wind up.' Intrigued, he glanced back at Maggie. 'You really think the silver get-up looks *good* on him?'

'I think,' she replied in that slow, careful way she

seemed to have, 'for a man to carry off a suit like that, he has to be really confident in who he is. And *that* is highly attractive.'

So, she fancied the pro dancer, did she? Seb instinctively looked down at her hand – slender and graceful, much like the rest of her – and noted the absence of a wedding ring. 'I guess you could see it that way.' What was so special about being sure of who you were, though? Couldn't a guy be attractive while he was still trying to find himself? 'Or maybe he was just too chicken to say no to the costume department. Hang on, make that too *turkey*.'

'Seb.' Sarah's sharp tone had him swivelling his attention to the woman on his other side. 'Don't you have some place else to go? Somewhere your conversation and schoolboy humour might be appreciated?'

Usually he'd shrug the comment off. He wasn't by nature insecure; he was a reasonably good-looking guy who had no problem getting on with people. So yeah, normally, he'd laugh that snide comment off and say something like *sure I have, but tonight I'm generously sharing myself with you.* After all, it's what Sarah was expecting, because that's what they did. Needle each other.

Tonight though? Yeah, tonight he wasn't in the mood.

Rising to his feet, he gave Sarah a mock salute and strode out of the room. He'd take a shower and head back out to the pub. A place where he didn't feel judged. Where he could talk to guys about offside rules and penalty shootouts, rather than costumes, posture and hip movements.

Chapter Two

The show was over, the girls fast asleep on Sarah's bed upstairs. Sarah had opened a bottle of wine, which Hannah and Alice were helping her drink. Maggie was tonight's designated driver.

'Do you think I upset Seb earlier?' Sarah turned to her sister. 'He's been a bit, I don't know, gloomy since he's come back.'

'You'd be gloomy if you'd been forced to ditch life in the Whitsunday Islands to come back here.' Alice took a large swallow of wine. 'He'll soon settle down. And he's an impossible guy to upset, you know that. Far too chilled to take offence at being told to get lost.'

Maggie was intrigued by the man who'd parked himself on the sofa between her and Sarah and gone on to both annoy and entertain them all for a while. 'Why is he back? Because of your dad?'

'Yes.' Alice glanced down at her glass, her face taking on

11

a sombre expression. 'His MI.' She raised her eyes to the ceiling when Sarah coughed. 'Sorry, for the non-medics, the heart attack was a major one. When I told Seb about it, I expected him to plan a visit. Didn't realise he'd drop everything and jump on the next plane.'

'That's our brother for you. Impulsive. He's never been afraid to up sticks and leave a place.' Sarah gave them a wry smile. 'Far more afraid of putting down roots.'

'He seems nice.' Hannah, who'd been quiet up till now, started to giggle. 'Okay, what I mean is, he's seriously hot.'

'You think so, huh?' Alice grinned at her. 'You know what, he's a pain in the arse but he is a good guy. You're what, twenty-six?' When Hannah nodded, Alice beamed. 'He's twenty-seven, so that works. As long as you don't want anything heavy, mind you, because one thing's for certain, he won't be sticking around for long.'

Hannah shrugged. 'I just want a bit of fun. I mean, is it too much to ask for a guy who's more interested in me than in taking moody selfies for his Instagram followers?'

Maggie gaped. 'Is that seriously what Giles did?' Giles was the boyfriend Hannah had ditched two months ago.

'Yep.' She eyed Alice and Sarah. 'Please tell me Seb doesn't have an obsession with selfies?'

The sisters burst out laughing.

'Seb's not even on social media, as far as we know. He's more your outdoors type. Scuba diving in the Great Barrier Reef, trekking through jungles, parachuting out of planes, that kind of thing.'

Hannah's eyes lit up. 'He sounds way cooler than Giles.'

'Anyone sounds cooler than Giles,' Maggie countered. 'You need to set your standards far higher than Instagram man.'

Slowly Alice swivelled her focus towards Maggie. Her heart sank when she saw the glint in her friend's eye. 'Sound advice, yet don't fall into the trap of Maggie here, who seems to have set the bar so high, nobody can ever hope to reach it.'

'I told you before, I've got enough going on in my life with work and the girls. Why don't you give Sarah a hard time, instead?'

'I do, often, but she keeps telling me—'

'I love my job more than I could ever love a guy,' Sarah interrupted.

'Exactly, and I respect that. Owning your own company, well, I guess it's like being married.' Alice's eyes swivelled back to Maggie. 'But you, dear Maggie, have been married for real, so you know how it feels to be in love. Don't you miss that? Miss sharing your life with someone special?'

Inside her chest, Maggie's heart ached, just a little, at the memory of the life she and Paul had once had together. Before he'd decided he didn't want to be her husband any more. 'I miss someone to share the girls with,' she admitted. 'The pride in their successes, but also the constant worries. Am I doing the right thing by them? I also miss someone to share that precious time after they've gone to bed, and the house is quiet.' Her mind filled with an image of her and Paul snuggled together on the sofa, glass of wine in hand, talking about everything, and nothing. But that had been before things had changed. 'I don't miss being berated for being late home from the surgery because my last patient needed to talk. I don't miss being told I'm too anal and pedantic just because I like things done a certain way, or that I make too many lists.' Fearing she was going down a depressing road, she forced a smile. 'And I certainly don't miss having to watch stupid action or comedy films on a Saturday night because,' she used her fingers to mimic quotation marks, '"*Strictly* isn't a programme a red-blooded male wants to watch."'

They all laughed, and Maggie hoped that was the end of the conversation, but no. Alice was like a bloody dog with a bone. 'You know what you should do.' Her friend didn't give her the chance to reply. 'You should go dancing again. I remember at uni you used to go to ballroom dancing classes, and even though we took the piss out of you, we were secretly envious because you'd come back all flushed and bright-eyed. You loved dancing.'

'I did. God, that feeling of floating across the floor, of all the crap from the day ebbing away until there was nothing left in my head but the music.' Even now, more than ten years since she'd last stepped onto a dance floor, tingles rippled down her spine at the memory. Dance lessons had been the highlight of her week. Protected time when, for a couple of hours, she forgot the seriousness of the career she'd chosen, the hard hours of study, and lost herself in something beautiful. 'But Paul didn't share the same passion, so...' she trailed off, shrugging to hide the knot of emotion in her throat.

'So what?' Sarah's expression turned fierce. 'He shouldn't have made you give up something you loved.'

'He didn't make me,' she countered, then immediately wondered why she'd defended him. It was a habit, one she should have broken by now. 'He let it be known he didn't like me going.'

'Which made it hard for you to carry on.' Alice reached across and squeezed her hand. 'We're not blaming you for stopping. We just think it's sad he couldn't support you, instead.'

And that kind of summed up her marriage, Maggie thought bitterly. Paul hadn't been someone she could lean on, a partner who would look out for her best interests. He'd looked out for himself.

'But don't you see, the fact that you used to love dancing, and that you still love watching it, means you should definitely take it up again.' Hannah almost bounced in her chair. 'I can totally look after Tabby and Penny if you want to.'

Could she? Dare she? Excitement hummed in her belly; butterfly wings dusting themselves off and learning to flap again. 'I wasn't good,' Maggie felt the need to point out. 'And it was a long time ago. I doubt I'll remember any of it.'

'You can learn again.' Hannah grinned. 'And then you can teach us. We could do some sessions when *Strictly*'s finished.'

'Maybe.' She was cautious by nature, and divorce had only magnified that. Still, she was talking about *dancing* again. And this time there would be nobody holding her back, nobody saying it was inconvenient. No annoyed husband to come home to afterwards. Hannah would look after the girls, so really there was nothing to stop her, except... 'I don't have a partner.'

'So? I'm sure that's not unusual,' Sarah pointed out in that assertive, some might say pushy way she had. 'Single people must sign up for dancing lessons all the time.'

Alice waggled her eyebrows. 'What's to say there isn't a tall, dark, handsome guy currently being forced to dance with... I don't know... a mop, because he hasn't got a partner.'

Maggie spluttered with laughter. 'Knowing my luck, I'll get the blasted mop. Though I suppose it would at least keep its hands to itself.'

Seb expected to find the place silent when he opened the door to his sister's house a few hours later. He definitely didn't expect to hear wild, drunken laughter. Nor did he expect to find Alice, Sarah and Maggie still camped in the sitting room when he popped his head inside.

'Me again.' He deliberately looked over at the now black TV screen. 'Do I take it talking is allowed now?'

Sarah smiled serenely back at him. 'Only if it's about ballroom dancing.'

'Very funny.' She kept smiling at him. 'Come on, you're kidding me, right? What was that about a mop I heard when I opened the door? That's not ballroom.'

'It is,' Alice asserted. 'It's Maggie's new dance partner.'

More laughter, though Maggie's was quieter than his sisters'; a more refined, dignified sound. As if she didn't really want to be laughing but couldn't help herself. When he sought her gaze, she gave him a small smile. 'It's a long story.'

How had he missed how attractive she was? With those grey eyes now gently amused, her mouth curved upwards... a zing of interest, sharp and hot, flashed through him. Pretending a casualness he didn't feel, he leant against the wall and crossed his feet at the ankles. 'Hey, I've got time.' *Especially to listen to you*, he wanted to add, but not with his sisters gawping. Besides, he really did have days of the stuff. Maybe weeks and months of it. God knows what he was going to do with himself now he was back, in between seeing his dad.

To his disappointment, Maggie shook her head and slowly rose to her feet. 'You might have, but I'm afraid I don't. It's time I was in bed.'

Okay, not a promising start. If he'd gone with the flirty addition, would she have knocked him back just as coolly? Really there was only one way to find out. With a nod he pushed back from the wall, and headed into the kitchen for a glass of water.

'Seb, do us a favour and help carry the girls down and into Maggie's car?' Alice shouted over at him a moment later. 'They're asleep on Sarah's bed.'

'Sure.'

He stepped into the hallway where he found Maggie,

who gave him a small smile. 'Just take care of Rebecca. I can manage my two.'

She's being protective, he reasoned. It wasn't personal. 'Worried I'll drop them?'

The look she gave him was steady and measured. 'I'm worried they'll wake to find themselves in the arms of a man they don't really know.'

Well, that shot his petty retort down in flames. 'Fair enough.' He indicated up the stairs. 'Ladies first.'

As he watched Maggie gently scoop up her eldest, Seb wondered what to make of her. She appeared distant, reserved, yet the way she was with her kids was quite the opposite. And there was no way his mouthy, larger-than-life sisters would be friends with a boring cold fish.

Picking up his niece, Seb followed Maggie down. Her eyes fluttered open when he settled her into the back of the car next to Penny. 'Sorry, Beccs, you'll soon be home.'

'Rebecca.' Alice glared at him over her shoulder from the front passenger seat.

His niece gave him a sleepy smile. 'Night, Uncle Seb.'

'Night, *Beccs*.' Smiling, he kissed the top of her head, saying a silent prayer of thanks to the inventors of Skype. Without it, he'd never have managed to keep up a relationship with his niece and nephew.

Straightening, he watched as Maggie walked out with Tabby in her arms. In what was clearly a well-practised move, she eased the little girl into the final seat in the back.

'You look like you've done that before,' he remarked after she'd put the seat belt round her.

'You could say that.' He received another small, careful smile before she opened the driver's door and slipped inside.

He wasn't sure what made him hold the door, stopping her from closing it on him. There was just something about her calm presence, those cool grey eyes that captured his attention. Made him want to unsettle her, as she was unsettling him. 'Well, it's been great to meet you, Maggie. I guess I'll see you around.'

'I guess you will.'

He continued to hold her gaze, not quite sure what he was hoping for, but whatever it was, his sister interrupted it. 'Will you shut that damn door, Seb. You're letting all the cold air in.'

Dipping his head, he nodded over to Alice. 'Catch you tomorrow at the folks?'

'Sure. I'll be the one with the humdinger of a hangover.'

Laughing, he pushed the driver's door closed. Within seconds the smart grey BMW eased away from the curb. Sleek and quiet, just like the woman driving it.

'So what was with the mop then?' he asked Sarah as he headed back inside.

'Oh, it was just a joke. We're trying to persuade Maggie to take up ballroom dancing again. She used to love it when we were at uni.'

'Did she study with you or Alice?'

'Alice. She's a GP.'

He thought of the woman he'd just seen carry her daughters into the car. Yes, he could see her as doctor.

Patient and caring, yet with a tough no-nonsense streak. 'Where's the husband?'

Sarah, who'd been clearing away, paused as she picked up a glass. 'He's now an ex-husband. They divorced three years ago, and wherever he is, he's keeping it quiet. Paul's no longer in her life, other than a few measly video calls to the girls now and then.' She angled her head. 'Why all the interest?'

He shrugged off the question, though inside he was asking himself the very same thing. 'No reason. Just learning about the people my sisters hang out with.'

'Well, it's Hannah you ought to be asking about.' Sarah winked. 'For some weird reason, she thinks you're hot.'

'Maybe because I *am* hot?'

Sarah laughed. 'Sure, maybe.' Seb had always found Sarah the easier sister to get on with. She was less loud, less liable to ask the searching, difficult question. More likely to smile at his jokes.

'What happened to Hannah tonight? Excitement of *Strictly* too much for her?'

'Funny. One of her friends picked her up to take her to a party.' She eyed him speculatively. 'So, how about it? We could facilitate things with her if you're interested.'

The thought of his sisters brokering him a date... He shuddered. 'It'll be a cold day in hell before I need either of you two helping me with my love life.'

'Okay, okay, message received.' Sarah picked up the remaining plates and headed towards the kitchen. 'But think about it. Hannah's not looking for anything serious and you could do with something to look forward to, in between visits to Dad.'

She wasn't wrong there, and Hannah definitely had what he'd call cute appeal. Not a beauty, like Maggie, but probably a lot more fun. He just wasn't sure he was in the right place to date anyone right now.

His world had gone from waking up to the sun rising over the reef, his only stress finding enough barracudas, turtles and rays to give the tourists their thrill, to – what? England in November. Grey skies, damp and dismal weather. Oh, and let's not forget his main role, helping to take care of an invalid. His life was on pause. He wanted to be back in the place where he'd found something he was good at, even if it was only entertaining tourists.

But then he thought of his mum, and how dramatically she seemed to have aged since his father's heart attack. Leaving now would be selfish. Like it or not, his family needed him, and he was damned if he was going to disappoint them. At least not any more than he had already.

Chapter Three

T he week had flown by and now here they were again, preparing for another Strictly Saturday. This time at Alice's.

Maggie had barely stepped through the front door when Alice pounced on her.

'Tell me you've signed up for some ballroom dancing lessons.'

'Sort of.'

The reply was never going to be enough for Alice, and clearly Hannah knew that too because she nodded towards where the girls were heading. 'I'm off to the TV room with them. I'll leave you to your inquisition.'

'Traitor.' Hannah just grinned, leaving Maggie to face Alice, who was looking at her with the expression she probably used on uncooperative patients. 'Look, I've rung a few numbers but most of them are full, or they started in September so I've already missed two months.'

'*Most* of them.' Alice gave her arm a nudge. 'See, I picked up on that.'

Damn, she hadn't meant to be so literal. 'Fine. There's one dance studio with vacancies on a Wednesday night.'

'Perfect.'

Alice, confident and spontaneous, would never understand Maggie's preference for taking things slowly. Even when it was something as important to her as dancing. 'I'm not fully convinced I should take lessons again. It means leaving Penny and Tabby—'

'It's a good job you've lots of willing babysitters then. Including their nanny.'

Maggie sighed. 'Okay, you've ripped through my cunning excuse. The truth is… damn it, Alice, I want to dance again, so much, but I'm also really, embarrassingly, scared.'

Alice's eyes flew open. 'Scared of *dancing*?'

'Scared of going to lessons. By myself,' she qualified, feeling more and more foolish. 'I know, I know, it's dumb, but God, the divorce has really done a number on me. I want to be this smart, confident woman who can walk solo into a dance studio and look forward to dancing, with anyone. But I'm not that woman any more.'

'Bollocks.' Alice grabbed Maggie's arms and stared fiercely back at her. 'Paul was a dick who didn't realise how lucky he was to be married to you. One day he will, but by then it'll be too late because you'll not only have realised the divorce was down to his inadequacies and not yours, you'll have met someone who values everything about you.' A lump of emotion lodged itself in Maggie's throat and Alice smiled. 'Even your need to plan things to death.'

The tears that had been brimming shifted into tears of laughter. 'Ouch, that's not fair.'

'No? Why do we always have pizza on Strictly Saturdays? Why do we have a rota detailing who's hosting when?'

'Because then we all know what's happening,' she protested. 'It's called organisation.'

Alice laughed and threw an arm around her. 'And it's just one of the many things we love about you.' Her face sobered as she caught Maggie's eye. 'Promise me you won't let Paul continue to interfere with your life. Take up dancing again.'

'I hadn't thought about it like that, but you're right. I refuse to let that man, hell, any man, tell me what I can and can't do any more.' Maggie drew in a breath and smiled back at her. 'I'll enrol tomorrow.'

'Good.'

After checking the kids were settled in front of the television, Maggie and Alice wandered into Alice's state-of-the-art kitchen to help sort out the food. Jack, who'd been opening boxes of pizza, grinned over at them. 'Thank God, the cavalry's arrived. I'm out of here.'

'Typical male,' Alice muttered as she watched her husband slink off. 'And I bet he's gone to grab the best spot in front of the TV.'

'Hey, don't knock him. At least he's happy to watch it with you.' More than Paul had ever done. Because she'd had enough of thinking of her ex, Maggie turned her attention to the mountain of food on the worktop. 'Wow, chicken wings as well as pizza. Did we agree on that deviation from the rules?'

'They were on offer, so I thought I'd make a unilateral decision.' Alice winked. 'I figured it was hard for the kids to make any more mess than they already do.'

'I admire your optimism,' Maggie said dryly, just as the doorbell sounded. 'That must be Sarah. I'll get it.'

But as she went to open the door, she spotted the outline of a tall male frame through the frosted glass. And when she opened it, her breath caught in her throat. Clad in a black jacket, grey shirt with several buttons open and smart black trousers, his too-long blonde hair loose around the collar, his chin sporting sexy stubble, the visitor looked like a cross between Thor and James Bond.

'It's you.'

Seb's lips quirked at her inelegant greeting, then angled his head down his body, before bringing it up again to look straight into her eyes. 'So it is.'

Damn, she deserved that. Usually she was much friendlier than this. Then again, usually she wasn't made to feel this unbalanced. Shaking herself, she managed a smile. 'Sorry, I was expecting you to be Sarah.'

'And I'm a poor substitute?' He clasped a hand to his heart. 'You wound me.'

'I didn't say that.' Why was he able to tie her up in knots?

'Then I'm a *good* substitute?'

Amusement lit up his vivid blue eyes and Maggie couldn't help but laugh. 'I didn't say that either.'

'Ah, but maybe you thought it. I can live in hope.' He winked, and she felt a small thrill to think this attractive man was, in a small, harmless way, flirting with her. 'I'm afraid Sarah can't make it tonight. Something's come up at work. She asked me to let you guys know.'

'Oh, I see. That's a shame.' Yet it didn't explain what he was doing here, in person, dressed like a surfing god going to an award ceremony.

He glanced towards the door she was still holding. 'Am I allowed in?'

Feeling stupid, she pushed the door open fully. 'You're not planning on joining us again, are you?'

'Is that a problem?' He leant towards her, the crisp, fresh smell of whatever he'd just showered with drifting deliciously up her nostrils. 'I mean, if it's a ticket-only affair, I think I should point out I've got an in with the woman hosting tonight.'

Enjoying him far more than perhaps she should, Maggie chuckled. 'I'm surprised you want to watch it with us, that's all. You didn't appear to enjoy it last week.'

The eyes that were so hard to ignore, pierced through her. 'You enjoy it, don't you?'

She blinked. 'Well, yes.'

'So much that you're going to dance with a… what was it? A broom?'

Now he was laughing at her. 'It was a mop, and it isn't my first choice.'

'Interesting.' His gaze sharpened. 'What, or perhaps I should ask who, would be your first choice?'

Though her heart bounced at the way he looked directly at her, she forced herself to meet his gaze. 'Someone who can dance.'

His lips curved. 'Sounds sensible.'

She couldn't help it, she had to know. 'Are you really here to watch *Strictly*?'

'I thought I'd give it another go.' He sent her a slow, seductive smile. 'I can enjoy the company, even if I don't enjoy the programme.'

There it was again, the cheeky flirting. Part of her admired his audacity – she was years older, yet he clearly wasn't fazed by that, or the fact she was friends with his sisters. 'Are you sure you've not just come to wind us all up again?' she asked as she stepped aside to let him in, closing the door behind him.

'Me?' His eyes widened in an entirely innocent expression.

'The thought had crossed my mind,' she answered dryly, more charmed than she wanted to be.

'Okay, you've rumbled me.' He dipped his head towards her, his lips so close to her ear that his breath fluttered across her skin. 'I thought I'd wind *Alice* up,' he whispered, before straightening and giving her a careful study. 'You, I suspect, are harder to rile. Where Alice is straight to boil, I'd put you down as more of a slow simmer.'

There was something about the way he said it, in that low drawl, with just the hint of an Aussie accent, that sent a flush creeping over her skin. A flush that wasn't appropriate for a thirty-seven-year-old woman. 'I can boil if the occasion warrants it.'

Seb wondered what it would be like to see Maggie boil. For her to let go of all that careful control. He had a feeling it would be quite spectacular. 'I'll consider myself forewarned.'

The alone time with Maggie he'd been enjoying was interrupted by the appearance of Alice in the hallway.

'Seb, what on earth are you doing here?' Her eyes ran up and down him. 'Why are you dressed up? And what have you done with Sarah?'

It was Alice's way, always straight to the point, and usually it didn't bother him. Yet as had happened last Saturday, he found being treated as the annoying younger brother in front of Maggie rankled with him. 'Okay, so in order: I'm here to watch *Strictly*. I'm wearing a jacket because I'm a smart guy, though it'll be handy when I go to the club later. As for what I've done with Sarah, you say that like I might have poisoned her tea, tied her up and pushed her into the boot of my car.'

Deciding he'd had enough of being interrogated, Seb walked through to where he could hear the TV, leaving Maggie to update Alice on the reason for his sister's no-show.

There he found Maggie's kids sitting on the floor next to his niece and nephew. Jack, who'd commandeered one of the armchairs, rose to his feet and gave him a manly handshake.

'Good to have some more male company for these evenings.' He nodded at Seb's outfit. 'Didn't realise we blokes were dressing up too, though.'

Seb laughed. 'I was told it was part of the rules.'

Tabby looked over at him with narrowed eyes. 'Are you going to watch with us again?'

'Yep.' He settled down in the middle of the sofa. 'I loved it so much last time, wild horses wouldn't drag me away.'

Rebecca giggled, but Tabby didn't seem convinced. 'It's Halloween night. That's one of the bestest shows. You have to be quiet when it starts.'

'I'll be mouse-like,' he promised.

As the jarring opening sounds of *Strictly* sounded on the television, the others rushed in carrying plates of pizza and wings which they set on the coffee table. Seb didn't miss how Maggie immediately went to sit on the other armchair at the opposite end of the room from him. Or how Hannah chose to sit on the sofa next to him.

'Yes, it's Halloween week.' On the TV, the Italian judge jumped to his feet, waving his arms flamboyantly. 'It's going to be a spooktacular night of dancing!'

Dancers took to the stage in a variety of ghoulish costumes, and it wasn't long before not making a comment was like not eating the last chocolate in the box: too hard to resist. 'This is definitely the stuff of nightmares,' he murmured. Almost mouse-like.

Tabby whirled round, eyes wide. 'You promised.'

He hung his head and whispered. 'Bugger, sorry.'

To his surprise, she grinned back at him. '*And* now you said a rude word.'

Of their own volition, his eyes sought out Maggie's, and he found her watching them. 'Your daughter's too sharp for me.'

'She's too sharp for all of us.'

Maggie's mouth curved in a smile that was echoed in her eyes, and the force of it hit him like a train. Wow, the ice maiden was intriguing, but the woman who'd just smiled at him? She was dynamite. Really, sit up and take notice. Gorgeous with a capital G.

All too soon, her attention was back on the TV screen.

'I'm going to be doing the tango,' a female contestant told the camera. She was dressed in a bizarre outfit he thought was supposed to resemble a playing card but actually looked like a cross between Frankenstein's monster and a Bavarian milkmaid. 'And I'm terrified.'

'Not half as terrified as I'll be, watching you.' The words slipped out before he'd had a chance to stop them and now it wasn't just Tabby who turned to stare at him. It was the whole room. Feeling most of them wanted to bury him alive, he mimicked zipping his mouth closed. 'Sorry. Again.'

He managed to keep quiet for a full ten minutes, until his sister started disagreeing with the judges' comments.

'No hip rotation?' Alice stabbed a finger at the television. 'That's ridiculous. Were they watching the same dance I was?'

Hannah giggled. 'You just fancy the pro dancer so you want them to go through.'

Seb cleared his throat. 'Perhaps they should go to VAR.'

Jack let out a boom of a laugh and Alice raised her eyes to the ceiling. When Seb glanced towards Maggie, he was certain he saw her lips twitch.

'What's VAR?' Rebecca asked him.

'Video assistant referee. They use it in football to correct clear howlers of a decision.'

'But this isn't football,' she protested.

'Quite,' her mother agreed. 'Your uncle was trying to be funny.'

'Hey, it *was* funny,' Seb protested.

'It kind of was,' Hannah agreed, sending him a flirty smile which soothed his ego but lacked the punch of Maggie's smile from earlier.

It was the turn of the waltz, and as they watched the next couple dip and turn, Hannah sighed. 'That's so beautiful. It's like they're gliding.'

'Exactly.' Maggie's eyes were on the television, her expression one of, well, it was beyond delight. If pushed, he'd have called it *enchantment*. 'The Viennese waltz is so elegant, so graceful. I love how they seem to float across the dance floor, as if they haven't a care in the world beyond the music and each other.'

For once, he had no ready quip. Sure, there was beauty in the dance, but that wasn't the reason he kept his lips sealed. It was the look of longing on Maggie's face as she watched it.

Chapter Four

It was the most hectic time of the day. That hour in the morning where things had to run to a disciplined timetable, yet could so easily veer off course if Maggie wasn't right on top of it all.

So far she could tick off getting herself up and dressed, and the girls awake enough to be sitting at the breakfast table in their uniforms, bar Tabby's socks. Twenty minutes for them to finish eating, clean their teeth and pack their school bags.

Twenty minutes during which Hannah would hopefully arrive, and Maggie could hand over the final responsibility of actually getting them to school. Oh, and getting socks on Tabby's feet.

'What happened with your project?' Maggie asked Penny as she slapped some pre-sliced cheese between two pieces of bread. It was one thing being a staunch believer in the benefits of healthy, wholesome, *exciting* lunches for kids.

Another having the damn time to make the Greek yoghurt and salad wrap/two-bean tuna salad/chicken satay with rice and diced flipping mango. That's if her fridge even contained ingredients beyond cheese, ham and tomato.

Penny kept her head bent, seemingly absorbed in the task of piling more Weetabix onto her spoon.

'Penny? Did you start it yet?' Her elder daughter, always the quieter of the two, seemed to have totally lost her tongue. 'Should I take your silence as a no? When does it need to be in?'

'Wednesday.'

And today was… 'But Penny, that's tomorrow. Have you started it yet?'

'I don't know what to do,' she protested. 'It's a crap title.'

'Crap isn't an appropriate word.' Though right now Maggie had a burning desire to shout it out loud and on repeat. 'Remind me what it was about again?' she asked with a heavy dose of guilt. Yes, Hannah was in charge of picking the girls up from school and supervising their homework, but she wasn't their mum. The shivvying, chasing, the encouraging, they were all down to her. And she'd ballsed this one up.

'We have to write about climate change. One example of it.'

'Well, that's not crap, it's important. I'm sure you can think of lots of things to choose from. How about the weather? Summers are getting hotter, weather becoming more extreme and more unpredictable.'

Penny yawned. 'That's so lame. Only old people talk about the weather.'

Tabby giggled, which made Penny grin, and Maggie took a precious moment from her tight schedule to gaze over at her daughters. How could Paul have just upped and left them? Even now, three years later, she still felt so angry about it. Him leaving her had hurt, but she was grown up enough to understand people changed and grew apart. Leaving these precious girls, though? That wasn't just incomprehensible, it was inexcusable.

'Mum?'

Maggie shook off the dark thoughts. 'Sorry. Okay, you don't want the weather. How about the effect on wildlife and loss of their habitats, like the poles losing ice, or the oceans getting warmer... hang on a minute, I might have an idea.' Flashbacks of the conversation she'd had with Alice and Sarah last Saturday played through her mind and she reached for her phone. 'You need to clean your teeth in two minutes.'

Used to her meticulous timing, they both gave her the long eye-roll, but then jumped down from the table and scrambled up the stairs.

A quick call to Sarah later, and Maggie was staring down at the digits she'd scribbled on the pad.

She couldn't explain why her pulse sped as she punched the numbers into her phone. Nor could she explain her body's reaction to the answering deep male voice. 'Hey, Seb here.'

Maggie found she had to clear her throat. 'It's me.

Maggie,' she added quickly, aware he wouldn't have a clue who *me* was. 'Do you have a minute?'

'For Maggie the Dancer? Of course. Shoot.'

Her brain, usually so sharp, was struggling to fire. 'Before you came back to England, you were taking people scuba diving on the Great Barrier Reef.'

'Are you asking me, or telling me?'

She could hear the amusement in his voice, and it annoyed her that he was so laid back while she sounded like an uptight school teacher. 'That part I remember Sarah telling me. What I'm asking, is would you be free later today to help my daughter with her school project?'

'The firecracker, or the mini-you?'

'Sorry?'

'Which daughter?'

She was still trying to get her head around the way he'd pigeon-holed them. Tabby was outspoken, yes, but was Penny really so much like her? 'Does it matter?'

'It doesn't matter, no. I was just interested. What's the project?'

Maggie explained how she thought her daughter could use the reef as an example of climate change. 'Penny has to hand it in tomorrow and I thought she might find it more interesting to chat to you than find information on the internet.'

'Wow, careful there. It sounds like you're saying I'm interesting.'

She knew, from the tone of his voice, that he was smiling. 'I wouldn't go that far.'

Soft laughter echoed down the phone. 'Ouch, you're a tough nut to crack. Just like your eldest daughter.'

'Penny's not tough,' Maggie countered. 'She's cautious with people she doesn't know.' There was a rustle of clothing, and in the background the hum of traffic, which made her suspect he was walking outside.

'As I'm one of those people, will she be okay with me interfering in her project?'

'It isn't the project itself I'd like your help with. More getting her interested enough in the subject that she'll actually do some work on it.' She hesitated, aware of the imposition. 'But only if you can spare the time.'

'Time is something I have a fair amount of at the moment.' There was a beat of silence. 'So when do you want me?'

Though it was an innocent enough question, Maggie felt her cheeks flush. God, what was wrong with her? 'Hannah brings the girls home around half three, so any time after that would be great.' Her nanny was finally going to get the chance to be alone with Seb. Well, Seb, two girls and a heavy dose of homework.

'And what about you? When will you be back?'

'It depends on my patient load.' She frowned down the phone. 'Why do you ask?'

'Just wondered if there's a deadline we need to be finished by.'

Maggie started to laugh. 'You haven't helped a nine-year-old with their school work before, have you?'

'Err, no. Why?'

'Because getting her to sit down for more than five minutes will be a miracle.' She glanced up to see the girls coming back down the stairs. Tabby still without her flipping socks on. 'Look, just do what you can. As long as she writes something. The moment she gets fidgety, you have my full permission to escape.'

'Okay. I might see you later, or I might not.'

'Oh, I'm pretty certain you won't.'

'You don't know how determined I can be, with the right incentive.'

Once again she could hear the smile in his voice. 'The incentive being?'

'If I keep Penny interested in her project for long enough, I get to see you again.'

Laughter burst out of her. God, he was incorrigible. 'Well, just in case the dubious incentive fails, thank you for helping out.'

'No problem. Thanks for trusting me with such an important mission.'

Maggie found herself laughing again as she ended the call, causing Penny to look over at her.

'Who was that?'

Maggie wrapped her arms around her. 'That, my darling daughter, is an expert on the effect of climate change on the Great Barrier Reef.'

———————

Seb winced as he watched his dad haul himself out of the

armchair. He still wasn't steady on his feet, yet he refused to use either a walking stick or a frame. 'I'm not a bloody invalid.'

His mum had the patience of a saint to put up with him. Then again, they'd been married for forty years, so she'd had plenty of practice.

'I told you, you don't have to see me out,' Seb protested. 'I'm capable of finding my way out of the house unaided.'

His dad straightened, resting a hand on the back of the chair to steady himself. 'And I'm capable of walking with my son to the front door.'

Stubborn sod. Seb glanced at his mum, who just smiled in that serene way she had. 'Fine, come on then, Dad, I'll race you.'

'Very funny.' Slowly he shuffled towards the door. 'So, have you sorted yourself out another job yet?'

Here we go again. For a few blessed moments he'd begun to think he'd escape the sermon this time round. 'It's taken you three hours to ask. Must be a new record.'

'Less of the cheek, son. When I was your age—'

'You were already climbing the career ladder,' Seb interrupted. 'What was it again? Marketing manager at twenty-seven?'

'Senior marketing manager.'

'Your parents must have been very proud.' The remark was tart, too tart for what he knew his father had only meant as a prod, a gentle push. Yet these 'gentle prods' had become more and more frequent. And Seb was feeling more and more battered by them. This was his dad, though. A man who'd nearly died two weeks ago, so he gentled his voice and gave him an honest answer. 'Look, Pops, I'm still considering what I want to do next.'

'How about, stay in one place long enough to actually make something of yourself?' His dad gave him a baleful look. 'And stop with that ridiculous name. You know it winds me up.'

Just as you know making my life feel insignificant winds me up, he wanted to counter, *so let's call it even*. He'd not come back to England to cause more hostility though. He'd come to build bridges and to help out his mum, so as they reached the front door, Seb swallowed the words. 'Same time again tomorrow?'

His mum, who had followed them to the door, leant forward and kissed his cheek. 'If you're sure that's okay.'

'I don't need babysitting, you know.' His dad glared at the pair of them, clearly recovered enough now to realise what was going on. 'I can be trusted to be in the house by myself.'

'We know that.' Seb clasped his dad around the shoulder in a hug. 'But I'd hate to deprive you of a chance of giving me another career lecture.'

It was just after four by the time Seb knocked on the door of the address Maggie had given him. A big detached house down a leafy lane. The sort of place owned by grown-up people with families and good jobs, he thought ruefully.

Hannah opened the door, a wide smile lighting up her face when she saw him. 'Hey there, come on in. I hear you're the reef expert.'

'Wow, expert.' He rubbed a hand over his chin. 'That's a word that's never been assigned to me before. Ever.'

Hannah laughed, ushering him inside. 'Apparently Maggie told Penny that's what you were.' She leant in closer, and he wasn't sure if it was accidental or not, but he felt the brush of her breast against his arm. 'I think she was disappointed when I told her it was you.'

He wasn't surprised. Just like her mother, Penny seemed cautious. Still, he'd back himself to charm a nine-year-old, given long enough. Her mother was a different matter. Not just a cautious nature, but with walls a mile high. He suspected there'd be a few surprise barriers, too, just when a guy thought he'd scaled the wall. Most of them probably courtesy of her ex – and yes, he'd gone to the trouble of asking his sister about Maggie. She fascinated him, the wary grey eyes in a quietly beautiful face, the sharp attitude. It was disappointing to know, despite his boast to her, he probably wouldn't see her tonight.

'Penny's in the kitchen.' Seb dragged his mind back to what Hannah was saying. 'She's doing homework but you can go on in. I think Maggie wants her to get the project done.' She flicked him a glance. 'Unless you fancy a drink and a bit of grown-up talk, first?'

Yep, he hadn't been imagining it. Hannah *was* flirting with him. His ego wagged its tail, yet he wasn't sure he felt anything more than that. Maybe it was down to the setting:

Maggie's house, Maggie's kids. 'I'd better see Penny.' He flashed Hannah a smile. 'But I wouldn't say no to a tea if you're offering.'

He took a quick scan of the rooms either side of the hallway as he followed Hannah down, trying not to feel too intimidated. The house was as he'd expected, impeccably neat, the furnishings tasteful, the muted colour scheme classy. Yet it was also so much more than he'd bargained for. More rooms, more space. More expensive.

He was pleased to find Tabby also in the L-shaped kitchen, though rather than sitting at the centre island like Penny, the younger sister was in what appeared to be a space designed for the kids to watch TV as Mum prepared tea. And... holy shit, what was that bright orange thing she was sitting on? No way was that Maggie's choice.

As soon as she saw him, Tabby jumped up from the satsuma of a sofa. 'We're not watching *Strictly*. That's for Saturdays but we get to watch *It Takes Two* if we're good. Penny has to do her thing for school now but I can watch the telly 'cos I've done my homework.' She pursed her lips as she glanced over at the TV screen. 'I guess you can watch with me. It's *SpongeBob*.' A grin lit up her face. 'He's well funny.'

God, Tabby cracked him up. 'That's quite some offer, thank you.' He glanced at Penny, who was staring at him with serious grey eyes identical to her mother's. 'First I need to see if I can help Penny with her project though.'

Aware of the elder sister's eyes on him, he walked over to where Penny was working and slipped onto the stool opposite her. 'Your mum tells me your project is about climate change.' Penny inclined her head, but remained silent. 'She thought you could use the Great Barrier Reef as an example of something that's been affected by it.' Another nod, and Seb felt the first knot of worry. What was he supposed to do if she refused to engage with him? Just bugger off home?

The thought of Maggie coming home to find Penny hadn't done any work towards her project, and he'd snuck off with his tail between his legs... nope, wasn't going to happen.

Resolutely he picked up the iPad in front of Penny and entered the website address of his home for the last few months. 'Did you know I was living on the Great Barrier Reef a few weeks ago?'

This time Penny's eyes caught his. 'You lived in the sea?'

'Not quite.' He found the picture he wanted and handed the iPad over to her. 'On the sea.'

Chapter Five

Maggie hadn't been sure what to expect when she let herself in. Penny and Tabby in front of the television, homework and project abandoned? A reasonable bet. Seb still there, flirting with Hannah as he watched her cook tonight's tea? Maybe.

It certainly wasn't the sight of Penny still working, pointing out something in her workbook to Seb. Nor was it the absolute focus on Seb's face as he listened to her.

Tabby was the first to notice her mum's arrival. She jumped off the sofa, the one Maggie hated with a passion because Paul had chosen it – *everything else in this house is so damn bland, Maggie* – and wrapped her arms around Maggie's legs. 'I did my homework and Hannah said 'cos I'd been good I could watch *SpongeBob*. Then I watched *Blue Peter*.'

Hannah, who was chopping up vegetables, looked up

and smiled. 'She's left out the part where she conned me into letting her have a cookie, too.'

Tabby gave Maggie a look of outraged innocence. 'I was good two times. Doing my homework and setting the table. That means two treats.'

'So it does.' Laughing, because it was hard to do anything else when Tabby used her special brand of logic, Maggie hugged her back before walking over to Penny and kissing the top of her head. 'How about you, Penny?' Maggie glanced briefly at Seb, who was now leaning back in his chair, before turning her attention back to her daughter. 'I didn't expect you still to be working on your project.'

'We're nearly done.' Penny pointed to the iPad, and a photo of a pontoon over the most beautiful turquoise water. Blue cloudless sky above, sun glinting off the water. Nothing else in sight but the ocean and the horizon. 'Did you know Seb used to live on the Barrier Reef?'

'Live on it? I think you mean he used to work on it.' Her eyes found Seb's, and once again she was struck by their colour, the blue so similar to the sea in the photograph.

'Yes, but he lived on it, too,' Penny protested, looking at Seb for confirmation. 'Didn't you?'

At the fond smile Seb threw her daughter, Maggie felt a small, but definite, squeeze in her chest. He might be too brash for her taste, and he might unsettle her, but it was hard not to like a man who treated her daughters with such respect, yet such indulgence, too.

'I did live on it.' Seb confirmed, his eyes drifting to the

photo. 'Not all the time, we had a rota, but for a few months, off and on, I lived on a pontoon floating right over the Great Barrier Reef.'

A shadow crossed his face, and though it was over in a flash, it was enough to make Maggie pause. 'You must miss it.'

Those bright eyes snapped to hers, his surprise clear. 'That's the first time I've been asked, since I've been back.'

She wasn't sure what it said about her that she'd recognised the sadness in his eyes, where his family hadn't. 'Well, look at what you've come back to.' She waved her hand towards the window, where the dark had already descended, and the lashing rain was making a din against the glass. 'Why would anyone think you'd miss life on a sun-drenched pontoon over the ocean?'

He chuckled, and when his eyes met hers, they shared a smile. A real smile, devoid of mick-taking or pretence. For the first time Maggie felt she'd seen the real guy behind the smart-mouthed, cocky drifter act he seemed to wear like armour.

Clearing his throat, Seb tapped a finger over Penny's workbook. 'How are we doing? Have you captured the part about the plastic, the bottles, the bags?'

Her daughter's eyes skimmed over the page. 'Yes.' She gave Seb a shy smile. 'It's in the bit about what people should do to help keep the reef from dying.'

'Okay, good stuff. Anything we missed?'

As Penny proceeded to turn over the pages to check,

Maggie's eyes nearly popped out of her head. 'Wow, there's a lot there.'

'There has to be, because there's so much that can hurt the reef.' Penny counted off the items on her fingers. 'There's the weather, and then the… the acid of the sea, and the way the sea's getting higher.' She looked up at Maggie, grey eyes alive with interest. 'Did you know where Seb worked, there's a bit of reef in the shape of a heart? It's so cool.'

'No, I didn't.' Again she glanced at Seb, her friends' kid brother, the wayward one who'd set off backpacking round the globe instead of settling down. She wondered if Alice and Sarah had ever actually asked him about his life, his experiences. 'How long did you live in Australia?'

'Long enough to develop a bit of an Ozzie twang, according to Alice.' Crossing one long, jean-clad leg over the other, he leant back again and smiled straight into her eyes. 'But if you're interested in the proper answer, I spent the last two years there, the last eighteen months in the Whitsundays.' He shrugged. 'The longest time I'd spent in one place since leaving the UK.'

'And before Australia?'

He gave her a long, steady look. 'You really want to know this stuff?'

Maggie was aware that Hannah had stopped chopping and was listening. Aware too that Penny was watching her. Yet she was right to be interested, wasn't she? His experiences were so different to her *got a job as soon as she left university, got married to a man who worked even longer hours than she had.* She could count on one hand the number of times she'd been abroad. 'If I didn't want to know, I wouldn't have asked.'

Her rather tart answer made him laugh. 'Fair enough. It's just some people ask out of politeness, and then glaze over when I start telling them how an orphan sun bear adopted me while I was teaching English to kids in Cambodia, or the time I was dive bombed by flying squirrels when I led a trek through the Borneo jungle.'

Penny's eyes grew wide. 'Are there really squirrels that fly?'

'It's actually more gliding than flying, but it's pretty awesome to watch.'

Penny turned to her, and Maggie had rarely seen her daughter so animated. 'Can we go to Borneo? It sounds so cool.'

Maggie laughed, though inside she felt a twinge of guilt. Holidays had never been a key priority for them as a family. Paul had been so focused on work, he'd never wanted to leave the country for long so they'd mainly stuck to UK holidays. And since the divorce, it had taken all her effort just to get by, juggling work with life as a single mum to two girls who'd not understood why their dad had all but disappeared from their lives, barring the occasional phone call. Holidays had slipped off her to-do list. 'Maybe one day.'

Uncomfortably aware she'd hogged too much of Seb's time, Maggie stepped back. 'I think we should let Seb go home now. I'm sure you can finish it on your own.'

For the first time since he'd come back, Seb could truthfully say he'd been enjoying himself. Two hours spent with a switched-on kid who'd fired questions at him as if he really was an expert, and who'd absorbed his answers with a focus he could only aspire to. Add to that the last five minutes he'd spent talking to Maggie, who'd seemed genuinely interested in what he'd been saying.

Well, until a few seconds ago when she'd suddenly closed up, his time apparently up. He wasn't ready to be dismissed though, not ready to leave the warm kitchen, the cute kids or the striking mother who, for a few precious minutes, had made him feel more than he was.

'I'm not in a rush,' he replied evenly. 'And I can't leave a job before it's finished, it's not in my nature.'

She clearly hadn't been prepared for that, but he was coming to realise Maggie was pretty good at hiding her real feelings because she gave him one of her polite smiles. 'Fine. I'll leave you and Penny to finish up while I help Hannah.'

Tabby, who'd been as good as gold while they'd been working, wriggled off the sofa and meandered over. 'I want to see the squirrel. The one with wings.'

Chuckling, he ruffled the top of her head. An instinctive gesture, yet one glance at Maggie, who'd stopped pulling a jug out of the cupboard to stare at him, and he realised it was too familiar. Snatching his hand away, he reached for the iPad. 'They don't have wings,

Tabs. They have this extra skin, called a patagium, that connects the front and back legs. Here, let me find you a photo.'

For the next twenty minutes, he had fun showing Tabby photos of weird animals he'd come across on his travels while Penny finished her project. If he ever needed another stroke to his ego, he thought, he'd come here. The girls had made him feel like a bloody king for a while.

All too soon though, Maggie declared tea was ready. 'Go and wash your hands, girls.'

As the pair of them disappeared, Seb wondered about his odds of bagging an invite to stay. Probably hovering around zero. Still, he'd always been partial to an outside bet. 'Smells good. What is it?'

'Lasagne. Hannah's signature dish.' Maggie turned to smile at Hannah. 'The girls pester Hannah to make it at least once a week.'

You can stay and try some if you like. The invitation didn't materialise. Clearly she didn't want him getting too familiar. A shame, because her kids were a real crack, and he could have done with another hour of fielding questions from their enquiring minds, while eating a plate of someone else's cooking.

And yes, okay, he'd like another shot at trying to impress Maggie too.

Instead all he had to look forward to was an evening rattling around Sarah's place, waiting for her to come home. It wasn't that he didn't have friends here – he'd enjoyed catching up with his old school mates at the weekend – but during the week they, unlike him, were too knackered to go out because they'd been at work all day.

'Right, well, I'll leave you to it.' He stood and picked up the coat he'd slung over the back of his chair.

At that moment the girls dashed back into the room. 'Is Seb going?' Tabby pouted. 'He can stay and watch *It Takes Two* with us after tea.' She glanced up to Maggie. 'Can't he, Mum? He doesn't have to be quiet in that.'

Maggie looked towards Hannah, and then back at him. 'Well, if Seb wants to stay, I'm sure Hannah won't mind, but he's probably got much better things to do.'

He didn't. Still, he wasn't quite sure what he was letting himself in for. Or why it was down to whether *Hannah* minded. 'What's *It Takes Two*? If it features another dude dressed as a sponge, I'm out of here.'

Tabby giggled. 'Duh, *It Takes Two* is about *Strictly*. It's where they talk to the dancers about costumes and stuff.'

Ah. Maggie must have seen his pained expression because she smiled. 'I think Seb might prefer *SpongeBob*.'

'No, it's fine.' It beat an empty house, anyway. 'I get to eat the best ever lasagne first though, yes?'

Hannah rolled her eyes at him. 'No pressure, huh?'

As it turned out the lasagne was tasty and the conversation, dominated by the girls, was easy. It was only as he helped clear the plates away with Hannah that Seb realised Maggie was making moves to leave.

'Is she going out?' he asked as he watched Maggie walk back into the room wearing a dark navy coat and clutching her handbag. She'd clearly given her hair a quick brush and applied a subtle pink lipstick.

'She's going dancing.'

He felt a small, but definite, tug of disappointment. 'The lessons she was talking about?'

'Yep. It took a lot of effort but we managed to persuade her. Apparently she used to be crazy about dancing before she got married.'

It wasn't his business. Still, Seb couldn't resist asking. 'Paul didn't like dancing, I take it?'

Hannah gave him a funny look. 'You know about Paul?'

'Well, not really,' he had to admit. 'Only what I've heard from Alice and Sarah.'

'Oh yes, I keep forgetting they're your sisters.' She shook her head. 'It must have been a real hoot growing up with them. They're like, what, ten years older than you?'

'About that,' he murmured as Maggie finished saying goodbye to the girls and came over to them.

'So, thank you for today, Seb.' Her smile was the warmest he'd received so far from her. 'Not just for helping Penny, but for making it fun, too. I have to say, I didn't think you'd still be working on it when I got home.'

He waited until her eyes met his and then smiled straight into them. 'I told you, I can work miracles with the right incentive.'

She shook her head, laughing softly. 'Seriously, have you ever thought about going into teaching? You've got a real way with the kids.'

'Thanks.' She was being kind, but not only had her

comment effectively deflected his flirty remark, it had also reinforced the chasm between them. Whether that was deliberate he didn't know, but now he felt like the chump who still wasn't sure what he wanted to do, being advised by the wise professional. 'Not all kids are as bright and receptive as Penny and Tabby.'

In what was clearly an unconscious gesture, Maggie glanced over to where her daughters sat on the satsuma sofa. The love, the pride, on her face, caught at him. Had his parents ever looked at him that way? They loved him, sure, but were they proud of him? Then again, what had he done to make them proud? Seb gave himself a mental shake. Nope, he'd done with the crappy pity party. 'Hannah tells me you're going to those dance lessons tonight?'

And there it was again, the shift in her body language from relaxed, when she was talking about her kids, to formal when the conversation turned to her. 'I am. I'll be hoping to avoid the mop.'

'Stuff the mop, you're going to get tall, dark and handsome,' Hannah interjected. 'I can feel it.'

'I've had enough tall, dark and handsome to last me a lifetime, thanks.' A cloud crossed Maggie's face and Seb guessed that Paul had been exactly that. 'I'll settle for a guy who doesn't stamp on my toes.'

'Hey, you should aim higher than that. I hear blonde is the new dark.' He waggled his eyebrows and though Hannah laughed, Maggie gave him a wary look. Either she thought he wasn't funny or, worse, she knew he was coming on to her and didn't like it.

An awkward pause followed, and Seb figured it was time for him to leave. It felt odd staying in Maggie's house without Maggie. Odd and, though he hated to admit it, not quite as appealing. 'I ought to go, too.' Maggie looked at him in alarm and he laughed. 'Chill, I don't mean to the lessons. I mean leave Hannah and the girls to watch their programme in peace.'

Maggie cast a glance at Hannah, and whatever they communicated, it seemed to be in favour of him staying because Hannah gave him a bright smile. 'We want you to stay. And you never know, with you being a fan of *Strictly* now, you might even enjoy *It Takes Two*.'

Once Maggie had left, Hannah threaded her arm through his and led him over to the sofa. It was nice to feel wanted, he realised as he settled down with them. Plus, Hannah was easy company; open, fun. A woman his own age, who laughed at his jokes and didn't seem like she'd be offended if he asked questions that were too personal.

And if now and again he wondered how Maggie was getting on in her dance lessons, well, it was only because *It Takes Two* was even less his thing than *Strictly*.

Chapter Six

It was Maggie's turn to host Strictly Saturday. The pizzas were out of their boxes and on trays beside the already warmed oven. Glasses and plates rested on the island, napkins by their side. A crisp salad waited in the fridge. Hannah was already here, sitting with the girls in the living room. All Maggie needed now were her other guests.

Right on cue, the doorbell rang.

After settling the pizzas into the oven, she went to open the door, finding not only the people she'd expected, but also one she hadn't. Her shock must have shown on her face, because Alice winced.

'He's promised to be good. Okay, that's a lie. When I went to pick Sarah up, Seb gave us the sad eye look and, well, we're suckers for it, so huge apologies but here he is. If it helps, Jack and Edward have ducked out. I tried to get Seb to meet up with them, but he insisted he wanted to come here.'

Seb, dressed smartly again, this time in black jeans, a light pink shirt that emphasised his tan, and a grey jacket, gave her a wide, winsome smile. She suspected it was the same one he'd given his sisters.

It was unnerving to realise she, too, was a sucker for it. 'The girls will be pleased to see you,' she told him, trying to ignore the butterflies in her belly. She suspected Hannah would be pleased, too. Her nanny had admitted to enjoying having Seb round on Wednesday, though Maggie had been surprised, and relieved, to find him already gone when she'd arrived home. It was one thing telling Hannah what a disaster the evening had been. Quite another admitting it to the man she still didn't feel entirely comfortable around. It wasn't that she didn't like him. Far from it. It was more that she didn't like the feelings he evoked in her.

Unconsciously she caught his eye and, as if to reinforce her thoughts, a ripple of awareness ran through her.

'It's good to know I have at least two fans,' he drawled, shooting her another of his easy smiles.

Ignoring the fluttery sensation, Maggie forced herself to smile back. 'Penny wanted to show you the comment the teacher put on her project.'

'Great.' He laughed softly. 'At least I hope it's great or I'll have to downgrade my earlier statement to one fan.' Then he laughed again. 'And Tabs will no doubt withdraw her vote the moment I open my mouth during *Strictly*.'

She wanted to tell him her daughter was called Tabby, but it felt petty, mean even, considering he was so lovely with them. And considering Tabby hadn't batted an eyelid when he'd called her that on Wednesday. It had been just after she'd watched him ruffle her hair in a gesture so affectionate, so natural, it had caused her heart to ache at what both her daughters were missing out on. Paul should have been the one helping Penny with her project, ruffling Tabby's hair.

'I'll head on in then.' Seb's voice brought her back, and she watched as he strode past her into the hallway, as if he was a frequent visitor. As this was his second visit in the space of a few days, maybe he now qualified as that.

'Good to see he's dressed for the occasion,' she murmured to Sarah and Alice, drawn to the view of his broad shoulders, enhanced by the jacket, and his trim backside, showcased by the dark jeans.

'Oh, he's got some woman picking him up later.' Alice shook her head. 'To think this is where women's liberation has taken us. Seems backwards to me.'

'To be fair, he's not got a car,' Sarah pointed out.

'True. To get a car, he needs to get a job, though maybe that'll change soon with this youth centre thing.'

She couldn't say why she was so interested, but she was. 'Has he applied for a job there?'

Alice shrugged. 'He said he'd been to see them. I know he's worked with youth clubs during his travels so hopefully it will work out.'

'He'll be good.' When they both stared at her, Maggie added defensively. 'He's got a knack with children. Alice, you must know that, from the way he is with Edward and Rebecca.'

'Eds and Beccs.' Alice shuddered as she mimicked her brother's drawl. 'I see he's taken to calling Tabby "Tabs" now too. The man might be good with kids, but he's a nightmare with their flaming names.' She shook her head. 'But enough about our brother, let's get onto more important matters. How was the dance lesson? Were you swept off your feet?'

'Did you get to trip the light fantastic?' Sarah added.

Maggie raised her eyes to the ceiling. 'Are there any more clichés coming or can I answer?' When they both looked at her expectantly, Maggie laughed. 'God, you're like dogs waiting for a bone. Sadly, it isn't the juicy one you're hoping for. The evening was like something out of a comedy show, only without the laughs.' Her voice cracked on the last word proving, annoyingly, that she hadn't yet put the disappointment behind her. Embarrassing enough that she'd cried the whole journey home. She really didn't want her friends to know how stupidly she'd raised her hopes of not just dancing again, but dancing with a man who made her knees weak and her belly sizzle.

'Tell us.' Alice took her hand, giving it a squeeze. 'It can't have been that bad, can it?'

Maggie sighed. 'Probably not.' If she'd only approached it with her usual caution, instead of letting her head get so carried away. 'Everyone was quite a bit older than me, which didn't help. On the plus side, there were several of us without partners.'

'That's... good?' Sarah prompted.

'It would have been, if the two males without partners weren't bald and boob height.'

'Boob height?' All three of them turned to find Seb lurking in the hallway, his eyebrows raised so high they were lost in his hairline. 'Does that mean what I think it does?'

Bugger, bugger, bugger. The last thing Maggie wanted was for Seb to hear her tale of humiliation. 'I was exaggerating, one of them possibly came up to my shoulder.' She released a breath, aware there was no point in not telling them the truth. 'Fact was, with my dancing heels on, neither of them could look me straight in the eye.'

'But they could look you straight in the—'

'Seb!' Alice and Sarah both frowned over at him.

'Hey, okay, I was only repeating what Maggie said.' Amusement made his bright blue eyes seem even brighter. 'Could they dance, at least?'

'They were learning, like I was.' Though after she'd had a blast of stale coffee breath from the taller, and a waft of ripe BO from the other, she'd worked hard to avoid them for the rest of the evening. Details she'd reserve for when Seb wasn't listening.

'Will you go back?' Sarah asked.

Much as she desperately wanted to dance again, Maggie wasn't sure she could put herself through that again. 'Maybe,' she demurred, aware that if she said no outright, they'd gang up on her.

'But you love dancing, you can't just give up on the idea.' Sarah glanced at Seb, and Maggie felt the bottom fall

out of her stomach. God no, she wasn't going to suggest…
'You have to give it another go.'

Relief flooded through her. Sarah had clearly read *no bloody way* from Seb's expression, which suited Maggie just fine. She absolutely didn't want anyone she knew witnessing her fumbling attempts to dance again. Nor did she want anyone to feel forced to dance with her. Especially not the man who unnerved her.

'Sarah's right. Maybe next time you'll get to dance with someone whose head isn't jammed against your—'

'Thank you.' Maggie cut off Alice's comment, keen to move the conversation away from her blasted boobs. Taking hold of her friends' hands, she gave them a quick squeeze. 'I appreciate you both looking out for me, but I'm a big girl. I can make my own decisions. Now we'd better get a move on because *Strictly*'s on in a few minutes and I haven't taken the pizzas out yet.'

They headed towards the sitting room, but Seb remained where he was and when Maggie stepped past him, he cleared his throat. 'Have you got a sec?'

Her heart gave out a loud thump – why was that? – and she eyed him cautiously. 'Of course.'

Seb wasn't sure what possessed him to call Maggie back. Was he really about to make the very same offer he'd silently begged Sarah not to make? Yet it wasn't that he didn't want to dance with her. More that he didn't want to be foisted on her.

Still, he couldn't get the conversation he'd overhead in the hallway out of his head... *The evening was like something out of a comedy show, only without the laughs.* Her disappointment, buried behind the stoic front, tugged at some deeply hidden chivalrous part of him. 'Look, I just wanted to say that if you think having, I don't know, a wing man I guess.' God, he was stumbling over his words like a gawky kid. 'If you think that would help next week, I'm happy to be that for you.'

To his surprise he didn't get the polite smile. He got the warm one, which made her eyes glint. 'Happy? Are you sure that's the right word?' Before he had a chance to reply, she lightly touched his arm. 'Don't worry. I know Alice and Sarah put you up to this, but I'm officially letting you off the hook.'

'They didn't.' He wasn't sure why he blurted that out. Only that he was sorry he had when her smile slipped.

'Oh, well, I must have sounded very sorry for myself then.' Her eyes avoided his and a faint flush entered her cheeks.

'No.' He was getting this all wrong, or she was too sensitive. Probably a bit of both. 'I can see how much you like dancing. It's right there on your face when you watch it. I guess I just figured if going with you would help you get some of that pleasure back, give you a sort of leg up, or whatever you want to call it, then I'd like to do that.' Trying to find his cool, his casual, he slipped a hand in his jeans pocket. 'We should all do stuff that gives us a kick now and again. Makes the crap and tedium easier to handle.'

'Thanks, I'll bear it in mind.' Though she smiled, he was pretty certain she had no intention of following him up on his offer. A lucky escape, he reminded himself. Just when he thought the conversation was over though, she surprised him. 'What about you? What are you doing that gives you a kick at the moment?'

His mind flashed to the Whitsundays. The beauty of the reef. The joy of sun on his face, of a white sandy beach. Of a life he missed. But then he thought of his parents, and the family he'd missed when he'd been out there. 'I'm driving my sisters crazy.'

Maggie laughed. 'You're certainly doing that, by all accounts.'

Their gazes collided, and once again he felt a pull, just like he had on Wednesday. There was something about this woman, about making her smile… maybe it was just an ego thing, proof that he had it in him to charm a beautiful woman.

'Mum, *Strictly* is nearly starting and the pizzas aren't out of the oven.' Tabby, hands on hips, shouted at them from the living-room doorway.

'Well, that told me,' Maggie said under her breath before giving her daughter a wide, amused smile. 'We'd better hurry up then.'

Seb followed Maggie down the hall, watching her slender hips sway, just slightly, from side to side, and her ponytail bounce – yeah, he'd noticed that straightaway tonight. Usually she wore her hair down, but the ponytail, well, it made her look younger. More approachable. He had a funny feeling he was deluding himself about the ego trip, and that what he was starting to feel for Maggie wasn't simply a detached interest in his sisters' friend. It was an attraction he could really do without. Jobless, homeless, unsure where his life was headed, what he absolutely didn't need right now was a crush on the unattainable Maggie Peterson.

Shaking the thought off, he walked back into the living room where everyone was gathered. The sofas here were a more tasteful muted grey, with cream scatter cushions. Hannah gave him a bright smile and patted the seat next to her. Realising it would be rude to ignore her, he went to sit down, hoping she wasn't getting any ideas. She was fun, he'd enjoyed her company the other night, but friendship was all he was interested in.

'You're looking smart,' she remarked, looking him up and down. 'Is this for our benefit?'

'I'm off out later.'

'Oh?'

'Blazers. The wine bar?' He'd somehow managed to bag a lift there off the sister of one of his old mates.

'I know it. I've never been.'

Ah. He didn't want to give any mixed messages so he kept quiet and the silence between them stretched, becoming uncomfortable. Thank God for the arrival of his sisters, who entered carrying the obligatory pizza. Maggie followed behind with plates and napkins, which made him smile. It wasn't that she was fussy – hell, she was letting them eat pizza in her fancy room – more that she was so meticulously organised.

After grabbing a slice, and ignoring the napkin – it was as close as he could get to living dangerously right now – he settled back against the sofa. A moment later the opening credits of *Strictly* jangled round the room and Seb realised with a touch of embarrassment that he was actually, sort of, looking forward to watching it.

Of their own volition, his eyes drifted over to Maggie, whose gaze was riveted on the screen, her expression one of utter absorption.

Was it the programme he was looking forward to? he wondered. Or seeing the emotions flit across Maggie's face?

Chapter Seven

A week later, Maggie opened the car door for the girls, who dived inside.

'It's going to be a quiet Strictly Saturday tonight,' she told them as she climbed into the driver's seat. 'Jack has taken Alice away for the weekend and Hannah just phoned to say she's coming down with a cold, so she won't be able to make it either.'

'Will Rebecca be there?' Penny asked, snapping her seat belt in place.

'Yes, and Edward. Sarah's offered to look after them for the weekend.' Alice had been so chuffed when her husband had announced he was whisking her away for two days, without the kids. 'I love them,' she'd told Maggie excitedly, 'but I'll love them even more after this weekend.'

'What about Seb?' Tabby demanded.

Maggie didn't like the way her heart reacted, just a little, at the mention of his name. 'I don't know.' *I hope not.* Call her a coward, but she could do without another dose of him tonight. His offer to dance with her had been kind but also really, really embarrassing. He must have her down as some pathetic divorcee trying to recapture her pre-marriage youth.

'If he is there, I'll have to tell him to be quiet *again*.' Tabby sniggered. 'He's funny. Last time he asked if people had to be orange to dance.'

'What do you mean, orange?' Penny asked, frowning.

Maggie glanced in the rear-view mirror and smiled as she saw Tabby shrug her shoulders. 'Dunno. I said Mum can dance, and she's not orange.'

'I'm learning to dance,' Maggie corrected, though she wasn't sure how long that statement would remain true. 'I think Seb was referring to the dancers having fake tans.'

'What's that?' Tabby looked confused

'It's where they spray a lotion to make your skin look a shade browner, like you've been out in the sun. People think a tan is more attractive than pale skin.' She glanced down at her hands as they rested on the steering room. Yep, there was skin that had barely seen the sun. Unlike Seb's, which positively glowed, making him look healthy, vital. His eyes vivid.

God, no. She shook the image away. The man made her uncomfortable enough. She didn't need to start thinking he was attractive.

Ten minutes later Maggie rang Sarah's bell. Only it wasn't Sarah who opened it. Of course it wasn't. 'Oh, hi.'

Seb, dressed casually tonight in faded jeans and a T-shirt

with the words *I'd rather be surfing*, gave her an amused smile. 'That's the second time you've sounded less than enthusiastic to see me.'

'It's also the second time I've been expecting Sarah.'

'Fair enough.' He glanced down at the girls. 'I'm afraid only *Strictly Come Dancing* fans are welcome here tonight.'

Tabby grinned. 'That's us.'

He nodded, as if considering. 'But I only have your word for it. How about some proof. Name me one of the presenters.'

'Tess Daly.' Tabby rolled her eyes. 'That was easy peasy.'

He smiled and opened the door wider. 'Okay, young lady, you can go in.' His gaze landed on Penny. 'Umm, the climate change wizard needs a less easy peasy question. Let me think.' He furrowed his brow, as if thinking very hard. 'Name me not one, but two of the judges.'

Penny gave him a shy smile. 'Craig Revel Horwood and Shirley Ballas.'

'Is she the one in charge?' When Penny nodded her head, he winked at her. 'Excellent, in you go.' Seb looked over Maggie's shoulder. 'Where's Hannah?'

'She can't come tonight, she's ill.'

'Ah.'

She'd been enjoying the little diversion on the doorstep, admiring how effortlessly he talked to her daughters, but now she felt a twinge of unease. 'Ah?'

He shifted awkwardly, and it was only then she realised he was barefoot. He caught her staring, and laughed softly. 'You want to tell me to put some socks on.'

Was she that transparent? That boring? 'It is November.'

'Yeah, but where I've been living, it's thirty degrees in November. Socks aren't something I'm used to wearing. They feel too restricting.' As if to emphasise the point, he wriggled his toes and, God help her, she watched.

'Can we get back to the *ah*?'

'Yes, right.' He rested a hand on the door frame. 'Sarah's got to work late.'

Maggie's heart plummeted. No Alice, no Sarah, no Hannah. No way could she stay. 'That's a shame. Don't worry, I'll grab the girls and we'll be out of your way.'

'What? Wait.' He removed his hand from the door frame and raked it restlessly through his mane of shaggy blonde hair. 'I promised Sarah I'd host. I've bought pizzas, as instructed. Lots of the ruddy things.'

She didn't know where the ripple of panic came from. Only that it was there, and she needed to leave. 'I'm sure you can enjoy them with Rebecca and Edward.'

'I'm sure I can.' He rested his arm back against the door frame, and those bright blue eyes unerringly found hers. 'I'm also sure I can enjoy them with Penny and Tabby. And you.'

Now, alongside the panic, was a flash of heat.

'So, can I tempt you to come in?' He flashed his sexy-as-sin crooked smile. 'I promise not to bite unless you ask me to.'

Maggie spluttered with laughter. She was being ridiculous, getting all flustered over nothing. Seb was Alice and Sarah's younger brother. He was fun, entertaining, *harmless* company.

Nodding her head, she stepped inside.

She found Penny and Tabby larking around with Alice's kids in the living room. A glance through the open doors to the kitchen revealed... okay, better not to look. She didn't want to interfere.

'I'll stick the pizzas in now, shall I?' Seb strolled past her into the kitchen. 'Bugger, I forgot to put the oven on.'

'Bugger's not a nice word,' Tabby announced.

Seb stilled and turned towards Tabby. 'True, but your mum will be calling me worse words if the pizza isn't ready in time for your programme.'

Maggie cringed. God, he must have her down as a total control freak.

'Mum doesn't say rude words.'

Seb glanced at Maggie and raised an eyebrow. Not just a control freak, but a squeaky clean head-girl type, too. The boring one. Damn it, she wasn't though. She'd become weighed down with the responsibility of raising a family while trying to work. That Paul hadn't been able to see past that. That instead of helping her, he'd chosen to ditch her for some young carefree model...

'Maggie?' Seb wondered where she'd disappeared to. She looked upset, no, more than that, she seemed angry.

But then she appeared to shake herself and wherever her

mind had taken her, she was back, and her walls firmly intact. 'I don't swear in front of the girls.'

'Ah, so you do let rip a juicy f-word sometimes?'

She smiled in that way he was starting to enjoy. A small, sort of surprised curve of the lips, as if she wasn't sure why she was smiling, but couldn't stop. 'If the occasion warrants it, yes.'

Her gaze left his and flicked towards the kitchen, which, granted, looked like he'd tried to empty the contents of the entire place, blindfolded.

'Bet you'd let one rip now if that was your kitchen, eh?'

This time she laughed. A gentle sound, but it crinkled her eyes and made him feel ten foot tall. 'Quite possibly.'

'In my defence, I haven't learned where everything goes yet. Plus I'd only just got home when you arrived. Sarah warned me you were always on time, but Becca and Eds dawdled after their swimming lessons, though it's fair to say the stop for an ice-cream hadn't been strictly necessary.' He grinned. 'Strictly… see, I'm getting into the mood of the evening already.'

Another bout of soft laughter. 'Glad to hear it. Do you want a hand in there?'

'No, no, I've got it.' When she gave him a sceptical glance, he grinned. 'What you see is organised chaos. There's a difference.' He gave her another study, noting her hair was loose tonight, falling in a curly wave around her shoulders. With that, the dark jeans and the same black sequinned top he'd seen her wear for previous Strictly nights, she looked both unshowy and strikingly attractive.

'Then again, if you want to help, I'm not about to stop you.'

'Maybe I could sort out some drinks?'

Damn, he was a crap host. 'That'd be great, thanks.'

'So, how are you settling in?' she asked as she went straight to the right cupboard to find the glasses. 'You don't seem short of friends to go out with.'

He gave her a quizzical look. 'I don't?'

Her eyes were focused on pouring the orange juice. 'Alice said you were going on to a club last weekend after *Strictly*.'

His mind skipped back to last Saturday. Was Maggie *interested*? Or was she making conversation? 'I went with a few of the guys I used to go to school with. One of their sisters gave me a lift.' For some reason he found himself willing her to ask more, and was disappointed when she simply smiled and nodded to the juice, indicating she'd take it out to the kids.

'How about you?' he asked when she came back. 'What do you do for entertainment, aside from watching *Strictly Come Dancing*?'

'Entertainment?' She said the word as if it was foreign. 'I'm nearly forty, and a single mum. Entertainment for me is being in bed at ten o'clock with a good book.'

He wanted to say she was thirty-seven, not seventy-three. That she was in her prime. And having kids didn't mean she had to put her own life on hold. The words died on his lips though as the opening sounds of the *Strictly* theme tune reverberated round the house.

Maggie disappeared out of the kitchen faster than Bruno doing a quick step.

See, he was learning something from these Saturday evenings.

He made it in with the pizzas just in time to hear the opening announcement. 'Tonight, the couples all dare to dream of a seaside resort two hundred miles north of here.'

'*North* of here?' he repeated. 'Who on earth dreams of a seaside resort that's not sunny?'

Tabby shook her head at him, as he'd kind of hoped she would. 'They don't want to go to the beach, silly. They want to dance in Blackpool.'

'Ah.' He placed the tower of pizza on the coffee table, wondering if he should have put a mat down first. Then realised even if he could be bothered, he didn't know where they were. 'Well, I can see why they don't want to go to the beach there. The golden mile might be a mile, but it sure as hell... heck isn't golden.'

'Shh.' His niece gave him an admonishing look.

'You have to be a mouse again.' Tabby grinned adorably at him.

Chuckling, he grabbed a slice of pizza and sat on the vacant armchair. 'I'll nibble on my pizza in silence,' he promised.

And stuck to it, in the main.

He'd cooked too many pizzas and made way too much

salad. Blame it on the fact that he'd forgotten, or maybe never consciously twigged, that kids didn't eat as much as grown-ups, women tended to eat less than guys, and nobody really wanted the green stuff, given the choice.

As the closing credits flashed up on the screen, Maggie looked over at her girls. 'I'm just going to help Seb clear away and then it's time to go.'

Seb watched as she began to pick up the plates. Clearly his guest was in a hurry to leave, which didn't say a lot for his hosting skills. Or his ability to entertain a woman considerably smarter and classier than he was.

'Can't we stay for a bit?' Penny gave Maggie a beseeching look that Seb wouldn't have been able to refuse. 'Rebecca wants us to play her new marble run game.'

Maggie glanced at him, and he wasn't sure from her expression whether she was hoping he'd turf them out, or encourage them to stay. 'You can hang here as long as you like. Sarah will probably be back soon,' he added, figuring it might push Maggie into staying for a while, and yes, he wanted that. A little bit of time, just the two of them, to see if he could nudge at that wall of hers. The one he wasn't sure was permanent, or if she just put up when she was around him.

'Okay, but not too long,' she warned. 'Just while we clear up.'

All of them dashed up the stairs and Seb grabbed a few empty glasses before going to join Maggie in the kitchen where she was meticulously rinsing plates under the tap before stacking them neatly in the dishwasher. The desire to rumple her, to turn the neat and tidy into a flustered, uninhibited mess, caught him by the throat. Shit, he really was developing a crush on his sisters' friend.

'How was the dance class?' he asked, needing to divert his thoughts. 'Any taller men come forward?'

Her attention remained on loading the dishwasher. 'It was fine.'

'You're going to keep going then?'

'I'm not sure. I've paid up until Christmas, but, well, we'll see.'

Her lack of eye contact was beginning to frustrate him. 'Where is it held?' That got her attention. Her head snapped up so fast he had to laugh. 'Hey, I'm not planning on going to watch.' Though actually, now he'd said it, the thought held a lot of appeal. 'I was just making conversation. I imagine these classes are held in some dreary hall with zero atmosphere.'

She gave him a tight smile. 'You're right.' She named the town, one over from theirs. 'It's a long way from the Tower ballroom at Blackpool.'

'Have you ever been?'

'No, well, not to dance, anyway. Paul and I drove along the prom once on our way to the Lake District, but he refused to stop. Said it was too tacky.'

'True.' Seb grinned. 'But they say that's part of its charm. And you can't deny a place that has the tallest rollercoaster in the UK.'

She screwed up her face. 'You'd never get me on there.'

He wasn't sure whether it was the emphatic way she

said it, or just this ridiculous crush raising its head again, but he took a step towards her, one hand on the work surface, the other on the island, almost trapping her where she was. 'Is that a dare?'

Her eyes widened, the grey looking less cool now, more... turbulent. He wondered if her pulse was racing as fast as his. If she was feeling the air between them crackle, as he was.

Wondered too, if the way her eyes darted to his mouth, and then away again, was a sign that she was thinking what it would be like to kiss him.

Because in that moment, it was all he could think of. Would her lips feel as soft as they looked? If he leant forward, if he pressed his mouth against hers, would she melt? Could he lower some of those walls, relax some of that stiffness? Or would she slap him round the face?

He'd never know, because at that moment the front door opened.

'I'm back,' Sarah called from the hallway. 'What did I miss?'

Me nearly kissing your friend. 'A bit of dancing. A lot of pizza,' he shouted back, turning to give Maggie a wry smile. She wasn't looking at him though. Her head was bent as she slowly, and with seemingly rapt attention, wiped her hands on the tea towel.

'There you are.' Sarah appeared in the doorway and glanced between him and Maggie, the question in her eyes making it clear he wasn't the only one aware of the tension in the room.

'I didn't realise we were playing hide and seek,' he answered, figuring sarcasm was his best route out. 'I'd have chosen a better spot.'

Sarah ignored him and turned her attention to Maggie, who'd finally put the towel down. 'I'm sorry I'm so late. I hope Seb looked after you properly.'

Was it his imagination, or did Maggie look less composed than usual? 'He did. The pizzas were plentiful and only a few minutes behind schedule.'

Sarah laughed and grabbed Maggie's hand. 'Well, I'm glad to hear it. And I hope you're not planning on dashing off just yet. I could really do with a big glass of wine, a few slices of that plentiful pizza, and a good chat with my friend.'

Seb cleared his throat. 'What about your brother?'

Sarah looked pointedly at the mess behind him. 'He can finish off tidying up, and then check on the little people he's supposed to be looking after.'

Thanks, sis.

As he listened to the faint hum of female voices in the other room a few moments later, he couldn't help but wonder what might have happened if Sarah *hadn't* come back. Would he have dared to kiss Maggie? Would she have let him?

With a resigned sigh he finished emptying the bin, and then trudged upstairs to play marble run.

Chapter Eight

Monday morning and Maggie was in a bind. Hannah had phoned an hour ago, and it had been clear from her voice, and from the constant coughing, she was still in the grip of the virus she'd caught. Though she'd offered to take the girls if Maggie was stuck, Maggie had told her not to worry, she'd manage. All Hannah needed to do was focus on getting better.

It had been easy to say, but now she was having a mild panic. She could drop the girls off to school early – yep, that idea had gone down well – and, traffic willing, just about make it in time for her first patient. But she couldn't pick Penny and Tabby up.

Sarah was working. Alice was working, and her two children were being picked up by Jack's mother. There was no way Maggie could foist another two onto the seventy-year-old.

Of course Maggie knew of one person who wasn't

76

working. A guy her girls seemed to like, probably because he acted like a big kid himself, but who she sensed, deep down, was far more responsible than he let on. Why else would he come back to England to help out his family? Still, she really didn't want to phone him.

Her belly gave a long, slow flip. God, they'd nearly kissed on Saturday night.

Even now, knee deep in Monday morning stress, her mind kept darting back, replaying every vivid moment. Seb's husky-voiced question, *Is that a dare*? Delivered with a sexy smirk. The way he'd moved towards her, caging her in with his tall, athletic, sun-kissed body. Never had she been so aware of a man before; his fresh, outdoor smell, the incredible blue of his eyes. The sensuous curve of his lips and the heat of his body. All that young, virile maleness.

Thank heavens Sarah had come in when she had. If she'd been ten minutes later… Maggie's stomach pitched. She didn't know how Sarah would have reacted to the idea of Maggie kissing her brother. No, it was worse than that. Seb was Sarah's *younger-by-ten-years* brother. One thing for certain, Maggie didn't plan on ever finding out. This crazy over-reaction to him was a sign she needed to get out there and date again. And she would, once she'd found someone suitable: a man nearer to her age and experience, who wouldn't make her conscious of her stretch marks, her wrinkles, her saggy bits. Who was looking for a meaningful relationship rather than a couple of hot trysts.

None of which helped her dilemma.

'Who's going to pick us up?' Penny asked as she shrugged on her coat.

'I'm not sure yet.'

'Will it be the woman Rebecca and Edward have sometimes? I don't like her.'

'No.' Alice's childminder had been efficient but horribly grumpy. Maggie had used her occasionally, in those dark days after Paul had left and before Hannah had arrived. 'She retired earlier in the year, which is why their grandma picks them up now.'

'What about our grandma?'

'She'd love to, I'm sure.' A white lie wouldn't hurt. Penny didn't need to know her mum's parents were still far too busy running their company to bother with things like wanting to help their daughter, or their granddaughters. 'But it's a bit far to come.' Damn it, she was going to have to grit her teeth and ask the favour of Seb. It wasn't fair on the girls to not know who'd be picking them up. 'If Seb is free, would you mind him picking you up?'

Penny shook her head. 'I don't mind. He's funny. And I can ask him some more about the reef.'

'Okay then.' Her children would be happy and safe with Seb. That was more important than her wobbly emotions. 'I'll give him a quick call while you get your shoes on and help Tabby with hers.'

Taking a deep breath, she pulled out her phone and called the number Sarah had given her a few weeks ago. The number she'd put into her contacts out of habit, and a need to be organised, without expecting to use it again.

'Hello?' The answering voice sounded deep and husky with sleep.

'It's Maggie. Sorry, did I wake you?'

A rustle of what she assumed was bedding. 'Morning, Mags. And yeah, I guess if it's still before eight, you did wake me.'

'Sorry.' Had he really just called her *Mags*? She hated that. Then again, she needed a favour, so maybe now wasn't the time to tell him.

'You already said that, and no worries. How can I help? I assume you need my help, and aren't just phoning to say you missed me.'

The smile in his voice was unmistakable, and made it pretty hard not to smile back. 'It's the first one.'

'Damn, I knew you'd be hard to charm. Go on then, ask away.'

Her smile faltered, and Maggie inhaled a deep breath. She hated asking for help, and hated even more asking it of a man she wasn't sure was flirting with her out of habit, to prove something or because he was genuinely interested. Whatever it was, she'd feel more comfortable seeing less of him, rather than more. 'Hannah's still not well, so I wondered if you were free later today to pick Tabby and Penny up from school? You could take them to Sarah's or to ours, whatever's easier.' There was a beat of silence. 'But no problem if you can't,' she added hastily, aware she sounded pushy. And awkward. God, she definitely sounded that.

'What time are you back? I need to be at the youth centre for six.'

Damn, she hadn't anticipated that one. 'Sorry, I didn't realise. I should be back in time.' Patients willing. Unconsciously she crossed her fingers. 'Are you working there now?'

'Sort of. I'm volunteering for a few days so we can both get a feel for whether it's a good fit.'

'It will be.' Oops, she'd not meant to say that out loud.

Again she heard a smile in his voice. 'I'm glad someone is confident.'

'I just meant that from what I've seen, you're a natural with children.'

'I don't know about that, but you're trusting me with yours, so I must be doing something right.' There was a pause, and as Maggie tried to work out how to bring the conversation back to more practical matters, he did it for her. 'So, you'd better give me the name of this school. And where you work, as I guess I'll need to collect your key if I'm taking them back to yours.'

Maggie rattled off the name of the school. 'I'll tell them to wait in the playground, as usual. And I'll leave the house key with the receptionist at the surgery.'

'Okay then, I'll catch you later. Oh, and no worries if you're running late. I'll take them along with me to the youth centre.'

As she thanked him, Maggie felt the stress of the morning slide away.

Seb slid his phone back on the bedside table and sank back against the pillow. Damn and blast, he hated being this guy. Not the one who was needed by Maggie, oh no, that felt frigging fantastic. But. She'd only asked him because he was the one person she knew who wasn't working.

And she'd assumed, of course she had, that he had the available means of transport to pick her girls up. He was guessing that didn't include his ten-year-old battered push bike.

Groaning, his head fragile from too many Sunday night beers – as the alternative had been staying in with sister and watching the *Strictly* results show, the beers had seemed like a good idea – he considered his options. He could ask to borrow his dad's car, but the fragile way he was feeling now, he didn't think he could stomach giving the man another opportunity to lecture him on where his life was going.

Public transport was out, because to get him to the school, and then to the surgery and on to Maggie's house would take all evening, the way the buses were around here. He could taxi it, but by the time he'd paid for that, he might as well hire a car. At least then he'd have the flexibility of being able to use it to drive to the youth centre later.

Grabbing his phone again, he found a local hire company and reserved the cheapest car he could find, putting yet more money onto his credit card. He hoped Maggie was right, and the youth centre thing worked out. With his savings currently sitting in an Australian bank, and his English account not exactly brimming with surplus cash, if he couldn't get work soon, watching *Strictly* was going to be his main form of entertainment.

The rest of the morning he spent with his parents, as had been the pattern since he'd come home – shit, had he really been here over three weeks?

'When are you heading back to Australia?' his mum asked as she walked him out.

He looked at her tired face. 'When Dad's back to being Dad.' Instead of the moody man he'd left slumped in front of the television.

She gave him a wan smile. 'You might be here some time then.'

Seb reached his arms around her and hugged her tight. 'He'll get there. And in the meantime, I'm here to give you breathing space.'

'You're such a good son.' Her eyes welled, and Seb felt a lump jump into his throat. 'I know your father gives you a hard time, but he only wants the best for you.'

'I know he does.' His dad had never understood him though. Had never twigged that Seb wasn't an over-achieving, super-bright version of him, like his sisters were. Seb was average, and still trying to find something he could stick at. Travelling had been fun, Australia had been fun, but it was only ever a short-term gig. He'd always known family would bring him home at some point. He only wished the trigger had been a happier one. And that his life plan had been sorted when he'd stepped on that plane.

Christ, there were kids everywhere, all dressed in green jumpers, white shirts and grey trousers or skirts. How the hell was he supposed to find the two he needed among this swarm?

But magically, the moment he stepped through the school gate and into the playground, Tabby and Penny dashed towards him.

'You're late,' Tabby greeted him. 'Hannah is always waiting for us when we finish lessons.'

'Hey, Tabs, good to see you, too.' He flashed her a grin, and as happy was Tabby's default, she dropped the pout and grinned back. Then he turned to her quieter sister. 'And how are you, young Penelope?'

She opened her mouth, he presumed to say hello, then frowned and closed it again. Finally, she spoke. 'Nobody calls me Penelope.'

'Is Penny not short for Penelope?'

'Yes, but everyone calls me Penny.'

He smiled. 'Ah, but I'm not everyone.'

'I'm Tabitha.' Tabby scrunched up her nose. 'Why do I get Tabs?'

'Because I can't cause Penny Pens, can I?'

The pair of them giggled, and Seb thought, not for the first time, what lovely kids they were. Happy, polite. Girls it was a pleasure to spend time with.

Following a fifteen-minute drive to the surgery, they all piled out of the hired Kia – he wasn't sure of the rules about leaving minors alone in a car. Herding them inside, he told the girls to sit down and headed to the reception desk.

The lady there greeted him with a smile that told him she was pleased he wasn't yet another pensioner. Then her eyes flickered behind him, and her smile widened. 'Well, well, you must be Seb. How… interesting.'

'He's taking us home today,' Tabby piped up, swinging her legs. 'Usually we only see him when we watch *Strictly*.'

Oh boy. Now, the forty-something-year-old was looking at him with blatant curiosity. Deciding the best way to handle the question in her eyes was to ignore it, Seb cleared his throat. 'Mags…' Shit. 'Maggie said she'd leave a key for me?'

'Yes.' The woman reached into a drawer and pulled out a dancing bear keyring, complete with pink tutu. A present from her daughters, he'd like to bet.

'Thanks.' Feeling faintly foolish, he shoved it into his jeans pocket.

'Before you go, she also left you a note. Well, it's more of a list.'

'Of course it is.' Smiling to himself, he read the neat handwriting.

Leave the key on the hall table once you've let yourself in.

Presumably so he didn't run off with it.

Make sure they take their shoes off and leave them by the door so we know where to find them tomorrow morning.

Please get the girls to do their homework. Tabby will say she doesn't have any but check her homework book. She'll also say she's finished when she hasn't, so please check what she's done.

They're allowed a cookie with their drink – they're in the cookie jar by the bread bin. Don't be conned into letting them have more or they won't eat their tea.

Please message me if you need to take the girls with you to the youth centre, so I know where to pick them up.

As if he didn't already know that.

One of the doors down the corridor opened, and Maggie stepped out. She caught his eye and, after a start of surprise, gave him an uncertain smile and began walking towards him.

He waved the paper in the air. 'Just getting my orders.'

'They're not—' She sighed when she saw him smirk. 'Okay, I deserved that.'

He scanned down the list. 'I wouldn't have run off with the key. And I wouldn't take them anywhere else without letting you know.'

He'd intended to sound matter-of-fact but it clearly hadn't come across that way because her expression tightened and that guard he hated came down. 'Noted. But you've not looked after them before, so I wanted to make sure.' Her gaze finally settled on his. 'I know my lists aren't always appreciated, but they're intended to help.'

Ah. It didn't take a genius to work out that lists must have been a bone of contention with her ex. And the realisation he'd reacted exactly like the jerk who'd left her annoyed him. 'You're right, sorry. Being the kid brother I was always the irresponsible one.' He gave her a half smile. 'I guess this made me feel ten again.'

She blinked. 'Looks like we both over-reacted.'

Her attention moved over his shoulder and she gave Tabby and Penny a wide smile. The one that made everything inside him sit up and take notice of her.

The one he wished she'd direct at him.

Going over to them, she gave them both a quick kiss on the top of their heads. 'Be good for Seb.'

'I'm always good,' Tabby protested, making them all laugh, and thankfully defusing the remaining tension.

'Okay, well.' Maggie glanced back at him. 'Thanks again for taking care of them.'

'No problem.' He nodded down to the sheet of paper in his hand. 'Thanks for making it easy by giving me such a comprehensive list.'

For a split second he feared she'd take his joke the wrong way, but then her mouth curved, and her eyes lit up with silent laughter. Damn if it wasn't one of the most beautiful things he'd ever seen.

She was late. Maggie parked in the youth centre car park and ran up the steps. Her job often overran – people needed time to talk to their doctor, not be herded through the system like cattle. It was fine when she had Hannah, a friend whom she paid to stay with her children. It hadn't been fine with Paul.

She didn't know if it was going to be fine with the man helping her out simply because she'd asked him to. A man who'd had to bring two children to his first shift in his new job. Bugger, bugger, bugger.

Feeling breathless, she marched down the corridor, pausing to look through the open doors. He wasn't playing pool in the games room.

Nor in what looked to be a computer room.

The double doors at the end had a glass window, and after a glance through them, she exhaled in relief. It was a large multi-purpose hall/gym and Tabby and Penny were at one end of it, trying to throw a ball through a hoop.

Seb was at the other end with a group of around ten kids in their early teens, showing them how to dribble with a basketball.

Edging the door open, Maggie slipped inside. Immediately the girls saw her and ran over. 'Hello, darlings, sorry I'm late.'

''S okay. We did our homework and watched some telly and then Seb brung us here in his new car which isn't really his car and we played trying to get the ball in the hole.' Tabby's words tumbled over each other. 'And he called me Tabs again, and Penny Penelope 'cos he can't call her Pens.' She sniggered. 'That was well funny.'

Oh dear. Maggie gave her eldest, and at times rather sensitive, daughter a hug. 'Do you want me to tell him not to?'

Penny shook her head. 'It's fine.' She shrugged, twisting her hands. 'In a way, I kind of like it.'

'Me too,' Tabby piped up.

Maggie glanced towards the man who seemed to have won her daughters over. Wearing a hoodie and scruffy jeans, laughing and mucking around with the kids, from this distance he looked like he was barely older than they were. She, on the other hand, in her prim work skirt and blouse, felt old and straight-laced.

He looked over and waved when he saw her, saying something to the group before jogging over, his loose-limbed style a dead giveaway that he was physically fit. As if the athletic body wasn't enough of a clue.

And yes, now he was standing in front of her, six foot something of virile male, flashing that grin, he no longer looked like a kid. He looked like a man who made her knees weak.

'I'm really sorry I'm late.' The more his eyes danced in amusement, the more flustered and defensive she felt. It was one thing being in his debt. Another finding herself embarrassingly attracted to him. 'I try not to be but it's not always in my control. Sometimes patients—'

'Hey, do I look annoyed? Worried?'

She bit into her lip, feeling like the up-tight woman he must have her down as. 'No, but when I asked you, I fully intended to be home in time. I didn't want to put you out even more by having to bring them to work.'

'Then it's lucky they're not bad company, for a couple of ankle biters.' He winked at the girls. 'Remember your bags, kiddos. You left them in the games room.' In a flash, before Maggie could ask them to wait, they'd all go together, they were off. As she followed them, Seb held the door open for her. 'Don't worry. They know where they're going.'

'I wasn't worried.'

He shrugged, leaning on the door. 'Okay.'

Damn, why did she always do this? Put up the defensive wall, when he was only trying to be kind? 'Right, well, thank you for today. It meant a lot to know they were in good hands.'

His mouth curved. 'Good hands, eh?'

'Yes.' She looked him straight in the eye. 'My daughters like you, and that's important to me.'

He nodded, folding his arms across his chest. 'The boy in me wants to ask if you like me, but the man in me thinks it'll make me sound like a prat, so instead I'll ask if you're okay for childcare tomorrow?'

A smile hovered across her lips. He seemed to have a knack of bringing it out of her. 'Thank you, but I spoke to Hannah on the way over here and she sounds better so you're off the hook.'

Silence descended between them. Oddly, it wasn't awkward. More of a tingling silence that crackled with awareness. It made her realise her worry hadn't really been whether he'd be cross she was late – that would almost have been a relief, because then she could have dismissed him.

Instead he'd made everything so easy: asking him the favour, pushing her luck with the timing so much he'd had to take them to work. Even the niggle about the list he'd smoothed out and turned into a joke. It all meant that this inconvenient attraction, instead of dwindling the more she got to know him, flared brighter and hotter.

Relieved to hear the girls clatter out of the room two doors down, Maggie gave Seb a quick smile and sped after them. Away from his lazy grin, his too blue eyes, and his chilled yet very powerful appeal.

Chapter Nine

He was dithering, and he never dithered. Seb usually made his mind up fast and got on with it. And he had made up his mind, hadn't he?

Frustrated with himself, he jammed on his boots – God, he missed flip-flops – shrugged on his parka and marched out of the house to the bus stop. The irony of riding to a fair maiden's rescue on a bus wasn't lost on him. Then again, successful, independent mum of two Maggie Peterson hardly needed rescuing.

So why was he heading out in the damp November cold, when he could be sat on Sarah's sofa watching soccer... no, football. He was English, even if some of his heart belonged in the Ozzie surf.

As he considered changing his mind *again*, the bus pulled up, and wasn't that a shocker. The one time he could have done with it running ten minutes late as usual. If he didn't get on the bloody thing now, he'd not only be a ditherer, he'd be a coward.

Half an hour and a change of buses later, his pulse, usually a steady fifty-five beats a minute, sped up as he pushed open the door to the community hall.

It wasn't hard to tell where the ballroom dancing lessons were being held. He could hear the low hum of chatter, and music that sounded like it came from a scratchy gramophone. Christ. If that was what they danced to, he'd not make it through the first ten minutes.

Make that five minutes, he thought as he pushed open the door and a dozen pair of eyes swivelled in his direction.

There was only one pair he was interested in though. Cool grey, they widened with shock as the owner realised who the late arrival was.

'Seb?'

He halted, stuffing his hands in his parka. 'Hi.' This wasn't quite as he'd planned it. Then again, he'd not factored in the change of buses, making him five minutes late.

'Now, now, don't be shy, come on in.' A twig-thin woman who looked to be in her sixties beckoned towards him. 'I'm Belinda, and I teach ballroom dancing here. I hope you're planning on joining us, because we're short on men.' Her eyes deliberately looked him up and down. 'Especially tall, handsome young men.'

'No.' Maggie's voice echoed sharply around the hall. 'He's not come for the lessons.'

Okay, so the awkward factor had just increased tenfold.

'Actually, I have.' And how ripper, how frigging awesome, that they had an audience for this conversation.

Belinda glanced at them both before clapping her hands, clearly deciding fresh blood was more important than pissing off one of her current students. 'Excellent. We can sort out the paperwork side of things later. For now, find yourself a partner. You've only missed two lessons, so I'm sure a smart young thing like you will find it easy to catch up.'

Young thing... He guessed, compared to Belinda and to everyone else in the room, he was, but twenty-seven didn't feel young.

Then again, the way Maggie was glaring at him as he strode towards her, did make part of him feel like a school kid again. Only a small part. A far bigger part of him – pun intended – felt all man as she coolly appraised him.

'What are you doing here?'

'I thought that was obvious.' Squeezing into the space next to her, he ran his eyes over the other men in the room. They were overweight, over fifty, two of them bald, and all of them considerably shorter than he was. 'I'm saving you from dancing with a partner whose head only reaches your—'

'I don't need rescuing,' she hissed as the class began to partner up.

'I know.' He blew out a frustrated breath. 'Look, I'd planned to turn up before the lesson and talk to you about it, but the buses didn't do me any favours.'

Her eyes widened. 'You came by *bus*?'

'Well, yeah. I don't have a car.' And okay, that had sounded a bit too defensive.

'You don't?' Her forehead wrinkled. 'Damn, now I think about it, I remember Sarah mentioning that a while back. So whose car did you use to pick the girls up on Monday?'

He didn't want to be having this conversation. 'Does it matter?' He nodded towards the now coupled up dancers who were taking an active interest in them. 'Shouldn't we be listening to Belinda?'

'No, because you're not... we're not.' She exhaled sharply. 'Why are you really here?'

Shit, he'd not planned for that question, either. 'I wanted to see what all the fuss was about, you know, with the ballroom dancing.' Her eyes narrowed and as she scrutinised his face he felt his cheeks heat in a way he hadn't experienced since primary school. 'Okay, okay, when we talked last Saturday you sounded unsure about carrying on and I didn't want you to give up. I thought maybe dancing with me would be better than a mop. And I promise to keep my head a long way from your boobs.'

Laughter spluttered out of her, and for the first time that evening, he felt a dart of hope. Maybe he'd not totally cocked this up. But then she sighed and shook her head. 'We'll talk about this later. For now, I guess we'd better pay attention or they'll throw us out.'

He smirked. 'You really think a bunch of oldies can throw me anywhere?'

'Belinda's a lot scarier than she looks.'

'Has everyone found a partner?' Belinda's voice cut through the general noise, making Seb jump, and earning him a *see, I told you* look from Maggie. 'I notice some of us have been luckier than others,' she added, with a pointed glance in their direction.

'Oh God,' Maggie muttered. 'Now I've bagged the one tall male, nobody's going to talk to me.'

'Err, please tell me I've got more going for me than my height.' Seb gave Maggie a pained look. 'I've also got a full head of hair. And my own teeth.'

'Neither of which is useful for dancing.'

'Ah, but they are useful for what might happen after the dancing.'

Her expression turned panicked. 'Nothing's going to happen after it.'

'I know, I just meant in general—'

Belinda interrupted them again. 'Okay, class, I want you all to begin with the box step we covered last week. Tonight, we're going to learn how to take that basic step and travel round the room.' She walked – actually, it was more of a glide – towards them. 'It's Seb, isn't it?' Before he had a chance to reply, she took hold of his hands. 'You need to hold your partner like this.'

Seb had fantasised more than once recently about having his hands on Maggie, but not like this. Not with her feeling so stiff and unyielding. Like a stranger, instead of a woman he'd spent a good part of Saturday night with. A woman he'd nearly kissed.

Belinda nodded. 'That's right, though you both need to work on your body language. You look like a couple of statues rather than a couple about to perform a romantic dance together.'

After watching her walk/glide away, Seb turned to his partner. 'Look, if we're going to get the most out of this lesson, you can't be pissed with me.'

'I'm not.'

'Yes, you are. You're annoyed I came here, and you're annoyed I might be scheming for us to go somewhere afterwards.' He bent so he could look her in the eyes. 'FYI, I'm not.' At least he wasn't tonight. If he made it to another lesson, all bets were off.

She exhaled, her shoulders losing some of their rigidness. 'Okay, yes, I am annoyed, but only because I don't like being surprised.'

'So if I'd messaged to tell you I was coming, you'd have messaged back to say whoopee?'

He was rewarded with a wry smile. 'Perhaps not.'

'I want to see you all rising and falling as you dance.'

Belinda's words floated over to them and Seb looked guiltily at Maggie. 'Sorry, we should be dancing.' He shook his head, laughing at himself. 'But shit, Mags. Rising, falling, boxes... I've no idea what she's banging on about.'

Maggie opened her mouth, as if to reply, but then her lips curved upwards, and she began to laugh. Not a genteel one, either. This was a real bend over at the waist belly ache of a laugh. He wasn't sure if she was laughing at him, or the situation, or something else he had no clue about, but right now he didn't care.

She was bloody gorgeous when she laughed.

Maggie knew Seb was staring at her as if she was bonkers. Knew too, the class were watching her. She didn't even know why she was laughing. Only that if felt good, and she hadn't laughed like this for a long time.

'Sorry.' She tried to pull herself together. 'That sort of burst out of me. I think it was the look of panic on your face.' Drawing in a breath, she held her hand out for him to take, and tried to ignore the shiver of awareness that ran through her when his hand found the small of her back. 'This is what she means.'

Maggie showed Seb what Belinda was asking them to do, and realised right away that he had a natural rhythm. Relaxed and loose-limbed, it didn't take him long to catch on with what Belinda was telling them.

And wow, being held by him, that long, lean body sliding against hers. She felt it right in the long-forgotten place between her legs.

'You can get closer, Maggie,' Belinda instructed.

'I know I would.' Shirley, who Maggie had come to realise was the most vocal of the dance group, bellowed across the room, much to the amusement of everyone. Including Seb, whose body vibrated with laughter.

'We should do as we're told.' His hand pressed her back,

drawing her more firmly against him, and her heart began to race, the heat from his body creating a sizzle across her skin. 'Is this okay?'

'Yes.' It came out as a croak and she had to clear her throat and try it again. 'It's fine.'

Another rumble of laughter in his chest. 'Trust me, this feels a lot more than fine.'

A rush of heat pooled in her core and her nipples hardened inside her bra. Please God he couldn't see it, couldn't feel it. Because she swore she could feel every inch of him.

Somehow she made it to the end of the lesson. While she waited for Seb to settle up payment with Belinda, Maggie hoped the women flashing her envious looks were putting her flushed cheeks and her too fast heart beat down to her poor level of fitness. Not an over-reaction to her admittedly very dishy dance partner.

'How did you bag him, love?' Shirley asked. In her late sixties or early seventies, she clearly wasn't going to let a little thing like age stop her from ogling.

'I haven't bagged anyone.' Maggie willed her cheeks to cool. 'He's the brother of my best friends.'

'Any more where he came from?' Shirley's friend, Pauline, gave Seb an admiring once-over.

'No, but if he comes next week, we can share him.'

That made them cackle so loud, Seb glanced over at them.

'What was the dirty laughter about?' he asked as he walked over a few minutes later, shrugging on his parka.

'Shirley and Pauline were telling me how much they're looking forward to dancing with you next week.'

'What?' She could have sworn he paled beneath his tan. 'That's not part of the deal.'

'I don't remember us having a deal?'

'Sure you do. I'm here to stop the boob-high guys getting anywhere near your, err—'

'Thanks, I've got it.' She cast a quick look in his direction, her lips twitching. 'And okay, I have to admit, you were very effective at that.'

'So, same time again next week? And you'd better say yes, because Belinda knows where I live now.' He mock-shuddered. 'I dread to think what she'll do to me if I don't turn up.'

Maggie spluttered out a laugh. 'Teacher's pet already. Unbelievable.'

'Trust me, that really is unbelievable. You only have to ask my parents.'

A little bit of the laughter left his face, and Maggie sensed there was a story there. One that would probably help explain why, even though he clearly loved his family, he'd found himself living at the other side of the world.

They halted by her car, and Seb thrust his hands in his pockets, shoulders hunched up against the biting cold. 'Well, thanks for the dance, Dr Peterson.'

'Do you want a lift back?'

He glanced towards the bus stop, and then back at her. 'The bus will be here soon.'

'Says the man who's clearly forgotten the unreliability of the English public transport system.'

He laughed softly. 'Okay, I was trying to be a gentleman, but sod it. I'm freezing my knackers off here. I gratefully accept your offer.'

He surprised her by grabbing the driver's door and opening it. She was about to tell him he'd got the wrong side, when he bowed and indicated for her climb in. Then ran round the bonnet and jumped into the passenger seat. 'Please tell me this car has heated seats?'

After turning the engine on, she clicked the button. 'You'll have to toughen up if you're going to hang around. It's only going to get colder.'

'I know.' He let out a deep sigh, his shoulders slumping, and she wondered what he was thinking.

'When are you planning on going back?'

'Good question. Now all I need is an answer.'

As she manoeuvred the car out of the car park, she snatched a glimpse at his face. He was staring straight ahead, and her heart did a little flip as she took in his profile. The square jaw, the straight nose, the blonde hair she'd first thought was messy, and now thought sexy.

Dragging her eyes away, she focused her attention forward. 'What does it depend on?'

'Dad, mainly. I want to see him up and about. Back to annoying Mum for the right reasons, like leaving the loo seat up and his towel on the floor, rather than being a moody git.'

'He might be depressed. Having a heart attack is a really traumatic experience.'

'Yeah. We've been warned about that.' He turned to look at her. 'You think I'm being too hard on him?'

'I think it must be tough for you to see your dad appearing vulnerable,' she answered carefully. 'Just as I think it must be tough for him to have his son see him like that.'

Seb blew out a breath. 'You're right. On both counts.' There was a beat of silence. 'He's not the only reason I might stay around for a bit though.'

'Oh?' She drew up at the red light, and as the car stopped, she glanced in his direction.

He smiled directly into her eyes. 'There's more to interest me here than I thought.'

'Oh?' Damn, she was sounding like a broken record. And why had her heart sped up? 'You mean the youth centre?'

'Yeah, I'm enjoying working there, especially now I'm officially part of the set-up. But there are other attractions, too.' His laughter was soft and low, and it made her stomach dip. 'I mean, it'll be hard to catch *Strictly* on a pontoon over the reef.'

He's teasing you. Yet his eyes held hers, and beneath the amusement there was a glitter of something more. Something hotter, darker. Something that made her blood feel twice as thick, and her pulse race twice as fast.

It was a relief when the lights changed to green, and she was able to focus on driving again.

At last she pulled up outside Sarah's house.

'Well, thanks for saving me from the bus nightmare. I guess I won't see you now until Saturday.'

She turned to look at him. 'You're joining us again?'

'Of course. It's Blackpool, darling,' he drawled in a very good impression of Craig Revel Horwood.

'Right, yes.' God, where had this jittery feeling come from?

'That's unless you need any more emergency childcare.'

'Hannah's back to full strength, thank you.' And that reminded her. 'You never did say whose car you picked them up in.'

Those eyes that could be so direct suddenly found something more interesting to look at outside. 'I hired one.'

Guilt wormed through her. She'd been in a blind panic that morning. She'd not considered the logistics, not thought beyond her own need. 'I'm sorry. You shouldn't have had to do that. I put you in a terrible position.' She hesitated. 'I don't suppose I can offer to—'

'Pay? No.' He huffed out a breath. 'And don't apologise. I wanted to do the favour.' Finally, he eyes met hers. 'In case you haven't realised, I like you, Maggie Peterson.'

All the saliva in her mouth drained away as her heart banged against her ribs. Maggie had to swallow, twice, before she could speak. And then she didn't know what to say. 'I… thank you. I like you, too. I mean, you're Alice and Sarah's brother, so that's not a surprise.'

He smiled, but it was a wry, crooked effort. 'I guess not.'

In a flash, he opened the door and jumped out. As she

watched him stroll up to the front door, her mind fretted. Had he meant he liked her, or he *liked* her?

Oh, for God's sake. She was being ridiculous. The guy was nearly eleven years her junior. He'd helped her out with the childcare, and turned up to the dance class, because she was a friend of his sisters.

He liked her. Full stop. No emphasis.

Chapter Ten

The kids, around a dozen thirteen to fifteen-year-olds, looked at Seb as if he'd just announced he was going to put on a sequinned leotard and parade down the high street.

Then again, maybe what he had proposed wasn't too far off the mark.

'That is like, so fucking lame.' Rylan, fifteen years old but packing around thirty years of attitude, hunched his shoulders as he stared down at the floor.

'If you've got any better ideas for fundraising, I'm open to hearing them,' Seb said mildly. 'I take it you do want an outdoor basketball court, Rylan?'

'Yeah,' he muttered, eyes still on the floor.

'Then we need to raise some money. This is one way. If there are others, shout them out.' Seb paused, eyeing up the group who were all sat, like he was, on the hall floor. They were good kids, in the main. Kids who'd either been cajoled, pushed or had the self-motivation to come to the centre rather than hang out on the streets, getting into trouble.

'What about street dancing?' Dark-haired Zayne's eyes flicked towards the exceptionally pretty Kiara, and Seb had to smother a grin. It wasn't hard to work out where the boy's thoughts were travelling.

'We could do that, but how many people are going to turn up to watch?' Seb wondered if the kids were right and he did have a screw loose. He'd never have thought of this a few months ago. 'Look, I suggested ballroom dancing because of the programme on the TV. You've heard of *Strictly Come Dancing*, yes?' They all muttered yes, so he pressed on. 'Well, it's watched by millions, so I figured we could tap into that popularity. Pitch this as like a local *Strictly*, and get people to enter to win a prize. We can ask local ballroom dancing teachers to be the judges.' Silence. 'You'll get lessons, so it's a chance to learn something new.'

'Yeah, like how to foxtrot,' Rylan said disgustedly. Sticking his chin in the air, he held his arms out and started to pretend to dance. 'Who wants to fucking foxtrot?'

He had a point. Still, Seb had only had one lesson, and yes, he suspected it had more to do with his partner than the dance, but already he was looking forward to the next one. 'Have you watched the programme? Ballroom dancing isn't what you might think. It's athletic, it's clever, it's fun. It's *sexy*.'

'Can't be. My gran does it,' Hayley piped up. She always

wore big hoop earrings, and had a matching big personality.

'Well, good on your gran. You can persuade her to enter,' Seb countered. 'Dancing's for everyone. Every age, every background.'

'Why do *we* have to do it?' Kiara shrugged. 'I mean, I see it might be fun to learn, but you don't need us to take part if you get loads of other entries.'

'My idea is to have three age groups,' Seb explained. 'Strictly teens, Strictly adults and Strictly over sixty. None of you has to enter, it's up to you, but I'd like you all to give the lessons a go. Some of you might enjoy it and want to take part. Others might prefer to help behind the scenes. We'll need both if this is going to work.' In fact the more he thought about it, the more he wondered if he was biting off more than he could chew. Still, it felt bloody good to be actually *doing* something again, something rewarding, and being paid for it.

'What about you?' Zayne looked over at him. 'Are you going to do the lessons?'

'Of course.'

'And you're entering?'

'I hadn't thought that far,' Seb replied honestly.

Zayne grinned. 'Well, we ain't if you don't.'

'Yeah, Seb.' Rylan started to laugh. 'You can't make us do it if you don't.'

He wanted to argue he wasn't making anyone do anything, but they were all looking at him expectantly now. 'Fine. I'll enter. But I'd like to see some of you doing the same. And before you ask, you can pair up girl with girl, boy with boy, or girl with boy. It's up to you.'

They all started looking at each other, and pointing. Then Rylan held out his hand to Zayne and as they pretended to dance together, the room erupted with laughter.

Hayley, standing on his right, turned to face him. 'Who's gonna be your partner?'

Seb's answering smile was totally unconscious. 'I've got someone in mind, but I don't know if she'll be up for it.' *Or if it's wise to ask her.*

Hayley started to giggle. 'Oooh, is she fit? Have you got the hots for her?'

Yes, and maybe. Okay, yes and yes. 'You don't have to have the hots for someone to enjoy dancing with them.'

'Yeah but it's kind of sexy if you do,' Kiara said quietly.

Seb watched as her eyes fell on Zayne, who was still larking around with Rylan. Clearly he wasn't the only one thinking of a potential dance partner. Trouble is, while he could now definitely confirm that dancing with someone you fancied was sexy, he also knew it wasn't always a good idea. Like, for example, if they were too classy, or too wary, for a quick fling, yet you weren't in the right place to date. Or if they saw you only as the brother of their friends... Memories of his ill-fated comment in the car flooded back to him.

Shit, he'd told her he liked her. Unsurprisingly, she'd deflected this in the same deft way she'd deflected his previous attempts at flirting, quickly turning it into an innocuous, bland *like*. It hadn't been the way he'd meant it, but he supposed it was something they could both continue to live with without too much embarrassment.

It brought him back to his original quandary. Now he'd started dance lessons with her, it was surely rude not to ask Maggie to enter the competition with him. Hell, who was he kidding, after last Wednesday he couldn't think of dancing with anyone else. Yet if she agreed, a big if, could he really continue to spend all this time with her and *not* fall for her? Not want to do more than thank her for the dance at the end of the evening? He'd not been lying when he'd told her he might stay in the UK longer than he'd originally planned. Though he yearned for a return to the sun and the reef, there were other attractions for him now, far closer to home.

What had started out as a simple crush on her was becoming more, and the realisation excited him and scared the crap out of him in equal parts.

Strictly Saturday was at Alice's that week. Maggie knew she'd arrived before Sarah and, she presumed, Seb, because the hostess cornered her the moment she stepped foot inside.

'Come on, spill the beans.' Alice watched as the kids disappeared into the TV room before adding, 'What's happening with you and my brother?'

Maggie felt the blood drain from her face. 'God, Alice, nothing's happening.'

'No?' She frowned, then let out a dramatic sigh. 'That's such a let-down. Not least because I owe Sarah twenty quid now.'

'You made a bet on whether I was... whether Seb and I were...' The blood rushed back into her face, the sting of it leaving her feeling heated and flustered.

'Shagging? Having a fling?' Alice let out a loud belly laugh. 'Of course not. But I did put twenty quid on him asking you out. He seems pretty smitten.'

Could her face get any hotter? 'He's not.'

'No?' Alice took hold of her hand and led her into the kitchen. 'He looked after the girls for you, then he went all that way by bus to your dance lessons. Sarah said he was being supportive, but I think there's more to it than that.'

'There isn't.'

Alice smiled as she let go of her hand and went to open the fridge. 'As your friend, I'll take your word for it and not point out the obvious colour to your cheeks. Now, what do you want to drink?'

The doorbell rang, and Alice smirked. 'Do you want to let them in? I say them, because I'm pretty sure my brother, who did nothing but take the piss out of our *Strictly* sessions a few weeks ago, will be with Sarah.'

'Only because it's something to do before he goes clubbing.'

'Perhaps. Or perhaps this is the main attraction and he only goes clubbing to put us off the scent.'

Maggie groaned. 'Oh God, you've turned into a crazy person. No, scratch that, you've always been crazy. I'm going to go and let in the sensible, mature, level-headed twin.'

'And her brother,' Alice shouted down the hallway.

Maybe he won't show, Maggie thought as she went to open the door. Then sighed as her stomach dipped in disappointment when she saw Sarah. Only for it to flip when she saw Seb's tall frame standing behind her. He's going clubbing, she reminded herself, taking in his collared shirt and smart jacket. But then he smiled, and her insides did that fluttery butterfly thing that's written about in books, yet rarely happens in real life. It had happened to her once before. Ten years and one divorce later, she should know better than to trust it.

'Can I have a word?' Seb asked once Maggie had hugged Sarah and given Seb an awkward kiss on the cheek. He glanced over to his sister when he realised she was taking an active interest. 'Sticky beaks can go into the kitchen. This conversation is for dancers only.'

Sarah quirked a brow, gave them both an amused, rather too knowing look and wandered away.

'Dancers?' Maggie tried not to inhale the invigorating maleness of his aftershave, or stare at the way his broad shoulders filled out the grey jacket. 'You've only had one lesson.'

'True.' He shifted, resting his arm on the wall above her, making her conscious of his height. Again she felt that squirmy sensation in the pit of her belly which totally wasn't her. She was too sensible for all of this. 'But I'm going to be having more lessons. With you, I hope.'

'Well, you did say you'd paid up until the end of the year.'

'I have.' He caught her eye and gave her a surprisingly sheepish smile. 'I've also, kind of, agreed to put on a ballroom dancing competition at the centre, open to the general public to enter.' He cleared his throat. 'And I've sort of convinced some of the kids to take part, and Belinda to give them lessons.'

Maggie gaped at him. 'Wow. That's, well…'

'Insane?'

'I was going to say very brave of you.'

He chuckled. 'I'll take that. The thing is.' His eyes left hers and he shook his head, straightening up. 'Hell, this is harder that I thought.'

It was this, the sweet vulnerability behind the confident façade, that made him so easy to like. 'Whatever it is you want to say, it can't be harder than me asking you to take care of my kids last Monday.'

'Nah, that was an emergency. Of course you had to ask. This is, well, it's more of a favour.' His eyes met hers. 'The kids said they'd only enter the competition if I do, too. So I'm looking for a dance partner.'

'I see.' She was a logical choice, but it didn't mean she was the right choice. Entering a competition would mean practice. She had a job, and children. *You're scared of being alone with him*. No, she told the inner voice. She was simply being practical. 'Obviously if you're going to enter a competition, you need someone with few commitments. Hannah might like to do it. She loves watching the dancing, and she did say she wanted to learn.'

That bright blue gaze wouldn't leave her alone. It was as if he could see her mind working. 'Hannah's great, but it's you I'm having lessons with, Mags.' A pause, as his eyes skimmed her face before settling back on hers. 'You I want to dance with.'

Her heart jiggled and bounced, and Maggie had to fight to keep her composure. 'It's Maggie. Mags are something you read in a doctors' waiting room.'

He laughed softly. 'God, I love it when you go all prim and proper on me. So,' he smiled down at her, 'is that a yes, Seb, I'll be delighted to be your dance partner in the very worthy fundraising event you're putting on at the youth centre, which I'm thinking of calling *Strictly Local*, by the way.'

Despite her reservations, a smile tugged at her. 'I like the name. And when you put it like that, it's hard to say no.'

'Hard, but I'm going to say no anyway, or hard so I'm going to give in gracefully?'

She'd been wrong. It wasn't hard to say no to him. When he looked at her like he was doing now, all sexy eyes and playful smile, it was impossible. 'The graceful bit.'

'Excellent.' He rubbed his hands together and nodded towards the television room. 'Now let's go to Blackpool.'

The show had already started when they slipped in, thank God. It meant no time for Sarah and Alice to voice the questions they were clearly burning to ask.

'This place has seen the best of the best,' the announcer

stated. 'The world champions have all danced here, in the Blackpool ballroom.'

The opening group dance was typically upbeat and then Claudia and Tess made their entrance, looking amazing in gold and silver outfits. After the judges had been announced, Bruno leapt to his feet and waved his arms theatrically. 'It's always magic in Blackpool.'

Across the room, Seb cleared his throat. 'I thought it was always blowing a gale and piss… pouring down with rain.'

'Shh.'

The exchange between Seb and Tabby caused a surprising warmth in Maggie's chest. Seb's 'whispered' comments, and Tabby's answering remonstrations, were fast becoming part of the Saturday night ritual.

She wasn't just being polite when she'd admitted to him the other day that she liked him. Her gut told her he was one of the good guys. The fact he was also young, without direction, without roots, and totally unsuitable for a thirty-seven-year-old mother to have a small crush on shouldn't take away from his core appeal. And as long as her crush remained her secret, it wasn't harming anyone.

'Now that's what I call a jive.' The judge's verdict brought Maggie's attention back to the show. 'The flicks and kicks were superb, though the sashays could have been a bit later.'

'Umm, I thought that,' Seb drawled from across the room. 'Those damn sashays are a killer, aren't they?' His eyes lifted to hers. 'We'll have to watch them if we decide to jive.'

Oh no. Suddenly everyone's eyes were on her. Not just Sarah and Alice, but all the children, too.

'Decide to jive, when?' Alice, as usual, was the first to say what others were thinking.

'I'm organising a ballroom dancing competition at the youth centre to raise funds,' Seb answered mildly. 'We're calling it *Strictly Local* and you guys are welcome to enter.' The grin he directed at his sisters was full of mischief. 'Now shut up, will you? I'm trying to watch.'

Alice huffed, then balled up her napkin and threw it at him. He caught it casually in his left hand, smirking before turning his attention back to the television.

Maggie felt her friends' eyes on her for several minutes afterwards and knew she'd receive a full grilling once their brother had left.

Chapter Eleven

S eb was shrugging on his coat when he heard a key in the lock and Sarah walked in. She took one look at him and raised her eyebrows.

'Going somewhere?'

'Putting on a coat would seem to suggest that.' She stared at him with the expression he knew she must use in her business deals; *I know you're up to something so I'll just wait it out, sucker*. Though maybe the last part was just for him. 'I'm heading to the bus stop.'

Removing her coat, Sarah placed it neatly on the peg. 'Let's make this easy, shall we? It's Wednesday, so I know that's the day Maggie goes to her dance lessons. The question is whether you're big enough to admit that last week wasn't just a one-off. Or whether you're going to carry on evading and avoiding me and Alice when we try to quiz you on it.'

Ouch. Those people who thought big sisters were all

kindness and support? It was a load of bollocks. They could be mean and meddling when they wanted to be. 'Fine, I'll be continuing with the dance lessons. I need all the practice I can get now I've been forced to enter the competition at the youth centre.'

'That explanation would work, if you hadn't started the lessons the week before you had the idea for the competition.' Sarah narrowed her eyes. 'Whatever you say next, remember I'm smart and I've known you all your life.'

Crap, why was lying to his sisters so damn difficult? 'Okay, okay. I'm going to the dance lessons because I want to dance with Maggie.' He swallowed. 'I like her.' That bloody word again. He wondered which way Sarah would interpret it.

His sister's face softened. 'I know you do, you muppet. The way you started joining us on Saturdays, but then spent more time watching Maggie than the television, was kind of a giveaway.'

He winced. 'That obvious?'

'To me and Alice, yes. To Maggie, no, because she has absolutely no clue how gorgeous she is.'

He smiled at that, because Sarah was spot on. 'Is there a subtle underlying message in there, along the lines of she's too gorgeous for me? Because if there is, I hold my hands up to knowing that.'

Sarah placed a hand on his cheek. 'No, there's no underlying message you dummy, because you're gorgeous, too. You're a great catch for someone.'

'Just not Maggie.'

Sarah bit into her lip. 'I don't know, Seb. She's older than you, she's got kids, a career she loves, financial security. She's *settled*. You're still figuring out what you want to do. Hell, you don't even know where you're going to be in two months' time. It doesn't seem the best fit to me.'

It was exactly how he saw it, too, but to hear the same thoughts echoed back to him from his sister, someone he really respected, hurt. 'I hear you. And you don't have to worry, I'm not about to do anything stupid.' Well, apart from the moment he'd come scarily close to kissing her. 'I'd better get going.'

Sarah smiled, her eyes still on him. 'You might not be right for her, but you are good for her, Seb. She told me last week how much better it was dancing with you than the other guys.'

So, he was at least a better *fit* than short, balding middle-aged men. Good to know.

He arrived at the dance class a few minutes late. Again. Blasted buses. Mind you, he'd never been a punctual sort of guy. Mainly because he hated watching the clock. Life was for living, not being tied down to dates and times. Another thing that made him unsuitable for Maggie, because as he knew from the Saturday night *Strictly* gatherings, she was a stickler for timekeeping.

If he ever did have the balls to ask her out, they

wouldn't make it past the first date. He'd turn up late, and she'd ditch him.

Peering through the window of the studio door, he spotted Maggie talking to two of the old dears he recognised from last week, Shirley and Pauline. Belinda seemed to share his unpunctual gene as she wasn't there yet. Maybe she'd had bus trouble, too. The thought of the frightfully elegant Belinda on a bus made him chuckle to himself as he opened the door. Immediately Maggie looked up and gave him a nice smile. One that made the trek on public transport worthwhile.

'Ooh, he's turned up again.' Shirley or Pauline, he couldn't remember who was who, they both had short white hair, portly middles and faces that looked like they'd spent most of their years laughing. Anyway, one of them gave him a wink. 'I'm bagging you for the first dance. Don't see why Maggie should get you all to herself.'

He looked at Maggie, silently pleading with her to intervene, but instead of the sympathy he was hoping for, her face lit up with amusement. 'No problem, Shirley. It's only fair we share Seb around.'

He was starting to feel like a piece of, well, not exactly meat. Maybe some sort of cake. Something these women fancied nibbling on. Involuntarily, a shudder went through him and Maggie smirked, as if she could read his mind.

Belinda chose that moment to make her entrance, and within minutes Seb found his left arm stretching round a sizeable body, his eyes looking into a pair of slightly sunken brown eyes, crow's feet radiating from their outer edge.

This definitely wasn't what he'd had in mind when he'd begun his epic bus trip.

Then again, though she didn't make his heart pump, or his hormones dance, Shirley did at least make the foxtrot memorable.

'Shirley, your hand shouldn't, at any point, need to be on Seb's backside,' Belinda admonished as she did her inspection.

Shirley cackled. 'You're such a spoilsport.' Seb felt a light squeeze on his right buttock before her hand, thankfully, moved back to the top of his arm.

Over Shirley's shoulder, he caught Maggie's eye and she gave him a pained look as the guy she was dancing with spun her too forcibly. 'You need to rescue me,' he mouthed to her.

'You need to rescue me,' she mouthed back, before she was jerked away from his line of vision.

'Shirley.' Seb gave the woman in his arms his best smile. 'Do you fancy helping me out?'

'Of course, love.'

'The thing is, I've not come here just to learn to dance.'

'Ooh, I knew it. You've come to pick up a girl. And look no further, dear. I may not have the body of one any more, but inside.' She patted her eye-wateringly large chest. 'Inside I'm twenty-one and game for anything.'

He felt the blood drain from his face. 'That's a great offer, Shirley, really, but what I meant is I've come here to learn to dance with Maggie.'

'Maggie?' Shirley looked over at Maggie, and then back

at him. 'What's she got that I haven't?' He must have looked as flustered as he felt, because she let out a loud belly laugh. 'Look at your face. I'm too much for you to handle, eh?' She glanced again at Maggie. 'Well, you certainly make a handsome couple.'

'Oh no, we're not a couple.' Christ, he couldn't have Shirley getting the wrong end of the stick. 'She's way out of my league.'

'She's a beauty, all right. If you want her though, lad, you can't be thinking like that. You need to pull your finger out and fight for her.' She chuckled, giving his bicep a quick squeeze. 'Seems to me you've got the right equipment.'

'I'll bear that in mind.' This was like wading through a treacle-filed bog. Still, he needed her on his side, so he kept smiling. 'First, though, before I do all that err… fighting… Maggie's helping me out with a dance competition I'm organising for the youth centre. She's agreed to be my partner and, well, frankly, we need all the practice we can get. Practice *together*,' he emphasised, just in case Shirley had missed the point.

Eyeing him shrewdly, Shirley nodded. 'I like your thinking. Get her to dance with you first, then she'll be putty in your hands. Us ladies do love being taken for a twirl by a strong man.' Before he could correct her – and he wasn't absolutely sure she was on the wrong path – Shirley let go of him and marched over to Maggie and her dance partner. 'Charlie, time to let go of that lovely young lady and partner up with this old bird.'

Charlie looked distinctly unhappy at the prospect, and

Seb had a smidgen of sympathy for him. Dancing with Maggie was probably the highlight of his year. Thankfully Shirley wasn't the sort of lady who took no for an answer, and two minutes later, Seb found his hand resting on the slim back of a sexy thirty-something-year-old, while gazing into a pair of dancing grey eyes.

'Whatever you said, thank you,' she whispered.

'I promised her I'd take her home and massage her feet.' Maggie's eyes flew open, her expression horrified, and Seb laughed, though privately he wondered if she'd be even more horrified with their actual conversation. Including the 'putty in his hands' part. 'Chill, I told her we had a competition coming up and we needed the practice.'

As if to prove it, he stumbled over the first few steps, wincing as she winced. 'Crap, did I get your toe?'

'It's fine.' She gave him a reassuring smile. 'Relax, or, what is it you said, chill?'

'Yeah, either works.' But he could feel the warmth of her skin against his palm, as if the blouse she wore wasn't there. And then there was the occasional brush of her breasts against his chest, the press of her thighs on his. It was heaven, and it was torture. As if that wasn't bad enough, his groin was twitching, excited to feel the object of his increasing obsession within such close proximity.

No, he couldn't think about this. He had to talk, to distract himself. He cleared his throat. 'So, have you thought about what dance you want to do for the competition?'

'I kind of assumed we'd do the simplest, like the waltz?'

Her hesitancy about something he knew she loved drove him nuts. 'Oh no. No way.' After navigating round a couple who needed hazard warning lights they were so off track, he bent so he could look into her eyes. 'We're not going with the dance you think we should do, we're going with the dance you *want* to do.' He smiled as she eyed him warily. 'So get thinking, Dr Peterson.'

If it happened on two successive weeks, did it mean it was becoming a habit? Maggie pondered the question as she drove Seb home. Again. She could hardly leave him to catch the bus though, could she? And what she definitely didn't want to do was put him off going again next week.

Admitting that was hard, but dancing with Seb was... An involuntary sigh escaped her. Dancing with him was *delicious*. Even the basic steps they were doing now, had never felt so intimate, so... okay, she had to admit it, so sexy. But why? Was it his physique, the cute smiles he kept shooting her when he mucked up, the heavenly smell of him? Maybe it was the natural rhythm he showed, once he relaxed into it. She needed it to be something she could easily explain, because then she could reassure herself what she felt was just a simple law of attraction: female to young, handsome male. 'Is Belinda right?' Maggie asked as she turned into Sarah's road. 'Have you danced before?'

He shrugged the powerful shoulders she enjoyed placing her hands on. 'I've not had lessons but I did a short stint as a cruise worker, and as part of that I was told some basics so I could smooch when needed.'

The image made her laugh. 'Funny, I can see you doing that.'

He slid her a look. 'You can see me charming the rich old ladies, huh?'

'You've got them all queuing up to dance with you at the studio.'

'What about you?' He asked as she pulled up outside Sarah's house. 'Could you see me charming you?'

I've got an awful feeling you already have. 'Why would you want to charm me?'

He smiled, his eyes skipping over her face, before resting for a beat on her lips. 'Who wouldn't want to charm you?'

Flutters rippled through her belly but she made herself remember why being attracted to someone wasn't necessarily a good thing. 'I can name one man who didn't want to, at least not once he'd seen someone better.'

Seb's browns came together in a frown. 'Your ex doesn't count because any man who decided to up and leave you and your kids is clearly mentally deranged.'

His words soothed her undernourished ego. 'He's got his own version of events, but thank you.'

'How long had you guys been together?'

Maggie had to think, it had been so long since she'd talked about Paul. 'Ten years. Long enough for us both to get on each other's nerves, I guess.' Though she'd never once considered throwing in the towel. Marriage had to be worked at, yet he'd not even wanted to try. Instead he'd decided to look at pastures new. 'What about you. Have you been in a relationship long enough to get on a woman's nerves?'

He clutched a hand to his chest. 'You wound me, but in answer to your question, I've not had the opportunity yet, no. Not that I'm against the concept – the relationship that is, not pissing women off.' He hesitated a moment, fingers drumming on his thigh. 'Can I ask why your marriage ended, or is that too personal?'

It was too personal. Yet sitting in the intimacy of the car, a street light the only illumination, Maggie almost wanted to tell him. 'I don't think we've reached that level of friendship yet.'

His soft laughter echoed round the interior. 'Neat evade, though I didn't miss the word *yet*. I can work with that.' His eyes zeroed in on hers and he stilled for a moment before leaning towards her. Immediately her heart began to thump against her ribs but his mouth didn't find hers, as she'd half dreaded, half hoped. Instead he whispered in her ear, his breath warm against her skin. 'I meant what I said before. I *like* you, Maggie Peterson.' Then he drew back and smiled. 'Strictly Saturday is at yours this week?'

Bemused, flustered, her heart galloping, she nodded.

With that he opened the car door and eased himself out. As she watched his long, loping strides take him up the path, she wondered whether to be scared or just plain flattered by his words. Damn it, she was going with the second. She enjoyed his company, enjoyed dancing with him, and from the sound of things, he felt the same way. It wasn't like the guy was going to make a move on her. He surely had his hands full with whoever he went clubbing with every Saturday night after *Strictly*.

Putting her key in the door five minutes later, Maggie caught a glimpse of her face in the reflection on the glass, and was surprised to find she was smiling. That's what dancing did. It was a happy place for her, though she had to admit a huge slice of the happy was down to the man she was dancing with.

She'd only been inside a minute, just long enough to wave hello to Hannah, who was sitting watching television, when her mobile began to ring. And when she answered it, the voice greeting her at the other end wiped the smile right off her face.

'Paul. What can I do for you?'

'Where have you been?' His tone was tight and irritated. 'I tried the home number and the girl who answered said you were out.'

'You lost the right to ask me questions like that three years ago.'

'Not if my daughters are involved. It's after nine o'clock on a school night.'

Maggie let out an incredulous laugh. 'You're seriously questioning my parenting ability when you've not actually bothered to see them for two years?'

Silence. Followed by a loud expulsion of breath. 'You're right, sorry.'

'You spoke to Hannah, my nanny, who was looking after

125

them,' Maggie told him, because he was still their father. As for her own whereabouts, that was nothing to do with him.

'Okay, yes, of course.' Another sigh. 'Look, I'm not phoning to fight. I know I've let the girls down recently—'

'Two years isn't recently, Paul.'

'I've FaceTimed them,' he countered, and she hated the arrogant way he said it. As if it was a perfectly acceptable alternative to actually seeing their father.

'And when was the last time you did that?' Another few beats of silence, and she imagined he was furiously glancing through the calendar on his diary. 'I'll save you trying to find the date. It was six months ago. And the time before that, it was five months ago.'

'Shit, was it really?'

He wasn't a bad man. Many times Maggie had reminded herself of that. He'd just turned out to be astonishingly self-centred. 'Yes, it really was.'

'Time seems to have run away with me, what with buying a new place and a promotion at work.'

'Congratulations.'

'Thanks.' He hesitated, probably because she'd been unable to put much warmth into the word. 'Look, I know I've been a poor father since I... since we split up, but I want to rectify that. In fact that's why I'm calling. I'd like to see Tabby and Penny.'

Maggie felt a crushing weight on her chest, and she had to take the phone away from her ear for a moment so she could just focus on breathing. He was their father. He had every right to see them. Plus she wanted them to have a relationship with him. So why did the thought of them spending time with him hurt so much? 'Will it just be you?'

'Err, no. Isabelle will be with me.'

And now she had her answer. Paul seeing them was fine. Paul and his new woman... *that* hurt. She wanted to tell him to go to hell. To slam the phone down on him, but how could she when he was their father? 'Why the sudden urgency for her to meet them?' The silence this time was so long, Maggie wondered if he'd heard her. But then he cleared his throat, and suddenly she had her answer. 'You're getting married,' she stated flatly.

Dimly she heard him say he'd wanted to tell her in person, and when her frozen mind couldn't come up with a reply, she heard him say he'd phone another time.

Then all she heard was the dial tone, and the sound of something in her chest shrivelling.

Chapter Twelve

Seb was worried about Maggie. The woman who'd opened the door to him and Sarah a few minutes ago for Strictly Saturday wasn't the same woman he'd danced with on Wednesday. That woman had been flushed, her eyes shining. This woman looked pale, her eyes a flat grey.

He glanced at Sarah, who shrugged. 'I don't know. I've not spoken to her all week.'

'She was fine on Wednesday.'

His sister gave him a sharp look. 'You didn't say anything to upset her, did you?'

'No, of course not.' But his gut twisted. Had she taken offence at what he'd said about liking her? Was this her way of telling him to back off?

'Seb?'

'I don't think I said anything,' he corrected. Unwilling to discuss it any further, he went to join the kids in the television room. Alice and Jack hadn't arrived yet, so it was only Tabby and Penny, currently fighting over the remote control.

'Mum said it was my go.' Tabby put her hands on her hips and gave Penny a good old pout.

'No, she didn't,' Penny argued. 'She said to take it in turns. And you did it last night.'

Seb coughed, drawing both of their attention. 'Hello, ladies.'

Tabby turned her pout on him. 'Penny won't let me put the TV on and it's my turn.'

He glanced at Penny, feeling like the referee in a fraught tennis match. 'Whose turn do you think it is?'

'It's mine.' Penny sighed, throwing the remote onto the sofa. 'But fine, whatever. Tabby can do it.'

Tabby snatched at it, grinning widely, and immediately after zapping it on began flicking through the channels. Penny went to sit quietly on the floor. Feeling for her, Seb went to sit next to her. 'Do you want to see what I learned at the dance lesson on Wednesday?'

She turned to look at him, her shoulders rising up and down in a shrug of indifference. 'I guess.'

He rose to his feet and held out his hand. 'Come on then.'

She stared at him. 'What, you mean like you're going to dance with me?'

'How else can I show you?'

Giving him a shy smile, she scrambled to her feet. 'I can't dance, though.'

'Neither can I. That's why I'm learning.' He bent his

head to whisper in her ear. 'Don't tell her I said this, but your mum is way better than me.'

As he began to show Penny the basics, Tabby's eyes left the television. 'I want a go.'

'No problem.' He nodded down to Penny. 'But it's your sister's turn first.'

Tabby gave a loud, dramatic huff. 'I suppose that's fair.'

He couldn't help it. He burst out laughing. Soon Penny did, too, and it wasn't long before Tabby joined them, even though he wasn't sure she knew why she was laughing.

It was because he was distracted, the television playing noisily in the background, that he didn't hear the front doorbell. The first he knew of Maggie's visitors, was when they appeared in the doorway. A tall guy, around six foot high, dark hair flecked with grey and brown eyes that stared antagonistically at him. By his side was a pretty blonde woman who looked to be in her early thirties.

Penny, whose right hand was in his left, her other hand on his arm, stilled. 'Dad?'

That's when Tabby also decided to take notice of the visitors. Unlike her more cautious sister, Tabby ran over to her dad and flung her arms around his legs. Then she looked up at the woman next to him. 'Who's that?'

It was only then Seb noticed Maggie, standing behind the man he presumed was her ex. 'Girls, this is Isabelle. Dad's friend.'

'What about you, Penny? Don't I get a hug?' Paul gave his eldest daughter a tight smile before raising his eyes to

Seb and giving him what could only be described as a death stare.

Realising he was still holding Penny in a waltz, Seb let go of her hand and stepped back.

Slowly Penny walked over to her father and tentatively put her arms around his waist. Paul, equally tentatively, kissed the top of her head.

Then he stared hard in Seb's direction. 'While we're making introductions, who are you?'

Seb took a second to glance at Maggie. A second he wished he hadn't wasted, because it gave Tabby the opportunity to jump straight in, feet first. 'That's Seb. He helps Penny with her homework and looks after us sometimes when Hannah is sick. And he dances with Mum.' Having detonated that minefield of information, Tabby plonked herself back on the sofa. 'And now we have to be quiet 'cos *Strictly* is about to start.'

Good God, the girl was priceless. He wanted to laugh, but Paul's face had twisted into an expression of... disgust? Horror? Suffice to say he clearly wasn't happy with what he'd just heard. As for Maggie, she looked like didn't know whether to laugh or cry.

Seb stepped towards Paul and held out his hand. 'Hi, I'm Seb. Alice and Sarah's brother,' he added, figuring it might remove some of the angst from Paul's expression.

'I see.'

Quite what Paul saw – Seb naked in bed with his ex-wife, Seb playing happy families with his ex and his daughters – he wasn't sure. He also didn't feel like enlightening him any further. The guy was stupid enough to walk away from the three Peterson girls, he deserved to feel whatever was currently giving him the expression of being punched in the gut.

The doorbell rang again, and figuring it was Alice and Jack, Seb took the opportunity to escape. 'I'll go and answer that.'

Maggie watched as Paul followed Seb's retreating body down the hallway.

'He even answers your door for you?'

He's Tabby and Penny's father, she reminded herself yet again. Even if he is being an absolute prick. 'He's answering it because he knows it's his sister.' She regretted the explanation as soon as she'd uttered it. Why not let Paul believe she was having a fling with a man ten years younger? He clearly didn't have an issue with an age gap, she thought bitterly, glancing at her replacement. Paul's future wife. The girls' future stepmother.

It was the latter that cooled Maggie's anger. She wouldn't antagonise the woman who'd be caring for her children when they saw their father. Even if it meant gritting her teeth, slapping on a smile and playing nice when inside she wanted to throw something.

'Everyone has come to watch Strictly Come Dancing, so

let's have this conversation in the kitchen and leave them to it.'

Giving Alice, Jack and their kids a quick wave, and ignoring her friend's shocked expression, Maggie led Paul and Isabelle into the kitchen where Hannah and Sarah were busy taking pizzas out of the oven. A task she'd totally forgotten about the moment she'd opened the door to her unexpected guests.

Sarah looked up with a start. 'Oh, hi, Paul. I wasn't expecting to see you.'

'That makes two of us,' Maggie added dryly. She made quick introductions to Isabelle and Hannah. 'Thanks for doing my job and taking care of the food. I'll join you in a bit.'

They both caught on to her unsubtle hint and hastily carried the pizza and plates out of the room.

'So.' Maggie turned to face Paul. 'What did you come round for?'

He grimaced. 'Do I need a reason to come and see my daughters?'

'You do when you've not been here for—'

'Two years,' he interrupted her, holding up his hand. 'Yes, I know. You've already pointed that out.'

The dig stung. It reminded her of the many slurs he'd thrown her way while he'd been explaining why he wanted out. *You're always nagging me. You're like a snappy terrier who won't let go of the damn bone.*

Paul sighed, leaning against the kitchen worktop. He

looks older, she thought, then realised he was probably thinking the very same thing about her. 'I realise I've been poor at keeping in touch, and I want to make amends.' He turned to Isabelle, giving her a tender smile. The sort of smile he'd once given her. 'We're getting married next spring and Isabelle would like the girls to be bridesmaids.'

'Oh.' She'd had three days to get used to the idea, so why did it hurt so much to hear him say it again? And to know there was a date. It was really going to happen.

'We thought it would be good for them to get to know me before the day.' Isabelle smiled at her tentatively. 'If that's okay?'

'Of course it's okay,' Paul butted in. 'I don't need Maggie's permission to see my children, Isabelle.'

Wow. Maggie felt a tug of sympathy for Isabelle, who was trying to be kind. And a wave of fresh anger at Paul for being a git to them both. 'I'm not going to respond to that, as we both agreed we didn't need lawyers to sort out our childcare arrangements.' She gave Paul a cool look. 'But don't think I'm afraid to go down that route, if I feel it's necessary.' Turning back to Isabelle, she forced a smile. 'Thank you for thinking of the girls. I'm sure when they get to know you, they'll be delighted to come to the wedding.' She deliberately kept it vague as she wasn't sure about the bridesmaid part. 'I'm sorry tonight has been a bit fraught. If Paul had phoned in advance, we could have arranged to meet at a less chaotic time.'

'We were in the area.' Paul shrugged. 'I guessed you'd be in, as it was a Saturday night.'

Isabelle elbowed him. 'That's rude.'

'What?' He started to laugh. 'Oh no, I don't mean it like that. Maggie's obsessed with *Strictly Come Dancing*. I knew she'd be watching it.'

There it was again, another dig. Because she enjoyed watching the progamme, did it really make her obsessed? It wasn't like she was watching it alone. 'We all enjoy watching it,' she corrected. 'Hannah, Sarah, Alice, Jack and the children.'

'And Seb?'

Interesting. The presence of Seb had definitely irritated Paul, and for once, Maggie felt she had the upper hand. 'Seb enjoys it too,' she answered, smiling serenely. 'So much so that we're having dance lessons.' *Stick that in your pipe and smoke it.*

Paul's expression tightened but it was Isabelle who spoke. 'Oh, that sounds lovely. It must be amazing to dance properly, like they do on the programme.' She squeezed Paul's arm. 'Maybe we can take lessons, too. Imagine being able to do a real waltz as our first dance at the wedding.'

While Maggie laughed silently to herself, Paul's face turned a fascinating shade of purple. Good luck with that, she wanted to say, but it would be catty and Isabelle was clearly trying her best to ease the tension. 'I can really recommend it,' she said instead, enjoying the way Paul looked daggers at her.

'Right, well, we'll be in touch.' Taking hold of Isabelle's arm, Paul almost frogmarched his fiancée towards the door.

Having seen them out, Maggie didn't immediately go

and join the others. Instead she rested against the door, drawing in a breath. She felt shaky, knots she hadn't realised had formed now slowly unravelling.

'Are you okay?'

She glanced up with a start to find Seb walking down the hallway towards her. 'Of course. Just taking a moment.' When he reached her, he thrust a hand in his jeans pocket, and it was only then she realised he wasn't dressed up. 'Not clubbing tonight?'

He slowly shook his head, eyes still fixed on her face. 'It's getting boring. Thought I'd hang around here and see what you all get up to when the kids have gone to bed.'

She laughed softly. 'Now that really is boring. We talk and we drink.'

His lips curved in a small smile. 'Sounds good to me.' God, those blue eyes of his, they were mesmerising. Especially when, like now, she was their sole focus. 'I'm sorry if me being here made things awkward between you and Paul.'

'Awkward?' This time she really laughed. 'Trust me, things between us have been a lot worse than that. And anyway, the only person who didn't enjoy Tabby's little outburst was Paul.'

Another smile, wider this time, so it crinkled his eyes at the edges. 'She was dynamite, wasn't she?'

'She sure was.' Maggie sighed, feeling her whole body finally relaxing. 'Call me a bitch, but I enjoyed seeing him think you and I were, you know.'

'Dating?'

'Yes. The breakup has always been about him. Why I wasn't what he needed. Why the marriage wasn't working for him. What he wanted out of life. It was so good to see him think, just for a moment, about me, and what I might gain from our divorce.' The blue of Seb's eyes darkened, their intensity making her heart flutter. 'Make him wonder what I'm getting up to, even if it was all thanks to Tabby's skewed version of things.'

Seb raised his hand, shocking her when he ran his thumb gently across her lips. As her pulse began to race, he smiled deep into her eyes. 'We could make him wonder for real.'

'What...' Oh God, her heart was hammering so hard she couldn't hear herself think. 'What do you mean?'

'I think you know.' He dropped his hand, and took a step back. 'You'd better and go and join everyone before they send out a search party.'

'I thought that's what you were.' Her voice was breathy, like she'd climbed a steep hill rather than taken a few strides down her hall.

'Nope. I was the guy with the dodgy bladder.' He flashed her a grin as he pushed open the door to the downstairs loo.

Maggie's heart rate struggled to calm as she stepped back into the TV room, settling onto the sofa next to Tabby. As she put her arms around her daughter, for the first time Maggie found herself unable to concentrate on what the judges were saying. Instead she kept going over Seb's words.

Had he meant they could make Paul jealous?

Or had he meant they could date, for real?

Chapter Thirteen

eb gave Maggie space, gave them both space, to think about what he'd said. He went to the lesson on Wednesday, but kept the conversation light and declined a lift home, pretending he was going on to meet friends. He also didn't join them for Strictly Saturday.

He didn't need to ask himself if acting on this crazy attraction was a good idea. He knew the answer.

Life wasn't neat and tidy, though. He only needed to look at his parents to see that. His dad was still struggling mentally and physically to get over the heart attack, his body taking longer to heal than they'd all hoped.

It meant Seb remained in limbo land. He couldn't go back to Australia, not with his dad like this, yet was he really ready to put down roots here? At the same time, just because he didn't know what he was doing with his life, did he really have to put it on hold? Stay clear of a woman he had these scary, increasingly out-of-control feelings for?

Wasn't that asking the impossible?

The thoughts churned through his mind as he picked up the phone to talk to her on Sunday afternoon.

'Hey, is now a good time?'

She sounded a little out of breath. 'Yes, sure. I'm walking to the park to pick the girls up. They've spent the morning with Paul and Isabelle.'

'Ouch. Bet that was tough, waving them goodbye?'

'Yes.'

Her voice caught, and he wondered if he should have kept quiet. The Maggie he'd first met, so very reserved, wouldn't have wanted him asking personal questions, but he'd hoped they'd gone beyond that. 'Sorry, if you don't want to talk about it—'

'Actually, I do.' She laughed. 'Or maybe I should say I'm sure it will do me good to talk. Your sisters have told me for years I keep things too bottled up. So anyway, yes, the morning was hard. Tabby was okay about going, but Penny's much more wary of people. She doesn't know Isabelle, and her father is nearly a stranger, too, because when you're nine, three years is a long time not to see someone regularly. Plus it's not like he was father of the year when he did live with us.' She paused. 'Wow, sorry. I'm nervous about finding out how they got on, so I'm afraid you've got the uncensored me.'

He smiled down the phone. 'I like the uncensored you. She's kind of ... normal.'

'Are you saying most of the time I'm not?'

This time Seb was the one who chose his words

carefully. 'You're a very put together lady, Mags. You've got this poise, this self-assurance. I'm not going to lie, to those of us who haven't got their act together, it can be a bit scary at times.'

For a few moments all he could hear was the wind, and the faint rustle of clothing. 'Most of that is an illusion,' she said finally, her voice quiet. 'Just like the swan, the real me does a lot of ferocious paddling below the water.'

'Then I hope I get to meet the real you one day. I think we'd have a lot more in common than I thought.'

'Maybe.' She didn't sound too convinced, but before he could quiz her further, she changed the subject. 'The girls missed you yesterday. They couldn't understand how you could be doing anything better than watching musicals week.'

'Damn, I didn't realise it was such an important one. How was it?'

'Amazing. There was a Foxtrot to *Oliver*, Samba to *Sister Act*. An incredible Jive to *Hairspray*.'

'How were the sashays?'

She laughed. 'Perfect. In fact the whole dance was perfect. The couple got tens from each of the judges.'

'Sounds like I missed a cracking episode. Instead me and a few old school chums were getting our arses handed to us by a bunch of testosterone-fuelled teenagers at five-a-side football.'

'Sounds painful.'

'It was. I'll never hear the end of it. Which is why I'm phoning you.'

'Oh?'

He smiled to himself, imagining her wary expression. 'These teenagers were from the youth centre and now I really, really – hell, let's make that three reallys – want to show them I can do something better than they can. Like dance. It's only twelve weeks until the competition, Mags. We need to get working on a routine.'

'Whoa, okay. But the kids have only just started lessons. You're weeks ahead of them.'

He ignored her protests, because this wasn't only about impressing a group of teens. It was about impressing his family. Impressing *her*. 'I've talked to Belinda and she's happy to go through our options after class on Wednesday. Does that fit with you?'

'I'll have to check with Hannah, but I'm sure she won't mind.'

'Then it's a date.'

An unfortunate choice of words, perhaps, because his comment was met by an eerie silence. But just as he was about to backtrack, she spoke. 'In the early days, I used to beg Paul to take me dancing on a date, but he never did.'

'Well, I'd be honoured to take you on a dance date at the Attlestone community hall. It doesn't get classier than that.' He winced. 'Err, unless you want me to *actually* take you there, in which case you'll have to go by bus.'

Her responding laughter was warm and amused, but after he ended the call, he made a promise to himself. He was going to buy a damn car. It would have to be a banger, the youth centre pay was lousy, but he was done with travelling by flaming bus.

Maggie was in her bedroom, getting ready for the dance lesson, which basically meant she was changing out of her black work trousers and into a pair of jeans. Not because they showed off her figure better... okay, exactly because of that. Tabby and Penny were sat on her bed, telling her about their day.

'And he had this worm and he put it on the desk and Lizzie screamed. It was well funny.' Tabby giggled. 'Then Miss came in and he was in big trouble.'

'What happened to the worm?' Penny asked, making Maggie smile. Since the project on climate change, her eldest daughter had started to take a real interest in the environment and wildlife.

'Miss made him put it back in the soil. It was all dirty and wriggly.' Tabby started to jiggle around, doing a good impression of a worm and making them laugh. Then, with typical seven-year-old logic, she bounced straight onto a different subject. 'When are we getting a tree?'

'A tree?' As she concentrated on sweeping a little more blusher on her too-pale cheeks, it took Maggie a moment to catch up. 'Oh, you mean a Christmas tree.'

'It's December now, and Miss said that means the school is going to put the tree up.'

'Then we can put ours up, too.' Maggie's heart sank at the thought of climbing the ladder into the loft. At least she knew exactly where the decorations were now. Unlike the first Christmas after Paul had left, when she'd had to scramble over suitcases, tripping over assorted abandoned cables and shifting mountains of dusty cardboard boxes to find the one she'd neatly labelled *Xmas*. Now she was in charge of the loft. And now it was organised. 'I'll get it down this weekend.' Tabby beamed, and Maggie kissed first her and then Penny. 'Okay, I need to go. Hannah is downstairs waiting for you to watch *It Takes Two*. You promise to be good for her?'

'Yes, Mum,' they chorused.

'Are you dancing with Seb?' Penny asked as they walked down the stairs.

'I'm going to dance lessons and I suspect Seb will be there, too,' she corrected. She didn't want the girls getting the wrong impression.

'Dad says he doesn't understand why we like dancing, but it's cool, isn't it?' When they reached the bottom stair, Penny put her arms out in a waltz pose and did the basic box steps.

'I think so, yes.' Watching her daughter, Maggie frowned. 'Where did you learn to do that?'

'Seb showed me that night Dad came round.'

The girls hadn't spoken much about the day they'd spent with their father, other than to say Isabelle was nice, the park had been cold and they'd had a hot chocolate afterwards to warm up. Since then though, they'd mentioned Paul several times in conversation, something they hadn't done in months, so Maggie guessed the relationship had started to form again. She hoped so, for their sakes. And perhaps, in time, for her own, because as hard as it had been to leave them with Paul, there was something to be said for having a bit of time to herself.

As for the obvious attachment they'd formed with Seb, she wasn't sure whether to worry or not. It was hard to believe spending time with someone so attentive, so in tune with them, could be a bad thing. *But what about when he goes back to Australia?*

Penny dropped her arms. 'Seb said he'll show me again, next time we see him.'

'You know I can show you, too.'

Penny smiled. 'Okay. But Seb would be better. I'd rather dance with a boy.'

It was funny how things turned out different than planned, Maggie thought as she climbed into her car. One of the reasons she'd been wary of admitting her attraction to Seb had been the girls, yet he'd become part of their lives anyway, with no help from her. There were other reasons to be cautious though, considerable ones, like their difference in age, their diametrically opposite personalities, the fact he was only here temporarily, and his sisters were her closest friends.

Then there was the biggest reason of all to squash her little crush. It was likely he was only flirting with her because he could, and not because he intended doing anything about it.

After the lesson was over and the class had trooped out, Belinda turned to them both.

'So, I understand you want to think about a routine, but first you have the most difficult decision. Ballroom or Latin? Waltz or Samba? Foxtrot or Cha Cha? Quick step or Rumba?'

Seb nodded to her. 'It's Maggie's choice.'

'I'm most comfortable with the waltz.' It was the first dance she'd learned, and the one she'd forgotten the least.

Seb shook his head. 'I told you before, we're not doing what you think we should, what you're comfortable with. We're doing the one you *want* to dance.'

'That's not how I make decisions. It's a case of weighing up the pros and cons. Choosing the one we'll have the best chance of success with, considering neither of us will be able to devote that much time to practising it.' Why, when she knew she was being sensible, did it sound so stuffy?

Seb sighed, rubbing at the back of his neck. 'I'm not asking you where you want to invest your life savings, Mags. I'm asking what you want to *dance*. Which one gets your blood flowing, your heart pumping at the thought of performing it? Which do you feel passionate about?'

His face lit up as he spoke. Handsome, full of vibrancy, energy and confidence. In that moment she didn't want to play safe. She wanted to be bold, like he was. 'The rumba.'

'Ah, the king of the sexy dances. Romantic and

seductive.' Belinda's face softened. 'It's one of my favourites, too.'

As quickly as it had come, Maggie's bravery began to take a nose dive. 'Maybe that's not a good choice though. The waltz would be better. It's more... elegant.' And a damn sight less sensual. God, why had she picked the flipping rumba? The "dance of love". The dance she knew, from all her *Strictly* watching, required serious chemistry between the dancers.

Seb laughed in that easy way he had. 'Elegant definitely describes you, but it's not a word that's ever been used to describe me.' He ran a hand through his hair, and there was something about the way the action caused his bicep to flex, about the way it drew attention to the leather straps around his wrist, that was unconsciously sexy.

That's why she'd chosen the rumba. It wasn't her, it was Seb: sultry and sensual. *Maybe it's what you want to be, too. At least for a few weeks.*

'It's your choice though, Mags. We'll do whatever you decide.'

'The rumba,' she repeated, then drew in a breath and forced out a smile. 'Let's give it a try.'

'You'll need to put in a lot of practice to pull it off,' Belinda warned, but just as Maggie started to wobble again, she added, 'But you've got a real flair for dance, a natural rhythm that can't be taught. I'm sure you won't have a problem picking it up.'

Seb coughed. 'And me?'

'You, dear, will need to get those hips of yours moving.'

Belinda smiled. 'But judging from the comments from the rest of the dance class, you've got the flirting down to a fine art.'

Seb gave her a wide-eyed innocent look. Then flashed a smile that proved Belinda's point.

An exhausting hour later – she hadn't realised how many different moves there were, how many possible routines – Maggie walked with Seb towards her car.

'Tomorrow I think I'm going to ache in places I didn't realise existed.'

He laughed, his breath visible against the cold, dark December evening. 'Looks like we're going to be seeing a lot of each other.'

She glanced sideways at him. 'Please don't tell me you're one of those hugely competitive people who has to win everything they take part in? Because if you are, we should have chosen the waltz, like I said.'

He shrugged. 'I like to win, sure.' As he held the car door open for her, he caught her eye and grinned. 'But mostly, I like to have fun.'

'I hope that's what it will be,' she continued as she manoeuvred out of the car park and onto the road. 'Because I can't dedicate much time to this. I work long hours, and then there are the girls to consider. It's hard enough finding time for the lessons once a week.'

'I know that.' The way her skin pricked told her he was watching her. 'But I figured I could come to your house a couple of times a week when the girls are in bed.' He let out a bark of laughter. 'And that came across way seedier than it sounded in my head.'

She was grateful it was dark, so he couldn't see the flush she knew was on her face. 'Or you could come while they're still awake, and we could dance with them. I know Penny would like that. She asked me tonight if you'd show her the steps again.'

There was a long pause before he spoke. 'That could work, too.'

When she pulled up outside Sarah's house, the car fell quiet and Maggie wondered if she'd said something wrong. There wasn't usually this awkwardness between them.

'Will you be joining us at Alice's on Saturday for the semi-final?'

'Yeah, probably.' He sounded distracted. 'Can I ask a question?'

'You don't usually request permission for that.'

He gave her a small smile. 'It's kind of sensitive.'

'Now I'm worried.'

'Sorry, I'm really ballsing this up.' His eyes found hers. 'Did you suggest I come round when the girls are awake because you felt you needed them as a chaperone, or because you thought they might enjoy it?'

'The latter,' she replied honestly. 'I'm a grown woman. I don't need to rely on a seven- and nine-year-old to look after my virtue.'

His shoulders relaxed. 'Good, because while I'd love to dance with the girls, I think sometimes it would be good for us to practice with no distractions.'

She eyed him thoughtfully. 'What happened to the guy who wants to have fun?'

He laughed softly. 'He's still there, don't worry. It's just… I guess I don't want to make a fool of myself in front of the kids.' His gaze shifted to hers. 'I want to inspire them. I mean, if I can get up there and dance, there's no reason they can't do it, too.' His eyes glittered in the dark interior. 'I also have this crazy need to impress you.'

'Impress me?' Her heart jumped. 'Why?'

'You mean aside from the fact you're the most attractive woman I've ever met?'

'Wow, that's…' She trailed off, completely thrown off balance. 'Thank you.'

He smiled. 'No thanks needed. I'm just telling you how I see it. As I said before, that ex of yours must have a screw loose.'

She wanted to believe the flattery, but she'd seen Isabelle. Blonde, pretty-faced, younger-than-her Isabelle.

'How did the girls get on with him the other day?'

Relieved at the change of subject – she wasn't sure how to handle his compliments – she launched into a too detailed description of where Paul had taken them.

If Seb noticed she was rambling, he didn't comment on it. 'Is he going to be a more regular fixture now then?' At her wary glance, he held up his hands. 'Hey, you can tell me to mind my own business.'

'I can, can't I?' She was a private person who only shared with people she trusted, so it surprised her when she went on to answer him. 'Honestly, I don't know how things will work out. Paul and Isabelle want the girls to go to their wedding, and the catty part of me thinks it's because Isabelle thinks they'll make cute bridesmaids, which they definitely will, but maybe that's not fair. Maybe she genuinely wants to include them in their life after the wedding, too. Maybe that's what they both want.'

'But until you're convinced of that, you're allowed to be catty.'

She laughed. 'Yes, that's what I thought. And I'm damned if I'm going to let him wriggle his way back into our lives, just for him to go and let them down again.'

'Ouch, look at those claws.' He opened the door and climbed out, then ducked his head and flashed her a grin. 'I reckon you're more tiger than cat. See you Saturday.'

A tiger, she mused as she watched him stride up the path. She liked the idea of it. Certainly it was a lot better than the doormat she'd felt at the end of her marriage, knowing her husband had been off flirting with another woman instead of coming home to her.

Chapter Fourteen

Visits to his father – not much change there – and work at the youth centre took up most of Seb's week. Belinda came by the centre to give the kids their first dance lesson, with predictable results. A lot of 'I'm not interested in this shit' posturing from the boys, and a fair amount of giggling from the girls. Belinda wasn't someone you ignored though, and she'd at least made them try, even if the comments he'd overheard in the corridor afterwards, 'I can't believe he's getting us to learn this dumb stuff' (Hayley), and 'I'm not gonna come next week' (Rylan), weren't exactly encouraging.

Saturday was *Strictly* night, hosted by Alice, and Seb had been disconcerted to find both her and Sarah giving him pointed looks on several occasions.

'What was all that?' he demanded afterwards when he'd come across the pair of them in the kitchen after Maggie, Hannah and the girls had gone home.

'We were just wondering why you came,' Alison answered, giving him a sly look. 'All you did was watch Maggie.'

'And you'd know that how? Because you spent the entire time watching *me*? Give me a break. You're doing the old needle Seb trick, and it's not going to wash, because guess what, I'm no longer ten. I'm wise to your little games.'

Their observation worried him though, because they weren't far off the mark. Truth was, though he'd begun to find *Strictly* entertaining – hell, at times it was downright funny – watching other people dance didn't really do it for him. He wanted to be the one dancing. More specifically, he wanted to be dancing with the woman currently taking up far more of his head space than was healthy.

In a few hours he'd be doing exactly that. In a community hall that had seen better days, and in the company of a dozen others, most of them pensioners, but none of that dampened the anticipatory fizz.

Of course it did assume the fifteen-year-old Fiesta he'd just bought would get them there.

Standing on his parents' drive, his mum cast a dubious eye over the silver dream machine. 'Is that the best you could find?'

'Way to crush a guy's manhood, Mum.' He ran a hand over the bonnet, trying to ignore the scratches, the small bubble of rust. 'It's the best I could find for under a grand, yes.'

His father grunted. 'Why the sudden urgency to buy a car? You'd be better off saving your money.'

'On a purely financial level, I agree with you. But that's not the only consideration here.'

'I thought you were okay getting the bus to that place you're working.' He shuffled his feet, and Seb wondered if he was already getting tired of standing. 'They hardly pay you enough to splash out on a car.'

'The pay goes up when I'm qualified.' No point telling his father it would take at least a year of study and cost over five grand if he wanted to do the course full-time. And yes, he'd looked into it.

'What's the other consideration?' His mum, scarily astute, started to smile. 'It's a woman, isn't it?'

God, was that really a blush he could feel creep up his neck? 'Buses don't always go where and when you want them to,' he protested. 'Cars are more flexible.'

'They're also more suitable for picking up a woman and taking her out,' she remarked dryly, before giving his arm a quick squeeze. 'I hope you'll tell us about her sometime.'

'There's nothing to tell, Mum.' Because he couldn't lie to her, he added, 'At least not yet.'

She chuckled. 'I knew there was someone. I hope she appreciates the effort you've gone to for her, buying this car.'

'Hey, I've not bought it for her.' Though he had, kind of, sort of, hadn't he? Because he couldn't ask her out and then get her to drive. But he wasn't going to ask her out. Was he?

'Of course you haven't.' She gave him that smile, the one

mums have that lets you know they can see right through you.

'How's the preparation for this competition of yours going?' his dad asked.

The question surprised Seb. 'How do you know about that?'

'I heard you telling your mother yesterday. It's my heart that's buggered, not my hearing.'

'Your heart isn't buggered. It's taken a hit and is recovering.'

'Too bloody slowly.' As if to prove it, he paused a moment, taking a laboured breath. 'So, are you advertising this event properly? Have you secured a sponsor?'

That was more like it. For a moment there, Seb thought he'd been genuinely interested in the dance competition but no. It was another opportunity to have a dig. 'I know what I'm doing, Dad.'

'Promoted a lot of events living on that pontoon of yours, did you?' When Seb rolled his eyes, his father humphed. 'Just as I thought. Now let me tell you how I used to go about promoting an event.'

When Seb finally managed to extricate himself, he cast a glance at them in his rear-view mirror, feeling an ache in his chest as he watched his dad lean on his mum as they made their way back up the path and into the house. For all his strut, his dad was failing. Always the man of the house, the 'strong' one, it was hard to see him like this. According to Alice, his heart muscle had been damaged by the attack, which explained why he was so frequently tired, and breathless just from walking down the path. The doctors were managing it with medication but so far hadn't found the right combination to really make a difference.

His dad was taking it hard, which meant he was making it hard for everyone else, too.

Shaking off the gloomy thoughts, Seb glanced at the clock on the dashboard. He had an hour to get back to Sarah's and give the car a clean – from the look of the inside it had recently been taken for a joy ride by a pack of golden retrievers – before heading over to Maggie's to pick her up.

He was losing his battle with Henry Hoover – who put a smiling face on a vacuum cleaner? It was just plain creepy – when Seb heard Sarah's car pull up behind his.

Bloody great. All those nights she worked late, and his sister chose today to get home on time.

'Well, well, well. My brother with a hoover in his hands. Wonders will never cease.'

'Funny. I've been using it on your place for the last two months.'

She tilted her head up to meet his eyes. 'You've really been back two months?'

'Give or take, yes.'

He held his breath, a faint hope that she'd leave the conversation there and not notice the metal object he was standing next to. 'You've bought a *car*?'

Sighing, he put the ruddy hoover down. 'Why is this

such a surprise? I work odd shifts, including evenings and weekends. I can't rely on the bus to always get me there.'

'Okay, I can go with that.' She nodded to the hoover. 'But cleaning it? That's what I'm finding suspicious. Especially considering the timing. Wednesday, 'Seb and Maggie go dancing' evening.'

Was there any way he could have a private life, living back here? God, to be thousands of miles away, where he'd dated women with nobody in his family knowing about it. 'Fine, I'm cleaning it because I'm going to pick Maggie up. It's about time I did, considering all the lifts she's given me.'

'In her three-series, two-year-old BMW.'

Yeah, he'd not needed the reminder. Not just a better car, and a newer car, but one that was always so frigging immaculate. How did she manage that with two kids? 'A lift is a lift.'

'Umm.' Sarah tapped a finger to her lips and his heart sank. It was her thinking pose. 'Well, I'm sure she'll appreciate the effort you've gone to, just to take her to a dance lesson. How are they going, by the way? Is learning the foxtrot everything you hoped it would be? I mean, I assume that's why you're carrying on with the lessons. And not just to follow Maggie around like a lovesick puppy.'

'Piss off.' Not eloquent, not nice, but he was getting a bit sick of all this.

Sarah frowned, and where he'd expected irritation, he saw only concern. 'You did say you weren't going to do anything stupid.'

'Thanks for the reminder.' He paused, looking back at

her. 'Purely out of theoretical interest, what would be stupid, in your book?'

She took a step towards him and cupped his face in her hands. 'Anything that resulted in one, or both, of you getting hurt,' she said quietly.

The worry in her eyes caught at his throat. They bickered, they annoyed each other, they needled, but when push came to shove, his sisters had always looked out for him. Swallowing down the emotion, he took hold of her hands. 'Roger that. And for the record, I have no intention of hurting her.'

'I know.' She smiled sadly. 'But it isn't always in your control. I worry that you're only here temporarily, so starting anything seems to be asking for trouble.'

'Am I only here temporarily?' His question surprised them both. Was he seriously considering not going back to Oz?

'Are you thinking of *staying*?' Sarah's expression held a mixture of both shock and hope.

'No. I don't know.' Where had this uncertainty come from? 'I'm not going anywhere while Dad's like he is.'

Sarah surprised him then by putting her arms around him and hugging him tight.

'What was that for?'

'To let you know how much I appreciate you coming back. You've been such a help to Mum, to all of us. I should have said something before now.' When she drew back, there were tears in her eyes. 'I feel so guilty, spending all this time at work when I know they're struggling.'

'Hey, you were there for them while I was on the other side of the globe. Besides, you see them when you can.' In a bid to dial down the emotion, he added, 'And I'm a bloody good substitute.'

Laughter burst out of her and, after giving him the sisterly thump on the arm he expected, and perhaps deserved, she went inside. Leaving him to his dog hair extraction.

————

Maggie had just started her car when a silver Fiesta screeched round the corner and parked up outside her house. She hoped it wasn't someone to see her. She had a dance class to get to. With a man who'd told her she was attractive – no, what was it, *the most attractive woman I've ever met*. The butterflies re-awakened in her belly. His words were such a massive, much-needed ego boost, but a level head was needed. The compliment had to be taken the way it had been intended, in the spirit of friendship.

Yet for all her talk, as she watched the tall blonde man climb out of the car and walk up the drive towards her, the butterflies began to flap in earnest. Putting the car back into park, she opened the door. 'What are you doing here?'

Seb placed one hand on the roof, one on the top of the door, and grinned. 'I'm picking you up.'

'But… why?'

'Because I figured it was about time I drove you. And because I thought we could go for a drink afterwards.'

More flapping in her stomach. 'Right.' *Come on, you can do better than that. Find more words with more syllables.* 'Hannah will be expecting me back after the class.'

'No problem.' He clasped her hand and helped her out of the car. 'You can phone her on the way.'

Thrown off balance, Maggie walked with him to the Fiesta and sank into the passenger seat. Instead of calling Hannah though, she stared down at her phone. She didn't do this: rush about, changing things round at the last minute. She planned in advance, that way everyone knew where they were.

'Everything okay?' he asked as he pulled off into the road.

It's just a drink. You dance together, why wouldn't you socialise a little? Stop being so anal. Hannah won't mind. And you have a late start tomorrow. 'Yes, fine.'

Before she could talk herself out of it, Maggie tapped out a text to Hannah.

Forgot to say, dance class is going for a drink after. Sort of Christmas-get-to-know-each-other session. Are you okay to stay a bit later? M x

She wasn't sure what stopped her from telling her friend the truth. Embarrassment that she'd jump to the wrong conclusion and assume she and Seb were becoming more than friends? Yet why should she be embarrassed if they were? If Hannah had been asked to go out for a drink with a sexy twenty-seven-year-old man, she'd be gleefully telling them all about it in a group chat.

But Hannah was young, bubbly, and outgoing. Maggie was none of those things.

Her phone dinged with a reply.

No problem, be as long as you like. Hope you avoid the guys with bad breath and BO :)

Maggie smiled, pushed the phone back into her bag and told herself to stop overthinking everything. 'Hannah's fine staying later.'

He flashed her a smile. 'Good.'

Maggie picked at a stray hair on the dashboard. It was blonde. The owner, or Seb's last passenger? 'I didn't think you had a car.'

'I bought her a few days ago.' There was a brief hesitation before he added. 'The bus was doing my head in.'

She could understand that, but buying a car when he was only in the country temporarily seemed an odd decision. 'Was the owner blonde?'

'What?' She held out the hair. 'Crap, I thought I'd got rid of them all. Owner was bald, but his canine friend was a golden retriever.'

'Ah.' She didn't want to think about the wave of relief she felt at the explanation. 'Well, I appreciate the lift tonight, though a few seconds later and you'd have missed me.'

He laughed, a lazy rumble that made her hormones dance. 'Yeah, we need to do something about this punctuality of yours or it's going to become a bone of contention between us.'

And suddenly her belly was fluttering again. 'I must have missed the part where we became an *us*.'

He cast her an amused look. 'You're my dance partner, Mags. From now until the competition we'll be seeing an awful lot of each other. And at very close quarters. I reckon that justifies an us.'

She willed the butterflies to keep quiet, but they ignored her.

By the last dance of the evening, it wasn't just Maggie's belly that was reacting to Seb. It was all of her body parts. She couldn't ever remember being so conscious of her partner before.

'Mags?' Seb's bright blue eyes looked questioningly down on her. 'You've gone all noodle arms on me.'

'Damn, sorry.' Maggie stiffened her elbows and tried to lose herself to the music, but there was no denying the flush of heat she felt every time the hard lines of his thigh pressed against hers. What would he feel like without the barrier of their clothes? That muscular thigh between her legs, soft blonde hairs brushing the sensitive skin of her inner thighs…

She lost her footing and stumbled.

'Whoa.' Immediately his arms tightened around her, and

she was crushed against him; breasts against the muscles of his chest, hips snug against hips.

'Oh God, sorry. Again.' Embarrassed, she tried to pull away, but his grip wouldn't allow her.

'No apology needed.' He eased them back into the frame position, his eyes alive with both amusement and something darker, hotter. 'I'm a huge fan of you falling into my arms, Mags.' Angling his body, he whispered into her ear. 'You can do it anytime.'

She laughed, flustered, turned on, and... yes, happy. Somehow he managed to do that, turn embarrassment into fun, while still maintaining an edge of sexual tension that left her hormones on full alert.

Thankfully for her equilibrium, Belinda chose that moment to end the class. Within seconds, Seb had placed his hand on the small of her back and was hurrying them out of the door.

'Wow, are you really that thirsty?' she asked as she struggled to keep up with his long strides.

He gave her a baffled look. 'What?'

'All this sudden urgency to get to the pub?'

'Ah.' He grasped her hand as they crossed the road, the gesture so natural she hardly noticed. Until she did. Then, just like when they danced, the feel of his warm, slightly calloused palm was all she could think about. 'I figured if we escaped early, they wouldn't follow us.'

'You have something against having a drink with our class?' She smiled as she said it, because she wasn't in the mood to be sociable either.

'I do if it means I have to share you.'

Her stomach did that squirmy thing again as he ushered her into the King George, which was exactly like pubs were supposed to be. Warm, inviting. Dark wood, open fire, a Christmas tree decorated in red and gold baubles. 'What would you like? And bear in mind as I'm driving, you need to drink for both of us.'

A few minutes later, Maggie found herself in a quiet booth, drinking a deliciously smooth merlot, on a school night. It felt wonderfully... rebellious. And yes, she was aware how sad that sounded, but she hadn't been to a pub during the week in years.

She'd also never been to one with a seriously good-looking man with overly long, sun-bleached hair, an easy, sexy smile, eyes the colour of the ocean. Oh, and ten years her junior. Go her.

'That's a smile I've not seen before.' Seb cocked his head to one side, appearing to study her. 'It's kind of secretive. Like you're thinking of something a bit naughty.'

'Me?' She settled back against the booth. 'This, having a drink in a pub, is about as naughty as I get.'

'I don't believe that.' Maggie watched as he lifted the Pepsi glass to his lips. Why was she starting to find everything, even the way his throat moved when he swallowed, utterly fascinating? 'Tell me what ten-year-old Maggie was like.'

She tried not to think about the fact that he hadn't been born then. 'Honestly, she was a bit of a swot. Even at that age I conformed to the rules, did as I was told. It was more than that at school though. I *wanted* to learn, especially about science.'

'Are your parents doctors, like you?'

'No. Dad was a finance director and Mum a lawyer.'

'A family of high flyers, huh?' For a fraction of a second, his smile seemed to slip. 'Are you close to them?'

'No.' Grateful he'd insisted on the wine, she gulped down a mouthful. 'They weren't what you'd call natural parents. I've got a younger sister, Emily, and I think we were more a tick box exercise than anything else. High earning career, check. Large house, check. Two children, check.'

He winced. 'Sounds pretty cold.'

'It does in hindsight, but as a child I didn't know anything else. It's only now I'm a mum I realise there was something missing.' *Love. A small slice of their precious time. Acknowledgement that while Emily was the prettiest, the funniest, Maggie deserved the occasional compliment. A tiny bit of their interest.* 'Being the eldest, I took care of Emily a lot.' *Because the childminder was lazy and their parents were always distracted.* Maggie raised her eyes to Seb's. 'That probably explains some of my more annoying traits.'

Sandy eyebrows scooted upwards. 'Annoying by whose definition?'

Damn, she hadn't meant to go down such a downbeat path. Then again, Paul would say it was all part of her personality, too. 'I just meant that I grew up having to be the sensible, responsible one. The annoying older sister who made sure Emily did her homework, brushed her teeth, went to bed on time. I guess it made me organised.' Attributes that had helped her become a GP, and then to juggle that profession with being a mum. So why did she sometimes feel boring? *Because next to Emily, you were.* Unwilling to speak about it any further, she threw the question back. 'What was ten-year-old Sebastian Armstrong like?'

He laughed. 'You can safely say I was the exact opposite. I wasn't planned, and by the time Sarah and Alice had gone off to uni, I think it's fair to say Mum and Dad had done with parenting and took a step back. It meant nobody was bothered when I didn't do my homework or got in detention for skipping lessons.' He gave her a dry smile. 'Being neither responsible or sensible, I made the most of it, so I guess you could say ten-year-old Seb was a teacher's nightmare.' A cloud passed over his face. 'By the time Mum and Dad cottoned on to the fact I was failing, it was too late. I scrambled enough grades to get on a degree course, but I missed out on the courses and universities they'd blithely assumed I'd go to.'

'What about what you wanted?'

'That's the thing. I didn't know what I wanted. Still don't, really.' His eyes dropped to his glass before lifting back to hers. 'Did you always want to be a doctor?'

'Will it sound obnoxious if I say yes?'

'Not unless you add that Imperial was your first choice and you got there with a grade to spare.'

She mimed zipping her mouth closed and he laughed. 'Wait, how did you know I went to Imperial?... of course,

Alice and Sarah went there.' For a while she'd forgotten the connection. She'd been talking to a hot guy in a pub. Not the brother of her best friends.

'Beautiful, bossy and smart.' His eyes found hers and he gave her a small, sexy smile. 'You do realise you push all my buttons, don't you?'

Oh God. Her heart lurched, and her brain scrambled for a reply. 'I don't know what to say to that.'

As luck would have it – or bad luck would have it, she wasn't sure which – she didn't have to say anything because Seb's expression had turned from flirty to... appalled? As he muttered 'For fuck's sake' under his breath, Maggie heard a familiar voice behind her.

'Well, look here, Pauline. It's the lovebirds.' She turned just in time to see Shirley pat her hair and smile at Seb. 'We're not cramping your style if we join you, are we dear?'

Not giving him a chance to reply, Shirley and Pauline squeezed their generous frames onto the padded benches, one on either side.

Chapter Fifteen

For fuck's sake.

Seb said the words again, though this time only in his head. He'd just worked up to asking Maggie out on a real date, not this poor excuse for one, cobbled together at the last minute with his sister's words of warning jamming through his head. Now he found himself thwarted – effectively cock-blocked – by a couple of OAPs.

When he'd gone to pick her up, Seb had fully intended to heed Sarah's words. That was before he'd seen Maggie sitting all cool and collected in her snazzy car, on the drive of her classy home, and he'd decided to screw being sensible. It wasn't in his nature.

If she was willing – a big if – why couldn't they have some fun? She was far too savvy to fall for him, but he liked to bet he could make her laugh, give her a taste of the spontaneity she seemed to have missed out on. Maybe even give her back some of that confidence her ex had snatched from her.

Now he had the Ugly Sisters to contend with. And yeah, that wasn't fair, Pauline and Shirley weren't ugly and they weren't nasty, but by God, he didn't want them here. He felt out of his depth as it was. He didn't needed a pair of witnesses to his seduction attempt. Which reminded him, note to self: when trying to impress a smart woman, don't bring up your ropey education and lack of career goals.

Shirley – of course it was her – broke the awkward silence. 'So, this is where you two hide after class, eh?'

He wanted to slide down the bench, under the table and right out of the pub. Holding tight to Maggie's hand.

'No.' Maggie cleared her throat. 'That is, it's the first time we've come here.'

'And we're hardly hiding,' he felt compelled to point out. 'If we were, you wouldn't have been able to find us.' Next time – please God there would be a next time – he'd make sure of it.

Shirley chuckled. 'Well, we don't blame Maggie for sneaking off with you. We'd do the same, given half a chance, wouldn't we, Pauline?'

'Given *any* chance.' Pauline winked at him before taking a big swig from the glass she was holding. A brown liquid, it could have been sherry. Or brandy, rum, tequila, whisky. One thing it clearly wasn't was alcohol-free. 'Are there any more versions of you?'

He nearly choked on his drink. 'Sorry?'

'Do you have brothers? Friends?' She let out a hearty laugh. 'Me and Shirley, we like a bit of male company.'

Good God, was this really happening? He glanced across at Maggie and was surprised to find her eyes brimming with laughter. The realisation she was amused by the ambush and not annoyed, brought his own frustration down a notch. Maybe she was right. If he couldn't beat these two young-at-heart crumblies, he'd have to join them. 'Sorry, ladies, no brothers, only a pair of pain-in-the-arse sisters. As for friends, most of them are back home, in Australia.' The words didn't sound as natural on his tongue as they had before. Was Australia still home? Or was he settling back here again, many miles from the sea, in a country even colder and damper than he remembered?

'Ooh, Australia.' Shirley picked up the conversation. 'I told you, Pauline, didn't I? Told you this man was exotic.'

His expression must have mirrored the *holy fuck* he was thinking, because Maggie started to giggle. A real, honest to God snorter of a giggle that, once she'd started, she couldn't seem to stop. 'Sorry,' she squeezed out, wiping her eyes. 'It's just, the word exotic.' It set her off again. 'I started to imagine Seb in a G-string, with peacock feathers in his hair, doing some shady dance routine on the beach.'

He didn't mind having the piss taken out of him. Especially if it meant seeing a glimpse of the real, uninhibited Maggie. The one not dragged down by responsibility, or dimmed by divorce. 'I can totally bring that image to life for you.' Shifting to his feet, he started to roll his hips suggestively, giving Maggie a big wink. 'Don't judge too harshly. If the table wasn't in the way, you'd be spontaneously combusting by now.'

'Oh heavens, I think I already am.' As Maggie pealed into further giggles, Shirley started to fan herself. 'You really shouldn't do that in front of women of a certain age. You'll give us palpitations.'

'Not to worry.' Parking his backside back on the bench, he threw a wink in Shirley's direction. 'Maggie's a doctor.'

'Ooh, are you, dear?' Pauline gave Maggie a thorough inspection. 'You don't look old enough.'

That started Maggie laughing again. 'I'm thirty-seven.'

Shirley tutted. 'That's no age at all, love. Wait till you turn the numbers the other way round. Then you'll have something to complain about.' She leaned towards Seb and whispered in a voice louder than her normal speaking voice. 'Have you asked her yet?'

'Asked me?'

Maggie looked over at him, wide-eyed, and Seb had to stifle a groan. Why had he decided to confide in a chatterbox? Before he could get a word in though, the chatterbox was off again, a wicked twinkle in her eye.

'Yes, dear. This exotic young man and I had quite an illuminating conversation when we smooched together last week.'

'*Smooched*? We were attempting the waltz.' Seb swallowed down his horror at the idea of him and Shirley in a smouldering embrace, and gave her his best flirty smile. 'Trust me, if we smooched together, you'd know about it.'

While Shirley guffawed with laughter, Maggie looked at

him in amusement. Seb only hoped she was still looking at him like that by the time Shirley had finished her tale…

'Careful, I might hold you to that, and we both know I'm not the woman you want to smooch with.' As Seb held his breath, Shirley glanced over at Maggie. 'This young man's smitten with you, dear. He wants to ask you out.' Then, as if she hadn't just detonated a ruddy great bomb into the conversation, she blithely added. 'I told him, a lovely thing like you is going to be snapped up by someone else if he doesn't pull his finger out.' She gave Seb's ribs a sharp dig. 'Didn't I say that?'

'You did,' he said soberly, not daring to look at Maggie. 'But then you say a lot of things, Shirley. It's not always easy to pick out the important stuff.'

Shirley let out one of those big, booming chuckles. 'You're a cheeky thing. I like that in a man.' She shuffled in her seat, seeming to adjust her ample chest. 'If I didn't like our Maggie so much, I'd give her a run for her money.'

'Noted.' It was his turn with the exaggerated whisper. 'And if I didn't like our Maggie so much, I'd chase after you.'

While Shirley cackled, calling over to Pauline to check she'd heard what he said, Seb screwed up his courage and glanced at Maggie. He wasn't sure whether to be worried or relieved when he saw her bite into her lip, clearly desperately trying not to laugh again. Was she amused at the banter, or the thought of him wanting to ask her out?

'Now then.' Shirley drained the bottom of her glass. 'Why don't you go and get us ladies another drink, and then tell me and Pauline about this dance competition you're organising. We might want to enter.'

———

As Maggie walked back to Seb's car – he was holding her hand again, and she liked it – she tried to remember how many glasses of wine she'd had.

One before Shirley and Pauline had arrived. Two with them? Maybe three?

She stopped abruptly, causing him to bump into her. 'Whoa, what's wrong?'

'Please tell me I didn't have four glasses of wine tonight.'

Seb screwed his face up, and wow, yes, he still looked cute. 'I think, maybe, yes?'

'Oh boy, I'm really going to feel that tomorrow morning.'

He opened the passenger door for her and smiled. 'You know the drill, doc. A pint of water before you go to bed, and a couple of paracetamol.'

She did know the drill, just as she also knew she shouldn't be finding everything about him so acutely sexy right now. Had he always smelt so divine? And was he always this warm, his eyes such deep pools of aquamarine?

Or was it the drink? Damn it, it had been a long time since she'd been so tipsy.

'Three is my limit,' she told him as he slipped into the driver's seat.

He gave her an amused glance. 'When did you set yourself that?'

'My wedding day.' Her brain might be sleepy, and finding Seb worryingly attractive, but she could still remember the moment all too clearly. 'It was after the meal and the speeches, when everyone starts to chill. We had this really cool band and Paul didn't want to dance, no change there, so I started to go round the room asking some of the men. Paul took me aside and told me not to drink any more, I'd clearly had enough.'

Seb was silent for a moment as he manoeuvred the car out of the car park. 'I hope you told him where to go.'

'No.' Her head felt heavy and she leant back against the seat. She'd been mortified that she'd embarrassed him. 'He was looking out for me.'

Seb grunted. 'You can remember it, Mags. Even after your wild four glasses of wine tonight, you can recall that happening on your wedding day, so you were hardly three sheets to the wind.' He gave her a sidelong glance, his expression pensive. 'Presumably these guys were your friends or they wouldn't have been at your wedding. What was wrong with asking them to dance? You were having fun.'

She wished her head was clearer, so she could point out the obvious flaw in his argument. And there had to be one, because why else had she decided to limit herself to three glasses from then on?

She must have nodded off, because the next thing she knew, the car had come to a stop, her door was open and

Seb was on his haunches, looking up at her. 'Time to wake up, sleepy head. You're home.'

Blinking her eyes open, Maggie stared at his tanned, ridiculously attractive, face. 'When are you going to... what did Shirley say?' She tried to drag her slumbering mind back to the conversation in the pub. 'Pull your finger out and ask me out?'

He laughed softly, reaching across her to undo her seat belt. 'Do you want me to?'

Crinkles formed around his eyes, and his mouth was tantalisingly close to hers. *I want you to kiss me.* Every cell in her body cried out for that, but was it just the drink? The wine had loosened her tongue, no doubt. Made her feel mellow and happy and yes, sexy. When she woke up tomorrow though, would she die of embarrassment when she remembered this conversation? 'Maybe ask me when I've not had four glasses of wine.'

He stilled, his expression turning more intense, his eyes seeming to reach inside her. 'I'll do that.'

'Good.' Or was it? She wasn't sure what she'd just invited. Only that when she thought of him asking her properly, of being the recipient of that intense blue gaze when she wasn't the worse for alcohol, her stomach executed a neat series of flips.

'Are you okay to walk?' He took hold of her arm, helping her out of the car, and when she tripped, the cold air a shock to her system, her legs not as steady as she'd thought, he smiled. 'I'll take that as a not sure. Here.'

Effortlessly, he lifted her into his arms. 'Let me sweep you off your feet.'

Arms around his neck, she laughed. 'How many times have you used that line?'

He shook his head, sliding her carefully back to her feet as they reached the front door. 'Never. Now where's your key?'

She opened her bag, finding them immediately because she always clipped them on a chain. It meant she knew where they were. Even after four glasses of wine. 'Thank you, for tonight I mean,' she said as she handed them over. 'I had a really good time.'

'Yeah?'

'Yes.' She stared into his twinkling blue eyes. 'Pauline and Shirley were hilarious.' As he pulled a wounded expression, she laughed for the umpteenth time that night. 'And you were quite funny, too.'

Seb deftly unlocked the door, the dancing bear key ring – a present from her daughters last Christmas – looking ridiculous, yet also weirdly adorable, in his large, manly hands. Instead of opening it though, he looked down at her, his gaze seeming to fall on every inch of her face.

'What is it?'

His eyes dropped to her mouth. 'I want to kiss you.'

Yes, please. The words stuck in her throat. Apparently she wasn't so tipsy she could throw away all her careful, cautious habits. 'What's stopping you?'

He let out a low laugh, rubbing at the stubble on his jaw. 'My dad.' He must have seen her silent question, because he continued. 'He always told me to treat women right, to respect them. I don't think he'd be too impressed if I took advantage of your currently squiffy state.'

'How drunk is squiffy? Because I'm not that inebriated.' Or was she? Would she really be flirting with him like this if she wasn't? 'I'm mellow,' she decided.

She felt the warmth of his breath against her ear as he whispered, 'Mellow enough to let me kiss you?'

A shiver ran through her, and she knew it had nothing to do with the cold December evening because inside she felt like a furnace. 'Yes.'

His eyes searched hers, as if checking she really was sure. Then he cupped her face in those big, warm hands. Tingles shot through her as he pressed his mouth to hers, and her bones seemed to melt as his tongue eased her lips open, deepening the kiss. And wow, the heat, the taste – Pepsi, with a hint of mint – the feel of him surrounding her. She shifted closer, seeking more contact, everything she thought she knew about kissing flying out of the window. This felt more, so much more than she could remember. More pleasure, more *connection*.

With a groan he dropped his hands to her hips, drawing her tightly against him. He was hard, deliciously, impressively hard against her stomach. Oh God, had kissing always felt this hot? Desperate for more, more friction, more heat, she shifted closer. She wanted to crawl up him, press herself against every male inch of him. Wanted his hands under her blouse, those calloused palms rubbing against her breasts.

He let out another groan, hoarser than the last, but this time he stepped back, his breathing ragged, his chest heaving in tandem with hers.

'Christ.' He ran a hand across his face. 'I knew there'd be sparks. I didn't reckon on the exploding fireworks.'

She laughed, feeling giddy. 'I thought I heard a fizz.'

'And a crack. And a bloody great bang.' His face sobered, the heat still in his eyes. 'I'm warning you, Mags, now I've had a taste, I want more.'

Her heart raced as he bent towards her again, his mouth hovering close to hers. Just one more kiss, she willed him. A little longer, a little deeper. Maybe he read her thoughts, because his breath hitched, and those pleasure-giving lips inched towards hers again.

'Oh, sorry.' Seb's head jerked back as Hannah came into view. 'I heard the key in the door, but then you didn't come in, so I was worried something was wrong.'

Hannah glanced from Seb, to Maggie, and Maggie wondered what she saw. Did she look like she'd been thoroughly kissed? And that she was silently begging Seb to kiss her again? Damn it, this was why she shouldn't drink. It loosened her control. 'Nothing.' She had to cough to clear the husk from her voice. 'Nothing is wrong. Seb was just seeing me to the door because I'm a little,' she nodded at Seb, 'what did you call it?'

He let out a deep sigh. 'Squiffy.'

'Yes, that's it. I'm a bit squiffy.'

'Okay.' Hannah looked like she wasn't sure what to say. 'Sounds like the class bonding session went well then.'

Seb's eyebrows rose and Maggie experienced a mild panic. 'You could say that,' she said hurriedly before he could blurt out the obvious 'What class bonding session?' 'I mean Seb was driving, so he probably didn't enjoy it that much, but I... well, it was fun.' The mellow feeling from the alcohol, the heat from the kiss, it was all fast disappearing. Now she felt confused, cold and desperate to escape the tension Hannah's presence had created. Turning to Seb, she gave him a brief, awkward hug. 'Thanks for seeing me home.'

'Of course.' But gone were the twinkly eyes and the flirty smile. 'Night, you two.'

With a curt nod he strode off down the drive, leaving Maggie with the distinct impression she'd disappointed him. No, more than that, she'd hurt him.

'So, are the pair of you, you know? An item?' Hannah asked as Maggie carefully – she had to concentrate, her brain wasn't functioning as it should – shrugged out of her coat and hung it up.

'No, God no.' That sounded wrong. Like she was horrified by the prospect, when really it was the other way round. She was scared of what Hannah would think, how horrified she might be to find Maggie had kissed the man she knew Hannah still had a crush on. A man for whom Hannah was surely far more of a match.

'Well, I think that's what he wants, because from where I was standing it looked like he was about to kiss you.'

'I'm sure you're imagining that.' She didn't want to lie to her friend, but nor did she want to talk about this. Not while she didn't have a handle on it herself. And not while her tongue might run away with her and say things Maggie wanted to keep private.

Like she wished he'd kissed her again. A real tangling of tongues, with wandering hands and skin on skin.

And she very much feared she'd still wish that had happened tomorrow morning.

Chapter Sixteen

He'd been busy, working long shifts and trying to squeeze in visits to his parents. That's why he'd got to ten o'clock on Friday evening and still hadn't phoned Maggie. It wasn't because he was a coward.

Seb parked the Fiesta up outside Sarah's house and shivered as he jumped out into the dark December evening. Bloody climate.

He couldn't blame the weather for the cold feeling he had on the inside though, the knotted stomach, the slight queasiness. That was all on him. Yesterday morning had been different. Then he'd woken up drowning in the same sensation he'd fallen asleep to. The heat of Maggie's lips on his, the soft feel of her body as it had writhed – yes, there had definitely been some writhing – against him as they'd kissed on her doorstep.

But then he'd had a text message from Sarah.

Just spoken to Maggie and she says her head feels like it's been taken over by aliens. What did you do to her last night? S x

Instantly the joy he'd woken with had flooded out of him, leaving him with a bucket-load of angst. She'd told him she'd had too much to drink, he *knew* she had – she'd never have flirted with him sober – yet he'd gone and kissed her anyway. He couldn't regret it – life was for living, for doing what made you happy, and kissing her had made him ecstatic. But his dad's words had floated back into his head, and he'd been left wondering if this was another example of him failing to live up to the man's high standards. And never mind his dad, what was Maggie going to think of him now? Was she dreading seeing him again? Embarrassed at what they'd done?

Those were the worries that had dragged through his mind yesterday, and had only magnified since. Usually he'd talk things like this through with his sisters – they'd always been his sounding board for advice on the female mind. Yet how could he do that, when they weren't supposed to know? At least he assumed that's how Maggie wanted it, as she'd clearly lied to Hannah about their drinks last night.

And yes, maybe now he was getting to the real route of this gut-churning unease. Maggie had clearly been too embarrassed to tell her friends she was going for a drink with him. There was no other explanation for why Hannah had called it a class bonding session, and for why his sisters hadn't bombarded him with questions over it.

'Is that you?' Sarah's voice called out from the kitchen as he opened the door.

'No. It's Kermit the Frog.'

'Excellent. I'm sure he'll be a better house guest than the morose guy I've got staying with me at the moment.'

Seb grimaced as he threw his jacket onto the bannister. He really had to get better at hiding his feelings. 'I'm not morose,' he told her as he wandered into the kitchen.

'No? Then why haven't I seen you smile these last two days?' Her eyes narrowed. 'Does it have anything to do with Wednesday night?'

He could feel heat creep up his neck. 'There's nothing wrong, other than working too much.' Turning away from her he went to open the fridge, dragging out a bottle of juice he didn't want to drink, which gave him an excuse to look somewhere other than at her. 'Thanks to this blasted competition, I've had two long shifts at the centre, and I've another tomorrow.'

'Umm. So you're definitely not feeling guilty about Maggie.'

Involuntarily his head snapped up. 'What do you mean?'

'I mean letting her drink too much.'

Shit, of course that was what she'd meant. Seb rubbed the back of his neck, trying to release some of the tension, but knowing Sarah's eyes were watching him like a hawk wasn't helping.

'Is there anything else you're feeling guilty about?'

He took a few deep breaths and slopped the orange juice

into a glass. 'I'm not feeling guilty about anything. Maggie's a grown woman. Nobody forced her to drink.' He finally managed to look Sarah in the eye. 'Maybe she needed to drop her guard for once and just let go and enjoy herself.'

Sarah's expression softened. 'Maybe you're right. And I guess if anyone is going to teach her how to relax and have fun it's the King of Chill himself.'

'She doesn't need teaching. Just the chance to turn her brain off now and then.' He caught Sarah's sharp glance, and wished he'd shut his bloody mouth, because now he could see the cogs in her brain whirling.

'Maybe you're right.' Because she was his sister, he knew not to relax when she agreed with him, unlike the poor suckers she probably did business with. 'You seem to know her pretty well.'

It was a trap, but he didn't know how to get out of it. 'Not really.' Sarah stared at him, making it clear that wasn't a sufficient answer. Taking a gulp of the juice he didn't want, he gave a non-committal shrug of the shoulders. 'When we dance, we talk. And she's been giving me a lift home.'

'Until you unexpectedly bought yourself a car.'

Okay, that was it. He didn't have sufficient interrogation training for this sort of conversation. 'It's been great chatting, but I need to get to bed. Some of us have to work tomorrow.'

'You mean you won't be watching the *Strictly* final, after all these hours you've put into it?' Sarah cocked an eyebrow at him.

He kept his face carefully schooled. 'We're not all lucky enough to get weekends off. Sweet dreams, sis.'

He darted off before she could ask anything further. Like had he deliberately volunteered for the Saturday evening shift, because he didn't know how to handle seeing Maggie again? Of course Sarah's line of questioning would have been more devious, but knowing his sister she'd have got there in the end.

And the answer, which he was keeping locked in a vault in his mind, was yes, he had. It wasn't that he didn't want to see Maggie – he desperately did – but not with the eyes of his sisters watching his every move.

The next time he saw Maggie, he needed it to be just the two of them. Though whether *she'd* want that, was another matter.

It wasn't just Strictly Saturday. It was Strictly *Final* Saturday. Yet even as Maggie dashed about the house with a vacuum cleaner, a duster and a bottle of bleach (not all at the same time), even as she straightened the wonky-looking Christmas tree that Tabby and Penny had lovingly decorated, she couldn't help but realise she felt a little... flat.

She couldn't blame the hangover. Thursday had been long and hellish, but by Friday morning she'd been back to being able to move her head without needing pain killers.

She couldn't blame the conversation with Paul this

morning, either. He'd been perfectly civil when he'd phoned to arrange to pick the girls up and take them out for lunch tomorrow.

There was only one other explanation for how she felt, and it didn't sit easily with her. It was day three since she'd shared a kiss with Seb – no, not just a kiss, a hot, mind-spinning, all-consuming few minutes of utter pleasure. Despite that though, he'd not contacted her. Or was he expecting her to phone him? And she didn't mind that, she really didn't, there was no reason she shouldn't be the one to make the first move.

Except she didn't know what to say.

Thanks for taking me home and sorry you had to carry me? But she wasn't sorry. She'd loved every minute of it.

Thanks for the kiss that was so good I've not been able to think about anything else? She didn't know how to be that forward. She might be older, but she wasn't more experienced. One guy before Paul, none since him.

How about that date? She'd already tried that though, hadn't she? He was the one who'd said he'd ask her when she was sober. And he hadn't.

So maybe she was taking this all way too seriously, as was her default. Some gentle flirting and a hot kiss to remind her she was still attractive was as far as he wanted things to go.

Paul found you boring. How did you expect to interest a fun-loving twenty-seven-year-old?

Angry at the way her thoughts turned, Maggie jammed

the plug into the socket and vacuumed the hell out of the carpet.

'Mum!' Penny's voice floated over the din of the hoover. 'The phone's ringing.'

Maggie took the phone Penny held out, and her heart skipped a beat when she saw the caller ID. Hastily turning off the vacuum cleaner, she drew in a breath and answered. 'Hi.'

'Hi yourself.' She could hear the smile in Seb's voice. 'How's the head?'

'It's been three days.' Biting into her lip, she scolded herself for sounding so testy. 'I didn't mean that the way it sounded. Just that hangovers don't last three days.'

There was a beat of silence, and Maggie slumped down on the sofa. God, she was a mature woman. Why was she acting like this?

'I'm sorry it's taken me so long to phone you back. I've been busy at the centre.' He swore under his breath. 'Okay, cards on the table, I have been working, but not so hard that I couldn't find five minutes to phone you. I just...' A sharp exhale. 'Shit, Mags, I didn't know if you'd want to talk to me.'

That made her sit up. 'Why wouldn't I?'

'Because you're angry I kissed you?'

'Did it feel like I didn't want you to? Like I wasn't enjoying it?'

His laugh was softer now, warmer. More like the man she was getting to know. 'No. It felt like the best kiss I'd ever had.' He hesitated. 'But I should have stuck to my guns and waited until you weren't, you know…'

'Squiffy.'

'Yeah.' Another pause, and she imagined him rubbing a hand over his chin, or dragging it through his hair. 'I've been torturing myself, imaging you waking up Thursday morning and being horrified at what you'd done.'

It was so different to what she'd imagined had been going on in his head. He wasn't as confident as he came across. The realisation caused the gulf she imagined between them to narrow a little. 'I was horrified by how much I'd drunk, considering I had to get up and go to work, though thank God it was only an afternoon shift. I wasn't horrified at what we'd done.' She paused. *Best kiss he'd ever had*. She could afford to be brave, if he was. 'I was glad you'd kissed me.'

'Glad, huh?' His voice lowered, and his delight was clear. In the background she heard his name being called, and then the bang of a door closing. 'Damn, much as I want to keep talking about kissing you, I'm at the centre on a break and it looks like they need me to calm a couple of the kids down.' It sounded like he was on the move. 'I'm going to get them to watch the *Strictly* final in a vain attempt to inspire them. The most vocal still think ballroom dancing is peak, which I gather means shit.'

'Oh, does that mean you won't be watching with us?' Stupid, needy-sounding question.

'I thought it would be better this way.' A pause, and she heard him inhale a deep breath. 'I wasn't sure how to act in front of everyone. You obviously want to keep this quiet, and I respect that. I'm just a pretty lousy actor, especially where my sisters are concerned.'

'Why would you think... oh, Hannah.' In a flash she remembered the text she'd sent off to her, before the drinks. 'I told her we were having drinks with the class because... because, oh God.' Was she really going to tell him?

'Hey, it's fine. You don't have to give me your reasons.'

'I'm thirty-seven, Seb. Hannah is far closer to your age, and she has a crush on you.' *Plus she's bright and bubbly, where I'm serious and overly cautious. The pair of you are a much better fit.*

There was another commotion in the background, and Seb sighed. 'Crap, I've got to go. Can I see you tomorrow?'

'The girls are with Paul from eleven till three.'

'Great, I'll pick you up at twelve. Take you to lunch.' She heard the creak of a door, and when he spoke again, he was quieter. 'It's not Hannah I want to see, Mags. Not Hannah I want to dance with. And certainly not Hannah I fantasise about kissing when I close my eyes.'

Chapter Seventeen

Maggie shrugged on her favourite black sequinned top, and teamed it with some new wide-legged black trousers she'd bought in the pre-Christmas sales. Staring at the mirror, her eyes looked bright, her cheeks flushed. *It's not Hannah I fantasise about kissing when I close my eyes.*

Several hours after Seb's phone call, and she still felt a little giddy. How had she got to this place, where a phone call could provide the excitement that the anticipation of the *Strictly* final hadn't?

But since he'd phoned, she'd found her buzz.

The doorbell rang and Maggie dashed downstairs.

'I'm going.' Tabby rushed down the hallway. 'I bet it's Seb.'

'Seb isn't coming tonight.'

Tabby screeched to a halt and put her hands on her hips. 'But he promised to teach us dancing. Didn't he, Penny?'

Penny nodded, looking down at her feet. It was clear she was upset, which worried Maggie. Her eldest daughter had been six when Paul had left. Old enough to be aware of having a father in her life, and then having him practically disappear. The last thing Penny needed was to form an attachment with another man who was going to drift out of her life.

As Tabby let everyone in, Maggie gave Penny a hug. 'He has to work at the youth centre tonight, though I'm sure he'd rather be here.'

Ten minutes later and the party was about to get started. The kids were bouncing up and down in the TV room, their disappointment over Seb's non-arrival thankfully forgotten. Jack was 'supervising' them, which meant he was keeping out of the way of the kitchen, where everyone else was gathered.

Alice opened the oven door with her left hand, the right clutching her champagne glass tight. 'Ladies, I do believe the pizzas are ready.' As Maggie donned her oven gloves, Alice picked up the pizza cutter and Sarah the plates, while Hannah grabbed Alice's glass before the contents upended over the pizza.

'Does anyone else feel it's odd watching the final without our annoying little brother?' Alice asked, hacking the pizzas into uneven slices and making Maggie wince. 'It shouldn't, right? I mean, he's only joined us for, what, eight of them.'

'Seven.' It was only when all three of them stared at her that Maggie realised how much she'd given away. 'I think it's seven. Halloween week was at Alice's and he was there for the one before that.'

Alice jotted it up on her fingers. 'But that's eight.'

'He didn't come to Musicals Week.' She remembered telling him about it when he'd phoned her the following day. In the same call he'd told her he wanted to see the real her, though she still didn't know how he could, when she wasn't sure who that woman was any more.

'That's a remarkably good memory.'

Sarah eyed her shrewdly, and Maggie felt a prickle of heat in her cheeks. 'You know me. I like details.'

'Here's a detail that Sarah and Alice might like.' Hannah's gaze skimmed them all, and Maggie felt a bubble of panic. *Don't tell them about Wednesday. Not yet. I'm not ready.* 'Maggie was so tipsy on Wednesday Seb had to carry her to the front door.'

Maggie's heart jumped. 'You *saw* that?'

She giggled. 'I was in the kitchen when I heard the car engine, and looked out of the window. It was like that final scene in *Officer and a Gentleman*, you know, where Richard Gere sweeps Debra Winger into his arms.'

'It wasn't like that.' Maggie could feel Alice and Sarah's gaze burning into her. 'I told you, I drank too much. Seb saved me from falling flat on my bum, that's all.' Before anyone could quiz her any further, Maggie gathered up the plates. 'Come on, pizza's getting cold and,' she did a little box rumba, 'the Final is about to start.'

With a loud whoop, Hannah and Alice raced out, but

Sarah didn't move. 'You can fool the others, maybe, for a short while, but the pair of you can't fool me.'

'I know.' Maggie placed her hand on Sarah's arm. 'And I don't want to lie to you, or keep things from you, but there isn't anything to tell you yet.'

Her eyebrow arched. 'Yet?'

Maggie raised her eyes to the ceiling. 'A figure of speech.' She gave Sarah a wry smile. 'You know me. I'm cautious. I'm not going to rush into anything. Right now I'm enjoying dancing with your brother.' And, in one drunk moment, kissing him. A fact she was going to keep to herself.

Sarah nodded, letting out a huff of breath. 'I suppose I can make do with that until you're ready to talk to me. But it won't stop me worrying.' She deliberately caught her eye. 'About both of you.'

Something tightened in Maggie's chest. This thing, whatever she might or might not be starting with Seb, had the potential to reach beyond the pair of them. She'd considered, and worried about, the effect on Tabby and Penny, but she'd glossed over the impact on her friendships. How annoyed would Hannah be? Would Alice and Sarah still talk to her when everything went sour?

Maggie felt Sarah's arm wrap around her waist. 'Damn it, I shouldn't have said anything. I can see your mind over-analysing everything already.' The sound of the *Strictly* theme tune echoed into the kitchen and Sarah smiled. 'Come on, it's Final time.'

Half an hour into the show, and Alice started to fan herself. 'Wow, that is one sexy, hot rumba. Look at the way his hips roll. And the intimate way she's moving against him.' She lurched to her feet. 'I need a glass of water.'

Transfixed, Maggie stared at the screen. Oh, to be able to dance like that. The couple's chemistry lit up the screen in a way that was beyond sensual and bordering on erotic.

Her phone, tucked in the corner of the sofa, started to vibrate. Picking it up, Maggie glanced at the message.

Are you watching our new dance routine? S x

She started to smile, but it froze as the full implication of what he'd said began to sink in. Did he really think they could do that? The thought of moving with him in that way, sensual, provocative. Of him holding her, looking into her eyes with such apparent intensity. Her pulse kicked up a gear and she tapped out a reply.

Afraid I'm not that bendy.

Did she put a kiss after it, or was that too forward? God, too much over-analysing. Hastily she added, *M xx*.

Then had a minor panic over whether two kisses was way over the top.

Trust me, my hips don't do… what did the judges call it, oily?

Like a garage mechanic's rag? Still, I'll enjoy practising with you. S xxx

She hadn't realised she'd laughed, until Tabby turned round. 'Mum, you're on your phone. That's against the rules.'

'Yes, sorry.' Hastily she tucked the phone down the edge of the sofa.

As the judges raved over the dance, declaring it beyond steamy and into melting point, Maggie felt the phone vibrate again. Checking everyone's attention was on the TV screen, she snuck a look at the message.

BTW, not sure about his sheer black shirt, but like the idea of you in a short black thigh high split dress. S xxx

Maggie glanced again at the gloriously toned professional dancer, with the legs, the body, of a supermodel. Her instinct was to tell Seb she could never pull off a dress like that, but she stopped herself. Paul might have rejected her, but here was Seb, younger and far sexier, *flirting* with her. So no, she wasn't going to lapse back into old habits. Screwing up her courage, she typed out a message, then deleted it and typed out another.

Crap, she was so out of practice with all this.

And damn it, now Alice was watching her. 'Are you going to tell us who's messaging you?'

'Your brother.'

Everyone turned round then, but it was Alice who asked the inevitable question. 'What did he say?'

'We're thinking about doing the rumba for our dance in the competition.' She glanced back at the phone. 'He's asking me if he should buy a see-through black shirt.'

Alice spluttered with laughter. 'Bloody hell, that would be some sight.' She narrowed her eyes. 'I thought he was meant to be working at the centre?'

'He told me he was going to get the group to watch the final in the hope of inspiring them.'

When Hannah, Sarah, and Alice all looked at her, rather than the television, Maggie knew they were wondering how many other conversations she'd had with Seb. 'Come on, this is the final. Let's focus on the dancing.'

Ignoring their smirks, their rolling eyes and their silent questions, she fixed her eyes on the television. And laughed silently when Tabby muttered. ''Bout time you were quiet. You're getting worserer than Seb.'

Seb wished he was sat in Maggie's front room and not on the floor of the youth centre. Partly because then he wouldn't be worried he'd got bubble gum/some other sticky substance he didn't even want to think about on his arse. Mostly, he wished he was there because she, and Tabs and Penny, and yes, Hannah and even his sisters, were a lot more fun to watch *Strictly* with than the bunch of moaners he was with right now.

'He looks like a dick, dressed like that,' Rylan grunted at the screen, where the male celebrity, dressed in a sheer black shirt, was doing a hot rumba.

'I dunno, I think he's kind of cool.' Hayley, gum in mouth, her oversize hoop earrings moving with every chew, seemed to be one of the few that were interested.

'You can see his nipples,' Rylan countered disgustedly.

'So?' Kiara grinned at him. 'You can see his muscles too. Can't say dancing is for wimps now, can you?'

Zayne, who was Seb's one hope from the male side, sniggered. 'Yeah, she's got you there. That dude's like seriously ripped.' He flexed his biceps. 'Do you reckon mine are big enough?'

'Yeah, for a waltz.'

Seb knew he should intervene, but his phone had just vibrated again, and the need to see if Maggie had replied to his flirty message – the third he'd tried – was just too much. Sneaking it a few inches out of his pocket, he angled his head, trying not to make it obvious, and scanned her reply.

I like the idea of you in the sheer black shirt M xx

Something warm and satisfying settled in his chest and he typed back.

It can be arranged S xxx

As he pressed send, he started to chuckle to himself. A bad idea when trying not to draw attention to yourself.

'You banned our phones and now you're looking at *yours*?' Hayley stared at him wide-eyed. 'You have to tell us what just made you laugh. That's the rule.'

'Whose rule?'

'Duh, doesn't matter. You have to tell us.'

'Yeah, Seb. What's so funny?' Rylan gave him a cocky look.

Bugger, bugger, bugger. Yet he couldn't be cross, because Maggie's words were imprinted on his brain and all he wanted to do was punch the air and high-five everyone. Her words felt like *encouragement*. She wasn't drunk – she'd probably had a couple of glasses, enough to lower her inhibitions, but the flirty nature of her text felt huge to him right now.

Distracted by his thoughts, he missed the way Hayley crouched down next to him. It meant he was a fraction too late to stop her from grabbing the phone he hadn't realised had slipped out of his pocket and onto the floor. The screen still alarmingly bright.

'Ooh, someone wants to see Seb's nipples,' she yelled, waving the phone in the air. 'They want him to wear the see-through shirt the bloke's wearing on the TV.'

'Thank you, Hayley.' If he gave the slightest hint he was embarrassed, or annoyed, they'd not let this go. 'Can I have my phone back, please? It's not cool to read someone else's messages.'

'I suppose.' She handed it back, but not before giving him a sly smile. 'It's the woman you're gonna dance with, isn't it? *She* wants you to wear the shirt.'

Kiara started to giggle. 'Is she your GF? *Girlfriend*,' she added when Seb looked at her blankly.

How easy, how bloody brilliant on so many levels, if he could answer yes. But they'd meet Maggie at the competition, if not before, so he couldn't lie. 'She's my dance partner.'

'Who wants to see your nipples.' Rylan smirked at him.

'Who wants to see his *muscles*,' Kiara added.

The group fell about laughing, and Seb couldn't help but join in. 'We're supposed to be watching the dancing,' he told them, in between chuckles. 'I was hoping to inspire you, show you how different modern ballroom dancing is from what you imagine.'

'Yeah, don't worry, we're inspired.' Hayley threw him a wink as she chewed on her gum. 'Well, us girls are anyway.'

There was another round of giggles, but just as Seb thought they were settling down, the next dance came on. And it was a sodding Viennese waltz. Beautiful, don't get him wrong, he could see the grace, the elegance. He could even see himself dancing it with Maggie, though he preferred it when his hand touched more than her shoulder blade. But it wasn't the sort of dance Rylan and co. were going to want to emulate.

'OMG, look at them.' Rylan bent over, clutching at his stomach, as laughter rolled through him. 'They're like summut out of... who's that woman who wrote that shit book we have to read for English?'

'Jane Austen?' One of the quieter of the group spoke up. '*Pride and Prejudice*?'

'Yeah. The dance is as stupid as the book.'

'Is it stupid?' Seb felt a spike of shame as he remembered how he'd sneered at *Strictly*, until he'd started to really watch it. 'I'm not sure you can call a book that's still read by millions, two hundred years after publication, stupid. As for the dance, have you watched their footwork? I sure as hell couldn't do that. Not without tripping over my feet and landing flat on my arse.'

'And with the dance partner you fancy landing on top of you.' Hayley started laughing. 'You wish.' Hayley nodded down to the phone. 'Ask her to come to one of our lessons on Thursdays. We want to meet her.'

'Oh no.' His fledgling romance definitely didn't need any help from Hayley and her sledgehammer approach to life. 'She works and has kids. She won't be able to spare the time.'

'Yeah but she came before, didn't she?' Hayley waggled her eyebrows. 'I remember you bringing some kids here, said you had to look after them. The woman who picked them up was her, wasn't it? Fair hair, slim. Peng but kind of reserved. And totally older than you.'

So this was what karma looked like. So many times he'd called Hayley out for not taking her eyes off her phone. Now was payback time.

'Fine.' Deciding not to comment on 'peng' – slang for beautiful and a comment he totally agreed with – or 'older', Seb snatched his phone out of his pocket.

Long story, but the kids here want you to come to one of their dance lessons. What do you reckon? S xxx

It was a long while before he received a reply. Long enough for Hayley to get bored of asking him, for the dancers on *Strictly* to have danced all their routines. And for Seb to wonder if he'd upset Maggie in some way. Was she angry he was talking to the kids at the centre about her?

But then finally, as the winners raised the glittery disco ball trophy aloft, his phone beeped.

I want to ask why, but suspect that's in the long story so if it helps you... yes. M xx

Just as he was reeling from that surprise, he got a second message.

Feeling emotional, watching the winners. I want a glitter ball M xx

The idea of winning something at all, never mind with Maggie, even if it was only a local competition he was ham-fistedly putting together, touched deep inside him. He had no clue how to reply without sounding like a sappy twit.

'What did she say?' Hayley's loud question barraged through his sentimental thoughts.

'Surprisingly, she said yes. Though she doesn't know you like I do.'

Hayley gave him a shove. 'Aw, come on. You like us

really. After all, we're entering your dumb competition.'

'You are?' A couple of them had put their names down, but he'd given up all hope of any more.

'Course. Kiara and Zayne and me and, well, I'll find someone.' Her eyes strayed to Rylan.

Seb followed her gaze, and winced. Hayley was in for rough ride if she decided to go down that route. In a way, Seb understood Rylan. He'd behaved in a similar way at fifteen. Acting up, pretending indifference to everything, because inside it mattered too much. In his case it had been about his grades. He wasn't sure what Rylan's issue was, but if anyone could help him out of it, he suspected it was the bolshie yet ultimately warm-hearted Hayley. 'Well I'm glad to hear it. Doesn't have to be a guy, you know.'

'I know.' But her gaze remained on Rylan.

'Have you asked him?' He nodded in Rylan's direction.

'What, Rylan? Are you mad?' She shook her head, earrings rattling. 'I don't want to dance with him.'

'Of course you don't.' He flashed her a smile. 'Just like I don't want to date my dance partner.'

Before Hayley could come back at him – and knowing her there was a volley of words ready on her tongue – Seb stood, turned off the TV and told them all it was time to head home.

As they meandered out, he opened up the message string to Maggie on his phone, and typed out a reply.

I want to help you win a glitter ball, but organiser is a bit tight and budget may not run to one. See you tomorrow @12. S xxx

Chapter Eighteen

Maggie sighed and slumped back on her bed, surrounded by half the contents of her wardrobe. If she was being this picky about what to wear for a casual lunch with Seb, there was no way she could actually date the man. She'd need a whole new wardrobe, for a start.

How had she turned from a sassy twenty-three-year-old to staid nearly-forty-year-old? She used to wear miniskirts and thigh-high boots, shorts with thick tights and chunky shoes. Skinny jeans and tight jumpers.

Why could she now only find jogging bottoms, ill-fitting jeans and work clothes?

As for her underwear drawer, it was a triumph of comfort over anything remotely sexy.

Not that she was thinking that far ahead. Though she had made a quiche, figuring why go out for lunch, when they had the house to themselves? No prying eyes, nobody to disturb them. Just her and Seb. Alone. In a place with a bed.

Groaning, she put her head in her hands. Watching that rumba last night had clearly ignited her long-lost libido. She had half an hour to pull herself together.

She'd only just dragged on a pair of leggings – the ones she usually wore for pilates – and a cashmere jumper that was her favourite go-to when she couldn't think of anything else to wear, when the doorbell sounded.

Heart racing a million miles an hour, she dashed down the stairs to open it.

'Hi.'

God, how did he do casually sexy so well? He looked like he'd thrown the jeans and Henley shirt on, not spent an hour deliberating over whether either or both showed off his figure. Which they did, beautifully.

He flashed her the smile she was growing to love. Easy, warm, yet when his eyes met hers, so intimate, too. 'Hi yourself.' Bending, he pressed a delicious, yet sadly all too brief, kiss to her lips. 'Tabby and Penny get off okay?'

'Yes.' She felt all tongue-tied and out of breath. All she could think was how heavenly he smelt, how fit and vital he looked. How badly she wanted to kiss him again. To run her hands over the muscled contours of his chest, amply shown off by the close-fitting shirt.

But they weren't at that stage, and she wasn't that woman, the one that could dive easily into a sexual relationship.

'I thought, well, I wondered.' She shook her head, annoyed at herself. 'I made a quiche.'

Amusement lit his eyes and before he could say anything, she found she was blabbering. 'In hindsight that wasn't the best idea, as they say real men don't eat quiche, but I think you're confident enough in your masculinity not to worry about that. We don't have to eat it though. We can still go out. I just thought it might be nicer to stay in, as we've got the place to ourselves.' And now she knew her face was going a bright shade of scarlet. 'God, I'm making a right hash of this. It's…' She exhaled a deep breath. 'It's been a long time since I've done anything like this.'

Those bright blue eyes glittered with humour. 'Cooked a quiche?'

'Cooked a quiche for a man.'

He reached for her hands, smiling into her eyes. 'No need to be nervous, Mags. You can bet whatever you have planned, I'm up for it.'

Remembering the rifle through her lacklustre underwear drawer, she let out a strangled laugh. 'That sounds like I've got this whole seduction routine lined up.' When he grinned even wider, waggling his eyebrows, she couldn't help it. She started to laugh. 'This is ridiculous. There's nothing planned.'

'Seriously? You, Maggie Peterson, have *nothing planned*?'

He gave her a wide-eyed look and she shoved at him. 'Very funny. So, are you coming in or are we going out?'

He stepped into the house and as he carefully shut the door behind him, Maggie felt a flutter deep in her belly;

part nerves, part anticipation. It grew stronger as his hands cupped her face, and he looked straight into her eyes. 'Real men can't resist a home-cooked quiche.'

She huffed out a laugh. 'It's bacon and tomato.' How could he make the word quiche sound intimate, yet she sounded like she was reciting a shopping list?

He smiled, staring at her mouth. 'My favourite.'

Her heart was hammering, her knees felt like jelly. 'What if I'd said spinach and goat's cheese?'

He licked his lips, eyes still on her mouth. 'Also my favourite.'

'Marmite and banana?'

His gaze bounced up to her face. 'Is that really a combination?'

'No. I just wondered how far you'd go.'

He laughed then, clasping her hand and kissing it. 'With you, Mags, I'd go all the way.' Before she could get too panicked, he tugged on her. 'Come on, let's go and eat quiche.'

They chatted as they ate at the kitchen table, dissecting yesterday's final, and Seb raised the subject of her coming to visit the youth centre again.

'You don't have to meet them. Hayley's the one who told me to invite you.' He smiled at her as he rocked back on his chair. 'She's trying to work out if you're my girlfriend or not.'

'Oh.' She wasn't sure what to think. Had he discussed her with the group?

As if he could read her mind, he reached across to touch

her hand. 'Relax. Hayley's loud but she's harmless. I get the impression she's ignored at home, so she comes to the centre to get some attention.'

'And you give it to her, by letting her nose about your private life?'

'I'm not sure I let her,' he countered mildly. 'More that she bulldozes her way in.'

Maggie eyed him curiously. 'Most men would tell her to mind her own business.'

He shrugged his wide shoulders. 'I'm not that private a person.'

And there it was, yet another reason to not just like him, but *really* like him. He was this cool, easy-going guy who didn't seem to have a side to him. He wasn't annoyed or irritated by the small things that wound most people up: lateness, nosey questions, having the mick taken out of him. 'Tell me about why you ended up on a pontoon over the barrier reef?'

He laughed. 'I said I wasn't private. Not that I liked talking about myself.'

'So? I'm interested. Why did you decide to go travelling after university?'

His eyes drifted away from hers, and towards the window. 'I didn't exactly decide. It just sort of happened. All my mates were applying for jobs, but I didn't know what I wanted to do, and the thought of getting stuck behind a desk so I could say I had a job...' He shuddered. 'I'd saved some money from holiday work, and decided to take the summer off and travel for a bit.' Finally his eyes met hers. 'The summer just kept stretching. I told myself I'd go back in October, then it was after Christmas. Then it was next year. Before long it became easier to keep travelling than to go home and face reality.'

She frowned over at him. 'You make it sound like you took the easy option, but that's simply not true. It takes guts to go travelling like you did. To stride into the big wide world by yourself. Most of us were too scared to try.'

'Scared? What of?'

It was so typical of him. He seemed to radiate cheer and optimism. As if he never saw obstacles, or danger. Only opportunities and challenges. 'Scared of having only ourselves to rely on, of not having enough money, of missing a few steps on the relentless career ladder, of... I don't know... getting eaten by a shark.'

Laughter rumbled in his chest. 'Sharks are given a bad rap.' Slowly his face sobered. 'Some people don't see it like you do. Some think I ran away and then put my head in the sand. That I didn't want to face responsibility. That I've frittered my life away so far and it's time to man up.'

For the first time since she'd met him, she heard vulnerability in his voice. 'What matters is how *you* see the direction your life is taking. Are *you* happy?' She felt the quiver in her voice and had to swallow before she could say the next words. 'For too many years I did what was expected of me, not what made me happy.' She supposed she should thank Paul for that insight, because it was only now, looking at Seb, and what was possible, that she realised how far her life with Paul had travelled down the wrong road. 'I refuse to make that mistake again.'

Seb searched Maggie's beautiful eyes, trying to understand what she was trying to tell him. 'Are you talking about Paul?'

'Yes.' She eased off the chair and began to clear the table. He knew he should help, but he couldn't take his eyes off her, and the gorgeous picture she made. Up to now he'd mainly seen her in what he guessed were her work clothes – neat trousers, smart blouses – or her Saturday night *Strictly* clothes, which seemed to be the one sequinned black top. She always looked elegant, and yeah, beautiful, but a little reserved. Today, in her stretch leggings and baggy jumper, her hair in a youthful ponytail, she looked so much more approachable. And so bloody sexy he was finding it hard to keep his hands off her.

'Paul was, I suppose you'd call it driven.' She walked to the dishwasher and stacked the plates neatly inside before turning and resting her back against the work top. 'I loved my job too, so I didn't think anything of it. It's only now, when I look back over our marriage, and when I talk to people like you, I realise how much he took away from me. Our life revolved around him, and what he needed. His ambition, his desire to reach the top, dominated everything.' She paused, seeming to gather herself. 'The girls have missed out on so many things other families take for granted: holidays, visits to grandparents, family days out.' Her eyes met his. 'And I'm starting to realise I've missed out on so much, too.'

Seb's heart knocked against his ribs. It wasn't so much what she said, as what her eyes seemed to be telling him. But he couldn't afford to misread their message, not now she was opening up to him.

'These things you've missed out on.' He stood slowly and walked towards her. 'Are there any I can help you with?'

And no, he wasn't mistaking the way her pulse was hammering in her throat.

'Yes.' Her voice was a whisper, but her eyes, now a stormy grey, didn't leave his.

He couldn't explain how honoured he felt that she was allowing him to show her. 'I want to kiss you again. Shit, I need to kiss you. Can I?'

She cleared her throat. 'Please.'

With a groan of hunger, of desperation, he pulled her into his arms, his mouth settling over hers, his tongue sliding between her parted lips.

Weeks of dancing with her, of watching as she laughed with his sisters, or fantasising about her as he lay in bed, all came to a head. 'Is this okay?' he asked as he ran his hand under her jumper, finding her soft, warm skin.

'It's better than okay.'

Her words were like petrol on a bonfire. Angling his head, he kissed her more deeply, his tongue, his hands, seeking and stroking, his hips pushing against hers, finding her core, her heat.

'The kitchen works for me,' he breathed between more long, drugging kisses. 'Or the sofa. But I'm better in a bed.'

Her felt her mouth smile beneath his. 'Promises, promises.'

Drawing back, he held her face in his hands. 'Let me show you.' There were so many ways he wasn't right for this incredible woman, so many things he couldn't give her, but making her feel good... that he could do.

Cheeks flushed, her eyes glittering, she nodded, but as she started to walk, he halted her with his hand. Then swept her into his arms like he had the other day.

'Oh God, no, you can't do this.' Instead of struggling though, she slipped her hands around his neck.

'Are you doubting my athleticism?'

She laughed, pressing her face to his neck as he began to stride up the stairs. 'I'm doubting your sanity. I'm not—'

'As light as you look.' Five steps from the top, and he was starting to regret the gesture. Shit, what if he *dropped* her? 'Do you bounce?'

That started her giggling, and if there was one thing harder than carrying a lady upstairs, it was carrying one who was wriggling. Especially as her breasts kept pushing against his chest. His knees were moments away from giving up when he reached the final stair. 'Thank Christ for that.'

'Oh God, this is crazy.' She shook her head, but laughter shone from her eyes. 'I've gone crazy. This isn't what a nearly forty-year-old mum should be doing.'

It niggled him that she kept mentioning her age, especially when she rounded it up. It was like she was reminding him this was just temporary insanity on her part.

'Why not, Mags?' He asked as he found her bedroom and laid her carefully on the bed. 'Why should age or having children be a barrier to doing anything you want to do?'

'I don't know,' she whispered, intelligent grey eyes scanning his face. 'I don't want them to be.'

'Then that's half the battle.' With one quick movement, he shrugged off his shirt.

'Wow.' Her gaze wandered over his bare chest. 'That's a lot more muscles than I'm used to.'

Laughing softly, he took hold of her hand and placed it on his chest.

Her eyes widened. 'Your heart is racing.'

He could have blamed the workout he'd had carrying her up the stairs, but he knew it had been hammering away before that. 'I want you.'

In what he'd like to bet was an unconscious gesture, she licked her lips. 'I want you, too. But I'm scared I won't be what you're expecting.'

He wondered what was going on in her head, betting Paul had something to do with it. 'You're already more, Mags, much, much more.'

Carefully he peeled off her leggings and eased the jumper over her head, revealing simple white underwear, against pale skin. And hell's teeth, was that a tattoo peeping out? The tip of a butterfly's wing?

Christ, that was so sexy. *She* was so sexy; coolly sophisticated on the outside, yet much of that was a veneer. On the inside he'd like to bet she was bolder and far less reserved than she thought she was.

'I couldn't find any snazzy underwear.'

Busy kissing the soft swell of her stomach, it took him a moment to register what she'd said. 'What do you mean?'

She waved a hand down her body. 'I've not thought to buy sexy underwear for a long time. This morning, I regretted it.'

The thought that she'd planned this in her head... he almost couldn't breathe with the ache it started in his chest. 'For future reference,' he told her, planting a kiss on her cleavage, 'anything with you in it is sexy.'

She hiccupped out a laugh. 'That can't be true. I've lost my flat stomach, nothing is pert any more.'

'This?' He nodded to the gentle curve of her stomach. 'That's far more special than a flat stomach. That's a stomach that has held two precious girls.' With almost embarrassing haste, he unclipped the bra, then drew in a sharp breath. 'And God, Mags. Look what you're hiding here. I think I'm in love.' He groaned as he cupped the luscious globes. 'These are spectacular. I'm going to revise what I said earlier. Anything with you in it is sexy, but you with nothing on is bloody sensational.'

Her body shook as she started to laugh.

'Hey, stop that.' He bent to suckle a ripe pink nipple. 'This is serious business.' He looked up, and caught her smiling at him. As he stared back, mesmerised by her, the amusement in her eyes started to fade, heat and desire taking their place.

She reached down to undo the button on his jeans. 'I want to see you, too.' Hastily he shoved off his jeans and his boxers, feeling a wave of fresh desire as she stared down at him. 'Did you say something about spectacular…?'

He laughed, tugging off the final piece of her underwear and easing her hair from the constraint of its jaunty ponytail. 'Flattery will get you absolutely everywhere you want to go.'

Then he bent to kiss her again, and soon he was lost to her, to the rose scent of her skin, the sexy sounds she made. The way her hand wrapped around the part of him that ached.

'Condom,' he managed, a second before all sense deserted him, and dived inelegantly off the bed to rummage through the contents of his wallet.

Then he was thrusting into her, drowning in her heat. Nothing in his life to date had felt so good, so right. Nor so *intense*. For a brief moment panic filled him. This had the potential to be more than a hot fling, more than him showing Maggie how to laugh again.

More than a beautiful distraction from where his life was heading.

For the first time in his life, he'd met a woman who had the potential to hurt him.

But then her husky moan chased away his thoughts and he angled his hips, deepening their connection, his kisses becoming distracted, impatient, messy. Life was for living, and while he had the chance, he was going to enjoy this smart, outwardly reserved, yet, he was coming to realise, inwardly passionate woman to the full.

Chapter Nineteen

As Seb rolled off her with a satisfied grunt, Maggie stretched out beside him, feeling... oh stuff it, there were no other words for it. She felt bloody fantastic. Sex was *the* best thing to do on a Sunday afternoon.

Fleetingly she thought of Paul, and tried to recall if they'd ever, even in the early days, had sex during the day. Her mind came up blank.

Early on in their relationship, sex with Paul had been... nice. Towards the end, it had been perfunctory. Done out of habit, not desire. At no time had it been as mind-blowing, all-encompassing or *fun* as Seb had made it. Nor had she ever felt so desirable.

Turning to face him, she found Seb propped up on his side, watching her.

'That was...' She trailed off, feeling suddenly uncertain. What if it hadn't been fantastic for him. What if it had just been ordinary?

'Incredible? Bonzer, ripper?' He smiled, giving her a tender kiss on the lips. 'The word spectacular comes to mind again.'

Satisfaction and delight rolled through her. 'It does, doesn't it.'

His eyes held hers and though his smile remained, it slipped a little, his expression mirroring the uncertainty she'd felt a moment ago. 'So now you've had your wicked way with me, will you go out with me?'

Her pulse scrambled. 'You mean like, on a date?'

'I kind of hoped there'd be more than one.'

She couldn't deny the joy, yet nor could she hide the worry. 'I'd like that.'

His smile broadened, but as his eyes searched hers, he sighed. 'Damn, I can hear a *but*.'

Unable to resist, she placed a hand on his face, running her fingers across the stubble. 'We'd be fooling ourselves to think this, you and me, could be simple.'

A furrow appeared between his eyes. 'Why?'

'You know why.' With the fog of lust cleared, the reality of their situation lay heavily over her.

'Because of my sisters?' He shook his head. 'They already suspect what's happening anyway, and they won't care.'

'They won't care now, maybe, but when it ends?' She wanted to go back to losing herself in him again instead of the awkwardness of this heavy conversation. 'I don't want to lose their friendship.'

'You won't. My sisters aren't fickle like that.'

'Then there's Tabby and Penny—'

'Who already know me.'

What about the fact that you're you, with your vitality, your rugged beauty, and I'm me, with my fussiness, my ordinariness. The words were trapped inside her. It was easier to admit to the practical than to her awful insecurity when it came to this, to relationships.

Raising his hand, he gently trailed a finger down her cheek. 'Am I the only one feeling something here?'

She swallowed, her throat tight, her mouth dry. 'No,' she admitted. 'I feel it too, but... oh God, Seb, I'm not this woman. I don't do this.'

His gaze narrowed. 'You don't date?'

'The last guy I dated, I married.'

She didn't miss his shocked look. 'Nobody since then?'

'No.' There had been a few offers, but none she could really remember. None that had made her want to risk trying again. Until now.

He watched her quietly with those incredible blue eyes. 'Dating doesn't have to be all deep and serious, you know,' he said finally. 'It can be fun and frivolous.' In a welcome change of mood, he flashed her one of his smiles. 'I'm a bloody master at fun and frivolous.'

Laughter bubbled, as it did so readily when she was with him. All of her life she'd been serious: as a child, taking care of her sister, as an adult, working hard to become a doctor, handling life and death decisions on a frighteningly regular basis. Then she'd gone and married someone even more serious than she was. No wonder it hadn't worked out.

Could she do carefree? Could she just relax and let this happen?

'What do you say?' His hands left her face and began to move down her body. 'Let's have some fun together, Mags.'

She gasped as his fingers found her core. 'Yes. Oh God, yes.'

She wasn't sure if that was a yes to the dating, or to him continuing his exploration. Just that she wanted more of whatever he was willing to offer.

Soon he was sliding back into her, this time with his front to her back, his hands caressing her breasts as his hips drove into her.

'You're beautiful, you know that, yes?' His words came out as pants, hot against her skin. 'So fucking sexy I can't get enough of you.'

Spectacular had been his word, yet it was exactly how she wanted to describe him, and how he made her feel. As if she was the most desirable woman he'd ever met.

Minutes, hours… she lost track of time as she lost herself to him.

'Mags.' Hands squeezed her shoulders, and she felt a kiss on the top of her head. 'Wake up, someone's ringing on the doorbell.'

'What?'

She jerked upright, belatedly dragging the duvet with her.

'The front door.'

And now she could hear it, a jarring, insistent sound disturbing the sensual haze she'd been luxuriating in.

'Oh my God, it's Paul with the girls.'

Panic filled her and she leapt out of bed, desperately searching for her clothes. Where the hell was her underwear? Her leggings?

'I think you're looking for these?' Calmly Seb climbed from the bed and picked up her discarded clothes. Clearly totally at ease in his skin, he crossed the room and handed them to her. Then dropped a kiss on her neck. 'Chill, Mags. They can wait.'

'No, you don't understand.' Frantically she started to dress. 'What's it going to look like?' She caught sight of herself in the mirror and her alarm escalated. 'Oh God, my hair, my face. I know exactly what it's going to look like.'

'So?' He shrugged, slipping into his boxers. 'You're a single woman. You've not done anything to be ashamed of.'

There was the slightest edge to his voice, enough for her to pause, and take a breath. 'I'm not ashamed. I just don't want Paul knowing my private business.' The doorbell sounded again, and she hastily dragged her jumper over her head. 'How do I look?'

His eyes skimmed over her face, and he smiled. 'Honestly? Like you've just had a couple of hours of amazing sex.'

'Oh God.' She went to the mirror and tried to scrape her hair back into a pony tail. Again the doorbell sounded.

'I'll get it.' Seb started towards the door.

'No.' She couldn't let him answer her front door. That seemed way too big a deal for someone she'd only just, tentatively, agreed to date.

'Why not? Give you time to straighten yourself up.' He winked. 'Though I'm a big fan of the mussy-haired, flush-cheeked, just-had-sex look.'

He was finding this so easy, in fact it was amusing him, yet she was drowning in embarrassment. Did it really matter what Paul thought? The man had been having sex with another woman while he'd been married to her. Why was she being so prim, so pernickety, about this?

Because that was the person she'd become. Responsible, cautious. Not one to make waves, to act out of character. Certainly not a woman to have sex for over two hours with a man ten years her junior. While her daughters were having lunch with their father.

'Mags?' Half in, half out of the bedroom, Seb stared at her in confusion.

'Sorry, yes, answer it, please.' She bit into her lip. 'But can we not make it obvious—'

'We've been having sex?' He exhaled a rough breath, dragging a hand through his hair. 'Of course.'

Seb bounded down the stairs, trying not to think too hard

about why Maggie was so twitchy about her ex knowing what they'd been up to. The girls he could understand, though they were too young to pick up on the subtleties of a just-had-sex appearance.

Paul, yeah, he might guess, but why did she care what he thought? The only reason he could come up with was one that chilled him to the core. She was still partly in love with the guy.

Pausing to take a breath, to settle himself, he opened the door. Then bit the inside of his cheek to stop from smirking when Paul gaped at him.

Dropping his gaze to the girls, Seb grinned. 'Who was making all that noise?'

Tabby pointed proudly to her chest. 'Me. I pressed the button but then Mum didn't answer so I runged it again.'

'And again, and again,' Penny muttered under her breath. 'I said Mum would have heard the first time.'

'She did, but she's...' Shit, he should have thought of this one before he opened the door. 'In the middle of something.'

'Why are *you* answering her door?'

Paul glared at him, jaw muscle ticking, eyes like flint. There was something about the arrogant tilt of his chin, the sharp cut of his cheekbones, the expensive cut of his hair, that made Seb want to slam the door back in his face. 'Because she's in the middle of something,' he repeated.

'What?'

It was an obvious question, and maybe if the guy had been half-way friendly, if he hadn't been such a bastard to

Maggie, hadn't chosen to desert his daughters for the last few years, Seb might have felt bad about his next words. 'I don't believe that's any of your business.'

Anger flared in Paul's eyes, and his jaw became more rigid, but whatever he might have been about to say was halted as Maggie came into view.

'Hey, girls.'

They dashed forward, throwing their arms around her, and Seb felt his chest tighten, just a little, at the obvious love. Easy for him, with his lack of any sort of responsibility, to dive into what, common sense told him, would only be a short-term fling. Not so easy for Maggie. As a fresh wave of respect flooded through him, he made a silent promise to her. He'd make sure she never regretted any of it.

'Did you want to come in?'

Maggie asked the question of Paul, and Seb could tell the guy was torn. 'Isabelle is in the car.'

'She's welcome too. If you want.'

How could she be so polite to him? Seb didn't understand. He wasn't aggressive by nature, nor did he anger or take offense easily, but there was no way he could be this polite to someone who'd fucked him over.

'Could we have a chat?' Paul glanced pointedly at Seb. 'Just the two of us.'

Seb stood his ground, not willing to go scuttling inside on the man's say-so.

Maggie glanced at him, her hair back together, her face reserved. Nothing left of the passionate woman he'd been buried inside only twenty minutes ago. 'Would you mind going inside with the girls? I'm sure they'd like to talk to you about last night's final.'

He wanted to stay, to protect her, stick up for her, and it gutted him to know she didn't need or want either from him.

He felt a little hand curl around his, and looked to see Tabby grinning up at him. 'That man won, the one who had greasy hips.'

'Oily.' Penny corrected. 'The judge said he had oily hips.'

Tabby stuck her tongue out at her sister. 'That's what I said.'

And Seb couldn't help but laugh as he was pulled down the hallway.

———

He wasn't laughing ten minutes later when Maggie walked into the kitchen. She looked subdued, the spark gone from her eyes, the flush of her cheeks a distant memory.

'Did you have a good time with your dad?' she asked, joining them at the centre island where the girls had jumped onto bar stools and were drinking the hot chocolate he'd managed to cobble together.

'We ate cheese that wasn't cheese and stuff that was green and slimy.' Tabby frowned and looked at her sister. 'Penny knows.'

'It was avocado salad with grilled hal... halum... something.'

'Grilled halloumi?' Maggie looked at Tabby. 'That was the cheese that wasn't cheese?'

'Yeah.' Tabby pulled a face. 'It was yucky.'

'Isabelle is vegetarian,' Penny supplied, making Maggie's eyebrows shoot up.

'Well, wow, that's interesting.'

Seb caught her eyes. 'Why?'

'Because Paul always liked his meat. On one occasion I made a vegetarian lasagna and he complained heavily. Looks like he's changed.'

His wife made him a meal, and he complained? Seb was starting to wish he had slammed the door in Paul's face after all.

As Maggie continued to ask questions of the girls, Seb began to feel more and more like the unwanted guest. She'd invited him for lunch. Considering they'd gone from that to her bed, and then to a visit from her ex… yeah, she had a lot to process. And if he knew one thing about her, she was a thinker.

'Well, I'd better be going.'

'What about the lesson?' As soon as Penny blurted the words, she flushed and stared down at her feet.

It left Seb momentarily confused – lesson, what lesson? Then he remembered his promise a few weeks back, and shame coiled through him. 'You want me to show you some dance steps now?'

She nodded, still not looking at him. In contrast, Tabby bounced up and down. 'Yippee, dance lesson. I want one too.'

Seb felt trapped between a rock and a hard place. Keep the daughters happy and his promise to Penny, or upset Maggie by outstaying his welcome. 'I can do a quick lesson now.' He glanced at Maggie. 'Or I can come and do one another day.'

She gave him a strained smile. 'I think the girls are hoping you'll stay.'

What about you? He wanted to ask, though he had a feeling he knew the answer. Was she already regretting sleeping with him? Regretting agreeing to date him, now that the reality of her life – her children, her ex – had burst back into their all-too-brief afternoon?

But two little people were staring up at him expectantly, so Seb pushed away the heavy thoughts and pasted on a smile. 'Who wants to go first?'

Chapter Twenty

Maggie sat at her desk, staring at the sandwich she'd thrown together that morning. She had twenty minutes to eat, stretch her legs and recharge until her next patient.

All she could do was fret over yesterday.

Not over lunch, not over spending the afternoon in bed. With Seb.

No, that she was not going to regret.

Her reaction to Paul's hurtful words on the doorstep after Seb had walked inside with the girls? Yep, that she was still stewing over.

'You're embarrassing yourself, Maggie,' Paul had told her dispassionately. 'A professional woman like you, a GP, for God's sake, cavorting around with some young beach bum. It's not only demeaning, it's unfair on the girls. What will people be saying behind your back? What sort of gossip will you subject Penny and Tabby to?'

She'd tried to argue. To ask why it was okay for him to run off with a younger woman, but not for her to date a younger man. 'It's not my fault society doesn't accept things that way round.' He'd stared at her, as if seeing her for the first time. 'I don't understand what's got into you. You're a mother, Maggie. You've always been a good, responsible one.'

And ouch, that had hurt, even coming from a man who'd been so irresponsible he'd practically abandoned his daughters since the divorce.

The thought of subjecting the girls to potential gossip, though… It made her feel sick. Were attitudes still so backwards that it was okay for a man to date a woman ten years younger, but not the other way round? She wanted to dismiss the idea, but hadn't she had her own misgivings on the subject?

Seb had noticed the change in her when she'd gone back inside, the distance she'd erected between them, because apparently Seb was an open book when it came to his feelings. His smile had gone from easy to strained, his expression from happy to worried.

That was the part she regretted. Not explaining to him why she'd got her knickers in such a twist that afternoon. God knows what he must be thinking of the way she'd blown hot and cold.

And it was that final thought that made her pick up her phone and dial his number.

'Mags.'

Alarm spiked at the sound of his voice. Usually so warm

and easy, with a dash of sexy, it slipped over her like brandy sauce over a Christmas pudding. Now though... now it sounded awful. 'Is everything okay?'

'No.' Some background noise, maybe traffic, and then the clunk of what had to be a car door. 'Sorry, I've got to go. It's Dad.' A harsh exhale. 'He's had another heart attack.'

The bottom fell out of her stomach. 'Oh my God, I'm so sorry. Do you need me to come with you?'

She heard the sound of his engine starting. 'Thanks, but Alice and Sarah are meeting me at the hospital. I've... I've got to go.'

'Yes, of course. Let me know if there's anything I can do.'

'I will.' Silence, long enough for her to wonder if he'd just forgotten not to end the call. But then he spoke again. 'Thanks.'

Her heart squeezed. 'I've not done anything.' *Except be a cow to you yesterday, which you didn't deserve.*

'For offering to come.'

'I meant it. Whatever you need.' She hesitated. 'Can I call you later? Or you call me? I want to know how he is.'

'Sure. I'll phone you.'

The call ended, and she leant back in her chair, her heart aching for Seb, for Sarah and for Alice. For their mum, who'd always greeted Maggie with a warm smile on the few occasions they'd met. A smile very much like Seb's. After pinging off two messages to her friends, offering any support they might need, she eyed up the sandwich in front of her. And knew she couldn't eat it.

The girls had just gone to bed and Maggie was sitting on the sofa with her phone in her hand, pretending to watch a programme on how to cook the perfect turkey. She didn't care. The girls would be happier with a plate of sausages wrapped in bacon, anyway.

When her phone vibrated, she snatched it up.

'He's gone.'

The anguish in Seb's voice caused a painful squeeze on her heart. 'I'm so sorry.'

'Yeah.' She could hear only his breathing, and knew he was struggling to keep his emotions inside. 'Turns out his heart was too weak from the first one to survive this.'

She was at a loss to know how to help. 'Where are you now?'

'Still at the hospital. We're going back to Alice's. She insists we need to eat and none of us are in the mood to tell her it's the last thing we want to do.'

Maggie could imagine her friend taking charge, doing what she thought was right. 'A bit of normality for a while is a good thing, Seb. And I'm sure Rebecca and Edward will be a good distraction for your mum.'

He heaved out a sigh. 'Probably you're both right. It's just the thought of sitting around like nothing's happened, eating when Dad's lying in the fridge of a mortuary... Fuck.' She heard him drag in a few hoarse breaths. 'Sorry.'

'Don't apologise. If you want a punch bag, a sounding board, just someone to talk to, you know I'm here.'

He didn't reply, and it made her worry. Had the way she'd left things yesterday, the brief kiss on the cheek she'd given him, which now seemed horribly dismissive, had they made him doubt he could come to her? Made him doubt she cared?'

Finally she heard his voice again. 'Alice wants a word.'

There was a muffled noise and then Alice's voice. 'Hi.'

Maggie could hear her friend start to cry, and it started her off. 'Alice, I'm so sorry. How can I help?'

'Can Edward and Rebecca come back to yours with Hannah for the next few days, until school breaks up? Mum's in coping mode already and said she'll pick them up as usual, but I don't want her to have to deal with that added pressure right now. Plus there's things that need doing, like registering his death, making funeral arrangements.' She sniffed. 'Oh God, this is awful, just awful.'

'Of course we'll take care of your kids. They can have tea with mine and I'll drop them back or you pick them up, whatever works for you.'

'You're a star, thank you.' Maggie heard Alice blow her nose. 'Right, better go.' A pause. 'Don't think I haven't noticed that Seb was the one to call you tonight, mind. Not me, not Sarah, but Seb. We'll have that conversation sometime... sometime.' Another sniff.

'Sometime when you're not blindsided by grief,' Maggie added softly. 'I'll see you tomorrow.'

Seb paced his mum and dad's... fuck, his mum's... living room floor. The Christmas tree stood in the corner, the cheery baubles a poignant reminder of what a truly crappy time of year it was to lose anyone.

It had been three days since his dad had died, and Seb didn't know what to do with all this anger, this emotion bubbling away beneath the surface. He wasn't this guy, the one who needed to punch something, or to scream at the top of his voice. Yet now it was all he wanted to do.

That or lose himself in the arms of a woman who could make him forget everything but the satin feel of her skin, the soft curve of her breasts.

Cursing, he smacked a hand against the wall. That option wasn't open to him.

If you want a punch bag, a sounding board, just someone to talk to, you know I'm here. Maggie had made it clear he could turn to her, at least as a friend. Yet how could he leave his mum?

'Seb, darling.' He lurched upright as the woman herself appeared in the doorway. Looking pale, older than she had a few days ago, yet bearing the same steely resolve she'd had ever since his dad's first heart attack.

'Shit, mum, did I wake you?'

'You think I can sleep, with my son wearing out the living room carpet?'

Guiltily he halted. 'Sorry.'

'Don't be sorry.' She walked over to him and hugged him tight. 'I'll be okay, you know. I won't fall apart if you go back to living at Sarah's.' She looked him in the eye and smiled. 'Or if you go and visit that woman you're seeing.'

'I'm not.' The lie – or was it a lie? Hell, he wasn't sure any more. Still, it didn't sit easily. So he took his mum's hand and tugged her gently down on the sofa next to him. Then proceeded to tell her all about Maggie, without mentioning her name.

'How do you know she won't want to see you, if you don't ask?' She squeezed his hand. 'You're the child I've always thought was most similar to me. The one who acts first, thinks later. Who lets his heart rule his head. Who dives into things feet first, because where's the fun in creeping in slowly?'

The emotion that had been so close to the surface these last few days threatened to overflow. 'I'm meant to be taking care of you.'

'You think you *aren't* doing that?' She touched his face, her look so full of fondness he almost couldn't breathe. 'You've shifted round your roster so you can help with the funeral arrangements, you've organised Sarah and Alice to be here when you're not. You're staying with me so I won't feel alone, sleeping on a mattress on the floor because the spare room is filled with junk, and the sofa's too small for you.' Her voice caught. 'But you need support, too. And I've a feeling this woman is just the one to help you.' Slowly she rose to her feet. 'Your dad always said the best cure for being unable to sleep was a jot of whisky so I'm going to pour myself a glass and take it to bed.' She smiled gently at him. 'I'll be out like a light until morning.'

Half an hour later, Seb found himself on Maggie's doorstep, his hand hovering over the bell. It was half past ten. Too late to be calling unannounced. Yet this burning need to see her was so acute, so sharp, he'd not dared message first, in case she said no.

Fumbling for his phone, he called her.

'Seb? Are you okay?'

He didn't know how to answer that. Physically he was fine. Emotionally, yeah, emotionally he was like driftwood, tumbling around in the stormy sea.

'Seb?'

'I'm...' Crap. He cleared his throat and started again. 'I'm on your doorstep.'

Silence.

His heart jumped into his throat and Seb slumped against the wall, feeling the bite of the December cold. 'It's okay,' he spoke into the phone. 'You don't need to let me in. I know it's late, and I—'

He nearly jumped out of his skin as the door opened. Maggie stood there dressed in an oversized fluffy dressing gown, her grey eyes giving him a quiet assessment. Then she held out her hand.

Wordlessly he took it, drowning in so much emotion he felt incapable of speech.

'Do you want a drink?' she asked as she closed the door behind him.

He shook his head.

'To talk?'

Again he shook his head. Christ, this was such a bad idea. He didn't know what he wanted, except to quieten his churning, tortured thoughts.

Eyes brimming with compassion, she kissed him gently on the mouth. 'Come with me.'

She led him up the stairs, and into her bedroom. Turning off the light, she slipped his coat off, then set about undoing his jeans. It wasn't sexual, more the deft movements of a woman who knew what he needed, even though he was unable to express it. When he wore only his boxers and T-shirt, she pointed to the bed. 'Lie down next to me.'

They both slipped under the duvet, and Maggie put her arms around him, bringing his head to her chest. It felt so right, like for the first time in days he had a chance to breathe, yet something niggled.

'If I'm here because you feel sorry for me—'

'You're not.' She brought her hands to his face, angling it so he was forced to look at her. 'God, Seb, I care for you, I ache for you and what you're going through. You're here because I want to help.' She bent to kiss him. 'Let them out,' she whispered. 'All those thoughts that are driving you crazy, let them out, so you can start to heal.'

'I can't.' God knows, he'd tried to talk to Sarah, but one look at her grief-stricken face, her sorrow-filled eyes, and he'd known he couldn't say what was on his mind.

'You can with me,' she said quietly. 'I'm not going to judge you. Whatever you have to say, I've said worse about my own father.'

Whether it was that, or the way her hand stroked a soothing pattern up and down his arm, he wasn't sure, but the floodgates opened.

'I'm so angry at him.' Ashamed, he rolled away from her, onto his back. 'I know that sounds terrible, but I can't believe he went and died on me before I'd made peace with him. The last conversation we had was about the blasted dance competition, for God's sake. He had a go at me for not promoting it properly.' Tears stung his eyes and Seb squeezed them away. No fucking way was he crying in front of this woman who was always so together. Except around her ex.

'I expect he enjoyed sharing his wisdom.' Maggie smiled. 'There's nothing parents like more than imparting knowledge. Just ask Penny. I drive her mad.'

He could see that, but there was more than the petty annoyance of a dad who thought he knew best. As Seb stared into her still grey eyes, he screwed up his courage and spoke the words he'd never dared utter. 'I never made him proud, Mags.' His breath caught on a sob. 'I was never what he wanted.'

That was it. Try as he might, he couldn't stop the damn tears rolling down his cheeks. Embarrassed, he turned away, but she wrapped her arms around him and drew him back to her.

Then she kissed him. Not a chaste kiss, or a sympathy kiss, but a proper kiss. One that stirred his blood, that reached inside him and curled around his heart. In seconds they'd shed their clothes and as he rolled on top of her, her arms clutching his shoulders, her legs wrapped around him, as he slid into her heat, enveloped by her, his mind finally cleared of everything but the feel of this incredible woman.

Chapter Twenty-One

M aggie woke to a note on her pillow.

Sorry, had to go, wanted to be at Mum's when she woke. I'll phone. And thanks. You helped more than you can know. S xxx

She'd never known a man allow himself to appear as vulnerable as Seb had yesterday. Her experience with Paul, with the boyfriend before him, with her patients, was that men kept their emotions tightly guarded. Heaven forbid they show a weakness. Such macho bullshit because, as women knew, talking, letting your innermost feelings out, was important. The way Seb had opened up to her, the way he'd talked long into the night, had revealed a maturity, a self-awareness and, yes, a strength she'd not given him credit for, before now.

Why had she worried about this age gap, when it wasn't the date on the birth certificate that counted? It was the age a person acted. The way Seb was handling his grief, supporting his mother – they were the actions of a mature, well-adjusted man. And the more Maggie saw of this man, the more she found to like and admire.

It was why, when Alice came to pick Edward and Rebecca up later that day, Maggie invited her friend in. 'Would you come and have a quick drink with me? I'd like to talk.'

Alice raised an eyebrow, but followed her in and waited patiently while Maggie poured the tea. Glancing at the kids, who were settled on the orange sofa watching TV, she led Alice to the sitting room.

'Seb and I… We…' She inhaled a deep breath, grasping at the words she'd rehearsed but now remained stubbornly out of reach. 'He was here last night.'

Alice's expression gave nothing away. 'When you say last night, you mean last evening, or—'

'Last night. All night.' Heat scalded her cheeks. 'Damn it, Alice, you know what I mean.'

She nodded, taking a sip of her tea. 'How was he?'

Maggie couldn't contain her surprise at the question. 'That's what you're interested in? You don't want to know what he was doing here?'

Alice waved her hand dismissively. 'Oh, we'll get to all that, but for now.' She frowned, a cloud crossing her face. 'We're all taking Dad's death hard, but Seb seems to be struggling with more than plain grief. Don't get me wrong, he's been a bloody rock, planning funerals and sorting Dad's things out with Mum during the day, then working at the centre in the evening. Sarah and I, we tried to help, but he said his work was more flexible than ours, and because it suited us, we selfishly agreed.' She bit into her lip. 'But that doesn't mean we're right to burden him with it all, and I'm worried how tired he's looking. How those bright blue eyes seem dimmer now.'

Maggie chose her words as carefully. 'I think Seb's taking it so hard because he feels things were unresolved between them. He didn't get to say the things he wanted to say to his dad.' She paused. 'Or hear the things he would have liked to hear.'

Alice looked at her long and hard. 'Does it make me a bitch that I'm pissed off my brother has confided in you and not me?'

'It makes you human.' Maggie found she couldn't hold her friend's gaze. This was what she'd been afraid of. And if it came to having to choose between keeping her friends and exploring this thing she'd started with Seb? She really didn't know which way she'd fall, which was terrifying because her friends were permanent. They'd been there before Seb, they'd be there long after he'd gone. Seb was a temporary madness.

Alice sighed, putting down her mug. 'I suspect I know what the issue is with Seb. Dad's always been so bloody hard on him. He thought Seb was drifting, wasting his life by travelling. He couldn't understand him, because he's so different from how Dad was, and how me and Sarah are. Seb's not driven. He doesn't plan life out, isn't organised, everything is always last minute.'

Maggie shot her a look. 'Is this your unsubtle way of warning me off?'

'No.' Alice gave her a wry smile. 'It's my unsubtle way of saying I wouldn't have put you and Seb together. He's so different from Paul.'

'You think I'm looking for a repeat of my last disastrous relationship?'

'Oh God.' Alice briefly put her head in her hands. 'You're right, and I'm totally bollocksing this up.' She sighed before lifting her eyes to Maggie's. 'Just be careful, yeah? You're both very special to me. I don't want either of you getting hurt.'

'I know.' Maggie hesitated, then decided to take a leaf out of Seb's book and open up to her friend. 'Everything you say is true, but the thing is, when I'm with Seb I don't feel like me. I feel like a *better* me. A less rigid version. A week or so ago I got drunk on a school night. Last Sunday, when the girls were out with Paul, I didn't do the laundry, didn't clean the house, as per my usual routine. You know what I did? I had sex. Glorious, mind-blowing, life-affirming sex. And more than once.'

Alice groaned. 'I'm not sure I want to hear about how good sex is with my brother.'

'Sorry.' But Maggie couldn't contain her smile. 'Really though? I'm not sorry, not in the slightest.' She leant over and patted Alice's hand. 'Everything you say, I've already said to myself, but this pull I feel towards Seb, this attraction? I've tried to tuck it neatly into a box and ignore it, but I can't. I'm fed up with being responsible Maggie, sensible Maggie. For once in my life, I want to be a little bit crazy, *do* something a little bit crazy, with a man who makes me feel good about myself. For however long it might last.' *And no matter how much it might hurt afterwards.*

'Okay.' Alice gave a decisive nod of her head. 'Then I'm going to cheer you on, and hope it works out.'

'Just to be clear, I know there's no future to this.' Funny how her heart twisted, just a little, at the words. 'That crazy I talked about doesn't extend to imaging Seb and I will walk off into some amazing sunset together. I just want to enjoy life again, with a man who makes me weak at the knees. I don't know what he's getting out of this, I really don't—'

'He's getting you.' Alice rose to her feet, and when Maggie stood up too, Alice hugged her. 'Paul's knocked your confidence, and if I get to see him again I owe him a knee in the balls. Seb can see you for who you are, and trust me, if he thinks you're worth chasing, you really are.'

Maggie swallowed, wrapping her arms around Alice just that little bit tighter. 'So, we're good?'

Alice pressed a hand to her cheek. 'We're good. Just don't crush his gentle heart. And be careful with your own.'

———————————

Three days before Christmas and here he was, watching his dad's coffin slip past the curtains in the crematorium, into the ruddy great furnace... Seb shuddered and gripped his mum's hand tighter.

As she began to cry he drew her to him, his heart heavy,

aching. People began to file out, casting them sympathetic glances, and Seb tried to smile his thanks.

That was when he caught Maggie's eye. Dressed in a simple black trouser suit, her skin looked pale, and those eyes, God, the compassion in them nearly tore him in two. For a few blessed moments he held her gaze, feeling a measure of calm for the first time since he'd left her bed the other night. Then someone walked in front of her, and the connection was broken. Immediately his heart was left beating painfully, his mind agitated once more.

'Come on, Mum.' He nodded behind her, where Alice was pushing his niece and nephew none too subtly off the hard wooden benches and up the aisle. 'Alice is in full sergeant major mode. If we don't get to the pub in twenty minutes, and then don't eat at least twice as much as we want to, she'll hunt us down.'

His mum elbowed him. 'Don't you be disrespectful to your sister.'

'Hey, I'm just telling the truth.'

Sarah appeared at his side. 'I'll take Mum to the pub. I think there's someone who'd like to see you.' She looked pointedly over to Maggie, who was hovering near the front door to the small chapel.

His mum caught the direction of Sarah's gaze, and blinked. 'It's Maggie? The woman you've been dancing with, the one you bought the car for? The one you went to see the other night?'

Sarah coughed. 'I'm not sure this is a suitable conversation for a crematorium.'

'Nonsense. Your dad was always interested in Seb's dalliances.'

'*Dalliances*? Christ.' Seb winced and briefly looked heavenwards. 'Sorry. But who uses words like that?'

'What would you prefer I used? Affairs? Sexual exploits?' Ignoring his grumbles, his mum glanced back at Maggie. 'Well, she's a lovely lass, so get yourself over there and say hello. I'll defend you against Alice should the need arise.'

The three of them shared a smile. A brief but much-needed touch of light, after a week that had been filled with so much dark.

Not needing to be told twice, Seb strode towards Maggie, his haste no doubt not fitting for the occasion, but his body unable to put on the necessary restraint.

'Hey.' The moment he reached her, he took her hand and tugged her outside with him. 'Did you bring your car?'

'Yes.' He caught sight of the BMW and began to lead her towards it, uncaring how it looked, the son dashing off with one of the mourners. He only knew he needed a dose of her; her serenity, her kindness, the unique way she had of making him feel like he could do anything, be anything.

He opened the driver's door for her, walked around the bonnet and climbed into the passenger's seat. The moment she was settled, he leant across and pressed his lips against hers. 'You have no idea how much I've needed this,' he whispered in between long, drugging kisses on her mouth and light, worshipful kisses on her cheeks, her forehead, the tip of her nose. 'How much I've missed you.'

Eventually Maggie drew back, placing a hand on either side of his face and searching his eyes. 'You look tired. How are you doing?'

It was the first time he'd been asked that since his dad had died. Everyone was so focused on his mum, which was absolutely right, but he couldn't explain how much it meant that she cared enough to ask. 'I'm okay.' He put his hands over hers and drew in a breath, letting it out slowly before replying. 'Our talk helped, and Alice has taken it on herself to be a kind of cheerleader for me, regularly dropping things into the conversation like 'Remember that time dad was so puffed up with pride when Seb won the school sports prize.' His eyes found hers. 'Something tells me I have you to thank for that.'

'I told her we're, well, that you'd come over to mine, and—'

'Please don't tell me you discussed sex with my sister.'

Maggie smiled. 'Not the specifics, no.' Her pale cheeks turned pink. 'Just that we've been… intimate.'

For the first time in days, he felt laughter bubble. 'God, I love your careful speech, Mags.' He rested his forehead against hers and inhaled, letting the smell of her, the touch, her innate strength, ground him. 'I can't wait to be intimate with you again.'

'Me too.'

Her words were no more than a whisper, but the promise they held, the knowledge that he had that to look forward to, had *her* to look forward to… it would get him through the next few days. So would this, he thought as his mouth found hers once more, driving them both wild for a few delicious minutes before he reluctantly drew back, giving her a wry smile. 'Making out in a crematorium car park is probably frowned on.'

Her answering smile held a touch of mischief. 'I didn't know your dad that well, but I think he'd approve.'

Seb laughed quietly, locking small details of her face – the freckles he'd missed, the small dimple in her chin – into his memory bank. 'He would have approved of you, that's for sure.' Seb could almost hear his dad's voice. *Smart woman like that? She'll not be interested in you until you sort yourself out.*

But she's here with me now, Pops.

'Are you coming to the pub? Help us eat some of the food mountain Alison ordered?'

Maggie shook her head. 'Sorry, I can't. I've got a full patient load this afternoon.'

'Hey, don't apologise. We appreciate you coming to the service.' Sighing, he took hold of her hand. 'I guess, with Christmas round the corner, this is goodbye for a while.' He hesitated, aware it had its faults, but needing to at least try. 'Unless... I don't suppose you and the girls fancy spending some time with us Armstrongs?'

She bit into her lip, then shook her head. 'You need to be with your family, and I need to spend some time with mine.' Her gaze strayed outside. 'The girls don't see much of my parents – their choice, not ours – but this is at least one time of year they make the effort. And my sister Emily always goes, so I have her company to look forward to.'

Disappointment settled heavy in his gut. 'When will you be home again?'

'I'm back at work on the Tuesday.'

'And that's the week I'm doing evening shifts.' He ran a hand down her cheek, savouring her while he could. 'Any chance we can meet for a rumba rehearsal early in the New Year?'

Her cheek lifted as she smiled. 'I'd like that.'

'Okay then, I'll be in touch. Happy Christmas, Mags.'

She caught his hand and squeezed his fingers. 'Happy Christmas, Seb.'

Chapter Twenty-Two

It turned out that a week during which she saw Seb and a week when she didn't were totally different time frames. The second felt about ten times slower than the first. Maybe it wasn't Seb, maybe it was just that the time at her parents over Christmas had dragged more than usual. Or that the post-Christmas rush of patients had been harder work.

Or that while Alice and Sarah had taken the news of her dating their brother in their stride, Hannah had been subdued when she'd told her. 'I guess I shouldn't be surprised. The way he looks at you, the way he carried you from the car that night. I knew then he wanted to kiss you. It's just...' She'd trailed off, sighing. 'I was kind of hoping he'd want to kiss me.'

Maggie hadn't known what to say. The word sorry had been on the tip of her tongue, but she'd swallowed it down because saying it would have been a lie. She wasn't sorry. She was wary, a little anxious, but she was also a woman with, it was time to admit, no longer a small crush but a great big fat one. It was the only way to explain why she'd spent the last fortnight with her hand glued to her phone, and why her heart had bounced every time it had vibrated with a text.

Some of them had made her smile.

Alice must have brought an ostrich, not a turkey. S xxx

We hid Sarah's laptop. She's threatening to put my balls in a vice if I don't tell her where it is. I told her you'd be cross. S xxx

At least I hope you would be. S xxx

Some of them brought a lump to her throat.

Lying in bed and wishing you were next to me. S xxx

Hope that doesn't sound too sappy? Or too much? S xxx

But I miss you, Mags. S xxx

Apparently another thing she'd found out this Christmas holiday was that being thirty-seven – and crap, another week and she'd be thirty-eight – still, being old enough to know better, didn't stop a woman from re-

reading all the texts she'd received, whenever she got the chance.

Probably she didn't need to actually read them now; they were burnt into her memory.

Penny put her toothbrush carefully into the holder. 'What time is Seb here?'

'Yeah, I ummmmmmmm.' Tabby spoke around a mouthful of toothbrush, rivers of frothy toothpaste flooding down her chin.

Maggie tapped her on the nose. 'Sorry?'

Tabby gave her a toothpasty grin. 'I want to see him.'

'You can both see him, and dance with him. Then it's bedtime.'

Tabby pouted. 'It's not a school night.'

'No, but you're seven and nine. You both need your sleep or you're cranky in the morning.' *And I need some time with Seb alone, or I'll be cranky, too.*

Seb arrived fifteen minutes later than advertised, and just late enough for the girls to have wound her and each other up to a fever pitch.

'Me first, me first,' Tabby yelled the moment Maggie opened the door.

'That's not fair. I'm the one having lessons with Seb,' Penny protested. 'You just butted in.'

Maggie raised her eyes to Seb, wishing she could hug him, kiss him, but happy just to see him. He was losing his tan but his eyes were still a vivid blue, his hair still too long, and the casual confidence that was so much a part of him flowed through his lean, athletic body.

God help her, his smile still totally undid her.

'Whoa, girls, let's start this again.' After one last, lingering look at her, he raised his hand for Penny to high-five him. 'Hello, Penelope, how are you? Did you have a good Christmas?'

She rolled her eyes, but gave him a sweet smile. 'Yes, thanks.'

'Excellent.' Then he turned to Tabby for another high five. 'And Tabs, how about you? Are you well?'

Tabby giggled. 'Umm, yes?'

'Well enough to go and help your sister get me a drink of water while I say hello to your mum?'

She huffed, putting her hands on her hips. 'I guess.'

As the pair of them charged down the hall, Maggie turned to Seb. 'Thirsty work is it, driving?'

He laughed, beckoning her towards him. 'Come here. I reckon I've bought myself two minutes.'

Feeling giddy, she took a step, he took a step. Then his mouth crashed onto hers, his arms wrapped around her, and Maggie felt her whole body go boneless.

'I forgot how sexy you smell.' His tongue darted between her lips. 'How sweet you taste.' His hand smoothed down her spine, and over her bum. 'How amazing you feel.'

On a groan, he stepped back, his eyes seeming to make the same inventory as hers. Then he smiled. 'How are you, Mags?'

She laughed, wanting to tell him she felt a lot better now she'd seen him, but stopping just before she did because it felt too much. They'd slept together twice, agreed to go out. Small steps were needed. Not a mad, heedless dash. 'I'm sorry about the girls, they're excited to dance with you.'

'And you?' His eyes turned darker, his lips curved. 'Are you excited to dance with me?'

'I'm excited to dance.' When his expression fell, she added. 'And with your oily hips.'

'You mean these?' He strutted down the hallway, rotating his hips from side to side in a totally over-the-top impression of the rumba progressive walk. 'Greasy enough for you?'

It was hard to focus on small steps, to remember to be cautious, when you were with a man who could make you laugh. And when that man was so good with your daughters.

As Maggie watched Seb patiently teach Tabby and Penny the waltz box steps a short while later, she wondered if Paul would ever really know what he was missing out on. He was at least making more of an effort now. He'd phoned them on Christmas Day, and come to see them last Sunday bearing presents she knew Isabelle had chosen. A sweet fluffy bunny for Tabby, which she'd said thank you for and promptly thrown onto the sofa, never to be touched again. A Barbie doll for Penny, who'd smiled politely, and afterwards asked Maggie if she could take it back and get a science set.

'Mum.'

Maggie gave a start. 'Sorry, I was miles away.'

'Watch what I learned.'

Tabby proceeded to take Seb's hand, and do a faltering but perfectly correct box step with him. 'That's amazing, Tabby.'

Seb ruffled her daughter's hair. 'It'll be easier in a few years, when she's not so much of a short-arse.'

Maggie knew the moment he was aware of what he'd said, because his gaze shot to hers. She also knew her smile must have frozen on her face, because he briefly closed his eyes, his shoulders rising and falling as he sighed.

As Seb waited on the Jaffa orange sofa for Maggie to come back down after saying goodnight to the girls, he wondered if it usually took this long to settle them. Or if she was hiding from him.

It's not as if he'd meant anything by his casual remark. He hadn't been sending her a coded message: *this isn't just a fling, I see us still together when Tabby's a foot taller.*

Yet for the first time in his life, the thought of planning that far ahead didn't send him into a panic. In fact, the more he tested it out, the more he tried to imagine still living here, still seeing Maggie next year, the more comfortably the idea sat with him. From the way she'd reacted, certainly more comfortably than it had for her.

He caught a movement out of the corner of his eye, and turned to find her walking quietly towards him. 'That took a while.'

Had there been an edge to his words? Maybe, because

she stared at him a moment, as if trying to puzzle him out, before she spoke. 'They didn't want to go to bed. They wanted to watch us practice.'

And now he felt like a git. Giving her a sheepish smile, he stood and walked towards her. 'Ah. Sorry.' He ran his hand down her arms, then took hold of her hands. 'I thought maybe you were avoiding me.'

'Because?'

'You know why.' He heaved out a sigh. 'It was a throwaway comment, Mags. Not a marriage proposal.'

It was definitely the wrong thing to say, because she snatched her hands away from his. 'I know that.'

'Then why did you look so panic-stricken?'

'Because I don't want the girls to get the wrong idea.' Her eyes, usually so tranquil, snapped back at him. 'I don't want them to have another man in their life they think is permanent, only to find he buggers off.'

And now he didn't just feel like a git, he felt like a total douchebag. 'Okay, sorry.' Tension filled the air between them, and Seb felt his evening slowly unravelling. 'Do you still want to practice? Or do you want me to go?'

She walked into the kitchen and pulled a bottle of wine from the fridge, followed by two glasses. 'I want to have a glass of wine.' Her gaze finally found his. 'And then I want to rumba.'

Relief flowed through him and he followed her into the kitchen, perching on a bar stool. 'Okay then.' He nodded when she pointed to the glass. 'Just a small one.' When she'd poured, he picked up his glass. 'What are we drinking to?'

She pursed her lips. 'Active hips and tight frames.'

He touched his glass to hers. 'And lots of flirting.'

He received a small, but yes, decidedly flirty smile.

Two hours later, he couldn't say his hip movements were any smoother, but he could say he'd felt every bit of the steamy intimacy, the sexual chemistry, the rumba was all about. The tease of her body as it wrapped around his, the glancing yet utterly erotic press of her buttocks against his groin... the warmth of her skin against his hands, those rhythmic, sensual movements she was so frigging amazing at. Christ, it was two hours of foreplay and the thought of leaving the evening there, of going home to his empty bed, was killing him.

Tugging her hand, he eased her down onto the sofa next to him. 'Are you working tomorrow?'

'Yes. Hannah's coming round at eight.'

With any other woman he wouldn't be this hesitant, he realised. Then again, the answer had never mattered so much. 'Can I stay tonight?' He picked up her hand, holding it against his chest where his heart pumped loud and fast. 'I promise to be gone before Hannah arrives.'

Her body stilled, and he swore he could see the cogs of her mind working out how to let him down gently. 'It's not that, not so much. And it isn't that I don't want you to.' She raised her eyes to his, and he could see how conflicted she felt. 'It just doesn't feel right, not with the girls here. Not when this is so new between us. And before you say it, I know you stayed the other night, but…'

'That wasn't planned,' he finished for her when she trailed off, remembering how lost with grief he'd been, and how generously she'd taken him in. Inhaling a deep breath, he planted a kiss against her hair. 'I understand.' And he did, it's just his body was taking a while to catch up. 'What about if we kiss for a while? You can boot me out as soon as you get bored.'

She laughed, which was a flaming relief because if kissing him really did bore her, he might as well quit now and become a monk.

As she snuggled against him, he began to plant a leisurely pattern of kisses all over her face, before finally touching her mouth with his. And that's when the concept of leisurely got blown out of the water. He *loved* to kiss, he could do it for hours with the right person, and Maggie was most definitely the right person. But settling for kissing after two hours of rumba foreplay… it was bloody hard. And yes, he meant that in every way possible.

Groaning, he shifted so she was on top of him, arranging them so her core rubbed against the part of him that ached and throbbed.

'I want… I need…' She wriggled over him, sending his blood to boiling point.

'What?' he gasped, wondering how far he was from totally embarrassing himself.

'I need more.'

Eyeing up the throw, he dragged it over them. Just in

case young eyes wandered downstairs. Then he trailed his hand down to the zipper of her jeans. 'I can give you more.' She moaned as his fingers found her heat and then, before he knew what was happening, her hands were diving into his boxers. 'Christ, Mags, if you touch me I'm going to go off like a rocket.'

Her laughter was muffled against his neck. 'There you go with the fireworks analogy again.'

He couldn't reply, because he was seeing stars in front of his eyes. Moments later, they both moaned together, finding their release.

'I've not done that since I was seventeen,' he told her once his breathing was under control enough to actually talk.

She reached up to kiss his cheek. 'I've not done that ever.'

'Not made out on a sofa?' he asked incredulously.

'Oh, I've done that. Just not, you know.'

'Finished with a happy ending?'

She let out a strangled laugh and curled up tighter against him. 'We must do that again sometime.'

'Well, give me ten minutes.' When she rolled her eyes, he gave her a cocky smile. 'Hey, recovery time is just one of the benefits of going out with a younger man.'

He felt her smile against his skin. 'And the other benefits?'

Ah. Now his cockiness looked woefully misplaced. He couldn't offer her fancy gifts, luxury weekends away, expensive restaurants. Maybe Maggie didn't want any of that, but she deserved it. Deserved far more than he could offer. 'I'm still working on that.'

He didn't know whether she'd heard his reply, because when he checked on her, he found her eyes closed, and her breathing rhythmic. Kissing the top of her head, he tightened his arms around her. He'd carry her up to bed, but not just yet. For now, he needed to hold her for a while.

Chapter Twenty-Three

It was the first Saturday of the New Year, and they'd woken to a blanket of fresh white snow. The girls were beside themselves, but all Maggie could think was how much more difficult the grocery shop was going to be. With the hectic pace at work, and the way days seemed to blur between Christmas and New Year, she'd somehow managed to miss the slot for doing her usual online order.

And okay, maybe seeing Seb again had helped to blur the days too.

Fact was, she had no food in the house.

'Sorry girls, we're going to have to go to the supermarket.'

Their faces fell. 'Can't we build a snowman?'

'Maybe later, but we need to get Penny a new pair of school shoes too. You start back next week.'

The doorbell rang as they were putting on their coats.

Distractedly, Maggie went to answer it, only to find Seb on the doorstep, grinning widely.

'Hey.' His eyes ran up and down her big puffy jacket, and her woolly hat. 'That's a good look on you.'

Her insides fluttered, not so much at the words – he had to be kidding – but the hungry way he looked at her. 'And that's flattery gone mad.'

He shook his head, eyes flirting. 'It's true a bin liner would look good on you, but seriously, I like the hat. It also happens to be perfect for what I had in mind.'

'Oh?'

The girls came to the door, and Tabby lost no time in opening her mouth. 'Hi Seb, it's snowing but we have to get food.'

'What, and miss all this amazing tobogganing material?'

Tabby's eyes rounded, but it was Penny who spoke, her voice filled with awe. 'Are you going tobogganing?'

He waved towards his car, and it was only then Maggie realised there were two wooden toboggans strapped precariously onto the roof. 'No, Penny, *we're* going tobogganing.'

'Bogganing, yay!' Tabby squealed.

They all looked so happy about the prospect, and Maggie wanted to join in, but all she could see was an empty fridge. Penny cramming her feet into shoes that had split the last day of term.

'Sorry, but we can't go today. We need to buy food and a pair of school shoes for Penny.' The girls gave her a look laden with disappointment and edged with annoyance. Immediately Maggie had a flashback to her childhood. Emily giving her the same dark look when she'd told her she couldn't go to the party their parents had banned her from, just before they'd buggered off, leaving Maggie to 'watch her sister'.

Seb, blonde hair trailing beneath the beanie on his head, eyes a vivid blue against the white backdrop, flashed her one of his lazy smiles. 'Come on, Mags, food and shoes can be bought any time. How many days can we dust off the toboggans in this country?' He turned to Penny. 'What do you reckon? Tobogganing or buying a pair of school shoes?'

'I've never been tobogganing,' Penny stated quietly.

Maggie felt a dart of shame. Nine years old and her parents had never found the time to take her tobogganing? Yet it was easy for Seb to turn up and promise fun. She had practical issues to sort out. 'Girls, go back inside for a minute please. I want to talk to Seb alone.'

Their shoulders drooped as they trudged back down the hallway, and Maggie's guilt turned to anger. 'Sorry, but you can't just turn up like this, Seb.' She waved at the toboggans on the roof rack. 'Why didn't you phone me first? We have plans, things we need to do.'

'I wanted to surprise you.' His eyes skimmed her face, and she could read every ounce of the disappointment he felt. 'I thought the girls would enjoy it.' He sighed, shifting on his feet. 'I thought we all would.'

Oh God, when he said it like that, when he looked at her like that – the cocker spaniel pup who didn't know what it had done wrong – the gap between them seemed like a chasm. Not just age, but *outlook*. 'It would have been fun, if you'd phoned first, if we'd planned it around the things I need to do today.' She looked him straight in the eye. 'If you hadn't put Penny on the spot like that, but talked to me, instead.'

His shoulders fell, and the wounded look in his eyes intensified. Dragging the beanie off his head, he sighed. 'I guess I didn't think. I saw the snow, and wanted to enjoy it with you.' Nodding, he took a step back. 'No worries. Say sorry to the girls.' Another step away. 'I'll see you soon.'

He half jogged back to his car, despite the snow which surely most adults would be cautious about slipping on. And he didn't look back at her once he'd opened the door, just ducked straight inside.

Her heart felt heavy as she closed the front door. She'd upset him, yet he'd upset her, too. This is what happened when you had two people with vastly different views on life. Paul, for all his faults, had never sprung anything on her.

Then again, he'd never said things like *I wanted to surprise you* or *I wanted to enjoy the day with you*.

Tears welled in her eyes as she recalled Seb's sweet words. They started to overflow when she thought of him racing around this morning, finding the toboggans and then strapping them to the roof of his car. Turning up to her house all excited and eager to see them, heck, to *please* them.

A band tightened around her chest, and Maggie sagged against the wall. Her girls were disappointed, Seb was hurt, and for what? Because she wasn't prepared to be flexible?

She hung her head, wiping her wet cheeks with the back of her hand. Sometimes she *was* every mean, angry word Paul had thrown at her: controlling, boring, irritating. It was beyond galling to have to admit it. And it was damn well going to change.

Seb cursed as he parked back outside Alice's house and turned off the engine. What a way to spend a morning. Wake to find snow – fan-bloody-tastic. Knock on his mum's bedroom door – yes, somehow he'd become a twenty-seven-year-old living with his mum – to locate their old toboggans, only to be told she'd given them to one of his sisters, she couldn't remember who. Drive to Sarah's, only to find that Alice had them. Annoy Alice by forcing her out of bed too early on a Saturday – her words – to try and find said toboggans in amongst the absolute shite that filled her garage.

'I know, I know. We'll clear it out one day.' A gleam had entered her eyes. 'I don't suppose you'd fancy doing it in exchange for the loan of the toboggans?'

He'd looked at her scathingly. 'You're proposing to effectively charge me for giving Tabby and Penny a go on *our* toboggans?'

She'd grumbled something along the lines of him not playing fair, and using the girls to win brownie points with the mother, at which point he'd had to shut her up.

'I'm not just doing this for the girls, you dummy. I'm doing it for Maggie. She'll love it.'

Only it turns out Maggie didn't love it, or if she did, she didn't love the way he'd gone about it.

And now he had two toboggans and nobody to enjoy them with.

When he knocked on Alice's door, she answered still in her pyjamas.

'I'm making myself a coffee because apparently I'm awake now, thanks to some pain in the arse who woke me up at stupid o'clock on a Saturday.' She narrowed her eyes at him. 'What are you doing back here. Were they out?'

'Nope.' He stepped inside, threw his hat onto the hook and peeled off his coat.

It might have been his tone, or what she read on his face, which apparently he'd never been able to really mask. Either way, her expression turned from griping to concerned. 'She didn't want to go?'

He sloped into the kitchen, dragged out a bar stool and slid onto it. 'She didn't like being surprised.'

'Ah.' Alice winced, sitting down opposite him. 'You didn't message her first?' She shook her head. 'Of course you didn't, because you're a single guy who does what he likes, when he likes.'

He wanted to say that was unfair, but for too much of his life it had been true. 'I ballsed up.'

She smiled sympathetically at him. 'We all do that from time to time, even me. Thankfully you'll discover Maggie is very forgiving.'

'If we're to stand a chance, she'll have to be.'

'This thing between you, is it getting serious?'

He was at a loss to verbalise his muddled thoughts. 'We've only been together a few weeks, and most of that we spent apart over Christmas, so no, I wouldn't say it's serious.' He shuffled on the chair, something not right about what he'd just said. 'Do I think it could become serious? Well, put it this way, it's been weeks since I went online, researching flights to Oz, or places I might want to go to next.' He shrugged. 'Could be because I don't want to leave you guys and Mum yet.'

'Or it could be because you don't want to leave Maggie.'

He was saved a reply, when his phone beeped with a message.

Apparently shoe shops open on Sundays. Groceries I've ordered online. Just need to get essentials to last us till they come. Could do that on the way back from whatever hill you've earmarked us to hurtle down. M xx

As a huge smile split his face, he received another message.

The hurtle was a joke. M xx

And then as he started to laugh, a final message.

At least I hope it was. M xx

'Something tells me you might be taking those ruddy death-traps out after all.'

Seb glanced up to find his sister smiling at him. 'Yep, looks like I am.'

'Well, I'm glad I didn't get woken at dawn for nothing then.'

Feeling like he'd just navigated a precarious ledge, Seb bent and gave Alice a smacker of a kiss on her cheek. 'It was eight thirty, sis. Doesn't the early bird catch the fat, juicy worm?'

'Go and take your too happy arse out of here and back to where it's appreciated.'

'You think she likes my arse?'

Alice gave it a stinging slap. 'Out of here. Let me enjoy my Saturday morning, my long Saturday morning, in peace.'

The girls loved haring down the slope every bit as much as he'd hoped.

And if he wasn't mistaken, there was an extra sparkle in their mother's clear grey eyes.

So far they'd tried most combinations: Seb with Penny, Seb with Tabby, Maggie with Penny, Maggie with Tabby.

Now, standing at the top of the gentle slope, Seb wound an arm around Maggie's waist and whispered in her ear. 'Are you ready to go down with me?'

She looked up at him. 'You did say with you, yes?'

He chuckled, kissing her nose. 'Surrounded by all this pure white snow, and your mind is in the gutter? Shame on you.'

'It isn't usually,' she muttered. 'You must be having a bad effect on me.'

He stilled, unconsciously holding his breath. 'Does this bad effect extend to forcing you to adjust your well-ordered plans?'

Her body rose and fell as she sighed, her eyes on Tabby and Penny as they threw snow at each other. 'I was a nightmare this morning. I'm sorry.'

His body relaxed in relief. 'No, I should have phoned you first. Next time I will.' He turned so she had to look at him. 'I'm going to balls up from time to time, Mags. I've not too much experience with relationships, and none where the lady was a mum. It's unchartered territory for me.'

Her breath came out in a soft exhale, and her hand reached to touch his cheek, the intimate gesture causing an unexpected pressure on his chest. 'I love that you wanted to surprise me. In fact that's kind of new for me too, but... I find it hard to be spontaneous. I make plans and then follow them through. It's what I do.'

It's what you've always had to do. He kept the words to himself, unwilling to upset the moment. 'I act spontaneously, as the mood takes me.' He tightened his arm around her. 'It doesn't mean I can't adjust, learn to think before I jump.'

Her head shifted, burying into his shoulder. 'And vice versa.'

He smiled against her head. 'Did we just navigate through our first argument?'

'It would seem so.'

They stood in a comfortable silence, her body nestled warm against his as they watched Tabby and Penny. He felt content, he realised with a shock. It was a word he used to sneer at, seeing it as a polite word for boring; used to describe people who were settled, stuck in a rut. Yet here on this hill, surrounded by sparkling white snow, his arms wrapped around Maggie, her girls laughing in front of them… here, content didn't feel like something to be sneered at. It felt like something to aspire to.

Chapter Twenty-Four

Maggie was in a flap. It was a day, just like any other day.

Yet it was also a day when she became another step closer to being forty. She was only two years away from it now. Closer to forty than to thirty-five.

And she was dating a man who wasn't even close to thirty yet.

Part of her wanted to whoop because hey, how flaming cool did that make her, being wanted by a younger man?

Yet it also scared her to death, because this younger man she was dating – and yes, she could officially say that – this man was starting to become the best part of her week. God, she was scared to admit how often she counted down the days to when she knew she'd see him again.

'You have to come out tonight.' Alice fixed her with a hard stare as they sat in the café next to the giant soft play area where their kids were currently letting off steam.

'Birthdays don't fall on Saturdays very often. Jack's happy to be in charge of all the kids. Sarah and Hannah are up for a night out.'

'I doubt Hannah is.

Alice eyed her shrewdly. 'Hannah's not invested in Seb, you know. It was more the idea of dating a dishy guy. She's already turned her eyes to someone down at the gym.' She gave Maggie a sly smile. 'So there's no excuse for you not to come out. I'm sure Seb will want to join us, once he's finished his stint at the centre. Unless...' She leaned back, raising her eyes to the ceiling. 'Crap, I'm so dumb. You don't want to come out with us, because you've already planned a cosy birthday celebration with my brother.'

'Umm.' Maggie stared down at her coffee, avoiding Alice's eyes. Around them she could hear the sound of over-excited kids, the chatter of exhausted parents, glad to put up with poor coffee and plastic tables, just to escape their children for a while.

'You have told him it's your birthday?'

A guilty flush stole over her cheeks. 'Why would I tell him that?'

'Because you're dating? Because he'd want to know?'

And that's where the guilt came from. A man who'd wanted to take her tobogganing the moment it snowed would definitely want to help her celebrate her birthday.

'Maggie?'

Drawing in a breath, Maggie raised her eyes to Alice's. 'I'll be thirty-eight, Alice. Your brother is *twenty-seven*. If this wasn't happening to me, I'd be laughing at how cringeworthy it was.'

Alice studied her. 'Has he said anything to suggest he's bothered by the age gap?'

'What? No! He's been...' She briefly closed her eyes. 'He's amazing. We're different.' She laughed. 'We're so different it's not true, but the age gap isn't a problem. Most of the time I'm not even aware of it.'

Alice gave her an understanding smile. 'Until a birthday comes up, and makes you think.'

'Exactly. I mean, what am I *doing*? If you'd told me a year ago I'd be dating a man ten years younger, who spent most the last year living on a pontoon over the Barrier Reef. Who treats life as a giant game, the sole purpose to be enjoyed. Who's only in this country temporarily, and will no doubt leave as soon as the whim takes him.' She shook her head. 'I'm crazy to be doing this.'

Alice reached for her hand. 'I thought you were having fun, Maggie?'

'I am.' Deep in her chest, her heart squeezed. 'I really am.'

'So relax.' Alice toyed with her cup, seeming to think before she spoke, which was rare for her. 'I don't know what Seb's plans are. He came over to help with Dad, and now Dad's gone.' She trailed off, her expression sad. 'Knowing Seb, he'll want to make sure Mum's okay before he goes anywhere though, so I think the word "whim" is a little harsh. Did you know he's still living with her because he doesn't want her to be alone in the house? That's got to be tough, being back in his old bedroom again. Especially as it's now a junk room and he's had to sleep on a mattress on the floor.'

Maggie felt a lump jump into her throat. 'I didn't know that. And you're right to defend him.' She took a sip of the awful coffee. 'When I first met Seb, I thought he was shallow, if I'm honest. I mean he was good-looking, and funny, and lovely with the girls, but he was easy to slot into this box marked "Alice and Sarah's brother".'

'Yeah, our annoying brother.' Alice looked at her quizzically. 'And now?'

Maggie swallowed. 'I realise I was way off the mark. He has this almost child-like exuberance, so it's easy to assume he doesn't feel things deeply.' Yet she'd seen him at his most vulnerable, heard him admit *why* he'd left to go travelling. 'Now I know he's more complex than that. He does feel deeply, does get hurt. And I'm worried neither of us will come out of this affair unscathed.'

'So stop. Nip it in the bud.'

Crushed was the only way Maggie could describe how that made her feel. To not have him to look forward to. No more kissing after dance lessons. No more holding his hand. No more afternoon sex. No more seeing this fun, carefree side of herself she'd forgotten existed. 'I don't think I can.'

Alice's expression softened. 'If it's any consolation, I believe Seb feels the same way.'

Maggie didn't know whether it was a good or bad thing when Penny interrupted them, tugging at her arm. 'Mum,

Tabby's at the top of the monster slide you said not to go on. You have to tell her to get down. It's too high.'

Alarm shot through her and Maggie lurched to her feet and ran behind Penny towards the slide. When she got there though, she found her youngest daughter grinning hugely, legs dangling over the top of the impossibly steep slide. Immediately her mind flashed to Seb, and she wondered if he'd looked just as fearless when he'd been seven.

Ignoring the panic churning her insides, she smiled up at her daughter. 'Do you want to go down?'

Tabby nodded. 'Pleeeeeeeease.'

'Are you sure?'

Tabby didn't hesitate. 'Yes.'

Heart in her mouth, Maggie nodded. Then listened to Tabby's delighted squeals as she zipped down.

It was only later that evening, when Maggie sat in front of the television, the girls having gone out like a light, she realised Alice hadn't raised the subject of going out again. It was a good thing, she told herself. Thirty-eight wasn't a birthday to be celebrated. It was one to let quietly slip by.

Seb dragged the carrier bags out of the boot and locked up the Fiesta, glancing up towards the house. The light was on in the kitchen, which hopefully meant Maggie was still up.

What a bugger he'd had to work late tonight. If he'd known, he could have swapped shifts, he could have... He exhaled heavily. Yeah, if he'd bloody *known*, he'd have done a lot of things.

Juggling the carrier bags, he went to press on the bell, but then froze. Damn it, yet again he was arriving at her house unannounced. Despite his promise after the tobogganing debacle, he'd not thought to message her.

He could message her from the car. Then kill time by driving around for ten minutes.

Satisfied with his plan, he began to head back down the drive.

'Seb?'

Her voice made him jump, and he turned to find her silhouetted in the doorway. 'Hi.' He gave her a bright smile, which must have looked as wild as it felt because she frowned.

'Are you okay? I heard the car pull up, but you seem to be heading in the wrong direction.' She bit down on her lush bottom lip. 'Unless you changed your mind about seeing me?'

'No, God no.' Walking back towards the door, he stepped inside and gave her a sheepish smile. 'Can we start again?' Dropping the bags to the floor, he brought his hands to her face and gave her a kiss. 'Happy Birthday.'

'Ah.' Her eyes searched his. 'You came to wish me happy birthday?'

She still looked confused, and it was hard to blame her. 'I came to cook you a birthday meal, but I was halfway up the drive when I realised I hadn't asked if I could come round, so I was heading back to the car to message you.' He gave her an awkward shrug. 'And then drive around a bit, hoping you'd say yes.'

Her gaze dropped to the bags, and up to him again. 'You're here to *cook* for me?'

And now, noting she was dressed in her pyjamas, a big hoodie over the top of them, he felt even more foolish. 'When Alice told me it was your birthday, it seemed like a good idea.' He trailed his thumb across her mouth, enjoying her sharp intake of breath, and the way her lips parted for him. 'She said you weren't up for going out, but birthdays are milestones in your life, Mags. They need to be celebrated.' He bent to kiss her. Just a brief touch of their lips, but enough to make his heart leap. 'I thought if you didn't want to go out, I could bring the celebration to you. But I had a late shift, and now I realise it's so late you've probably already eaten.'

'Seb, I don't know what to say.' For an awful moment he thought she was going to tell him to go home, but then she reached for his hand. 'I can't believe you've come here,' she waved at the carrier bags, 'with food.'

'Is it *okay* that I'm here?' He thought it was, by the way she clutched at his hand, but he didn't want to make a misstep. Not again.

Her face broke into a beautiful smile. 'Is it okay that a gorgeous hunk of a man has turned up on my doorstep wanting to cook me a birthday meal?' Laughter tumbled out of her. 'God yes, it's more than okay. I was sitting here feeling sorry for myself, wishing I hadn't been such a moody cow and said no to Alice. I couldn't even face eating any of the tea I made the girls.'

Happiness flowed through him. 'Then come and sit in the kitchen and watch me make you a chicken Pad Thai.'

Her eyes widened. 'Good God, who are you?'

He laughed, dropping another kiss on her beautifully soft lips. 'I could keep up the mystique, but when the next meal I make you is also a chicken Pad Thai, and then the one after that, you're going to twig that it's one of the few things I can cook. Courtesy of a five-month stay in Phuket.'

'Next meal.' She smiled. 'I like the sound of that.'

So did he, he thought as he emptied out the contents of the bag and set to work chopping up the chicken. Maggie watched, nursing a glass of wine. She'd poured him one too, and he sipped slowly at it, unsure if he was going to have to drive home.

'Why didn't you want to go out?' he asked once everything was sizzling in the pan. 'Are you usually so reluctant to celebrate your birthday?'

'Not usually, no.' Avoiding his gaze now, she stared down at her wine glass.

'So why this year?' He prompted. When she remained quiet, he stepped to stand in front of her, turning the stool so she faced him, and bending so she had to look at him. 'Mags?'

'I'm thirty-eight.' Her voice caught. 'A few months ago, if you'd asked me if I minded being nearly forty, I'd have told you not to be daft. I've never had a thing about age.'

Finally she met his eyes. 'But that was before I started dating a twenty-seven-year-old.'

'You think it bothers me, how old you are?'

'No, I don't.'

He relaxed his shoulders. 'Good.'

'But I think it should bother me.' She rubbed at her face. 'Paul told me I was embarrassing myself. Worse, that I was embarrassing the girls.' He watched as she swallowed, her voice shaking, ever so slightly. 'While I hate to listen to anything he says, I wonder if he's right.'

Irritated, Seb pulled her to her feet, and then lifted her onto the island so they were eye to eye. 'Are *you* embarrassed to be seen with me?' He couldn't shake off the feeling that this wasn't about his age, but about who he was. And that wasn't a man who wore a suit and drove a BMW.

But she didn't duck from his gaze, and when she answered her voice was firm and steady. 'Of course not.'

'Then why on earth are you paying any attention to a guy who's so stupid he actually let you go?'

For a few humming seconds she didn't say anything. But then a smile broke out across her face. 'I don't know.'

He heaved out a breath, staring into her beautiful clear eyes. 'When did Paul say that to you?'

'The day he came to pick the girls up after we'd…' She trailed off, a slight blush on her cheeks.

'Been intimate?' He teased.

Laughing, she buried her head in his chest. 'I don't

know why I worry about my age. Around you I feel like a blushing schoolgirl again.'

He smiled, thinking back to that day, and to how close he'd felt to her, only to have that ripped away the moment Paul had arrived back on the scene. 'I remember you being distant with me after you'd spoken to him.' He'd been hurt, but also jealous, driving himself crazy with thoughts that seeing Paul had reminded her who she really wanted. 'I thought maybe you were regretting what we'd done.'

'Absolutely not.' Her arms wrapped around his neck, and he edged closer, breathing her in. 'I don't know what this is, where it will take us, but I know that when it's over I will remember it for the rest of my life.'

When it's over? His heart stuttered. Was she already planning an end, when he was starting to see a future? 'I didn't realise we had an expiry date.' He meant it to sound jokey, but he guessed he was feeling too upset to carry it off because her gaze snapped to his.

'I'm not telling you something you don't already know. You're the one who's heading back to Australia.'

'Am I?' He touched his forehead to hers, something shifting in his chest. 'I don't know what I'm doing, Mags.' It was part of his problem, he'd never known. 'But I do know that just because I am casual, you shouldn't assume I can only do casual. At least not with you.' Ignoring the sizzling pan, he stared deep into her eyes. 'I'm falling for you, Mags.'

Instead of pleasure, he saw fear. Worry. 'This is meant to be fun, Seb. Dating doesn't have to be deep and serious,' she repeated his words back to him. 'It can be fun and frivolous.'

He remembered saying it, yet it seemed a million years ago now. Before he'd lost his dad, before he'd started to realise exactly what he'd found in Maggie. Not just a beautiful face, a dry wit and a sharp intellect, all of which absolutely did it for him. There were also the attributes that others didn't always see, because they lay deep beneath her surface. There was her calm, and her strength. Her compassion – he'd never forget the way she'd been there for him in his darkest hour. Then there was the hidden surprise; all that simmering passion she kept so well controlled until she had a few drinks, or lost herself on the dance floor. Or in his arms.

But he was racing ahead, and Maggie was taking small, cautious steps. Of course she was, because unlike him, she'd been here before, and she'd been badly let down. He needed to reel himself in, stop wanting to gallop and enjoy walking for a change. Gently he kissed her. 'Sorry. Fun and frivolous. It's still my specialty.' It was all he'd ever known, all he'd ever wanted, up till now. How ironic that this time he was the one wanting more, and being told no. It was a dose of his own medicine, and it tasted bitter.

Slapping on a smile, he dug out the candles he'd bought, lighting them and placing them on the island. After serving out the meal, he sat opposite her, raising his glass. 'To reaching the grand old age of thirty-eight.'

This time she laughed off the age, as he'd wanted her to, because seriously, what did it matter which year was on your birth certificate? It mattered how a person felt inside, and he wanted to help her feel young and carefree.

'Why aren't you drinking?' she asked a moment later, noting he'd barely touched his wine.

'Because I'm driving.'

'Oh.' Disappointment flooded her expression.

'I don't *have* to drive back tonight,' he added quietly.

The air hummed between them and he watched, heart thumping, as she reached for the wine bottle and filled his glass. 'Then don't.'

Because he needed her to be certain, he pushed. 'Are you sure?'

'It's my birthday.' A hint of mischief entered her eyes. 'I think I should have fabulous sex on my birthday.'

Everything inside him tightened, and he reached for his glass. 'I'll drink to that.'

Chapter Twenty-Five

I t felt as if Seb was determined to prove his boast, that he was the master of fun and frivolous. Yes, they went to dance lessons every Wednesday, and yes, when he came over to rehearse he did it with full concentration. In between dancing though, he was pulling out all the stops.

For example, last weekend, she'd received a phone call after his shift on Friday. 'I'm off tomorrow and I want to take you all ice skating.' He'd paused. 'That's if you don't have any shoes to buy.'

The girls had loved it, especially when they'd seen how wobbly he was at first. 'Crap, I remember skating being a lot easier than this.'

Maggie, who'd taken the girls ice skating every Christmas since they could walk, had smiled smugly. But she'd loved it too, every moment, from seeing him happily make a fool of himself, to having his hand discreetly hold hers as they'd watched the girls have a second go.

In between the fun, there was the passion. There had been another Sunday afternoon spent in bed, while Paul and taken the girls out. And a steamy session in the car after dance lessons one Wednesday, when he'd taken a detour down a dark, unlit country lane, parked in a lay-by and told her. 'I've spent the last two hours with my hands on you, not being able to really touch you. I need to do that now, before I explode.'

She'd never felt so... Heck, she was only admitting it to herself, so she could be honest. She'd never felt so sexy. Perhaps she'd never even felt sexy, before now. Paul had wanted her, in the early days, but that desire had come at carefully ordered times: Friday and Saturday night, when they were in a bed. It had been sedate, safe. He'd never made her feel like he *had to have her*. That he was desperate for her. Beneath Seb's heated gaze thoughts of her wrinkles, her stretch marks, her it-will-ever-be-flat-again stomach, melted away. As did her natural caution.

What hadn't melted away was her fear about where this was taking them. When she lay in bed at night, the last thing she saw was Seb, his expression earnest, his eyes intense. *I'm falling for you.* It wasn't part of the plan, not for either of them, and it frightened her to think feelings were becoming entangled with the fun and the sex.

Yet when she thought of putting a halt on things, on going back to the life she'd had before she met him, the world appeared dull and lifeless. With no Seb, where was she going to get this buzz, this feeling that she could take on the world?

Turning into the youth centre car park, Maggie pushed the thoughts to one side. She was looking too far ahead, trying to plan something that was impossible to tie down like that. Look what had happened to the carefully constructed plans she'd made with Paul. They'd had children far earlier than intended, not gone on any of the holidays she'd longed for. And the happily ever after had crashed and burned.

Walking to the main hall where she'd found Penny and Tabby the last time she'd been here, Maggie pushed open the double doors. Immediately everyone inside turned to look at her, and Maggie felt the first flutter of nerves.

She wasn't here as Dr Maggie Peterson. Or simply Maggie. She was here as Seb's... damn it, they hadn't even discussed what she was supposed to be. His friend? His dance partner? Whatever it was, she realised that she cared what this group thought of her, and that was sobering.

'Hey.' Seb, his face wreathed with smiles, jogged over. 'Perfect timing, as always.' He bent to give her a chaste, yet perfectly natural, kiss on the mouth. 'Belinda's just gone to get herself a drink. Why don't I introduce you?'

As she struggled to find her composure, he took her hand and turned to the dozen or so kids – youths – who stood in a group, watching them. 'This is Maggie, everyone. She's going to be my dance partner in the competition.' He gave her a sidelong glance, and smiled. 'She's also my girlfriend.'

Well, that resolved who she was here as, Maggie thought as she listened to the chorus of whoops and whistles.

'You kept that secret.' A girl/young woman with dyed black hair and huge hoop earrings looked her over.

'Maggie, this is Hayley. She's the one who asked to meet you.'

'Yeah, only 'cos he was acting all coy, messaging you while he forced us to watch that *Strictly* programme.'

'There was no forcing, Hayley.' Seb laughed, shaking his head. 'And I seem to remember you enjoyed some parts of it.'

Hayley started to laugh, and as the others around joined in, Maggie had the feeling they were sharing a secret joke.

'Oh yeah, the parts where we watched that guy with the see-through shirt.' She flicked a look a Maggie. 'The shirt Maggie wants you to wear.'

Maggie froze, dread pooling in her stomach. Had he really shown them her text? Embarrassment hurtled through her and she didn't know where to look, what to say.

Thankfully at that moment Belinda came in, clutching a mug. 'Right then, class, today, as we have Maggie joining us, I thought we'd do the rumba.' She threw a warm smile in Maggie's direction. 'It's the dance Maggie and Seb have chosen to do for the competition.'

Belinda went on to discuss the origins of rumba, and the kids, thank God, turned their focus towards her, and away from Maggie.

'Hey.' Seb stepped up to her, reaching for her hand. 'It isn't like it sounds.'

Maggie snatched her hand away, too hurt, too angry to

be consoled right now. 'I hope not. Because it sounds like you were discussing a private text with a group of kids.' It was more than that. Maggie could vividly recall how long and hard she'd considered her words. The first time she'd tried flirting again for so, so long.

'It wasn't like that.'

He had no chance to explain any further though, because Belinda had said their name. And oh joy, now she and Seb were going to have to demonstrate the most sensual, sexy dance in ballroom, when all she wanted to do was run out of the room, back to her car, and return to the sanctuary of her home.

Seb's hips wouldn't glide, his body wouldn't bend. He felt stiff and inflexible. About as sexy as a sheet of MDF.

It didn't help that the group were laughing at him, though in all honesty he'd have been happy to have the piss taken out of him, if Maggie had been laughing, too. She wasn't, because she believed he was the sort of guy who got a flirty text from a woman and then, what, bragged about it to everyone he saw?

'Seb, you've missed the spot turn to the left.'

Shit, there he went again. He gave Belinda an apologetic smile.

'What's wrong with you this evening? I've seen Maggie dance better, but you Seb, you're more wooden than my pine dresser.'

The group tittered. 'Yeah, sorry, Miss but I don't get this rumba thing.' Rylan smirked over at him. 'Seb's kind of hard to watch.'

'Umm, on tonight's performance I have to agree. Why don't you dance with Maggie instead, Rylan,' Belinda suggested. 'I'll show you what to do. Heaven knows, you can't do a worse job.'

His humiliation now complete, Seb reluctantly stepped back. Rylan strutted over and took Maggie's hand. The worse of it was, she actually looked relieved.

'You're pretty rubbish,' Hayley told him as he went to stand next to her.

'Tonight, yes.'

He was aware of her studying him. 'Is that 'cos of what I said, about you messaging her? Are you, like, angry with me?'

Hayley was tough as nails, but there was something in the defensive way she stood, the way she didn't meet his eyes, that told him she was worried. 'No, Hayley, I'm not angry with you.'

She was silent for a moment, chewing on the inevitable gum. 'You didn't tell her I read the text, did you?'

'No. To be honest, I'd forgotten all about it.' Not the text itself, that had been a real high spot. It simply hadn't occurred to him how she might feel about others seeing it. It wasn't as if it was crude, or wildly intimate.

'I don't think she was happy when I mentioned the see-through shirt.' Another few chews. 'Sorry.'

Surprised, he glanced at Hayley. 'What for?'

'I shouldn't have read what was on your phone.'

'No.' He dug his hands into his pockets. 'But it's not like you deliberately hacked into it. You stole it for a laugh, and then read it because it was there, on the screen.'

Whatever Hayley had been about to say was interrupted when the doors to the hall swung open and Winston, one of the other youth workers, ran in, carrying a kid in his arms. 'Is there a Maggie here, Seb's friend? The Maggie who's a doctor?'

Maggie, who'd been in the middle of demonstrating an underarm turn, cleared her throat. 'That's me.'

'Thank God. Seb said you were coming tonight, and I remembered him saying you were a doctor.' He nodded down to the kid he was carrying in his arms. 'Josh here was complaining of feeling tired and then he started fitting.'

Immediately Maggie rushed over, and Seb watched in a kind of awed fascination as she calmly took over. Josh was laid on the ground and Maggie began to talk to Winston, asking questions. Seb could hear bits of the conversation: epileptic, diabetic, injection.

'Is he gonna be okay?' Kiara stared, almost in a daze, and Seb realised this was probably the first time most of them would have seen such a trauma.

'He's in great hands.' He squeezed Kiara's shoulder. 'Come on, everyone, let's go to another room and give them some privacy.'

Belinda was brilliant, her no-nonsense attitude the perfect distraction. In no time she had them dancing again, and Seb couldn't help but notice the way Rylan's gaze never strayed far from Hayley.

'You were pretty good dancing with Maggie earlier,' he told the boy as they watched Hayley and Belinda demonstrate a short routine.

Rylan snorted. 'You're only saying that 'cos you were an epic fail.'

'I'm saying it because it's true.' He nodded over to Hayley. 'Why don't you enter the competition and ask Hayley to be your partner?'

Rylan shoved his hands in his pockets. 'Not interested.'

'That would make sense, if I hadn't spent the last five minutes watching you watch her.' Seb paused, trying to order his thoughts. 'You saw how rubbish I was this evening, but the world didn't end. You all had a bit of a laugh, but that's okay, I deserved it. I suspect you'll continue to rib me about it next time I see you, but again that's okay, because I'm going to keep practising. And maybe when it comes to the final, I'll be better.'

'Couldn't be worse,' Rylan muttered.

Seb laughed. 'True, but the thing is, worrying about looking stupid, about failing, isn't going to stop me from doing what I want to do.' He paused, trying to catch Rylan's eye, but not succeeding. 'Don't let it stop you, either.'

It was half an hour later when Maggie popped her head around the door. Immediately Seb left Belinda's side, where he'd been watching the group dance, or more particularly watching Hayley trying, and failing, to get Rylan to dance. So much for his pep talk.

'How's Josh?' he asked, studying her face, trying to gauge how serious the situation was.

She smiled, eyes calm. 'He's fine. He's a diabetic and experienced a hypoglycaemic attack. Winston found his glucagon injection and he came round straight away. His parents have just picked him up.'

'Thank God.' Seb ran a hand through his hair, and then laughed softly. 'Or maybe I should say thank *you*.'

'No need, believe me. Winston and Josh's parents have said it far too many times already. I only gave him an injection.'

'You worked out what was wrong first.' He wanted to hug her, but it wasn't the right place, and she was still unhappy with him, so he pushed his hands into his pockets.

'Winston would have got there in the end.' She glanced up at him. 'I suspect you've done first aid as well, so you would have done too.'

'Yeah, maybe.' He could still remember the way his heart had raced when Winston had come rushing in. 'It's one thing learning about it, another dealing with it when it happens in front of you.' His eyes found hers and just in case she couldn't read what he was feeling, he told her. 'I'm in awe of you.'

Her breath hitched, but anything she might have said was halted when Hayley suddenly appeared in front of them.

'Is Josh...' She swallowed. 'Is he okay?'

'He's fine, Hayley.' Maggie gave her a warm smile. 'His blood sugar just got too low, so we gave it a boost.'

'Cool.' Hayley's eyes darted to Seb. 'Can I talk to Maggie for a minute? Like, by ourselves?'

Seb's heart bounced. What on earth was that about? The last thing his relationship with Maggie needed was a dose of Hayley's subtle-as-a-brick, though no doubt well-intentioned, help. Yet if he said no, wasn't he just doing what he suspected others in Hayley's life had done: dismissing her?

'Sure.'

With a last, lingering look at Maggie, he turned and walked back to the group.

Maggie was quiet as Seb walked her back to her car. He itched to ask what she and Hayley had talked about, but realised it was none of his business. When they reached her car, he gave her a tight smile. 'Thanks for coming tonight.' Placing a hand on the roof of the car, he leant in towards her, his body wanting the connection though his mind knew he shouldn't push it. 'It's not usually so... fraught.' Maggie nodded, fiddling with the car keys in her hand, and Seb wondered if that was it. She was just going to get in the car and leave him in limbo land. 'Look, about—'

'Hayley told me she'd pinched your phone and read the message I sent.'

'Yeah.' He pushed his hand off the car roof and took a step away from her. 'I'm sorry. I was distracted and didn't realise what she'd done, until it was too late.' He found her eyes. 'I should have told you, but at the time it didn't seem important.'

'No.' She sighed, and he waited tensely, knowing her well enough now to realise she was picking out the words she wanted to use. 'I overreacted.' Again, she began to play with the keys. 'I'm so out of practice at all this: messaging, flirting. I imagined you all laughing at what I'd written.' She winced, shaking her head. 'It made me feel stupid, and foolish, and *old*.'

His hands flew to her shoulders. 'Good God, Mags.' He tried to order his thoughts, like she had, but his brain was going a million miles an hour. 'Sure, I laughed at it, that's what got me into trouble, made them realise I was messaging you, but it wasn't laughter in the way you mean. I remember feeling so happy, I almost punched the air. I was so high I didn't even care that Hayley was blabbing about it to everyone a few minutes later.' He forced his hands to relax their death grip on her, his voice to soften. 'It was the first time I felt I really had a chance with you.'

On a soft exhale, Maggie leant forward and rested her head against his chest. 'I'm sorry. I should have let you explain before assuming the worst.' Placing her hands on his chest, she looked up at him with sad eyes. 'I really put the kibosh on our rumba, didn't I?'

He tucked a wayward piece of hair behind her ear. 'It is

kind of hard to dance sexily with someone when you're half afraid they're about to knee you in the groin.'

She laughed, the sound muffled against his chest. 'I wasn't about to do that. In fact, I was rather hoping to play with those important parts next weekend.'

He groaned, hugging her closer, feeling his body twitch and harden. 'How can you say you're out of practice at flirting? From what I've seen, you're a real pro.' And only then did her words sink in. 'What's happening next weekend?'

'Paul is taking the girls to see his parents. They live in Cornwall, so they'll…' He felt her body heave as she sighed. 'They'll be staying overnight.'

'Something you're not looking forward to, I suspect.'

'It's the first time I'll have been away from them in, well, so long I can hardly remember. I'm trying to be stoic, and plan how I can use the time, so I don't spend it sitting at home and fretting.'

He kissed her nose, her cheeks, and finally her lips, his mind already plotting. 'Leave it to me. I have an idea how to distract you.'

She smiled up at him. 'Does it involve a bed?'

'Absolutely.'

And maybe that's all she really wanted from him, the fun she'd been at pains to point out. A break from the stress of parenting, and the hard career she'd chosen. A distraction when things got tough. It wasn't all *he* wanted though, and this was his chance to show her.

Chapter Twenty-Six

This was the worst moment. No, scrub that, watching Penny and Tabby climb into Paul's Jaguar had been the worst moment. This, sitting by herself, twiddling her thumbs while waiting for Seb to come and pick her up, was only awful because she couldn't stop thinking about her daughters. Had she reminded Paul that Penny got car sick if she read? That Tabby liked a light on in the landing and her bedroom door open just a little to let the light in at night?

Paul's got your mobile number. He'll phone if he has a problem.

Shaking off her worries, she tried to focus on the positive. She had a weekend to look forward to. One she hadn't organised, didn't even know where she was going. She was trying to see that as exciting, though the not knowing, being a passive passenger rather than the driver, was rubbing against every instinct.

Where was Seb? How was she, always on time, dating a

guy who had such a fluid concept of it? 'I'll pick you up at ten' meant at any time between ten and eleven.

Finally, she saw his car pull up, and his long, lean body jump out of the driver's side. Dressed casually in a hoodie and jeans, his hair in its characteristic loose style around his face, he looked sexy, handsome. Young. So different to Paul, who'd turned up in smart chino trousers, collared shirt and cashmere jumper. One was raw, vital. The other sophisticated, yet now, with the benefit of distance, she could see her ex was also staid.

'Hey.' Seb greeted her with a kiss that made her breathless. 'All packed?'

Heart pounding, knees weak, she glanced at the case next to the door. The one containing new, matching lacy underwear. Not flesh-coloured, or white, oh no, nothing so sensible. These were in shades of black, midnight blue and red. 'I wasn't sure what to take, as you've not told me anything about where we're going.'

'Ah, the great planner being forced to sit back and let someone else take over.' He smoothed a hand over her hair, and down her ponytail and smiled. 'Do I sense some tetchiness?'

'Maybe,' she grumbled, handing him the case.

'Well, we've got a bit of a car journey ahead of us, so plenty of time for you to interrogate me.'

It was the first clue that he really had planned something. 'Can you define a bit? Far enough that we'd be better taking my car?'

His shoulders sagged, just a little. 'My surprise, Mags, my car.'

Guilt pricked. He was right. No matter how hard it was, she had to take a step back. He'd planned this, he had a right to expect her not to interfere. Damn it, and a right to expect her not to belittle him. 'Sorry.' Reaching up, she kissed his cheek. 'I'm not used to someone else taking over, I'm finding it a bit of an adjustment. I should warn you it probably won't be the last time I'll get on your nerves this weekend.'

He didn't say anything until he'd settled her case in the boot. Then he pushed her gently against the side of the car, crowding her, his eyes locked on hers. 'The only thing that will get on my nerves this weekend is you assuming I'm anything like your ex.' Planting a soft kiss on her lips, he straightened up. 'I'm a pretty laid-back guy. It takes a lot to annoy me and you haven't even come close to my threshold.'

She thought back over the time she'd known him. She'd seen him upset, when she'd treated him clumsily, frustrated, too, but she'd not seen him angry. 'Just wait till you're locked in a car with me asking you a million questions about where we're heading.'

He laughed, opening the door for her. 'Bring it on.'

For the first two hours, the only clue she got out of him was that he hadn't been there before. Thinking she might be onto something, she phoned Alice to ask where in the North, because that appeared to be the direction they were heading, Seb hadn't visited.

'Look at a map, cross off York because I know he went to the transport museum there once, and after that, it could be anywhere,' Alison had replied.

'I want a better clue.'

He flicked her a grin. 'What do you mean? You know we're not going to York.'

'I knew that because we're on the M6 now and not the M1.'

'Well then, you're ahead of the game.'

Okay, this was starting to become a competition. Instead of getting the hump, she needed to think. 'The Lake District.'

'A quaint old cottage with a four-poster bed and a wood-burning stove? Just across the road from a cosy pub? All that beautiful scenery?' He let out a dramatic sigh. 'It would be romantic, wouldn't it?'

It did sound rather perfect. But the mischief in his expression told her that wasn't it.

'Liverpool?'

'You have a hankering to do the Beatles tour? Visit the Albert Docks? I hear it's great now it's been renovated.'

'I do like the Beatles.'

'Really? I'll file that away for future reference.'

'What under? Old-fashioned taste in music?' she grumped, getting ever so slightly wound up now.

'Old-fashioned, are you kidding me? They're ageless.'

'But we won't be visiting the Beatles museum this weekend.'

'No.' He turned to glance at her. 'Does it really matter

where we're heading? Can't you sit there and relax for a few hours?'

'How many hours? Does that mean we'll be beyond Liverpool?'

He let out a huff of exasperation. 'Mags, turn your brain off and the radio on. It's basic, but I'm sure it plays Radio 1.' He smirked. 'Or Radio 2.'

'Fine.' She twiddled with the nobs, finding Radio 2 because yes, she did prefer that. Lying back against the headrest, she thought about what he'd said. Did the destination matter? The answer came to her immediately. It didn't, because all she actually wanted from the weekend was some time with Seb. A man who made her laugh, made her relax, and made her *feel*.

As the junctions came and went, Seb glanced over at Maggie, relieved to see she'd closed her eyes. Boy, was he now regretting making the destination a surprise. He thought it would add to the fun of it all, but instead not knowing seemed to have wound her up.

Worse, she'd started to guess, coming up with places she clearly would have liked to go.

Shame the place he'd booked them into wasn't one of them. And now he thought about it, why would it be? A seaside town that, even in the summer, wouldn't be on most people's list of top ten places to visit in England.

Indicating, he turned off the motorway, following the

signs to the promenade. He wasn't flush with cash, but as February was clearly not the time of year to visit the place, he'd got a good deal in one of the traditional old hotels on the front. Even splashed out a few quid more for a view of the murky Irish sea.

As he pulled into a car park space and killed the engine, Maggie stirred. Then sat up with a start. 'God, did I really go to sleep?' She looked mortified. 'Some company I am.' It was only then it seemed to occur to her that they'd stopped. 'Are we here?' Her head spun round, taking in the huge red brick Victorian building in front of them. The hotel looked impressive from the outside, at least. When she looked the other way, towards the sea, she drew in a sharp breath.

'It's Blackpool, isn't it? We're spending the weekend in Blackpool.'

Surprise he could read, but was it good surprise or bad surprise? 'It's what I'd planned, yes, but we can abandon it and go to Liverpool or the Lakes for that matter.'

'So I have a choice of wandering round the docks, climbing a small mountain or…?' She was smiling at him, a glint in her eye.

'Or we're booked to have afternoon tea and a spin around the Blackpool Tower Ballroom at four p.m.'

'Oh my God, Seb.' Her eyes lit up, a huge grin splitting her face. 'I'm going to be dancing in Blackpool.'

'Better hope we make a better job of it than we did at the youth centre.'

'Oh, we will, of course we will. How can I not dance brilliantly in the Blackpool Tower Ballroom?' She yanked open the door and jumped out of the car. 'Come on, what are you waiting for? We've only got an hour.'

Amused, he climbed out and hauled their cases out of the boot. 'You told me you dismissed the place as too tacky when you drove through it.'

'Paul dismissed it, not me. I wanted to come when the girls were small, but he said, and I quote, "Blackpool is full of stag parties, drunks and fish and chip shops."'

Seb held the door open for her as they stepped inside the hotel. 'He's probably not wrong.'

Maggie halted, gazing up at him. 'Yet you brought me here anyway.'

He felt another flicker of doubt. 'I thought you'd enjoy dancing in the ballroom.'

Her arms wrapped around his neck, and he dropped the bags on the floor so he could hold her. 'I will enjoy the ballroom. I'll also enjoy the rest of the tower, the sea, the slot machines, the fish and chips.' She went on her tiptoes to kiss him. 'I'll enjoy it all, because I'm here with you.'

'Christ, Mags.' His arms tightened around her, and he felt himself falling that little bit further in love. It wasn't what she wanted from him, yet he was powerless to stop it. He didn't even want to stop it, because it felt so right. Like his world was suddenly starting to make sense. 'That hour we've got?' He whispered, his hands slipping lower than was decent in a hotel foyer. 'I'm going to need thirty minutes of it with you, and a bed.'

They ended up having to run along the prom to get to the ballroom in time, the wind whipping in their faces, Maggie's laughter echoing around them. Any lingering doubts he'd had about bringing the sophisticated, elegant Maggie Peterson to Blackpool were squashed the moment they stepped into the ballroom.

She gazed around in awe at the rows of balconies, laughed giddily, then spun around the polished wood floor like a big kid, as he imagined Tabby would do.

'It's spectacular. Look at the ceiling, I don't think the television cameras ever showed us how incredible that is. The paintings, all that intricate gold carving.' Her eyes darted around the room, as if she couldn't bear to miss a single detail. 'And the chandeliers, they're amazing. I've never really noticed them before.'

'They lower them to the floor to clean. Takes them over a week.'

There was a beat of silence, and then he heard giggling, quiet at first, but getting louder as she clearly tried to stop herself, and couldn't. 'You've been reading up on the ballroom.'

'I might have done.'

She nudged him in the ribs. 'Why? Did you want to impress me?'

'Did it work?'

He expected some further ribbing, but instead she sighed and reached for his right hand, holding it in both of hers. 'You brought me to a place I've longed to come, but in the rush of day-to-day life, had forgotten I could. You read up on it to impress me.' He felt her hands squeeze his. 'I don't know what to say, how to thank you.'

His heart feeling full, he bent to touch her forehead with his. 'You don't have to. Being here with you is my reward, trust me.' Because his throat was now clogged with emotion, he drew in a breath and took a deliberate step back. 'Of course if you really want to thank me, I can think of a few ways. Some of which will involve taking off that sexy red underwear I know you're wearing.'

She laughed. 'That sounds like a reward for me, too, but first—' She nodded over to the tables, draped with blue tablecloths and each furnished with a large cake stand overflowing with sandwiches and scones. 'First we have to make our way through that, and then dance it all off.'

Chapter Twenty-Seven

F or the first time in years, far more years than she'd been divorced, Maggie woke to find herself being cuddled from behind. Paul hadn't been a cuddler, even when he'd supposedly been in love with her.

Seb liked to put his arms around her, both in and out of bed. It was a sensation Maggie was becoming addicted to.

'Morning.' He rolled her over so she was facing him. Hair a shaggy mess, eyes the blue of the Indian ocean, he looked like a hot dream. 'I thought you'd never wake up.'

She'd slept like the dead. That's what sea air, sex and a bottle of champagne did for you. They'd smuggled two bags of greasy fish and chips back into their room the night before, along with the champagne. It had been a perfect end to a perfect day. A day where she'd thought of her daughters, of how much they would have enjoyed it, but the thoughts hadn't consumed her. 'You could have woken me up.'

'You looked far too peaceful.' He shifted, pressing himself against her so she could feel every inch of his hot, naked body. 'Especially for what I had in mind to do to you.'

She smiled up at him. 'Well, I'm awake now.'

'Umm.' He threw back the duvet, his eyes trailing over her breasts, across her stomach and down to her hips. A small smile broke across his face when he came across her small butterfly tattoo. 'Did I tell you how much I love this? And what a shock it was to find it?'

'It was a shock to me too, when I woke up the next morning.' She cringed, remembering the horror of finding the permanent reminder of the alcohol-fueled freshers night. 'I'd just started at uni, and for the first time in my life I felt like I could really, I don't know, let loose somehow. Only I went too far.'

'No way.' His lips settled over the tattoo, kissing it, licking it. 'It's beautiful, and surprising.' His eyes met hers. 'Just like you.'

An hour later they sat in the dining room with a full English in front of them; reason one hundred and seventy-two she was glad she'd come to Blackpool. Maggie looked out at the choppy grey sea.

'It's not quite the Whitsundays, is it?'

Seb laughed, the rich, carefree sound fast becoming one of her favourite things to listen to. 'I don't fancy taking groups to scuba dive in it, that's for sure. Considering we're in Blackpool, in February, I'm just grateful it's not raining.'

She wanted to ask him again if he missed his other life,

like she had that day he'd come round to help Penny with her homework, but she was too afraid of the answer. Instead she took a sip of her tea and made a vow to focus on now, rather than the uncertain future.

'So, yesterday we ticked off all the things you mentioned, I think?' Seb spoke into the silence. 'We danced in the ballroom, walked by the sea, played the slot machines and ate fish and chips.'

Ah, the ballroom. Automatically a smile tugged at her. It had been more beautiful, more ornate than she'd imagined. And dancing in it, dancing with *Seb*, had been sublime.

'Mags?'

'Sorry, I was thinking I must bring the girls to see the ballroom. They'd go nuts.'

Seb smiled. 'I can just see Tabby hanging from a chandelier.' His eyes dipped to his plate and when they met hers again, he seemed... not quite nervous, but perhaps uncertain. 'What I was trying to say was I have an idea of what we can do today, but it wasn't on your list.'

'Oh?'

'The Pleasure Beach is open this weekend, I think because it's the start of half-term.' He paused. 'And I seem to remember promising you a ride on the rollercoaster.'

'Oh no, no way.' The sausage and bacon she'd just eaten felt like a congealed, greasy lump in her stomach.

'Hey, I'm not going to force you.' His eyes sought hers, his gaze steady. 'I do think we should go to the Pleasure Beach, though. If only so I can win you a big fluffy something and you can carry it around as proof of my manly prowess at hooking a duck, or whatever it is they do now.'

The unease lessened – fairground games she could do – but it didn't go away. A guy like Seb, he'd want to go on the rides. What was she supposed to do – send him on his way and sit in the café with a hot chocolate? Yet the thought of going on them turned her stomach.

They checked out of the hotel after breakfast, put the cases in the car and took a tram along the prom to the South Shore.

'Pleasure Beach sounds entirely the wrong name for the place,' she muttered as she looked up at the monster rollercoaster.

Seb laughed, throwing an arm around her shoulders. 'Come on, let's find some ducks to hook, or some tin cans to demolish.' He winked at her. 'Then we can tackle the rides.'

Maybe he meant it as a joke, but Maggie's stomach turned over, and a tiny bit of the joy she'd felt from waking up with him left her.

An hour after they'd arrived, they sat in the café, Maggie with a giant bumble bee on her lap.

Seb smirked. 'Look at the smile on the dude's face. He's clearly happy sitting on your lap. Can't say I blame him.'

'The feeling's mutual.' She gave the bee's antennae a gentle tug. 'I'm looking forward to taking him home. The girls will love him.'

Seb glanced at his watch. 'Well, speaking of home, we'd better head off soon. Just enough time to do the rollercoaster.'

The bottom fell out of her stomach and she tightened her grip on the bee. 'I told you, I can't do it. I'm sorry. I'm the wrong person for you to bring here.'

A rare flash of irritation crossed his face. 'What's that supposed to mean?'

'I like control, Seb. I don't even drive over the speed limit. I've never whizzed down a hill on a bike without clinging to the brakes. I've never been skiing because the thought of hurtling down a mountainside terrifies me.'

'You enjoyed tobogganing.'

'Yes, because you asked me which hill we should go down and I chose the one with the gentle slope.' She tried to rein in her panic. 'Why on earth would you think I'd want to plummet through the air upside down on a rickety rollercoaster?'

He didn't reply immediately. Instead he glanced down at his coffee cup, turning it round and round on the table. When he finally spoke, his voice was softer. 'The woman I dance the rumba with, she doesn't need control. She lets go. Just like the Maggie who got that tattoo.'

'I was nineteen and drunk.'

'Maybe drunk you, the person with her defences lowered, her control switched off. Maybe she's more like the real you than you think.'

'Or maybe she's the woman you want me to be.'

His gaze snapped to hers. 'You think I want to *change* you? That I don't think you're absolutely bloody perfect, just as you are?' He dragged a restless hand through his hair. 'All I'm saying is I think you've spent so long having to be sensible, you've suppressed the part of you that wants to be a little crazy, a little wild now and again.'

His expression was so earnest, it was hard to hold on to her anger. 'You make me both.'

He huffed out a laugh. 'Yeah, I'm sure I drive you crazy.' Reaching across the table, he touched her hand. 'Just one ride, and then we'll head back. Do you trust me to find one you'll enjoy?'

Trust was something she'd taken for granted, giving it easily, until Paul had broken it. Yet Seb hadn't given her any reason to doubt him. 'I trusted you to plan this weekend, and look how that turned out.' She glanced down at the bee. 'But what about him?'

'He's used to flying through the air, he'll be fine.' She must have blanched, because he laughed. 'I'm kidding, come on.' He stood, holding out his hand. Taking a deep breath, she clung onto it and allowed herself to be led outside.

———————

Maggie was still laughing as they climbed into the car.

'Hey, you were supposed to find that scary,' he told her as they buckled their seat belts.

'Looping the loop is scary. Ghosts and Dracula I can cope with.' She reached out and touched his cheek, her eyes bright. 'Thank you, the Ghost Train was the perfect end to a perfect weekend.'

He couldn't resist. He bent to kiss her, groaning as she

opened so easily for him. Would he ever have enough of this woman? So damn beautiful, so smart, yet so careful and guarded. He loved the two sides of her: the confident professional, the cautious lover. When he drew back, his heart was thumping, his mind full of words he wanted to say, yet knew would scare her off.

'What is it?'

Maggie's eyes regarded him questioningly, and Seb knew he couldn't hold back. It wasn't in his nature. 'I think I got it wrong, when I said dating doesn't have to be serious.'

Her throat moved as she swallowed. 'What do you mean?'

He had a feeling she knew exactly what he meant, because her voice was no longer steady. 'I don't think it's possible to date you and not fall in love with you.' Alarm crossed her face, and even though he'd expected it, the punch to his gut hurt like a bugger. 'Don't panic, I know the rules and besides I'm not there yet.' Though he felt like he was teetering on the edge of a precipice and didn't know how to stop himself from free-falling right into it. Running his thumb gently across her lips, he tried to steady himself. 'If I didn't say it though, you might never understand how special you are. If you take nothing else from this time, I want you to at least have that. To know how unbelievably stupid Paul was, to not see what is so blindingly obvious to me.'

Her eyes began to glisten and he knew she was considering how to respond, which careful words to select.

Unlike him, who'd just blurted everything out without thinking.

'I don't know what to say. Your openness, the way you're not afraid to express your feelings, it both staggers and touches me in equal measures.' Her hands gently clasped his face. 'But I'm terrified once the rush of conquest has gone away, I won't be the person you've built me up to be.' She swallowed again, blinking away the hovering tears. 'Don't get me wrong, I'm proud of who I am, but Paul had a point, and at times I *am* some of the things he accused me of: rigid, too serious, tiresome with my need to plan, to be careful.'

She wiped at her eyes, and as he watched, he ached for her. Naturally cautious anyway, it was no wonder she was doubly so after the way Paul had treated her. Yet what hurt more than anything was the false perception she had of herself. 'You act like nobody else has faults. Paul was disloyal and selfish, to name but two. And my lack of discipline, my chaotic approach to life is as annoying as fuck, according to my sisters.' He ran a finger down her cheek. 'I bet you were getting frustrated when I picked you up half an hour late yesterday.'

'I was. And I know none of us are perfect. It's just, when somebody who's supposed to love you, faults and all, turns round and tells you they no longer do, that actually they've found someone else, it bloody hurts. Not just the heart, but the ego.' Her breath was a half-sob. 'Suddenly you question everything, including yourself. And you wonder if it's worth taking the risk again.'

'God, Mags, don't let him do that to you. You're incredible. You're raising two happy, well-adjusted, amazing children while working in a high-pressure career. I can't even organise my own life.'

'No.' Her hand reached for his. 'Deciding what you want to do, where to settle. That all comes from the heart, not the head.' She gave him a watery smile. 'It will come, when you're ready.'

He thought maybe, just maybe, he *was* ready, but it was too heavy a topic for now and besides, he owed it to her, to both of them, to be certain before he made any drastic move. So instead of pushing the conversation in a direction he suspected neither of them was ready for, he forced a smile on his face. 'Right, better get you and Justin home.'

She gave him a confused look. 'Justin?'

He cast a look behind him to the bee sat on the back seat, wearing a seat belt. 'Justin Bee-ber.'

Maggie groaned. 'That's terrible.'

'Well, the challenge is on.' He started the engine and pushed the Fiesta into gear. 'You have around four hours to come up with a better name.'

Bee-yonce, Bumbledore, Buzz Lightyear, Barack Obeema… Maggie had plenty of cracks at it as they headed back down the motorway.

It was only when they passed Birmingham she started to look at her watch. 'Are we going to make it in time? Paul said he'd bring the girls back at four.'

He glanced at the dashboard clock. 'I think so.' She didn't answer, and Seb felt the anxiety creep over her. 'Hey, it's not like he's going to abandon them on the doorstep if we're a few minutes late.'

'No.' She drew in a breath and let out a small laugh. 'Sorry, I know it seems overly fussy, but I hate being late, especially for the girls.'

Guilt slithered, coiling in his gut. He hadn't been thinking of the timings when he'd pushed her onto that ghost train. 'It's not fussy, I suspect it's called being a mum.'

Glancing over at her, he caught her small smile. 'I appreciate the cop out, but I was anal about being on time before I had children.'

'Well, as long as there's no traffic, we should be fine.'

Of course he should never have said that, because half an hour later a sea of red brake lights flashed ahead of them. Thankfully the accident was starting to clear so the holdup was only twenty minutes, but it meant they definitely weren't going to be back for four.

He glanced again at Maggie as they finally left the motorway. 'Sorry, won't be long now.'

'It's fine.' She looked down at her phone. 'I've not heard from Paul yet, so it looks like he's not running to schedule.'

'Does he usually?'

'Oh yes. I'm sure that's one of the reasons I fell for him. His obsession with being on time makes me look chilled.'

Seb smiled, but inside her words were like sharp needles, pricking where they touched. It made him wonder if what she'd said earlier, the so-called faults she'd listed, had been a warning to him. She might enjoy his company, enjoy the fun and flirtation, but she wasn't going to risk her heart on a man who was so different to her. And with no firm idea what he was doing with his life, fun and flirtation were all he could reasonably offer, anyway. Especially to a woman like Maggie, who was so *together*, so competent and self-sufficient.

What a shame he'd gone and buggered things up by letting his own heart become involved.

The sound of Maggie's phone ringing bounced him out of his thoughts.

'Paul. Yes, we're nearly with you.' A few beats of silence, then Maggie drew in a sharp breath. Seb felt the hairs on the back of his neck prick as the air around them seemed to fill with a sense of dread. When she finally spoke again, her voice sounded tortured. 'We'll head straight there.'

His fingers clenched at the steering wheel. 'What's happened?'

'It's Tabby.' Her voice sounded flat, as if she'd put all her emotions firmly on lockdown to deal with whatever was facing her. 'They went to the playground to wait for us. She… she…' Maggie let out a muffled sob. 'She fell off the top of the climbing frame.'

Seb's heart almost exploded in his chest. 'But she's okay?'

Maggie bit onto her lip. 'He doesn't know. He didn't want to move her, she fell so badly, so he rang for an ambulance. They've taken her to hospital.' She turned to him. 'You need to take me straight there.'

'Of course.'

As he drove, his mind raced, showcasing reels of Tabby,

telling him to be quiet, pouting, giggling. It was only when Seb finally pulled up outside A&E that Maggie's words fully sank in. *Take me straight there.* Not take *us*. A slip of the tongue, or did she not want him with her?

He turned to tell her he'd park and meet her inside, but before he could, she'd thrust open the car door. He watched, helplessly, as she ran through the double doors and disappeared.

Chapter Twenty-Eight

All Maggie's medical training drained away when she saw Tabby lying on the hospital bed. She didn't see a patient, one she could assess, understand what was wrong, work out how to fix. Only her precious daughter, hurt, her face as pale as the sheets she lay on.

Before she'd gone in to see her, the doctors had assured her they didn't think there was an issue with Tabby's spine, but they were going to take more x-rays to be certain. She had broken her ankle, so would need to wear a special boot, and they wanted her to stay in overnight for observation.

'Mum, you're here.' Maggie's heart squeezed as Tabby blinked up her. 'I fell off a climbing frame and I hurt bad. I had to go in an amb… amblance and then they took pictures of my bones.'

Desperately trying to hold in her tears, Maggie kissed her forehead. 'You've had quite an adventure.'

'Where's Penny?'

Slipping onto the chair next to the bed, she held her precious daughter's hand, aware it was more for her than for Tabby who, typically, appeared unfazed by her experience. 'Your sister went with one of the nurses to find something to eat.'

'Dad brung me here.' A cloud crossed her face. 'He wasn't happy I fell off.'

Maggie could imagine Paul's reaction. 'That's because he was worried you'd hurt yourself.'

'Where is he?'

'He's gone to phone Isabelle. Apparently she had to leave.' For a brief moment Maggie's mind shifted to Seb. She'd been so numbed by fear, so focused on seeing Tabby, she hadn't even said goodbye to him.

A little while later, the male nurse came into the small side room Tabby currently had to herself, and checked Tabby's chart.

'You're going to have to wear a special boot for about six weeks to help the ankle heal.' He grinned at Tabby. 'It means you can boss your parents and your big sister around for a while as you won't be able to walk easily. You can be like, "Penny, can you get me a drink please," and she won't be able to complain.'

Maggie glanced over at him. 'Speaking of Penny, have you seen her? One of the nurses took her to a vending machine but I thought she'd be back by now.'

The nurse smiled. 'Don't worry. She met your friend, the one waiting outside the ward, and said she wanted to stay with him.'

'My friend?'

It was the nurse's turn to look anxious. 'He said he was your friend, and Penny seemed very happy to sit with him. Tall guy, fair hair, looks like he'd be more at home riding the waves or on a beach than sitting here.'

'Seb's waiting outside?'

The nurse breathed in a sigh of relief. 'Yeah, that's what he said his name was, Seb.'

'I want to see Seb.' Tabby's eyes pleaded with her. 'I want to show him my hurt.'

'Yes, fine.' Her mind racing, Maggie rose to her feet. 'I'll go and fetch him.'

He'd stayed. Maggie couldn't explain why the realisation made her chest hurt, and her eyes well. She'd not thought to ask him, but he'd come to support her anyway. *I don't think it's possible to date you and not fall in love with you.* Her heart had nearly broken when he'd told her that. Especially when she'd looked into the deep blue of his eyes and seen everything he'd told her mirrored there. There was no guile to Seb, no playing it coy. He absolutely believed he was falling for her, and wasn't afraid to let her know.

Of course he'd not had a serious relationship before, so it was entirely possible his natural enthusiasm for life was running ahead of him. A life, she had to remind herself, that didn't belong here.

She, on the other hand, knew the cost of giving her heart away too soon. And to the wrong person. Yet when she pushed open the door to the ward and saw Seb and Penny sat on two plastic chairs, their heads down as they stared at

Seb's phone, her heart flip-flopped in her chest, confirming her fears.

No, she thought, swallowing hard. Seb wasn't the only one falling in love. Not the only one who might get hurt.

They both looked up when she cleared her throat.

'Mum, Seb's been quizzing me on the map of the world. I got nine out of ten.'

Though she was talking to Penny, somehow Maggie's eyes wouldn't move from the bright blue of his. 'What did you get wrong?'

'Guyana. It's in South America.'

It took a huge effort to force her gaze away from Seb and onto Penny's. 'Did you find the vending machine?'

'Yep, I got a bag of Minstrels.'

'Do you want to show Tabby? Maybe ask the nurse if you can share them with her? I'll be along in a minute.'

Penny darted off, and Maggie looked once again at Seb, her heart now firmly lodged in her throat. 'I didn't realise you were still here.'

'You thought I'd just drop you and go?' He looked so offended, so hurt.

'I wasn't thinking at all. My mind was too full of Tabby.' And guilt, she thought. There'd been plenty of that, too.

His expression softened. 'How is she? I asked the nurse but she wouldn't tell me as I'm not family. Penny said she's got a broken ankle. Is that right? Is she okay apart from that?'

Maggie nodded. 'They're keeping her in tonight as a precaution but they're pretty confident it's just the ankle.'

Maggie sat on the seat Penny had vacated and leant into him. How stupid to think he hadn't been worried, too.

'Thank God.' Immediately he wrapped his arms around her, hugging her to him. 'Don't shut me out,' he said quietly, his voice rough with emotion. 'Lean on me.'

'I didn't mean to shut you out.' Reacting to his warmth, to the strength in the arms that held her, her body relaxed and she nestled closer. 'It's been me and the girls for so long, and I'm talking years before my divorce, too. I'm not used to having someone else to share things with.' She'd also pushed him into an 'only for good times' box, she realised shamefully. It had been both thoughtless and unfair.

He kissed the top of her head, but when he spoke again, his voice sounded sad. 'When Dad died, the thought of seeing you, of talking to you, was the only thing that anchored me.'

He didn't say the words, but she read the subtext clear as day. It hurt to know she didn't need him in the same way. 'This wasn't on that scale, Seb.' She twisted her hands on her lap. 'I'm also fighting a heck of a lot of guilt. If I hadn't gone away with you—'

'If I hadn't pushed you to go on the Ghost Train.'

Hearing the agony in his voice, her heart crumpled. All this time he'd been sitting out here, fighting his own brand of guilt. 'You didn't push me. Heck, I wasn't even keeping track of the time. How irresponsible was that?' And how rare, for her, to have turned off her brain to such a degree.

His arms tightened around her. 'Thoughts like that don't

help. The number of times I've beaten myself up over the last conversation I had with Dad, wishing I'd thanked him for his advice instead of turning defensive. Wishing I'd told him how much I loved him.' He drew in a shaky breath. 'None of that soul thrashing brought him back though. It just made me more miserable, which was of no use to anyone. Myself included.' Soft kisses on her nose, her eyes, her cheeks. 'Don't go there, Mags, because once you do, it's a real struggle to haul yourself out of that mindset.'

He'd been wrong to think she hadn't needed him. She just hadn't known how much, until now. Placing her hands either side of his face, she looked him straight in the eye. 'You have no idea how much it means to me to have you here.'

'Good.' Briefly he touched his forehead to hers, before straightening up. 'I guess you'd better get back to the girls. Stop Tabby from smearing chocolate all over those pristine white sheets.'

'Good point.' When she stood, she reached for his hand. 'But this is a job for both of us.' Surprise shot across his gorgeous face, and she smiled. 'Come on, I know a little girl who wants to see you.'

Seb nearly bawled his eyes out when he first saw Tabby. Christ, seeing a kid in a hospital bed, especially if you'd grown ridiculously fond of her, really grabbed a guy by the throat and squeezed, hard.

Thankfully Tabs was her usual perky self, at least for a short while, keeping them all entertained before tiredness crept up on her and her eyes slowly drifted closed.

That's when her father chose to march into the room.

'What's he doing here?'

Paul's eyes snapped to his, and Seb sighed inwardly. This was one of the reasons he'd stayed outside the ward. The other being he wasn't sure if Maggie had wanted him with her or not. The last thing she needed was a confrontation. 'I stayed to see how Tabs was doing.'

'Tabby.'

Seb kept quiet.

'Are you the reason Maggie was late?'

God, the guy was an arsehole. 'Technically it was the traffic that made us late.'

Paul narrowed his eyes. 'Where were you on your way back from?'

'Blackpool.'

'Blackpool?' Paul started to laugh. 'You took Maggie to the tackiest seaside resort in the country. In February.' His eyes skimmed over Seb's well-worn jeans, his hoodie. 'Good God, you've got a lot to learn about how to treat women.'

So many things Seb wanted to say. That's rich, coming from the guy who cheated on his wife... who made an incredible woman feel less about herself... who hardly bothered with his daughters after the divorce. He settled for, 'We both have.'

Paul snorted. 'Well, next time you plan a tacky jaunt,

make sure you're back when you say you'll be.' He turned his attention towards the bed, and Tabby. 'This could have been avoided.'

Despite his determination not to let the bastard get to him, Seb flinched. Looks like Paul had seen Seb's festering wound and decided to grind a tonne of salt straight into it. He'd meant what he'd said to Maggie, going through what-if scenarios weren't healthy, yet neither could he deny the facts. Maggie had trusted him to get her back in time, and he'd failed.

'Stop it, Paul.' Maggie gave her ex a long, cold look. 'Nobody is to blame for this. Not us for being late, not you for taking the girls to the park while you waited for us.'

Paul's eyes flared and tension crackled around them. Seb had never been prone to violence, but the desire to grab Paul by his expensive leather jacket and haul him out of the ward burned hot in his gut. It would certainly make him feel better, but sadly it wouldn't help defuse the situation. He caught Maggie's eye. 'I'll go and wait outside.'

'No.' She gave him a too-bright smile. One he sensed hid her weariness, and her frustration. 'Would you fetch my bag from the car, please? I'm going to stay here with Tabby tonight.' She glanced down at Penny. 'Is that all right, darling? Will you be okay if I ask Hannah to stay over?'

Penny nodded at her mum, and then raised her head to look at him. 'Will Seb take me home?'

Paul glared at him before looking at his daughter. 'I'll take you home.'

But Penny shook her head. 'I want Seb to take me.'

His chest felt like it was in a vice. How was it possible for these two girls to have wormed their way into his heart as much as their mother had? Maggie's gaze settled on his and he nodded. 'Whatever you and Penny prefer.' He hoped Paul read the underlying message. *This isn't your choice, mate.*

'I'm her father.'

Where were you the last three years then? The words were there, right on the tip of Seb's tongue, but one glance at Maggie and he swallowed them down.

It was Penny who spoke. 'I'll be okay with Seb, Dad. You can go back to Isabelle.'

Her quiet words took the heat out of the situation. Clearly mollified, Paul patted Penny's head. 'Okay, thanks, honey. She's sorry she couldn't stay.' He bent to whisper. 'Between you and me, she doesn't like hospitals.' Straightening, he smiled at his daughter. 'I'll see you next week, yes? Isabelle wants to go looking at bridesmaids' dresses for you and your sister.'

Seb saw Penny stiffen, but she didn't say anything.

After Paul had left, they stayed with Maggie and Tabby until Penny started yawning.

'I think someone needs to get to bed.' Maggie looked at her watch. 'Hannah said she'd be round at seven.'

Seb stood, wanting to kiss Maggie so much he ached, yet aware she wouldn't want the display of affection in front of Penny.

As if she knew what he was thinking, Maggie rose to her feet and his heart faltered when she put her arms around his neck. 'Thank you for the weekend, for being here, for taking care of Penny.' She drew up on tiptoe and whispered. 'And for not punching Paul when I know you wanted to.'

Swallowing down his emotion, he told her quietly. 'Thank you for coming away with me, despite the tackiness of the destination, and for keeping your cool when I failed to get us back on time.'

Her face fell. 'Please don't take any notice of Paul. He's never understood me, not really.'

Seb wanted to believe her. Certainly, Paul had never understood Maggie's passion for dance, and that was one thing Seb knew he could give her. He wanted to give so much more, yet realistically how could he, when he didn't have his own life in order?

Chapter Twenty-Nine

Maggie had never danced so much in her life. There was work, a break when she had a few hours with the girls, and there was dance. At least that's how it had felt in the past week. She knew Seb was starting to worry about the competition: not only their dance, but the evening itself.

'What if nobody turns up?' he mumbled as they walked into their usual Wednesday dance class.

'I thought you'd sold a lot of tickets?'

'It depends on how you define a lot. And just because they've bought a ticket, doesn't mean they'll turn up. It's not going to be much of a competition if nobody's there to vote. Or those that entered don't turn up to dance.'

'Hey.' She tugged his hand, halting him before they entered the studio. 'Where's all this coming from?'

He dropped his gaze to the floor, drew in a breath and then seemed to shake himself. 'Sorry. It's just I haven't done anything like this before, put on an event. I'm getting jittery.'

'This from the man who rides roller coasters, jumps out of aeroplanes and swims with sharks?'

'Turns out sharks are a piece of cake compared to putting on a dance competition.'

'So it's the event that's giving you jitters, not our rumba?'

She'd meant it as a tease, and though he smiled back, his eyes locked on hers with an intensity that surprised her. 'I'm dancing with you. Even if I balls up, I know you'll be there to carry us through.'

'Who's carrying who?' Shirley burst through the doors, breaking the moment. 'It'll take a strong man to get me up in the air.' She waggled her eyebrows at Seb. 'But I'm game for trying out a lift if you are.'

'That's quite an offer,' he murmured. Then, to her astonishment, and clearly to Shirley's too, because she shrieked like a teenager, Seb scooped the older lady into his arms. 'Bloody hell, Shirley, you're not exactly light.'

As Maggie bent over with laughter, Shirley cackled. 'I'm a lot of woman to handle, I'll give you that.'

Panting, Seb eased her back onto her feet. 'Sorry, but I need to do some serious weight training before we can do that lift.'

'You do that, dear. I'll be waiting. Might even squeeze myself into a slinky sequinned number for the occasion.' Maggie had to bite into her lip to stop from laughing again as Seb's face paled. Clearly oblivious of the alarmingly vivid image she'd created, Shirley moved the conversation on. 'I'm glad I've caught you. Me and Pauline want to enter this competition of yours. We figured who needs a man to dance with in this day and age? Especially as the ones here are about as useful as a glass hammer. Present company excepted.' She reached up to give Seb a loud smacker of a kiss on his cheek. 'Anyway, Pauline and me, we're going to pioneer the way for same-sex dancing in Attlestone. You did say there was a group for us not so youngies?'

'There's an over-sixty category, yes.' Seb treated Shirley to one of his trademark smiles. 'Though I'll need proof of ID from you both, obviously.'

Shirley boomed out a laugh, looking over to Maggie. 'He's a right charmer, this one, isn't he?' She bent and whispered in a volume loud enough they probably heard it through the door and in the studio. 'Did you two get it together after we had our little chat in the pub?'

Dear God. Maggie looked helplessly at Seb, who was no help, his face wreathed with silent laughter. 'I... err, that is we—'

Seb interrupted her rambling to lift her in the air. With their mouths aligned, he proceeded to give her a very thorough, toe-curling kiss. When he finally let her down, sliding her slowly, sensuously against his body, he turned to Shirley. 'Does that answer your question?'

Shirley's eyes were so wide they were in danger of popping out of her head. 'Oh my. That's going to be quite a rumba.'

For the second day on the trot, Seb's dancing wasn't quite as sharp as it had been BB – before Blackpool. The steps were there, but the fluidity wasn't. As she mused on it while Seb drove her home, Maggie realised it wasn't just his dancing that was different, it was Seb. She'd put it down to worries about the competition, but now she wondered if there was more to it than that. He seemed distracted. As if he was thinking heavily about something. Her thoughts kept circling back to the same conclusion.

Was his time up here? Was he heading back to Australia?

Seb pulled to a halt outside her house and turned to look at her. 'You've been quiet since we left the class. Is everything okay?'

She shook her head. 'Funny, I was going to say the same to you.'

His eyes rounded. 'Me? I'm fine.' But when he didn't look her in the eye, she knew for certain something was up. He was the most open person she'd ever met. She could usually tell what he was feeling just from searching his eyes.

Not now.

'Do you want to come in?'

Since her birthday, he'd started to stay over a few nights a week, but had always been careful to leave before the girls woke up.

Finally his gaze met hers. 'You don't need to ask.' But then he sighed. 'Damn, I've an early start tomorrow, and I need to catch Mum before she goes to bed, so can I take a raincheck on that?'

The creeping worry she'd felt earlier intensified. 'Fine, no problem.' Trying not to let her disappointment show, she reached for the door handle, but before she had a chance to pull it he'd run round to open it for her. 'Thanks.'

He held her hand as they walked up the path to her front door. 'I didn't ask about Tabs. Is she still causing havoc with her crutches?'

'Of course. I caught Penny trying to hide them from her yesterday. She said, and I quote, "Tabby was a pain without her crutches, Mum, but with them she's, like, really annoying."'

Seb laughed. 'Poor Penny, she's got a handful for a sister, that's for sure.' When they reached the door, he hesitated a moment. 'Have you spoken to her about being a bridesmaid?'

'No, why?'

'Might be nothing, but when Paul mentioned it at the hospital I got a feeling Penny wasn't very enthusiastic about the idea.'

'She hasn't said anything to me. Neither has Paul.'

'Maybe he hasn't realised.' Seb shifted on his feet, clearly uncomfortable with the conversation. 'Penny's a lot like you. She's responsible, likes to do the right thing.' Exhaling heavily, he jammed his hands in his pockets. 'Sorry, you don't need me to tell you that.'

'No.' But wow, the fact that he understood her daughter so well touched her more than he could know. 'Thank you for looking out for her. I'll talk to her about it.' Her heart felt full, her emotions wild and heavy as she reached a hand to his face. 'You know if you want to talk about anything, I'm here.'

He inhaled, trapping her hand with his, his eyes fluttering shut. When they opened again, they blazed with raw feeling. 'I've got stuff on my mind, stuff I need to sort through.' He let out a soft, humourless laugh. 'I'm a twenty-seven-year-old guy currently living with his mum, Mags.'

'There are reasons for that. Loving, decent, *kind* reasons.'

He acknowledged her words with an incline of his head. 'When I came back I didn't factor in Dad dying.' His gaze pressed hers, his voice softening. 'I didn't factor in meeting you.'

Maggie's pulse quickened, her voice barely making it through the lump in her throat. 'And now?'

He ran a hand down his face, his gaze a whirl of blue: indigo, cobalt, cornflower. 'Now I need to go before I do what I really want to do. Follow you in and get lost inside you.' His lips touched hers, tender, sweet, belying the heat in his eyes.

A moment later she watched him stride back down the path, broad shoulders braced, blond hair ruffled in the wind. A man too bright, too bold, too adventurous for her to hope to hold onto. What had Shirley called him? Exotic. Seb wasn't meant to be caged, hemmed in by the monotony of everyday life. The very life that Maggie didn't just live, she thrived on. Seb had tried to persuade her, and himself, that she wasn't that person, but career, family, responsibility… it was what she knew, what she did well. She needed the stability it provided.

Seb needed action, unpredictability. It was why he'd end up going back to his life on the Great Barrier Reef before no doubt packing up again and setting off somewhere new and exciting.

The knowledge was heartbreaking, because while she was careful and cautious with every other part of her life, it seemed that, once again, she hadn't been careful and cautious with her heart. Still so fragile, it was irresponsible of her to give it to someone so casual in his approach to life.

Yet when Seb left her, she knew he would take it with him.

As Seb drove away from Maggie's, his heart felt heavy. Funny, he'd always imagined when he finally fell in love, it would feel the opposite – light, filled with excitement and joy for the future. Then again, he'd also always imagined having a fair idea what that future held, by the time he met the woman he wanted to spend it with.

The sound of his phone ringing was a welcome distraction. Pulling into a side road – none of that fancy hands-free stuff for his old Fiesta – he pressed answer. 'Seb here.' There was a long pause at the other end. 'Who is this?'

Finally a gruff young voice. 'Me, Rylan.'

Seb felt a sliver of alarm. 'What's up, buddy? You okay?'

'Yeah. Just chillin' with me bro' and his mates.' He sounded fine, and Seb's pulse began to return to normal. 'You said to call, if I wanted.'

'I meant it. How can I help?'

'This lot all say dancing is for pansies.'

So Rylan had been talking about the lessons to his brother. Interesting. 'What does your dad say?'

Rylan snorted. 'Like he cares what I do.'

Damn. Seb had expected that, but still, it angered him to realise he'd been right. 'Okay, you know what, it doesn't matter what anyone else thinks. The only person's view that's important here is yours, Rylan. If you enjoy dancing, if you like the idea of entering a competition, of showing people what you're capable of, then go for it. You know it's bloody hard to dance properly. Your dad, your brother and his mates, none of them can do what you can. Be proud of that, whether you choose to carry on with it or not.'

Silence. Had he even been listening? But just as Seb began to give up hope, Rylan spoke again. 'If I want to enter the competition... I mean, not that I will, but if I did... when do I have to decide?'

'Just let me know a few days before.'

''Kay.'

As Rylan ended the call, Seb wondered if a man who couldn't work out his own life, was really the best person to be advising a kid like Rylan.

His mum was still up. Seb could tell because when he opened the front door he was hit with a blast of Frank Sinatra. His dad's favourite. An oldie but goodie, he'd always retorted when anyone had dared to take the piss.

Seb's heart twisted at the memory.

'I'm back,' he called out. 'Can you tell Frank to quieten down before he decimates my eardrums?'

The volume lessened, and Seb breathed a sigh of relief as he chucked his coat over the bannister – yeah, his mum would have a go at him later, but she always did it with a gleam in her eye.

'I hope you've hung your coat up,' she called from the sitting room.

'Why would I do that, when you enjoying nagging me about it so much?' Smiling to himself, he walked down the hall and into the kitchen. 'I'm making myself a tea. Do you want one?'

There was a moment of silence, long enough for him to worry and pop his head around the door. 'Mum?'

She looked up and gave him a small smile. 'For the conversation I think we're about to have, maybe a whisky would be more appropriate.'

He felt a dart of surprise, then wondered why, because unlike his dad, his mum had always been able to read him. 'Two whiskies it is then.'

It was only when he sat down next to her, he realised he didn't have a clue where to start. So much was going through his head, so many things he needed to work through.

She nudged her elbow into his side. 'Don't look so worried. It's time, my dear son.'

He frowned, not understanding. 'Time for *what*?'

'For me to no longer be your responsibility.' He opened his mouth to protest, but she cut him off. 'You have no idea how much I appreciate all you've done for me.' She laid a hand on his, her voice catching. 'But it's time for you to live your own life. You only came over to help me with your father, and yet you're still here, four months later.'

He took a large swig of the whisky. 'Shit—'

'Language. I'm still your mother and I can still tell you off.'

'Sorry.' He gave her a sheepish smile. 'Has it really been that long?'

'Long enough for your tan to have faded.'

He rolled his eyes, but inside he thought, *long enough to have fallen in love*.

He felt her fingers curl around his. 'It's time for you to stop thinking about me, and start thinking about yourself. What do you want to do next, Seb? And if that involves going back to Australia, don't you hesitate, not for a second. I'll be fine. I have to start getting used to being by myself, and your sisters will keep an eye on me. Make sure I don't get into trouble.'

Emotion balled in his chest and he struggled to form his words. 'Isn't that what you tried to get them to do for me?'

She smiled fondly. 'I suspect I'll give them an easier time than you did. Always dashing off, you were, never telling us where you were going. It drove me potty.'

'I didn't tell you, because I didn't know.'

Her eyes, once blue like his but faded now, searched his face. 'Do you know now?'

'I think so.' It scared the shit out of him, had done ever since he'd come back from Blackpool, but he hadn't made a move yet because he needed to be sure. He also had to acknowledge that whatever he decided – go back to Oz, or stay and make a go of things here – Maggie shouldn't be the driving force behind his decision. It was brutal, but he couldn't afford to kid himself. The woman he'd fallen in love with didn't see a future for them. 'Don't worry, Mum, I won't do anything until I'm absolutely certain it's what I want.'

'And in the meantime?'

He stared into his whisky. 'I've got plenty to keep me occupied.'

'You mean the dance competition? Your father wouldn't stop harping on about it. Kept bothering me with questions. *Has Seb thought of this, has he done that.*'

The guilt he'd spoken to Maggie about, that last conversation with his dad, came crashing back. 'I should have listened to him,' he admitted. 'Picked his brain more, rather than assume I knew what I was doing.' He hung his head, the worries from earlier weighing down on him. He wanted so badly to prove to himself, to his family, to Maggie, that he was more than a backpacking traveller who'd drifted in and out of jobs, moving on when the mood took him.

His mum caught his eye and furnished him with one of

her steely looks. 'Your father was a wonderful dad, and a wonderful husband, but there was one thing he didn't do well, and that was understand you.' She patted his hand. 'You weren't, and never will be, driven to succeed like he was, and like your sisters are. You were always more about the journey than the destination. It means you take time to appreciate the small things, like wanting to get your hands on those blasted toboggans the moment it began to snow.' She chuckled, shaking her head at the memory. 'It also means you notice things others miss, like the fact that the youth centre could do with an outside basketball court. And you listen to people, like your old mum, who said she was fine when your dad died, but you knew she wasn't, so you moved in with her.' She eyed him speculatively. 'That's why you're so good with kids. Maggie has girls, doesn't she?'

He wasn't sure where this was going. 'Yes, two. Penny is the more studious, the more careful, but she's sharp as a tack and has a real caring side. Tabby is a handful, into new experiences, not afraid of anything, including speaking her mind. A giggler. She cracks me up.'

A smile lit up his mum's face. 'There, you've just proved my point. You don't see them as kids, you see them as *people*. That sort of empathy is rare, so don't keep knocking yourself for what you aren't. Be proud of what you *are*.' A lump rose to his throat, and it threatened to choke him when she leant forward and kissed his cheek. 'And what you are, my beautiful son, is capable of doing anything you set your mind to.

Chapter Thirty

S he'd spent the last hour wrapping her legs around Seb's hips, being twirled round and round, then sliding suggestively down his thigh. It felt more intimate than sex. Especially when one of the hands he was supposed to be using to hold her upright shifted from her back to her stomach, and then sensuously up towards her breasts.

'I don't remember that being part of Belinda's routine.' Maggie leant back up, still straddling his thigh, her voice sounding breathless. And it wasn't from exertion.

He gave her a smile loaded with sexual promise, hand gliding across her breasts, down over her stomach, and then back up again. Leaving a trail of heat wherever he touched. 'She said we could add our own touches.' For a moment his gaze dipped to where his hand now covered her left breast, which tingled and ached beneath her sports bra. 'I'm a big fan of this particular touching.'

The heat in his eyes made her feel desirable, wanted, and she arched her back, encouraging his exploration. Two hands returned to support her spine, but then she felt the heat of his mouth as it trailed across her bare stomach. 'Christ, you're so fucking sexy.'

She almost purred with pleasure. 'If I am, it's because you make me feel that way.' Again she brought herself upright, this time bringing her hands to his face. 'But much as I love the new addition to the routine, we're performing in front of children, including my own. We need to stick with the PG version.'

He smiled into her eyes. 'Understood. We'll save this one for the bedroom.' Then he winced, holding her by the hips and easing her off him. 'And maybe wait until my quads recover.'

Laughing, Maggie flopped, exhausted, onto the sofa. Whatever *stuff* Seb had needed to sort through a few weeks ago, it seemed he'd made progress because he was no longer distracted. In fact he appeared fully focused on two things: the youth centre *Strictly Local* dance competition and her.

The former meant he was often tired and had less free time to spend with her. The latter meant that in the time they were together, she'd never felt so cared for, so doted on or so listened to. And when they ended up in her bed, as they inevitably did, she'd never felt so needed. She tried not to worry that this hunger, which at times bordered on desperation, was because he'd be leaving soon.

But at night, when she heard him creep out, and in the

morning, when she woke alone, it hovered over her like a dark rain cloud.

Seb sat down next to her, drawing her against his chest while he nuzzled her neck. 'Umm, you smell different today.' He kissed behind her ear. 'Just as hot, but different.'

'It's a new body lotion.' She laughed as his mouth tickled her, wondering if Paul had ever noticed how she smelt.

His mouth curved. 'Body lotion, huh? As in you've rubbed it all over you?' He brought his nose to her cleavage, and inhaled deeply before planting another kiss just above her breast. 'I think I'm going to have to investigate further.'

He'd got as far as lifting the right side of her sports bra, when her flipping mobile began to ring. Snatching it from the lamp table beside her, she stared at the screen. 'It's Paul.'

With a sigh, Seb straightened, and Maggie immediately felt the loss. 'Remember where we were.'

He laughed huskily, staring down at the breast he'd revealed. 'Trust me, I'm not going to forget.'

As she pressed answer, Seb rang his tongue over her nipple, making her gasp.

'Maggie?'

'Yes, Paul, I'm here.'

'I need to talk to you. I'll be round in half an hour.'

Assuming she'd drop everything for him, presumably. 'That's not convenient.'

'I don't care whether it is or not. I've got Isabelle in tears, telling me you phoned her earlier to say Penny doesn't want to be a bridesmaid.'

Maggie knew Seb must have heard the conversation because he tugged the bra back over her breast. 'Fine. I'll see you soon.' When she ended the call, she gave Seb a rueful smile. 'I'm sorry.'

'Don't be.' He kissed the top of her nose. 'Better to clear the air.'

He was so easy to be with, she was discovering. How refreshing, and also how freeing to know she didn't have to mind her step, watch what she said. 'You really don't mind?'

'Hell, of course I mind.' He licked his lips, staring down at her now covered breasts. 'I had plans for that body, with all its seductive smelling lotion.' His eyes met hers. 'But it's not like you have a lot of choice in the matter. I take it you had a chat with Penny?'

'Yes.' And what a revealing conversation that had been. 'She said she didn't know Isabelle very well and if she had to go to the wedding she wanted to sit next to me. Not stand with Isabelle and her dad, wearing a frilly dress and smiling until her face ached.'

Seb burst out laughing. 'She gets more like you every day.'

Surprised, she stared at him. 'Why do you say that?'

'Because it's the dry, coolly cutting way you'd phrase it, too. I should know. I've been the recipient of a few of those verbal hand grenades.'

'Ah, but only before I realised how cute you were.'

He grimaced. 'Cute is for babies and soft furry animals.

Men are handsome, sexy, hot.' He flashed her a grin. 'Pick the one that's most suitable.'

She pretended to think. 'Can I use all three?'

Laughing, he gave her a smacker of a kiss. 'That's my girl.' As her stomach dipped at the term, Seb's face sobered. 'I should go.'

He made to stand, but she reached out to hold his arm. 'You don't have to.'

'I don't think Paul will be too impressed.'

'I don't care what he thinks. I care that we had plans, sexy plans, and he's interrupting them.' It seemed safer to blame sex, than admit she wanted the intimacy of going to bed with him. God, she wanted to wake up with him, too, but she didn't want to confuse the girls, not when she was so uncertain of Seb's future plans.

'Well, if you put it like that.' He settled back, sliding his arm back round her. 'While we're waiting for him, you can give me the story behind the satsuma we're sitting on.'

'The what?' But she laughed, knowing full well what he meant.

'Maybe it's more of a tangerine.' Pulling her against him, he tapped her nose. 'Whatever fruit it is, I have a feeling you didn't choose it.'

'I hate it,' she admitted, 'but when Paul left, the girls refused to get rid of it. With irrefutable logic, they said it was where they watched TV, and wouldn't be persuaded that they could still watch TV from a more tasteful sofa.'

He chuckled and the conversation moved on to favourite

colours – his were bold, hers neutral – and then to favourite television programmes – his were *Friends* and *Family Guy*, hers *Strictly*, of course, and *Countryfile*. She didn't worry about how different their tastes were though, because while they chatted he drew absent circles on her arms and nothing seemed more important than how close she felt to him right now.

The moment was shattered by the doorbell.

Seb let out a deep sigh and shifted so they were sitting upright. 'I'll go and put the kettle on. Your job is to get rid of him as fast as you can.'

Giving Seb a wry smile, she slipped on her discarded jumper and went to open the door.

The sight that met her was unexpected enough to send a bolt of alarm through her. Paul's usually impeccably combed hair was awry, as if he'd been jamming his fingers through it. His shirt was crumpled, his tie hanging half way down his neck.

'Is everything okay?' she asked as he stepped inside.

He laughed, the sound bitter. 'No, everything isn't *okay*. It's a bloody disaster.'

'What is?'

'This blasted wedding, for a start. Isabelle doesn't have any children on her side and she thinks it will look bad if her step-daughters aren't bridesmaids.'

As she led him down the hall, Maggie struggled to keep her temper. 'So she wants to force Penny into a bridesmaid's dress just for *appearance's* sake?'

Paul tugged again at his hair. 'For God's sake, Maggie. She's the bride. She wants them as her bridesmaids.'

'And what about you?' she asked as they walked into the family room. 'Do you want them to be part of your wedding?'

He glared at her for a brief moment, but then his shoulders slumped and an agonised sound tore out of him. 'Honestly? I'm not sure I want a blasted wedding at all.' Slowly his eyes zeroed in on hers. 'I think I've fucked everything up, Maggie. Including us.'

Shocked, Maggie glanced over to the kitchen, where Seb was pulling three mugs out of the cupboard.

What on earth was Paul trying to tell her?

————————

Seb stilled, the ramifications of what he'd just heard weaving inexorably through his brain.

Turning, he found Paul staring back at him with narrowed eyes, his expression cold. 'Looks like you're making yourself at home.'

Looks like you gave up the home when you walked out of it. He added the silent retort to the long list of insults he wanted to throw at Paul, but hadn't.

Yet as he stood in Maggie's kitchen, why did he now feel like he was encroaching on another man's turf? Why did Paul no longer feel like Maggie's git of an ex-husband, but his competition?

Logically, Seb knew Maggie wasn't interested in rekindling the relationship with Paul, at least not as things stood. It didn't stop the niggling doubt though. *What if things changed*? What if Paul, who no longer looked like a Pringle model but a man with a huge tonne of regrets weighing him down, what if he'd come to pour out his heart to the woman he realised he still loved?

A shudder ran through Seb and he shoved one of the mugs back into the cupboard, clattering the remaining two onto the worktop. 'I've just realised there's somewhere I need to be.'

Smooth, Seb. Damn it though, he didn't feel smooth, or chilled, or any of the usual labels thrown at him. He felt a mess, his emotions jangling, his gut churning. No doubt he was making way too big a deal out of this, but right now he couldn't find his inner calm.

All he could see was the proprietary look in Paul's eye, and the stunned expression on Maggie's face.

He had to get out.

But he wasn't going to leave with his tail between his ruddy legs. Dragging in a lungful of air, he forced his body to relax, and his face to smile. When he felt he had his balance back, he walked up to Maggie, clasped her by the shoulders and gave her a humdinger of a kiss. One that let her know he didn't *want* to go, and let Paul know he was staking his claim. It was primitive, probably it was crass, but Seb didn't have the luxury of experience in matters of the heart. He could only go with his gut, and that was ringing alarm bells.

When he drew back, Maggie looked as dazed as he felt.

'I'll...' She cleared her throat and started again. 'I'll walk you out.' Turning to Paul, she said. 'I suggest you make us both a drink.'

Paul nodded, and as he walked wearily towards the kitchen, Seb had a brief flash of sympathy for him. Then reminded himself that the bastard had made his bed. He couldn't now complain he didn't want to sleep in it. That actually he wanted to sleep in Maggie's instead.

Maggie's hand curled around his as they walked towards the front door. 'I don't want you to feel you're being pushed out. I don't care if Paul's uncomfortable talking in front of you. He was thoughtless enough to barge his way over here.'

Seb halted by the door, his heart and his mind a tangle of emotion. 'I think you should hear what he has to say.' *But don't fall for him again. Don't forget what a bastard he's been to you and your daughters.*

'I don't owe him anything, not after the way things ended between us.'

He ached, right there, in his chest. What was he doing, leaving her, when he wanted to stand guard by her side? But the man who stood at the end of the hallway, hands in his pockets, watching them, wasn't going to hurt her. Judging from the look on Paul's face, he'd come to mend wounds, not create new ones. So Seb had to suck this up. 'You owe yourself the opportunity to get some closure on your marriage.' He bent to kiss her, just one, gentle press of her lips. 'If you want to phone me when he's gone, don't worry about the time. I'll be awake.' That he could guarantee. No way was he going to sleep easily tonight.

She smiled sadly. 'Okay.'

Seb had been home – okay, back at Sarah's, though depressingly it felt like home after staying with his mum. He'd been back only two minutes, just long enough to slump in front of the television and put some mindless quiz game on, when Sarah began her inquisition.

'I didn't expect you back so soon. Usually you sneak in at dawn. Have you and Maggie had a tiff?'

Feeling as he did, the question stung. 'Leave it. I'm not in the mood.'

Sarah studied him a moment, then sighed and went to sit next to him. 'Talk to me.'

He was too confused, too miserable, to put a voice to the emotions churning inside him. 'I'm watching this.'

Sarah picked up the remote control and in a flash, the screen went black. 'You hate quiz shows. If you don't want to talk to me, then listen. I know you've been seeing a lot of Maggie. I know the pair of you have become close, probably far closer than either of you expected.' She paused. 'How am I doing so far?'

'C+.'

She huffed, settling properly onto the sofa and tucking her legs under her. 'I've never been anything less than an A.'

'About time we found something you're only average at, then.'

'No, I can do better. I wasn't focusing properly.' She eyed him shrewdly. 'You took her to Blackpool, kudos to you. Seems you do know how to give a girl a good time.'

He gave her a sharp look. 'She enjoyed it.'

'Hey, I know she did. She wouldn't stop talking about it. Blackpool was the perfect place to take a *Strictly* fanatic.' Sarah's eyes searched his face, and then her expression softened. 'You're not usually this touchy when it comes to women. Or this lacking in confidence.'

He swallowed, trying to lubricate his tight throat. 'It's never meant this much.'

'Oh, Seb.' Sympathy brimmed in her eyes.

'Yeah. Apparently when I said I wasn't going to do anything stupid, I lied.'

Sarah reached for his hand, clutching it in both of hers. 'Have you told her?'

'That I love her?' He shook his head. 'Not quite.' He inhaled, letting the breath out slowly as he tried to formulate his thoughts. 'And after tonight, I don't know if it matters any more.'

'Why, what happened?'

He told her about Paul, and about what he'd said when he hadn't realised Seb had been listening.

'And now you're sitting here, terrified he's going to, what, somehow convince her the last three years didn't happen?' She rolled her eyes. 'Come on, Maggie's far smarter than that.'

On one level, he knew that. But on another level. 'I know she is. She's also smart enough to realise she can do way,

way better than me.' Divorce, the belief she'd been somehow at fault, had dented her confidence. He hoped tonight's conversation with Paul would start to heal that, to make her realise what he, and everyone else who met her, already knew. That rather than being ordinary, she was in fact extraordinary. And when she did... yeah, the rest wasn't difficult to work out.

It was just after midnight when Seb's mobile buzzed. Being wide awake, he snatched it up, heart pounding.

'Hey. Is everything okay?'

Her voice sounded sleepy. 'It's fine. He left about fifteen minutes ago. I'm tucked up in bed now.' She paused, and his heart went into free fall when she added softly. 'I wish you were here.'

'God, I wish I was, too.' He could be, he thought for a wild moment. He could dive into his car and be there in fifteen minutes.

She needs time to work through whatever it was Paul said to her. Time and space. And so do you.

'Do you feel better having spoken to him?'

A gentle breath, then a rustle. Seb imagined her shifting on the bed, her hair fanning the pillow. Her lips pursed a little as she considered her reply. He had to blink, to count the number of items of dirty washing piled on his chair, to stop the building arousal.

'Yes, I think I do,' she answered finally. 'He was very honest with me, for once. Even admitted the fault wasn't with me, but with him. He thought he wanted something different, and now wonders if he got that wrong.' She laughed softly. 'Apparently Isabelle's lack of organisation drives him nuts.'

Just as yours would drive Maggie nuts, too. Seb pushed the thought aside. 'So there won't be a wedding?'

She hesitated. 'I don't know. It's not my business.'

She yawned, and he realised he had to let her go. 'I'm working tomorrow, but can I see you after?'

'Of course.' He heard the smile in her voice. 'I'm going shopping with your sisters, but I'll try to leave enough energy in reserve to make you dinner.'

'If the energy supplies are going to be that low, I'll skip dinner and get straight to the good stuff.'

She laughed, and as they said goodnight Seb consoled himself with the thought that she sounded *happy*. Then worried himself to sleep over whether that was a reflection of the time she'd spent with Paul, or the phone call with him.

Chapter Thirty-One

As Alice and Sarah pulled out dresses left, right, and centre, Maggie started to go cross-eyed. No wonder Maria, the assistant in the specialist ballroom dancing shop they'd trekked into London for, was getting ever so slightly ruffled.

'Stop.' Maggie held up her hand. 'I've got a suggestion. Why don't we all sit on this very comfortable velvet sofa and let Maria use her expertise to select the dresses she thinks will suit me.'

Alice snorted. 'But she doesn't know you as well as we do.'

'No.' Maggie looked over at her friends. 'But maybe I don't want to look like me next Saturday.' Their eyebrows raised in unison, and Maggie burst out laughing. Most days she forgot they were twins, they were so different, but right now their facial expressions were identical. 'Don't look at me like that. I'll be dancing in front of an audience, with the guy who's organised the whole competition. I want something a bit... different.'

Alice turned to Maria. 'What she means is, she wants a sexy outfit that'll blow the socks off her dance partner.'

Maggie started to laugh harder, part embarrassed, part impressed. 'That's not... oh, what the heck. Yes, I'd like something sexy. Tasteful,' she added quickly, 'but definitely an outfit that'll make him see me in a new light.'

'Seb doesn't need a new light,' Sarah said quietly once Maria had gone to rifle through the rails. 'He already sees you like that. It's you who needs the costume.'

She was about to protest, when she thought of how Seb had looked at her last night while they were dancing. His eyes had caressed her long before his fingers had. 'I want to feel the way he sees me. The rumba is such a great dance, but it's so easy to get wrong if we don't find that chemistry.'

They both burst into giggles. 'Trust me, you two have enough chemistry to set up a lab. It was clear even before you got together.' Alice nudged her shoulder. 'But I don't think that's the real issue, is it?'

'No.' Maggie sighed. 'Is it terrible of me to wish right now you were my friends, and not his sisters?'

'We're both.' Sarah squeezed her hand, just as Alice did the same. 'But today we're your friends, and friends don't blab intimate secrets to their mate's boyfriend.'

'Okay.' Maggie drew in a breath. 'I want the people watching to believe in the performance. To believe that Seb, who'll be a knock-out even if he turns up in jeans and T-shirt, is performing this dance of sensual, passionate love for me. And not because he took pity on a middle-aged woman at a dance class.'

'That's absolutely not—'

Maggie silenced Sarah. 'I know it's not how he feels now. But it is sort of how it started.'

'It was never about pity, Maggie. From the moment he saw you, his interest was snared. Even when you were sniping at each other, he had a twinkle in his eye.' Sarah let out a frustrated exhale. 'Only you see the age gap as a problem.'

'Actually, I don't, not any more.' There were more significant gaps, like outlook on life and where they saw themselves in six months. *Stop planning, you ridiculous woman, enjoy now.* Maggie straightened her back. 'Right, GP to rumba queen; let the transformation begin.'

'Looking at the state of that lot,' Alice waved her hand towards the returning Maria, whose arms were laden with feathers, sequins and sparkle, 'this is going to be a breeze.'

Of course it wasn't. Maggie puffed, squirmed and squeezed into the costumes, mesmerised by the choice. Long or short, split to the thigh or higher. Low back, high back. How much cleavage to show.

Frazzled, she looked at herself in the mirror: hair sticking out of its ponytail, cheeks flushed. Twenty costumes later and she still wasn't sure what was *her*.

'Has Seb said anything about what he likes you in? Colour, style.' Alice edged the curtain open. 'Even my Neanderthal of a brother must have complimented you at some point.'

'He likes my tattoo.' Maggie smiled. 'And my new underwear, though I do remember him saying me wearing nothing was—'

Alice put her hand up. 'I know we said we're your friends today, but there are limits. Discussing my brother's sex life is gross.'

'Noted.' Maggie glanced at herself again in the mirror. 'You know, he did send me a text the night of the *Strictly* final.'

'I remember. He asked you whether he should buy a sheer black shirt.'

'Actually, that wasn't entirely true.' Maggie held Alice's eyes in the mirror. 'He actually said he liked the idea of me in a short, black, thigh-high split dress.'

'Wow, so that's why you couldn't take your eyes off your phone, even though it was the *Strictly* final.'

'Umm, yes?'

Alice burst into laughter. 'Well then, I think we can now safely cut the choice down.'

In the end there wasn't a choice, because as soon as Maggie slipped on the knee-length black dress Maria found her, they all sighed. It had a low front and back, but was covered in a fine lace so it wasn't too obvious. The split was daringly high, allowing her the freedom of movement she needed. It would also show off her legs, and Maggie was convinced they'd become more toned with all the dancing she'd been doing. The fabric was covered with tiny sequins, which sparkled under the lighting.

She felt like a million dollars. More, she felt like a woman who deserved to be dancing with Seb.

'It feels like the day I found my wedding dress.' When Alice and Sarah winced, Maggie shook her head. 'I know that didn't end well, but the day I put the dress on, it felt right. And when I walked down the aisle, I knew I looked like a bride should: radiant, the best she could be.' How sad the marriage had never matched the fantasy of the day. Yet equally, how incredible that she could stand here and talk about it quite openly, without the anger, the despair, the rejection that had hung around her for the last few years.

She knew who she had to thank for that, and it wasn't the man who'd come to see her last night. Paul's frank talk about his own failings had soothed her ego, but the fact that her ego was alive and kicking at all was thanks to another man entirely.

'I wonder if my brother is putting the same degree of effort towards his costume,' Alice remarked dryly as they squeezed themselves into the packed tube, huddled protectively round the dress.

'I'll ask him tonight.' They looked at her. 'What? I'm making him dinner.'

'He comes back from work to a home-cooked meal.' Alice smirked. 'How cosy. Don't tell me you greet him wearing an apron.'

'Actually, if the girls are in bed, I might just greet him wearing—'

'Aggh.' They both put their fingers in their ears, and Maggie laughed along with them.

It was only later, as she was making the dinner – Tabby had requested spag bol – she realised how easy the day had been, with none of the awkwardness she'd once feared, dating the brother of her best friends.

In fact none of her original worries about dating Seb had come to light so far. He found her ways amusing, not irritating. He laughed off the age gap. He enjoyed her kids almost as much as she did. The only complication was something she hadn't anticipated. That she'd fallen in love with the man who'd only ever been on loan to her.

He's not said he's leaving. She'd cling to that hope for all she was worth.

On Tuesday, Seb finally had a day off. The centre had been full on recently, what with his usual rota and the extra time he was putting in trying to get everything ready for Saturday. And… yep, there it went, his stomach doing its usual series of nervous twitches every time he thought of the competition. Only four days to go. Fingers crossed, everything was in place. Thanks to Belinda and her friends, he had a panel of judges. Thanks to old school friends he had a live band doing the music, with a back-up stereo for the less obvious requests. Competitors were lined up in all the age groups, including the youth group he'd been worried about. He'd had to work very hard not to fist bump when Hayley had handed him an entry form yesterday with her and Rylan's names on it.

So the people were in place, the hall would be decorated Saturday morning and all the tickets had been sold.

It meant today, he didn't have to get up or go anywhere. Yawning, he stretched, relishing the prospect of a lazy day.

A second later, Sarah burst into his room.

'Christ, sis.' He did a quick check to make sure none of his naked body parts were on show. 'What happened to knocking first?' He did a double take at the clock, which said eight thirty. 'And why aren't you at work?'

'I've taken the morning off.' She plonked herself on the end of his bed. 'What are you going to wear on Saturday?'

It felt all sorts of wrong to have his sister sitting on his bed while he was naked beneath the covers. Self-consciously he shifted the duvet tighter around him. 'I work on a one day at a time principle. I'll work out what I'm wearing on Saturday, on Saturday.'

'God, why are guys so dense.' She stood up and began to pace. 'Do you know what we did with Maggie last Saturday?'

Was this a test? He took his mind back to the weekend. Eating at Maggie's on Saturday night, Tabby's giggles as she sprayed them with sauce as she sucked up her spaghetti. Dancing with Penny, who was getting better than he was. Making love to Maggie, twice; once when they'd gone to bed, a second time before he'd left as daylight had started to creep through the curtains. 'You went shopping?' he hazarded.

'Exactly.'

'Err, is that meant to be a light bulb moment for me?

Because I've got to confess, I'm not feeling it right now. Isn't shopping what girls *do*?'

She let out a noise he imagined a cat might make if someone stood on its tail. 'Did you even ask her what she bought?'

'Should I have done?'

'No, yes. Aggh, what am I doing, trying to have a conversation with an imbecile.' She waved her hands in exasperation. 'When Maggie stands up to dance the rumba with you on Saturday night, she's going to look a-ma-zing.' Her eyes locked onto his. 'How are you going to look?'

'Well, I hadn't given it much thought, but I reckon Maggie likes me in my jeans. I mean she's not said as much, but I have seen her eyeing up my arse a few times...' As Sarah raised her eyes to the ceiling, her expression one of complete exasperation, the penny began to drop. 'Crap. I guess the jeans are out?'

After uttering the biggest sigh he'd ever heard, she picked up a pair of the said jeans from the towering dirty washing pile, and threw them at him. 'Put your dubious arse in these. Your big sister is about to dig you out of a bloody great hole and take you shopping.'

Ten minutes later, feeling like he'd been battered by Storm Sarah, Seb sat in the passenger seat of his sister's Audi and pulled out his phone.

Help. Sarah's taking me shopping. S xxx

Maggie's reply pinged back a few minutes later.

Why? M x

He frowned.

Only one kiss? S xxx

A few weeks ago she'd confessed to her worry about the first text she'd sent him, and how relieved she'd been when he'd replied with three kisses.

Sorry. Busy. M xx

Swallowing his disappointment, he replied.

Okay, will catch you later. S xxx

Immediately he got another text.

Never too busy to hear from you. M xx

He grinned, affection curling through him. How had he got lucky enough to get this lady's attention?

B4 I forget Rylan and Hayley entered the competition. S xxx

A line of smiling emojis came back at him.

You've got a soft spot for that pair, haven't you? M xx

He chuckled, fingers flying over the phone.

Nothing soft about me. S xxx

'I hope you're not going to act like a lovesick puppy all morning. It's going to get really boring.' Sarah glanced sideways at him as another text came through.

Obvs! So, why the shopping trip? M xx

'What does Maggie want?'

He didn't have to ask how Sarah knew who he was texting. No doubt the tongue rolling out of his mouth gave it away. 'She wants to know why you're dragging me shopping.'

'Tell her your sister is making sure you don't embarrass her.'

Chuckling to himself, he typed out:

Sarah thinks we need some sex toys. I told her I was enough for you, but she insisted. S xxx

He received a string of ??????? followed by emojis of monkeys hiding their face, puzzled expressions and finally an aubergine, which caused him to snigger.

'For God's sake, put the phone away,' Sarah muttered. 'You're making me feel sick.'

Figuring he'd better not piss off the woman who was

giving up her morning to save his arse, he sent Maggie a final message.

All will be revealed on Saturday (but the aubergine is FYE). S xxx

FYE? M xx

Okay, so he couldn't not reply to a question.

For your eyes only. S xxx

Returning his phone to his pocket, he settled back to mentally prepare himself for a morning of clothes shopping. With his sister. 'I can handle colour and don't mind snug fitting, but frills are out. And sequins.'

'What about feathers?'

He grimaced, but when he turned to look at her, he found she was now the one smirking. 'Very funny. Just find me something Maggie will want to rip off later. With her teeth.' Sarah shook her head. 'What?'

'She gave us the same instruction.' She paused a moment, before adding, 'Though she phrased it much more elegantly.'

Any comment he would have made – and for the moment he was feeling too buoyed by Sarah's remark to think of one, was halted by an eerie sound coming from his mobile.

Sarah visibly jerked. 'What the hell is that?'

'That, dear sis, is a didgeridoo.' He grabbed the buzzing phone from his pocket, not needing to look at the screen to see who was calling. The ring tone had done that for him. 'G'day mate. How's it going?'

'Sunshine all the way,' drawled Bruce, the mate he'd shared a house with in the Whitsundays. 'I got a message saying you'd called. Figured you would, eventually, when you got sick of all that English gloom.'

Seb closed his eyes, picturing the place they'd shared, backing onto the beach. He'd almost forgotten the feeling of warmth on his face from the sun, the sparkle of the water. 'It's not all gloom here but yeah, I wouldn't say no to a dose of sun. Are you going to be around first week in March?'

Chapter Thirty-Two

The day of the competition had finally come around, and Maggie gasped as she stepped inside the youth centre hall.

'It looks amazeballs,' Tabby breathed, her gaze jumping round the room.

'It really does.' Maggie gaped in admiration at the transformation from multi-use hall to ballroom. There were silver and purple balloons, purple velvet drapes covering the walls, fairy lights along the small stage where the band were setting up. Oh, and strings and strings of lights dangled from the ceiling, too. It wasn't the chandeliers of Blackpool, but the effect was similar, casting a twinkling light that made the place feel special.

And God, speaking of special. Her heart stuttered as she caught sight of Seb. It had only been a few days, but it felt like forever since she'd last seen him.

As soon as he saw them, his face lit up. 'My favourite people.'

Tabby hobbled on her crutch towards him, giggling as he pretended to swipe it away from her as she high-fived him. Penny showed none of her cautious side as she, too, exuberantly high-fived him and then, as he held her hand up, executed a perfect underarm turn.

Finally, his attention fell on her. 'Hi.'

She grinned back with the foolishness of a teenager. 'Hi yourself.'

Taking her hand in his, he looked around the hall. 'So, what do you think?'

It was only then Maggie realised how tense he was beneath the casual clothes and the wide smile. 'Tabby said it looks amazeballs.'

'Yeah?' He nodded, but his eyes searched hers. 'What do *you* think?'

'I think my daughter summed it up perfectly.'

He smiled, but still it wasn't the Seb she knew. Lines she hadn't seen before were etched on his face. 'You don't think it looks naff? There was so much we could have done, but it all cost and we're here to make money, not spend it, so we tried to stick to stuff we could borrow.' His breath came out in a fast exhale. 'The theatre lent us the drapes, the DIY place donated the fairy lights…'

Maggie gave him a gentle nudge in the ribs with her elbow. 'Seb.' He turned, and she could read everything he was feeling in his expression. The fear it wasn't good enough, that what he'd *done* wasn't good enough. It brought her back to the night he'd come to her after his dad had died. *I never made him proud, Mags.*

This man was so special, so gifted in ways he couldn't see: empathy, compassion, inspiring others, especially children. He wasn't afraid to take a risk, to show his emotions, to make a fool of himself. To dive into life with his eyes open to new possibilities. 'This is... God, it's incredible. Not just what you've done with the hall, but the whole idea, getting the people here to agree to you doing it.' She shook her head. 'No, it's more than that, you got the whole community to buy into the idea, young and old. You made it happen, Seb. You proved to everyone, but most importantly to yourself, what you're capable of. Never, ever forget that.'

She watched his Adam's apple move in the column of his throat. 'Plenty of time for it to go pear-shaped.'

'It won't.' She gave him another nudge. 'Do I need to remind you that *you're* the optimist? I'm the one who'll envisage at least a hundred things that can go wrong.'

His features finally relaxed. 'True, but you'd also have at least a hundred plans in place to counter the issues. All I've got is this.'

He brought his hand up, and she burst out laughing when she saw he was crossing his fingers.

People began to enter the hall and sit on the seats that surrounded three corners of it. 'I guess I'd better go outside and wait for Paul.' Maggie checked her phone. 'He messaged to say he'd be here in five minutes.'

Surprise shot across Seb's face. 'I didn't realise he was coming.'

'The girls told him I was dancing in a competition, and when he came round last week he said he wanted to come and watch.'

Seb's jaw tightened. 'To see what he missed out on, I presume.'

'What do you mean?'

'You said Paul never took you dancing.' He gave her a half smile. 'After tonight, he's going to regret that, big time.'

'I think it's more a question of him wanting an excuse to escape his rented four walls for an evening.' Seb raised an enquiring brow. 'He told Isabelle he wasn't sure he wanted to get married again and she threw him out.'

A muscle ticked in Seb's jaw. 'So you've been in contact with him then?'

'He's the father of my children. Yes, I've been in contact with him.'

Hearing the edge to her voice, Seb's shoulders slumped. 'Sorry. Jealousy is a pretty shitty trait.' His eyes snagged hers. 'I can't say I've ever felt it, before now.'

And just like that, her irritation slipped away. 'I'd hate it if you were in contact with any of your exes, too,' she admitted.

He took his phone out of his pocket and pointed to the list of people he'd been messaging recently. 'Only ladies I've been in contact with this week other than my family are Belinda, Pauline and Shirley.' He gave her a wry smile. 'I'm clearly a magnet for the older woman.'

It was a measure of how far she'd come, how confident he'd made her in her own sexuality, that the only feeling his quip elicited was laughter.

While they'd been talking, two faces she recognised had come up alongside them: Rylan and Hayley.

'Yo, Seb.' Rylan, wearing a hoodie and grey tracksuit bottoms, greeted Seb with a half smile.

'Afternoon, Rylan, Hayley. Are you both ready for later?'

'Err, yeah, about that.' Rylan shuffled his feet, his gaze dropping to the floor.

The unexpectedly nervous-looking gesture made Maggie's heart squeeze. The teen might act cocky most of the time, yet here was another side to him. By all accounts, Seb had been very similar when he'd been Rylan's age: confident on the outside, full of insecurities on the inside. No wonder he felt a connection to the boy.

'What Ry's trying to say is he's got nothing to wear tonight.' Hayley levelled the teenager a dark look. 'The dumb arse thought he could wear what he's wearing now.'

Rylan bristled. 'Fuck off, Hayley. I ain't dumb. This isn't a fucking fancy dress competition.'

'Right, but you watched the *Strictly* programme, Kiara and Zayne showed you what they're gonna wear.' Hayley chewed hard on her inevitable gum. 'We're gonna look stupid if you turn up like that.' She waved dismissively at him.

'Whoa.' Seb raised his hand. 'Let's dial this right back. Rylan's not being dumb, he's being a *guy*.' In that easy way he had, Seb took the tension out of the situation by winking at Hayley. 'I'd be dancing in jeans tonight if my sister hadn't stepped in.'

Rylan smirked as Hayley gaped first at him, then at Maggie. 'Seriously?'

Maggie smiled. 'Seriously. Men don't always think. Or plan ahead,' she added with a sly glance at Seb.

'Can't disagree with that.' Chuckling, he turned to Rylan. 'It's up to you, mate. You won't look stupid if you dance in what you've got on now. You're going to smash it out there whatever you wear. Still, it's a team effort, so Hayley's wishes are important, too.'

'Yeah, I suppose.'

Hayley giggled. 'Don't look so scared, Ry. It's not like I want you wearing anything weird, like a see-though shirt.' She gave Maggie a wink, and Maggie couldn't help but laugh. It seemed Seb wasn't the only one fond of these two.

Aware that a crowd had gathered around them now, all clearly needing to talk to Seb, Maggie squeezed his arm. 'Look, I'll sort something out for Rylan and Hayley. You go and be important.'

Relief flashed across his face, but still he hesitated. 'You sure?' When she nodded, she swore his shoulders eased down a fraction. 'You're a bloody star.'

'Not yet, but wait till we get onto that dance floor.' She kissed his cheek. 'Next time I see you, we'll be ready to rumba.'

His eyes went so wide, it was comical. 'Did you just do a Michael Buffer joke on me?'

Had she? 'Maybe?'

'Let's get ready to rumble? His famous catchphrase when he introduces a fight?'

'Of course. I knew that.' He clearly didn't believe her, because his eyes brimmed with amusement, the earlier strain now vanished. 'Go, be brilliant.' As he walked away, the relaxed demeanour, the easy stride were back in place. She'd helped do that, she thought proudly.

And Seb had done that, she thought, equally proudly, when she turned to find Rylan and Hayley sniggering about what he should wear.

It was going to be a hit. Earlier he'd wobbled like a... hell, a spinning blancmange. Thank God Maggie had been there to calm him down. She was so good at that: quietly yet firmly taking control of a situation. First his nerves, then Rylan and Hayley's wardrobe calamity. Now, watching the first dancers step onto the dancefloor, he knew her confidence in him hadn't been misplaced. He bloody could put on an event.

Immediately he thought of his dad, and how much he wanted him sitting on the front row, next to his mum and sisters. Burning with the same pride he could see in their eyes. *I hope you're watching up there, Pops.*

The over-sixties dancers – Seb had put them on first, figuring they were the least likely to get stage fright – wowed. To see that generation strut their stuff, grey hair shining in the lights, arthritic joints and bad backs forgotten, heightened his already sky-high emotions. And that was before Shirley and Pauline came onto the floor. Not the most competent, but their sheer gusto, the delight they showed... He reckoned he wasn't the only one having to blink a few times.

Now it was the turn of the middle group, and Seb was waiting outside the ladies for Maggie – yeah, *Strictly Come Dancing* had big posh changing rooms; *Strictly Local* had youth centre toilets. Unless you wanted to take your chance on a back room without a lock. He'd changed in the gents.

The door creaked open, and Seb nearly swallowed his tongue. 'Jesus, Mags.'

She grinned, giving him a twirl. The vibrancy of her face, the confident way she moved, the sparkle in her eyes. She radiated beauty, elegance. And sex. Oh yes, the seemingly endless legs, the cleavage peeking through the lace. The low, sultry back. They were all pure sex.

'Our shopping spree last Saturday wasn't wasted then?'

'God no. Though how you expect me to dance with you, when all I want to do is push you against a wall and...' He let out a ragged breath. 'Please tell me I can at least go home with you when this is all over.'

'Of course.' She stepped towards him, then ran her hand down the silk of his black shirt, stopping at the third button. After undoing it, she took a step back and gave him a smile loaded with promise. 'Now I see why Sarah took you shopping on Tuesday.'

'Apparently jeans aren't appropriate.' He could hardly

get the words out, his throat, his whole body, felt so tightly wound.

She smiled. 'I do like you in jeans.'

'You like my bum in jeans,' he corrected.

'I do.' She raised her eyes to his. 'But black silk is now my favourite outfit on you.'

'It's not see-through. Turns out I don't have the balls.'

She laughed softly. 'I'm glad. I don't want all those other women out there seeing what I get to see.'

He smirked, enjoying the possessive glint in her eye. 'Are you sure about the third button?'

'We're about to perform a sensual, erotic ballroom dance.' The smile she gave him was pure sin. 'Trust me, I'm sure.'

They waited by the double doors for Winston, compère for the evening, to call them out. 'In case I forget, thanks for earlier, sorting Rylan and Hayley, and calming me down. I was a basket case.' He jammed a hand through his hair, wondering how she was so collected while he felt those same nerves jangling again. Could he really do this? Last time he'd danced in this hall, Belinda had told him he'd been more wooden than a pine dresser.

His heart jumped as he felt Maggie's hand curl around his. 'Whatever you're thinking now, stop.'

Okay then. Taking a deep breath, he squeezed her fingers. 'You're right. It's just I'm only now realising that if I cock up, they won't see how good you are.' His eyes found hers. 'And that would be a crying shame, because you're bloody amazing.'

'Thank you.' Maggie's laughter fluttered over him. 'Only realising now, huh? That really is last minute.'

'Yeah. We should have planned for this scenario. I blame you.'

A pair of slender arms circled him, their hold surprisingly strong. 'We did plan for it. That's why we put in all the practice. Now all we have to do is go out and enjoy ourselves, because that's what dancing is all about. Joy. And that's one of many things you've given me, Sebastian Armstrong.' Her breath warmed his neck as she reached to kiss him. 'Now let's go and show them what a real rumba looks like.'

And they did.

To the tune of 'Aint No Sunshine' – yes, they'd copied mercilessly from *Strictly* – Seb didn't just dance the steps, he felt them. With Maggie looking at him the way she was, her hands running over his chest, teasing him, twirling away and then falling back into his arms, his nerves were forgotten, her sensuality, her vibrancy, carrying them both through.

When the final note sounded, Seb looked at Maggie and didn't try to hide how he felt. Totally swept away, not just by the dance, but by her. 'I have no words to do that justice. To do *you* justice.'

She gave him a tremulous smile and if he wasn't mistaken she looked like she'd been squeezed through the emotional wringer, too. 'Me neither.'

The moment was broken as the crowd erupted around them, cat whistles in amongst the applause. Usually he'd lark about, bowing, hamming it up, but it all felt too much, his emotions too on the edge. Finding Maggie's hand, he turned them towards the judges, where Belinda winked, thankfully dialling the emotion down a notch. In common with the TV show, the judges had their say – sexy, hot, x-rated, he'd take all the plaudits. Hell, he'd felt them all. The final vote on the performances though – a show of hands – was down to the audience, when all the contestants had danced. It was crude, but Seb figured if anyone was taking it that seriously, they'd come to the wrong place.

As they stepped out of the hall, Alice caught up with them. 'That was incredible, darlings.' It was a reasonable imitation of the *Strictly* judges – the real ones, not the group who were out there now, happily bestowing compliments on everyone.

Maggie glowed – there was no other way to describe her. Laughing, she threw her arms around his sister. 'We killed it, didn't we? I think it was the dress, in fact I'm sure it was. I felt so sexy in it.'

He cleared his throat, about to tell her it was the woman inside the dress that had blown them all away. Before he could though, Penny and Tabby burst through the doors and threw their arms around their mum.

They were followed by Paul, and the moment Seb caught sight of him, his euphoria took a nose dive.

The girls chattered away to Maggie and Alice, words like 'sick', 'awesome' and 'wicked' a few he could make out. Paul stared stonily at him.

'She's quite a dancer, isn't she? But then you must have

known that.' *Bet you regret not dancing with now though, you prick.*

Paul shifted on his feet. 'I was aware she danced, yes.'

Maggie looked up with a start when Paul spoke. 'Oh, hello, Paul. I didn't see you there.'

'I came to congratulate you.'

'Both of us.' Maggie's gaze fell on Seb. 'I couldn't have done it without Seb.'

There were degrees of awkward Seb could put up with, and then there was now. It wasn't that he didn't mind facing off Paul. He'd have continued to do so, happily, if he didn't think the atmosphere was killing Maggie's buzz and confusing the girls.

'Right, well I'm going to check out the youth dancers.' He forced a smile on his face. 'I'll catch you all later.'

As he pushed open the doors back into the hall, Seb tried not to think about how Paul was now congratulating his ex-wife.

The next couple on the floor were Kiara and Zayne, who performed a very classy waltz. Kiara looked stunning in what he'd been told was her sister's prom dress, and Zayne wore his dad's suit. It was a couple of sizes too big for him but nobody really noticed. Not with the way he led Kiara confidently round the dance floor. Seb didn't need to look at Belinda's proud smile to know how well they'd done.

'No way are we beating that,' Rylan huffed beside him. 'The dude can actually dance. We might as well not bother.'

Seb put an arm on Rylan's shoulder and squeezed. 'You're not going out there to win. You're going to show your mates, the people in the audience and, most important, yourself what you can do if you put your mind to something.' He glanced across at Hayley who was standing on his other side. 'Plus you're going to dance with a, what do you call it, a really peng girl? So shit, Rylan, go out and enjoy yourself.'

Rylan smirked over at Hayley. 'Yeah, I guess.'

Eyes shining, she gave him a small shove. 'Yay Ry, did you just call me peng?'

'Nah, Seb did.' Rylan grinned at her. 'But maybe he's not wrong.'

A moment later, Rylan and Hayley walked out onto the floor. The sight of their interlocked hands, the way they looked, so smart, so chilled, caused his heart to lodge in his throat. Maggie – the same Maggie who was probably still with Paul, but no, damn it, Seb wasn't going to think about that – anyway, somehow she'd managed to find Rylan some dark trousers, a white shirt and even a bow tie. It meant he nicely matched Hayley, who wore a flirty black and white skirt, along with her inevitable huge hoop ear rings.

As they waited for the music, Seb felt a rush of unexpected nerves. If Rylan tripped, if it went badly... would the kid ever forgive him for pushing him into this?

The music began, and he held his breath. The jive was... enthusiastic he decided was the kindest way to describe it.

But hell, it really didn't matter. Not when you could see how much they were enjoying it.

When it was over, Rylan fist pumped the air. Then, as the crowd cheered, he picked Hayley up and spun her around. After the judges had finished giving their glowing verdict – no way were they going to say anything but good things to these amazing young dancers – Rylan's eyes found Seb's and he flashed him a cocky grin. It said he'd done it, he'd pushed himself out of his comfort zone, dared to try. And hadn't fallen flat on his face.

Shit. Seb wiped at his eyes. He was going to bloody miss these kids when he left.

Chapter Thirty-Three

Maggie didn't want to be in the TV room, playing happy families with Paul. Alice had discreetly disappeared, saying something about getting back to Sarah and her mum, and Paul had somehow persuaded her into this room, on the pretext of keeping the girls entertained. As if watching the dancing wouldn't do that.

How little he knew his own daughters still. And how little he knew his ex-wife, if he seriously thought she was going to listen to what he had to say about Seb.

'I know I'm not one to dish out advice, considering my own confused situation with Isabelle, but do you really think you should be dancing like, well...' He cleared his throat, glancing over at the girls, who were watching some random cartoon channel. 'Dancing like *that*, in front of your children?'

'Dancing like what?' Oh, she knew, but she hadn't

realised what a prude he was, until now. 'The judges said we performed an excellent rumba.'

'That's what it was? It looked more like foreplay.'

Delighted, she laughed. 'Then I guess we really did smash it out there.'

It had been more than sexy, though. The moment the music had begun, the connection between her and Seb had been palpable, yet it had been when the dance had ended, that her heart had almost stopped. The look Seb had given her, the tenderness, the adoration in his eyes. Paul had never looked at her like that, nobody had. She knew now that whatever Seb planned on doing with his life, she meant something to him, as he did to her.

It's just she'd taken it a step further, and fallen headlong in love with him.

'I don't understand. This isn't like you at all, dancing like that, taking up with someone so... unsuitable.' Paul looked not only puzzled, but concerned. 'Is it serious?'

'That's between us.' Because she sensed beneath his prissy tone he was trying to understand, actually trying to be a friend to her, Maggie added. 'Whatever the future holds, I don't regret it. Seb's given me back something you managed to take away for a while. Myself.'

He flinched. 'What do you mean?'

'You chipped away at my self-confidence, without me realising it. And I'm to blame too, because I let you. Yes, I'm organised, yes, I like to plan and I'm naturally cautious, but you made me feel like these were bad traits. That I was dull.

Well, guess what, the woman who just danced out there isn't dull. She can let go, she can have fun. And more than that, she can attract a gorgeous twenty-seven-year-old man.' One, she knew, had held the attention of every female out there tonight with his snake hips and his shirt unbuttoned enough to give glimpses of his ripped torso.

It had taken her until now to realise Paul, for all the years she'd spent with him, had never really understood her. Seb, on the other hand, understood her more than she understood herself. *You've spent so long having to be sensible, you've suppressed the part of you that wants to be a little crazy, a little wild now and again.* How right his words seemed now.

To his credit, Paul looked shamefaced. 'I'm sorry, I never meant for any of this. I did love you, part of me still does, but as the marriage went on… I guess I felt hemmed in. Instead of talking to you, telling you how I felt, I took it out on you and lashed out.' His eyes were bleak when they sought out hers. 'The girls, they came too soon. I wasn't ready to be a dad.' His voice shook as he dragged in a breath. 'If I'm honest, I'm not sure I ever will be.'

Because she sensed he was struggling, Maggie placed a hand over his. 'You can talk to me now.'

'God, this is so hard to admit to.' His chest heaved and when he spoke again, his voice sounded full of guilt. 'I worked crazy hours, and when I'd finished, I wanted to play. To go out to the theatre, to eat out. Not watch blasted cartoons in front of the television. I love the girls, don't get me wrong. They're great kids. It's just…' He trailed off, shaking his head.

'You don't enjoy them,' Maggie finished for him, remembering the day it had snowed. Seb's first thought had been to take them all tobogganing. Paul's would no doubt have been, could he still get into work. 'It wasn't just the girls though, was it? You didn't want to do what *I* wanted to do, either, even before they came along.'

'You mean the dancing,' he said flatly.

'Yes, the dancing was one, but there were others, like going on holiday, spending time with *my* friends. You were only interested in what you wanted to do.' Judgmental and self-absorbed, Paul was the exact opposite of Seb, who'd left a life he loved in Australia because his dad was ill. Who'd put his heart and soul into helping the kids at the youth centre. Who'd been there for her, unasked, when Tabby had been in hospital.

Yet none of that meant Seb was any readier to be a father or a husband, than Paul had been. He was unselfish, yes, but he was also untamed.

Paul stared at her with a pained expression. 'I thought you liked what I wanted.'

'I liked pleasing you, yes.' She looked at him sadly. 'But our marriage didn't work because you didn't feel the same way.' Her eyes searched his. 'And if you're not prepared to put Isabelle first now, to do things to please her, then it's not fair to marry her.'

Paul clasped his hand over hers, his face sombre. 'I hear you.'

At that moment the door opened, and Maggie looked up with a start to see Seb standing in the doorway. His gaze jumped from where she had her hand in Paul's, to her face. Hurt flashed in his eyes before he looked away. 'Sorry. I didn't mean to interrupt.'

Maggie disengaged her hand and rose to her feet. 'You weren't interrupting anything.'

He nodded, but wouldn't meet her eyes. 'I came to tell you they're ready to announce the winners. Thought you might like to watch.'

Paul stood too. 'Reckon you're going to win, do you?'

'I know we're not,' Seb countered mildly. 'I'd already agreed with Belinda that we wouldn't put our dance towards the vote. It didn't seem fair, me being the organiser.' His gaze strayed to her. 'But Maggie still has a chance at best overall dancer.'

Seb's tone, so formal, didn't sit with the man she knew, and she worried that it wasn't because of Paul's presence, but because of what he thought he'd seen. 'I didn't realise there was an individual category.'

'Belinda and I discussed it this morning.' His gaze pinned hers. 'I didn't want you to lose out on the chance of picking up a glitter ball.'

Her eyes widened. 'You got glitter balls?'

Finally he smiled, just a small lift of his mouth, but his eyes blazed with affection. 'You told me you wanted to win one. This might be your best shot.'

The conversation with Paul was forgotten. 'Then what are we waiting for?'

Seb couldn't get the image of Maggie holding hands with Paul out of his head. Logically he knew what he'd seen hadn't been sexual. It was nothing more than Maggie showing compassion to a man she'd shared her life with. Still shared her children with.

Fuck, it hurt though. If he couldn't cope seeing her with Paul, a man who'd hurt her, how could he cope knowing she was with a man who might actually deserve her?

But that was for the future, and he wasn't a guy who dwelled too long on that. Now was more important, because in reality, that was all anyone had.

And for now, he had Maggie.

'God, I can't believe how nervous I am.' Maggie, her hand holding his tightly, gave him a wry smile.

They were standing with the rest of the contestants at the side of the small stage. Winston, very dramatically, opened an envelope containing the list of winners. Seb didn't know who'd been chosen because he'd asked not to be involved, figuring then nobody could say the results were rigged.

Best dance couple in the over-sixties... wasn't Pauline and Shirley.

Pauline sighed, but Shirley waved her hand in a dismissive gesture. 'Blah, what do the judges know. We were fabulous, dear.'

Seb laughed, giving them both a hug. 'If it helps, you had my vote.'

Best dance couple in the adult category was a couple with no connection to the centre.

'Should have been you,' Shirley said to Maggie, rather too loudly. Seb couldn't help but agree, but please God Maggie would get her glitter ball anyway.

Best dance couple in the youth category went to... Kiara and Zayne.

Seb's chest filled with pride as the pair of them giggled their way onto the stage to collect their glitter ball – okay, it was more tennis ball than the football-sized one on *Strictly*, but his budget was considerably smaller. In front of him, Hayley clapped vigorously and Rylan, well, at least he clapped.

'Bummer it wasn't us,' she told Rylan, 'but they were good.'

'Never mind, babe, we'll win it next year.' Rylan turned round and cocked a brow at Seb. 'We're doing it again, yeah?'

Seb shrugged. 'That's not going to be up to me.' He glanced from Rylan to Hayley, and warmth seeped through his chest. 'But you two should keep up the lessons. You make a great pair.'

'If this guy had sussed that sooner,' Hayley replied, nudging Rylan, 'we'd have aced it today.' Then, clearly only just realising what he'd said, she frowned at Seb. 'Why isn't it up to you? You're still gonna be here, yeah?'

Ah. Seb was saved an awkward reply when Winston stepped back up to the microphone. 'And now, the award to beat all awards.' He raised the glitter ball trophy – soft-ball sized, he'd gone all out on this one. 'This one is for the best dancer of the evening. And it goes to... Maggie Peterson.'

As joy and pride flowed through him in equal measure, he turned to Maggie, expecting to find her face wreathed in smiles. Instead she looked... frozen. 'Mags?' Her eyes were glazed, her expression blank. 'Your glitter ball is waiting for you.'

'My... what?'

He couldn't work out what was wrong with her. 'Your trophy.' He waved towards the stage. 'Go, pick it up. Winston's waiting for you.'

'Oh, I won?'

Was it the shock of winning? Something had scrambled her usually razor-sharp brain.

With the help of Pauline and Shirley, they pushed Maggie towards the stage. Whatever it was that had spooked her, she recovered sufficiently to give him a smile when she put her hands on the glitter ball.

Maggie was quiet when they arrived back at her house. Seb left her to take the exhausted Penny and Tabby upstairs to bed, and when she came back down he patted the space next to him on the sofa. 'Is everything okay?'

'Of course.' He loved to see her smile, but now it seemed forced. 'I could ask the same of you.'

'Me?' he asked, surprised.

'Paul opened up to me today. He admitted he wasn't ready to be a husband or a father.' She turned to face him. 'What you saw was me—'

'Comforting him,' Seb interjected.

'If you knew that, then why did you act so weird? I thought maybe you were jealous.' Her gaze dropped away from his. 'Now I feel stupid.'

'Are you crazy? Of course I was jealous.' He wrapped her up in his arms. 'I hated seeing you with him. I want to be the only one holding your hands, talking that intimately to you.'

'It wasn't intimate.' Her voice was muffled against his chest. 'Not in the way you mean.'

'But you were sharing feelings.' And that had hurt. She and Paul shared a history, children. It made his few months with her appear insignificant, even though how he felt couldn't be more significant. 'Look, can we forget about him now? Focus on you and me.' He lifted her chin so he could look directly into her eyes. 'And the fact that we've got the whole night together?'

'The whole night?' She glanced down at her watch. 'It's ten o'clock already.'

He dipped his head to kiss her, feeling the spark shoot through his body the moment their lips touched. 'You'd be amazed what I can do in the time that's left to us.'

Her eyes turned smokey. 'Then I look forward to being amazed.'

It was only as his mouth descended greedily on hers that he remembered he hadn't got to the bottom of what had been troubling her earlier. The way she responded though, the way she shifted so she was sitting astride him, her hands in his hair, her body hot and needy over his, suggested it was no longer important.

Chapter Thirty-Four

M aggie woke to the sound of the bathroom door being slammed shut.

Tabby.

Her youngest daughter hadn't learned the art of being careful about anything.

Beside her, Seb let out a muffled sound, his arm tightening around her.

And Maggie stilled.

He was still here. In her bed. And Tabby was already awake.

Logically it wasn't that big a deal. The girls had seen him around her. He'd held her hand in front of them. Him staying over was simply the next step.

Except yesterday he'd told Rylan that running the competition again next year wouldn't be up to him. Not *yeah, let's do it*, or even *we've got to see what the boss says*. Seb wasn't careful about his words, so the only explanation for why the youth centre holding a competition again next year wouldn't be up to him was because he wouldn't be there.

The hurt she'd felt yesterday burned again and no, it didn't help that Seb leaving had been inevitable. A foolish part of her had held out hope, and now that hope had been snatched away.

Seb shifted, moving closer. 'Umm, warm, soft.' His nose nuzzled her neck. 'Smells like roses.' He let out a long, sleepy sigh. 'This is how I want to wake up every morning.'

Until you leave. The thought made her stiffen, which in turn woke Seb properly. Propping himself up on his elbow, blue eyes as dreamy as a summer's day, he gazed down at her. 'Morning.' He gave her an easy smile, but as his eyes took her in, his expression changed to worry. 'Crap, I forgot to set the alarm last night.'

'It's okay.' But it wasn't, because there was no next step for them. Not now he would be leaving. 'Tabby's in the bathroom.'

He sat up, the muscles of his chest sliding over each other. 'What do you want me to do?'

'If I distract her when she comes out, could you...' She trailed off, because *sneak out* sounded awful.

'Could I creep out of your room and out of your house, like a... trespasser? An uninvited guest?'

She didn't need to look into his eyes to see he was hurt. The way he flung the covers back, walked stiffly to his jeans and yanked them on, said it all.

'I'm sorry.'

He nodded, but she could tell from his tight expression

he was still upset. 'You really think Tabby would care if she walked in and saw me in bed with you?'

Tabby no. Penny would have questions, and Maggie didn't have the answers for her. 'This isn't about how they might feel now. It's about protecting them.'

He thrust his T-shirt over his head. 'Protecting them? From what?'

'From heartache.' She'd failed to do it for herself, but by God she was determined to do it for them. She knew what it was like to have parents who didn't look out for you. She would always be there for her daughters, always.

Picking up his shoes, he stared at her, his expression not just confused, but crushed. 'You think I'd hurt them? Hurt you?' They heard the toilet flush in the family bathroom, and Seb sighed. 'Go, do what you need to do. I'll be gone when you come back.'

His unhappiness was clear and her heart tugged painfully. Yet much as he cared for them all, perhaps even loved them, to some degree, he wasn't going to be sticking around. He was going to hurt them, however unintentionally.

So she swallowed down the words she wanted to say. *Stay. Have breakfast with us. Spend the day with us.*

Instead she walked out to find Tabby.

Later that day, she met Alice and her kids for lunch in the park.

'Have you and Seb fallen out?' Alice asked as they lingered over a coffee in the warmth of the café, the kids now blowing off steam in the playground outside.

This, she thought, taking a deliberate sip of her coffee. It was exactly what she'd been afraid of. Was Alice asking as her friend, or as Seb's sister? 'Why?'

'Because he popped round to ours this morning and looked really out of sorts. Upset, I think. I wasn't sure if you'd had a tiff, or if it was these calls he keeps getting from Australia.'

Maggie clutched onto the mug, dread pooling inside her. 'What calls?'

Alice's look was full of sympathy. 'He hasn't said anything to you?'

'No.' Had he been too afraid of her reaction? Worried she'd cling to him and beg him to stay? Or had he just not thought it was important enough, considering he'd always planned to go back?

'Well, if it's any consolation, he hasn't said anything to me, either. It's just Sarah mentioned she'd overheard him talking about meeting up with some guy called Bruce, and I know he took another call this morning from him because he said his name when he answered. Before sloping out of the kitchen.' Alice toyed with her coffee cup. 'I also heard him talking to someone at the youth centre. It sounded like he'd handed his notice in, but I couldn't be sure. I tried to listen in, as any nosey big sister would, but it was hard to make much out.' She glanced up at Maggie. 'Might be that

Bruce is coming over here. And I totally misheard the other conversation.'

'Maybe.' Maggie fought to speak past the tightness in her throat.

Alice exhaled heavily. 'This thing between you and Seb, it's not the neat and tidy fun affair you wanted it to be, is it?'

As understatements went, it was a beauty. 'It's not, no.'

'More a messy, tangled, steaming emotional cowpat?'

Maggie looked at Alice, at the sympathy in her eyes, the concern, and managed a strangled laugh. 'God, Alice, what have I done?'

Alice slid an arm around her. 'You've opened a heart that had been closed for too long.' She squeezed her. 'But that's a good thing. It means you've avoided becoming a bitter, wronged woman. In fact, judging from last night, you've become a sexy, vibrant one instead.'

Maggie forced a smile. Yes, okay, she could do this. Be happy that she'd met Seb, rather than miserable he was going to leave her.

But the ache in her chest told her she was kidding herself.

Monday morning, and Seb stood outside the small modern office building where Sarah worked, ringing on the intercom.

'Seb Armstrong, here to see Sarah Armstrong.'

A few seconds later, the door clicked open. It wasn't the first time he'd visited her at work – he'd had to pick the house key up from her all those months ago when he'd first arrived back – so he wasted no time bounding up the two flights of steps to her floor. Once outside her office, he tapped on the open door.

She glanced up and narrowed her eyes. 'Sally said there was a Seb Armstrong to see me but I didn't believe her. What are you doing here?'

'Good to see you too, sis.'

'We live together. I see enough of you at home.'

'Yes, about that.' He stepped inside the office and shut the door behind him. 'Is there an evening this week when you can, maybe, not come home? At least not until late?'

'You're throwing me out of my own place?'

'I'm asking you, very nicely, if you can go somewhere else after work for few hours this week.' He eased back against the fancy leather and chrome chair. 'You know, this would be a lot easier if you had a boyfriend.'

'Right, so I need to get a boyfriend so I've got somewhere to stay when my brother needs to turn my place into some sort of, what, shagfest?' The moment she realised what she'd said, her eyes widened in horror. 'Oh God, no, I don't want to think about what you and Maggie are going to be doing in my place.'

Seb grinned. 'So we will be getting it to ourselves?'

'Maggie has a great home. Why aren't you using that?'

'I could.' He crossed one leg over the other, wondering how he could put this without sounding like a prat. 'We always go to hers though, and for once, I'd like to invite her to mine. Even if it isn't actually, mine. At least that way I can cook for her without dragging carrier bags round. And I can take her to bed without worrying if the kids will wake up.'

Sarah put her fingers in her ears. 'God, Seb, will you stop talking about your sex life. I don't want to hear it. Especially as I've not got one of my own.'

'Your choice, sis. I keep telling you work is no substitute for a good—'

'Stop, now.'

The look on her face was so comical, Seb burst out laughing. 'Relationship, sis. Work is no substitute for a good relationship.' He paused, shooting Sarah his most charming smile. 'Back to me commandeering your place. Hannah is happy to stay over and take care of the girls any night this week. Though we did, only tentatively of course, agree on Friday.'

Sarah's eyes rounded. 'Let me get this straight. Without asking Maggie first, you've arranged for Hannah to look after Tabby and Penny while you entertain their mother. In my home.'

He screwed up his face. 'Yeah, it doesn't sound great when you put it like that.'

Sarah sat back on her chair and studied him. 'Are you going to tell me why you're going to all this effort?'

'No.' There were some things a guy had to do by himself, without his big sister's help.

'Umm.' Being the shrewd woman she was, he knew she

wouldn't leave it there. 'Does this have anything to do with the calls you've been making to Australia?'

He felt a flush creep up his neck. 'Sort of.'

Sarah exhaled a long slow breath, her expression turning from mildly irritated to concerned. 'Can you at least let me know if Maggie is going to be upset at whatever it is you're going to all this effort to tell her?'

Sarah pinned him with her stare, and Seb felt the weight of his decision press heavily down on him. 'Truthfully, I don't know how she'll react to what I have to say. I only know that it's time to say it.'

'You once told me you loved her.'

He swallowed, hard. 'Nothing's changed.'

'So why all the drama?'

He picked around for the right words. 'I can't carry on like this, sis. Living in your house, earning not very much. I need to... move forward.' His eyes found hers. 'That's all I can say. The rest, Maggie needs to hear first.'

'Fair enough, but please, treat her with care.'

'You seriously need to say that to me?'

Her eyes locked with his and she gave him a sad smile. 'You're right. I guess you both went into this with your eyes wide open.'

They had. Yet he could never have anticipated how hard he'd fallen. 'So, Friday?'

'Fine. I'll talk to Hannah. Might be best for me to sleep at Maggie's with the kids. Let Hannah have her Friday night to go out on the town, like young folk do, apparently.' She shook her head. 'You know it would have been a lot easier if you'd dated Hannah instead.'

Seb rose slowly to his feet and leant across the desk to kiss Sarah's cheek. 'Thanks, sis.' When he got to the door, he looked back at her. 'I didn't want easy. I wanted deep, complex, serious, fascinating, challenging. Beautiful. I wanted Maggie. I still do.'

But what he wanted, and what he could have, were two very different things.

_____

Later that evening, after Sarah confirmed Friday was fine, Seb picked up the phone to call Maggie. She answered on the second ring.

'Hey.' He heard the click of a door, and imagined she'd moved into another room. 'I'm sorry about asking you to leave yesterday morning.'

'No need. I understand.' She didn't want her kids getting the wrong idea, that he was a permanent fixture. He respected her decision, though it bloody hurt. Whatever the future held for him and Maggie, he still wanted to be part of their lives. All of their lives. 'So, this Friday.' He was alarmed to find his voice shaking. 'I wanted to invite you over to mine. Technically to Sarah's, though that kind of sounds naff so let's stick with how I phrased it the first time.' *Get a grip.* 'Would you like to come over for a meal?'

There was a pause, long enough to nearly give him a

heart attack, before her voice came back on the line. 'Well, with an invitation like that, how can I refuse?'

He exhaled in relief, wondering when talking to Maggie had become so difficult. *Since you decided what you want to do.* 'So that's a yes? Sarah's happy to come and stay at yours with the girls.'

'This is an overnight offer then?'

'Of course.' Was he imagining it, or did she sound uncertain? 'Does that change your answer?'

'No, no, that's fine.'

Fine? Sleeping with him was only *fine*? 'Okay then, it's a date.'

'It's a date,' she confirmed.

Yet when he put down the phone, it didn't feel like a date at all. It felt like the beginning of the end.

Chapter Thirty-Five

Friday evening, and Maggie's heart was in her throat as she knocked on Sarah's front door. Seb had offered to come and pick her up, but she'd wanted the comfort of knowing she could go when she wanted to.

She wasn't sure she could stay, once he told her he was leaving. Yet the way he'd set this up, getting Sarah to babysit, he was clearly expecting her to. Is that how he saw this playing out? They carried on seeing each other until she... God, would he expect her to put him on the bloody plane?

'Hey.' The door opened, and in the space of a blink, Seb's face went from welcoming smile to concern. 'Mags?'

No regrets. She could do this. 'Hi.'

He ushered her in, hands on her shoulders, eyes burning into hers. 'What is it? What's wrong?'

You're bloody leaving me.

She inhaled slowly, fighting for her composure. None of

this was his fault, it was hers for taking things too far. Of course he was going back to the life he'd had. He was young, with no responsibilities. Why be trapped here, when he was free to start his next adventure? She was lucky to have this time with him. Swallowing down her emotions, she smiled. 'Nothing is wrong.' To prove it, she gave him a brief kiss, savouring the sensual feel of his lips against hers. 'Just a bad day at work. Something a meal cooked by you will surely rectify.'

He scrutinised her face, and though she was sure he didn't fully believe her, he let the matter drop. 'Come on in and have a drink. Wait, where's your overnight bag?' He looked around, his expression falling. 'Please tell me you're going to stay?'

'It's in the car,' she answered truthfully.

'Okay.' Relief flickered in his eyes. 'Shall I get it?'

'Later.' She couldn't see a scenario where she would need it, but she'd packed it anyway because that's what she did, plan for every eventuality, however slim. 'First, I'll have this drink you promised, and you can tell me what we're eating.'

He led her through to the kitchen, and she drew in a sharp breath when she noticed the table, and the effort he'd gone to. The twinkling tea lights, the silver place mats, folded napkins and, oh God, a small vase of snowdrops and crocuses. 'It looks beautiful.'

He gave her a small smile. 'It's Sarah's candles, Sarah's table decorations. The flowers I managed to sneak from the park.'

She reached for his hand. 'It's the flowers I appreciate most of all.'

His eyes searched hers, a swirl of blue. 'Shit, Mags, there's so much I want to say. I had all this planned, the wine, the food, but now I don't know if it was a good idea. Maybe we should talk first.'

But then she wouldn't want to sit at his beautifully laid table, and eat his carefully prepared food. 'In my experience, it's always better to stick to a plan.'

He laughed softly. 'Yeah? Even if it's a bad plan?'

'When you decided on it, you thought it was a good plan.'

'You're the expert on these things so fine, let's stick to plan A.' A tenderness entered his eyes, one that made her heart swell and her chest tighten. 'But we need to rewind, because we skipped the most important part.'

'Yes?' Her voice sounded husky.

'Umm.' He ran a hand through her hair, eyes never leaving hers. 'First, we kiss. A proper one this time.'

It had taken Seb to make her realise there were different kinds of kisses. With Paul a kiss had been a straightforward press of lips and tangle of tongues; a signal he wanted to have sex.

With Seb, a kiss was like an enchanted journey. It didn't need to arrive at a destination; the journey was a treat in itself. He could kiss for seconds, or for hours, but always, always, he kissed like he didn't ever want it to end. Sometimes the kiss was gentle, often it was hungry, every time it left her breathless.

As his hands slid down her back, cupping her buttocks, drawing her against him, his tongue teased, his lips caressed. Just when she was losing her mind, her body on fire, her heart dancing, he eased away. Pressing his forehead against hers, he groaned. 'I could kiss you for ever.'

Then do it. Don't leave me.

But that wasn't fair. After all he'd given her, she wouldn't let him feel bad about going. She'd accept it with a smile on her face, even as her heart tore in two. 'Maybe you should feed me first.'

He kissed her briefly on the end of her nose, then took a step back. 'No diverging from the plan. Got it.'

'What are we eating?' She asked as she watched him slide some diced chicken into a wok. 'No, let me guess. Chicken Pad Thai.'

He smiled. 'Well remembered, but I did say it was *one* of the few things I could cook. The other is Thai red curry.'

'Wow, even your cooking is exotic.'

He raised brow. 'Even?'

'Shirley once called you exotic, and at the time it made me laugh, but in a way I think she was right. All that travelling, living abroad, has made you different from most guys. You're sort of, I don't know, not domestic.' She paused, catching his eye. 'You like to roam free.'

He regarded her questioningly for a moment, but made no comment as he sliced and stirred.

It was only when they sat down at the table she realised she wasn't the only one feeling strained. Seb looked – she could only describe it as twitchy. Nervous. Whatever he had to say, he'd wanted to blurt it out earlier, and she hadn't let him.

Now she regretted it, because now both of them were sitting here pretending everything was normal, when it wasn't.

Seb started to join all the dots together in his head. Her hesitation on the phone when he'd first invited her over. The anxious look on her face when he'd opened the door. Her reluctance to bring her overnight bag in, if she even had one. The gasp when she'd seen the way he'd set the table. The way she'd hardly touched her wine, presumably so she could still drive home.

Maggie had guessed what he was about to say, and was dreading it.

Shit. What did he do now? Go through with it still, despite pretty much knowing her response? *You like to roam free*. Had that been her subtle way of telling him that's what he should be doing?

Maggie settled her fork onto her plate and sat back in her chair. 'I think, for both our sakes, we need to talk.'

The mouthful he'd just taken stuck in his throat, and Seb had to fight to swallow it. Abandoning the rest of his plateful – it had tasted like cardboard, anyway – he stood, collected the plates and dumped them on the side of the sink. 'Let's go to the sitting room.' At least when it all went up in flames, his bum would be comfortable.

She sat down first, shifting right to the end of the sofa, but Seb wasn't having that. Deliberately he sat next to her, and took hold of her hand. Though she froze for a second, he felt her body relax as she squeezed it back. 'I...' He cleared his throat. Where were those bloody words he wanted to say? Why the fuck hadn't he planned this? Because however hard it had seemed, it was a thousand times worse now he was pretty certain what her response was going to be.

'It's okay,' Maggie said quietly. 'I know about Australia.'

He jerked his head up. 'What do you know?'

'Your sisters told me about the phone calls.' Her eyes flicked away from his. 'How you're flying out there the first week in March.'

He sighed, wondering how much his interfering siblings had overheard. 'They're such bloody gossips.'

'Maybe they thought I deserved to know.'

Her tone was mild, but he sensed she was upset. 'Obviously I was going to tell you, but me going to pick the rest of my stuff up and sorting out the loose ends over there didn't seem to be such a big deal.' He looked down at their clasped hands, trying to find his rhythm. 'There's so many more important things I need to tell you. Things you might not want to hear, which is okay, because I kind of expect that, but I have to say this anyway, just in case there's some chance—'

'Sorting out loose ends?'

Her strangled question made him look back up at her. 'That's what I said, yes.' Her eyes were like saucers, her expression one of utter confusion. 'Holy shit, you thought the trip to Oz was it? That I'm *leaving*, leaving?' She nodded, and as he watched the tears well in her gorgeous grey eyes, his heart began to thump into life. 'Christ, Mags, I could never leave you. Don't you realise this yet? I'm in love with you. I'm yours, totally and utterly, if you want me.' He clutched her hands with both of his. 'Hell, even if you don't, I'm here. I'm going to hang around just in case you change your mind.'

She looked dazed. The good news, she hadn't pulled away her hand. He'd hold onto that flicker of hope.

'But Alice said you'd handed your notice in at the youth centre.'

'She *what*? Bloody hell, she's like some super spy. Why the hell is she discussing my business with you?' But then he shook his head, realising exactly why. 'Because she's your friend as much as she's my sister.'

'She was trying to forewarn me.'

'Yeah, might have been better if she'd got her facts straight first.'

'She's right though? You are leaving?'

'I'll be working at the centre right up to September, but then yes, I'll be leaving.' He'd told her he loved her, that he was hers, yet she'd kept quiet about her own feelings. That spark of hope began to fade but he ploughed on, determined to give it his best shot, even though he'd always known it was a long one. 'I've signed up to do a master's in youth and community work at one of the London universities.'

Her eyebrows shot up, her face losing some of its shock. 'Seb, that's... amazing. I'm so happy for you.'

'Yeah?'

Her hands, previously still, shifted so she was now holding his tightly. 'Yes. It means you've decided what you want to do.'

'I have.' He met her eyes. 'I've also decided where I want to be, and who I want to be with. If she'll have me.' Before she could say anything, he played his final cards. 'I can't offer you what Paul did, or what others can. What you deserve. For the next year I'll be earning pretty much zero, and the savings I have will be decimated by university fees and living expenses.' He dragged in a breath, his chest tight, his pulse racing. 'All I can say is nobody could love you more. If you want to take a risk on seeing me still, on giving you and me a real go, I'll always put you and the girls first.' From the dodgy start, the words now poured out of him. 'Just one more thing, Tabby and Penny. You know I'm besotted with them, don't you? That I know they come as part of the package, but that only makes it even more precious.'

Chapter Thirty-Six

M aggie felt like she was coming out of a deep sleep. One in which she'd imagined Seb was leaving her. A nightmare she'd now found out wasn't real.

Her brain was still playing catch up though, her thoughts muddled. 'I came here tonight expecting you to tell me you were leaving.'

His body, usually so fluid, tensed in front of her eyes. 'Would you rather that was the case?'

The uncertainty of his voice, the vulnerability in his eyes… Maggie's heart clutched painfully. He'd bravely laid out all his feelings and she'd given him nothing in return.

How much could she trust what he was saying, though? By his own admission he ambled through life, not thinking ahead, living for now. He was still young, what if he changed his mind?

'Mags, you're killing me here.'

'Oh God, I'm sorry.' She flung her arms around his neck, inhaling his essence: fresh, vigorous. So unlike the expensive, sophisticated smell of her ex.

In a heartbeat she knew she wanted to carry on inhaling Seb's unique scent for the rest of her life. That meant taking a giant risk though, one she'd be taking not just for her but for the girls.

He pulled away, his gaze skimming her face. 'Talk to me, please. Even if it's to say things you know I don't want to hear.'

'Okay.' Her hands lifted to his face, her thumbs running over the unlined skin around his eyes. He was young, but she'd been younger when she'd got married. *Look how well that worked out.* 'Before I say anything else, it's important that you know I love you, too.'

Hope flared in his expression. 'That's… wow.' As he watched her though, the light in his eyes began to dim. 'You don't look happy about it.'

'I am.' She caressed his face gently with her fingers. 'But I'm worried you're doing this for me, and it isn't right for you. What if in six months you get itchy feet and you want to go travelling again?' She drew in a breath, trying to order her words. 'I don't want you resenting me. Feeling trapped.' Her voice began to break. 'I've already had one man do that, and I can't bear to go through it again.'

'No, no.' His hands flew to hers, dragging them to his chest. 'You've got this idea I'm some adventurer, but that's not the case at all.' His expression intensified, as if he was willing her to believe him. 'Think back to that first conversation we had, about why I went travelling. Do you remember it?'

How could she forget? It had been just before they'd made love for the first time. 'You said it was because you didn't know what you wanted to do, except to avoid being stuck behind a desk.'

'Exactly. I sloped off abroad not because I wanted to explore, not because I had a thirst for adventure, but because *I didn't know what I wanted to do.*' His eyes burned into hers. 'Now I do. I want to work with kids. I want to put down roots here, near my family. I desperately want you in my life, too, but if you don't want that, if you're not ready for it, I'm still going to get my master's, and I'm still going to pursue a career in youth work.'

Inside her chest, her heart began to beat so fast, she feared it was going to trip over itself. Was this really happening? 'I thought I'd have to put you on the plane.' She buried her face in the crook of his neck, squeezing the words out past the giant lump in her throat. 'I'd told myself I could do it, smile while I waved you off, even though inside my heart would be breaking.'

He groaned, hugging her tighter. 'When you were so keen for me to leave that morning I overslept, and then so hesitant about coming here tonight, I thought you were getting ready to break up with me.' His voice faltered. 'Then you looked upset when I opened the door, and when you saw the table set out. You hardly drank any wine. I thought you'd guessed what I was going to say, and were thinking of a way to let me down gently. Before you scarpered.'

God, they'd both jumped to the wrong conclusions. As she relaxed into his arms, Maggie tried to collect her scattered thoughts, going back through what he'd said and processing it again, this time without the fog of shock. All the while his hand stroked her thigh, and his heart beat strong and steady where she lay her head.

'You still haven't said if you see me in your future.' As he spoke, his heart beat faster.

She straightened, so she could look into his eyes. 'I do. I'm just...'

'Scared of making a mistake.'

'No.' She pressed her mouth to his, closing her eyes at the power of the connection. 'Nothing about knowing you would ever be a mistake. I'm cautious though, Seb. I don't want to rush this.' She smiled. 'Not when I'm really enjoying the journey.'

'Yeah?' He laughed softly. 'That works for me.'

But still her mind couldn't help but plan ahead. 'Then again I am thirty-eight, so time isn't necessarily on our side.'

'Bloody hell, you're hardly at death's door. Men pop their clogs earlier than women anyway, so our age gap evens us up...' He trailed off when he saw her expression. 'Ah, you don't mean in that way.' He pressed his mouth to hers, the gesture tender, his gaze full of love. 'The way I see it, as long as this unrushed journey takes us to the place I want it to, Tabby and Penny will have a dad, and a stepdad. And the latter couldn't love them any more if they were genetically his. If you wanted more kids, that would be your decision. You, Tabby, Penny, and me. That's all I need.'

Maggie felt her heart burst open, and tears roll down her cheeks.

His thumb scooped them up. 'Please tell me these are happy tears and I've not said something monumentally stupid, because, fair warning, I will do that. I don't think before I speak, so sometimes crap comes out of my mouth before I realise it.'

She hiccupped out a laugh. 'You said something monumentally right.' Her body moved so she was sitting astride him, face to face, nose to nose. 'This slow pace I mentioned.' She kissed him. 'Do you think we can up it, just for tonight? I'm kind of in a rush to see your bedroom.'

The following afternoon, Seb climbed out of his car in front of Maggie's house. She'd left him early in the morning to, as she'd called it, rescue Sarah, though Seb knew she was keen to get back to her girls.

He also knew she planned on telling them he was her boyfriend.

And yes, nervous butterflies were now flapping around in his stomach. Maggie and he had talked about a lot last night, but one thing they hadn't discussed was what happened if Tabby and Penny weren't happy with their mum having a boyfriend. Or worse, with him being her boyfriend. He knew they liked him, but would that change if they were forced to see more of him? If they thought they no longer had their mum to themselves?

While he was having his minor melt-down, the door opened, revealing Tabby, crutches under her arm, her ankle still in its boot.

'We heard your car.' She put her fingers in her ears. 'It's noisy, not like Mum's.'

Okay then, at least she was still talking to him. Then again, maybe that's because Maggie had decided telling them was a small step she wasn't ready to take yet. 'It's old, and its engine has worked hard. Now and again it likes to complain.'

She nodded, as if that made perfect sense, then shifted to let him in. 'We had Auntie Sarah stay with us last night 'cos Mum was with you.'

He figured explaining whose house they'd actually been in wasn't strictly necessary. 'Did you have fun?'

'Yep. She said she's your sister, like Penny is my sister.'

'That's right. Only Penny is a cool sister.' He bent to whisper in her ear. 'Sarah is a bit goofy sometimes.'

Tabby giggled, hazel eyes sparkling. 'Mum said you're her boyfriend now.'

Seb sucked in a breath, but forced his legs to keep walking down the hallway, his face to remain relaxed, and not give in to the *holy shit what do I say now* expression it wanted to. 'Is that okay with you?'

'Does it mean you have to kiss her?'

God, this girl was an incredible, wonderful, handful. 'I don't have to, but I do want to, yes. Though you don't have to watch.'

She nodded, expression turning sober. 'Will you live here? 'Cos my friend's mum has a boyfriend and he lives in the same house as them.'

Oh crap. Hunkering down on his haunches, he looked Tabby right in the eye. 'I don't know, that's up to your mum, but I do plan on being round here a lot.'

Her face burst into a wide grin. 'Good, 'cos when you're not talking all the time when we want to listen to the telly, you're funny.'

Then she did something that made his chest tighten so painfully, he thought for a moment he was having a heart attack. She dropped her crutches and threw her arms around him.

As Seb struggled not to give in to the tears that stung his eyes, he saw Penny's face appear in the family room doorway.

Picking up Tabby's crutches, he handed them to her. Clearly oblivious to the fact that she'd totally shattered him, Tabby manoeuvred them skillfully under her arms and hobbled towards her sister. 'Mum's *boyfriend* is here.'

'Hey, Penelope.' Seb smiled over at her, his heart racing. Tabby was like him, she wore her heart on her sleeve so he knew exactly what she was thinking. Penny was altogether different.

'I have another project. I have to choose a region, like

North America or South America, or Europe, and then write about it.' Her big grey eyes looked up at him. 'Can you help?'

He swallowed, hard. 'Of course.'

'I thought maybe North America, as that has Canada and Canada has mountains, doesn't it?' In a gesture that gripped his heart as painfully as Tabby's hug, Penny clasped his hand as they walked into the family room and to the table where she'd clearly been working.

'Yes.' He had to clear his throat before he could carry on. 'The Rockies is the most famous mountain range.'

'Have you been there?'

'I have.'

'But you didn't live on a pontoon there.'

He laughed, but he knew it came out hoarse because he was still so choked full of emotion. 'No. I stayed in a log cabin.'

Her eyes widened. 'Did you see bears? I read there are lots of bears there.'

And before he knew it, Seb was talking to Penny about his holiday in Banff.

It wasn't until the girls went to bed that Seb had a moment alone with Maggie. When she came downstairs and joined him on the satsuma sofa, he stretched out so she could lie alongside him, cradling her head against his chest.

'I got a text from my sisters,' he told her, reaching for the phone he'd left on the coffee table and showing her the messages.

The first was from Alice.

If a smart cookie like Maggie is willing to put up with you, maybe you're less of a dork than I thought, A x

The second from Sarah.

I sure hope this means I get my house to myself a bit more. You're a grumpy sod in the morning. Does Maggie really know what she's letting herself in for? S x

Maggie laughed. 'They love you really.'

Yeah, he knew they did, even before reading the further messages they'd sent, telling him they were chuffed he was staying, and even more chuffed he and Maggie were really giving this a go. 'The girls seemed okay about us?' he asked, his mind turning to the other two people whose views were important.

She laughed. 'As if you had any doubts. The Peterson females are all putty in your hands.'

'All of them, huh?' He smiled, kissing the top of her head. 'Does that mean I get to rule the roost?'

'Oh no. I said we were besotted with you. Not pushovers. In fact we've already drawn up a set of rules.'

Lists he could cope with; rules made his neck hair stand on end. 'Oh yes?'

'We're going dancing once a week. All four of us. And Saturday night will always be *Strictly* night.'

Relieved, he snuggled her further into him. 'It's a deal. Hell, if it makes you all happy I'll even buy some sequins.'

Epilogue

M aggie looked along the row. There were Alice and
Sarah, chatting away to their mum, who looked
proud as punch, and very elegant in her floral print dress.
Next to her on her right sat Tabby and Penny. Tabby, now
eight, was fidgeting around in her seat... just as much of a
liability as she had been at seven. Penny, now ten, kept
craning her neck.

'I can't see him.'

Maggie pointed across the packed hall of the Barbican
Centre to a group sitting at the front wearing black gowns
and mortarboards. 'He's the one—'

'Pretending his cap is a Frisbee.' Penny grinned. 'Found
him.'

It was no wonder her daughters adored Seb, Maggie
thought with a rush of affection. He was basically a big kid
himself. Only kids didn't knuckle down to do a master's
degree while also commuting back from London every

evening to give their undivided attention to their step-daughters. He'd originally planned to rent somewhere closer to the university, but she'd questioned why he wanted to waste money on rent when, she hoped, he would spend most of his time with them.

'You said slow,' he'd pointed out.

But Maggie had soon got fed up with slow. What was the point, when she'd met the man she wanted to spend the rest of her life with? He'd moved in with them last summer. And they were still adjusting. She was learning to say yes more than no to whatever wacky idea Seb came up with for the weekend; they'd been skiing (fake snow), rock climbing (climbing wall) and skydiving (indoor, over a tube of air) to name a few. He'd committed to keep his mess to his side of the bedroom, rather than across 80 per cent of the house. He still failed to adhere to her list system regarding shopping, but each time he scratched around in the biscuit tin for his favourite Oreos, only to come up empty, she ignored his cute puppy eyes and pointed to the list. Trouble is, he'd flash that full-on, twinkling, blue-eyed smile and she'd find herself writing the damn biscuits on the list herself.

Between the adjustments though, there was laughter. And there was love.

The chancellor stepped up to the microphone, and quiet descended.

If he'd gone straight to the award ceremony itself, what followed later might never have happened. Seb was collecting a higher level degree, and his surname was

Armstrong. It was highly likely his name would be one of the first ten students to be called up.

The chancellor chose to make a speech first though, and it went on. And on.

Tabby let out a loud huff. 'That man's boring. I want to see Seb get his 'tificate.'

'Certificate,' Maggie whispered, ignoring the glare of the woman in front of them. Seriously, had she forgotten what her darling son or daughter was like at eight? 'And you will, soon.'

Alas, there was more the chancellor had to say, and Tabby was now bouncing her knee up and down.

Finally, thank God, he started to announce names. First came the doctorates.

Tabby stared at the stage, a frown on her face. 'Why's he not going up?'

'It's not his turn yet. You have to listen out for his name. Sebastian Armstrong.'

Next came the masters. Grace Ackerwell.

'That's a girl.'

'Listen, Tabby.'

Stuart Anderson.

Tabby climbed to her feet, and Maggie felt a flutter of panic. 'No, Tabby, you have to sit down.'

'Why?'

Sebastian Armstrong.

Wriggling away from Maggie's grasp, Tabby ran down the aisle. Seb, who was making his way to the stage, turned as the audience gasped. And his face broke into a huge grin as Tabby flew at him.

Laughing, he bent to pick her up, plonking his mortarboard on her head before stepping up onto the stage. Taking it all in his stride, because that was Seb. Nothing really fazed him.

The chancellor, who, to be fair, was now laughing too, handed over the certificate and the applause picked up.

As Seb stepped down from the stage, he eased Tabby to the floor, his eyes skimming across the hall to where they were sitting, and to Penny. He handed Tabby the certificate, and whispered in her ear, nodding over to Penny.

Tabby ran back to her chair, and shoved the certificate at Penny. 'He said I have to look after his hat and you have to look after this.'

That was when the tears began to stream down Maggie's face. Seb never let Tabby overshadow Penny, like she'd always been overshadowed by Emily.

Finally they made their way out of the hall to find Seb. He was waiting for them by the exit, unbelievably handsome in his dark suit, white shirt, blue tie and black gown. As the girls rushed towards him, Maggie wondered again at the amazing stroke of luck that had brought him into their lives. Paul, as she'd guessed, had decided not to marry Isabelle in the end. He was, by his own admission, too selfish to marry. And too selfish to be a proper father. He was still in their lives, the occasional phone call, the even more occasional visit. Their dad in name and DNA. In everything important though, Seb was there for them. He was the one Tabby wanted to tell when she'd fallen over/got picked for the school football team/remembered a joke/got detention for talking in class. He was the one Penny wanted to see when she aced a test/needed help with homework/wanted to know how to get rid of the boy who kept asking her out.

He was the one who offered them constant, unconditional love.

Unconsciously Maggie's hand rested on her stomach, and the new life she'd found out that morning she was carrying.

Seb loved his mum and his sisters, was besottedly in love with his step-daughters. But he wanted some time alone with Maggie.

They were all eating in a restaurant round the corner from the Barbican. It was a sunny July day and Tabby and Penny were playing in the courtyard, having demolished their lunch. God, Tabby had killed him when she'd run up to greet him. Then to see the pride in Maggie's eyes, the sweet smile from Penny as she'd hugged him afterwards. Sod the master's, being part of their lives had been his greatest accomplishment so far.

He wanted to take it to the next level though, and now, with his master's behind him, a job already lined up… yeah, it was time. Never mind he'd not rehearsed it in his mind, not planned anything around it, like the venue, the ring.

He'd known he was going to do this from that moment in Sarah's flat, eighteen months ago, when Maggie had admitted she loved him.

While Maggie chatted with his sisters, his mum caught his eye. 'Your dad would have been so proud of you.' Her voice caught. 'And I'm not just talking about the master's.' She nodded to the girls. 'You've stepped up, Seb.'

He shook his head. 'I've fallen in love. The rest was easy.' He glanced over at Maggie, saw she wasn't listening, and leant closer to his mum. 'I could really do with your help with one... vital matter.'

'Of course.' Her gaze skimmed his face, and whatever she saw there made her smile. 'Oh Seb, are you about to do what I think you are?'

'I'm not getting the bill, if that's what you mean. I don't start earning till next week.'

'You know full well I said I'd get that.' But her eyes shone with a light that hadn't been there much since his dad had died. 'We'll take the girls home. You and Maggie can follow us home later.' She put a hand to her mouth, her expression gleeful. 'Oh, you arranged a night in a hotel, didn't you? That's so romantic. See what I mean about stepping up?'

'Ah.' Bugger it. Why hadn't he thought this through more? He'd known for eighteen months he wanted to propose, and yet he decided to actually do it on the spur of the moment?

'You didn't?' His mum's shoulders fell. 'Oh, well, never mind. I'm sure you'll think of something. You usually do.' Rising to her feet, she waved over to Penny and Tabby, who were chasing pigeons. 'Girls, we're going to take you home. Your mum and Seb will follow… later.'

They rushed over, Penny's face flushed, Tabby's hair half out of the plait he'd watched Maggie try to tame it into this morning.

'Why aren't we going home together?' Penny asked.

'Seb has something he wants to ask Maggie,' his mum announced, making Seb wince, his sisters sit up with a start, and Maggie's eyes widen so they looked like a couple of shiny silver ten-pence pieces.

'He can ask her now,' Tabby protested.

'It's something *important*.'

Christ. Seb slunk further down his chair. She might as well just announce he was going to propose and be done with it.

'Oh, well.' Alice and Sarah stood, laughter in their eyes. 'I guess we'd better get out of here.'

Tabby looked at Penny, who glanced up at him and gave him a secretive smile.

That's when Tabby started to jump up and down. 'I know, I know. You're going to ask Mum to marry you!'

Maggie's gaze fell on his, eyes so full of laughter she looked like she was going to burst. 'Well? Are you?'

There was no alternative but to go with the flow. So with a flourish, Seb stood, walked over to Maggie, and dropped to one knee.

He didn't know what he said, only that his proposal was messy and chaotic, just like he was. Yet despite that, Maggie looked him straight in the eye, her gaze full of love, and agreed to be his wife.

'I have something to tell you,' she whispered as they hugged. 'But we're definitely saving that for when we're alone.'

He drew back to study her face. Beautiful, though perhaps a little pale today. Her eyes glowed back at him, flickering briefly down to her stomach before finding his again.

And his heart cartwheeled in his chest.

It looked like his life was going to get messier and even more chaotic. Yet as he gazed at the woman he loved, the one smiling serenely back at him, he knew he didn't have to worry. She'd have it all under control.

ONE MORE CHAPTER

YOUR NUMBER ONE STOP

FOR PAGETURNING BOOKS

One More Chapter is an award-winning global division of HarperCollins.

Sign up to our newsletter to get our latest eBook deals and stay up to date with our weekly Book Club! <u>Subscribe here.</u>

Meet the team at <u>www.onemorechapter.com</u>

Follow us!

🐦 <u>@OneMoreChapter_</u>
📘 <u>@OneMoreChapter</u>
📷 <u>@onemorechapterhc</u>

Do you write unputdownable fiction? We love to hear from new voices. Find out how to submit your novel at <u>www.onemorechapter.com/submissions</u>